D1525575

# DAVID ABARE

# The Swing Over the Ocean

Salbare Publishing LLC

# Copyright

*The Swing Over the Ocean*

Copyright © 2017 by David Abare

Cover Art by Jeremiah Metzcar

Interior Illustration by Christopher Johnston

Published in the United States of America by Salbare Publishing LLC

*FOR POPPY*

# *Prologue*

*Stephen* sat on the edge of the doctors table, swinging his legs back and forth like a nine-year-old-not a man of twenty-four-whistling and bobbing his head to the awful Muzak version of "Don't Worry, Be Happy" playing in the cramped, sterile room. He let his eyes work their way over the charts and colorful graphics that peppered the walls of the Urologist's office, some about E.D., others highlighting symptoms of B.P.H. It was the largest collection of flaccid peckers he'd seen at one time since he was in seventh grade when several of the eighth-grade kids came into the locker room during gym and yanked their shorts and underwear down.

"So, Mr. Alexander," the doctor said, popping through the door off to Stephen's right side. "I had a chance to review the sample you brought in, and what's unique in this sperm sample is that, well, there's no sperm."

"Come again," Stephen asked, his head tilted to the right. "No pun intended, Doc but, I did a good job there. The website costs me twenty-nine bucks a month and I can assure you it's worth it, and that I definitely *delivered*, if you know what I mean."

The doctor chuckled. "I've no doubt it was a successful emission but what I mean is that, in the sample itself I've found no sperm. It's a condition called *Azoospermia*, meaning a lack of sperm. You still ejaculate, because that's made up of more than just-"

"Wait, doc, hang on. What are you saying?" Stephen interrupted. "That I have no sperm at all? I'm cumming but there's no little swimmers you mean?"

"Well, yes that's precisely what I'm saying. There was no actual sperm present in your sample. I'm sorry. But, of course in these scenarios we want to be extra thorough so we're going to do additional tests and check your Testosterone levels to see if-"

"Huh. Been pretty careful most of my life but, there's been some accidents...never got anyone pregnant though," Stephen said, his volume trailing off at the end as his eyes looked down at the white tile floor.

"As I said, Mr. Alexander, we definitely need to do some more tests and-"

"No, no it's OK," Stephen interrupted again. "I brought the sample in out of curiosity doc, was here for the peeing thing and...no need to do more tests. Last thing I want or need right now is a kid anyway. Almost thirty years old and I barely feed myself, never mind another little bugger. Thanks for letting me know."

The doctor looked at him, watching his eyes trail off towards the floor. "Please see Cheryl at the desk and set up another visit for the urination issues and, I do hope you reconsider on more testing," the Doctor said.

"How many of these patients that have this 'Zoo Sperm' or whatever you called it," Stephen asked, hopping off the table. "How many, after more tests, show they have sperm? What percentage?"

"Well, I don't have an exact number but-"

"Just give me a ballpark, doc."

The doctor hesitated, then, "I'd say less than 1%."

Stephen nodded, then grinned back at him. "I don't gamble much, but those odds sound pretty abysmal. Thanks again, and I'll check in with Cheryl about a follow up on the other stuff."

He made his way to the Receptionist and booked another appointment a few weeks down the road, then headed out to his car where he sat-staring out the windshield into the Medical Center garage-for an hour before dialing the last number that had called his phone.

"Hey. So, that thing you were worried about, you don't need to anymore," he said to the voice on the other end of the line. "No, definitely don't need to, unless you've been hooking up with that dude from High School that moved in next door. Sorry, I was kidding. No, kidding about the High School guy, not kidding about that. I'll explain later when I come by. Yeah, you too. See you soon."

He snapped the cell phone cover down, tucking it back into his pocket and starting the silver Nissan Altima, whose exhaust leak startled a mother and her son walking in the garage several feet away. He watched her pull the child closer to her after the noise had frightened them, and they quickened their pace towards their car. Stephen took a few long breaths as he watched them get into their SUV and drive away, then sat there motionless in his vehicle as a stream of tears rolled down onto his cheeks.

He wiped his leaky eyes on his sleeve, then pushed the gear lever into drive and sped out of the parking garage into the breezy, overcast October day.

## Chapter 1

*The* man threw the phone down onto the pile of rags, disgusted that no one picked up, and unwilling to be an idiot that leaves a long message on voicemail. He reached down and grabbed a gray rag, then wiped his hands vigorously before tucking it into the back pocket of his jeans. An hour cleaning with chemicals and the place looked decent, especially considering its age and location beneath the ground. The odor of sanitizer permeated the confined space and he felt a wave of nausea creep over him along with a looming headache. He needed air, yet still had tasks to finish and items to store away. In the corner of the room lay a pair of flimsy, light gray skater-style sneakers that he needed to take up with him when he left as well.

There was noise coming from the other room, which he'd need to deal with, but there were more pressing matters to address before leaving for his trip. He went over to the sneakers, picked them up from the floor, lacing the two of them together, as always, then draped them over his shoulders and headed into the next room. The noise lessened-but continued-as he walked past and he ignored it still, making his way outside.

The air was brisk and dry, swirling around him as he stepped into it, with the early Spring sun offering only a hint of warmth in the early hour. He looked over into the back of the yard, knowing there was hours of work ahead there as well-a byproduct of life on a farm and his chosen avocation-then walked towards the front of the house, the sneakers bouncing against his back and chest as he took each stride. As he got to the porch, he pulled the rag out of his pocket and slid the sneakers off his shoulder, then walked up the stairs with them in his hands, held out in front of his stomach like a platter.

The porch was covered in scattered twigs and debris, some of which he kicked aside as he made his way to the left corner and knelt in front of the stack. A pile of shoes, mostly sneakers, all laced to its identical other and layered in an imperfect but deliberate symmetry. The tower rose almost three feet from the floor of the porch and contained more than forty pairs of shoes-earth tones mainly-resting up against the corner of the wall-railing. The last pair placed on top were purple and white with several tiny stickers adorning the white sole. The man stared at the structure, closed his eyes and breathed in deep, then took the shoes he'd been carrying and placed them on top of the others. He slid one of them back at a forty-five-degree angle-not liking its original position-then moved the other a few inches as well. He made final, subtle adjustments, then got up off his knees and stared at the pile of footwear.

"Beautiful," he said, as the left side of his mouth curled upwards and he slipped his hand into the front of his jeans.

# *Chapter 2*

"*I* need to die."

"You always say that. I think death after three orgasms in an hour, though, is a pretty voracious wish. Forbidden in the Constitution, even. Specifically, the preamble I believe."

"So, you think our founding fathers were more concerned with rules governing climaxing versus how to build the framework of our fledgling country?"

"Ugh, baby. *Climax*? Come on, that word is the 'moist' of sexual dialogue. Maybe you *do* need to die because I won't be getting an erection for four score and when-the-fuck ever."

"Wanna bet?"

She slid her hand under the scratchy lime green motel blanket and across his inner thigh.

"Ohhh no, that's it for you. I should get back to my office and at least pretend I'm working for a while. Someone has to pay for these tacky rooms of debauchery you love so much," he said, motioning with his hand across the landscape of the bedroom as he hopped off the bed.

"Yeah, well, I may have a penchant for kitsch and seventies-era cheesy but I'd give that all up for a stint at Casa Stephen, you know that," she replied, her eyes widening.

"I know, hon. I'm sorry," he replied, rubbing his hand over the side of his neck, then glancing back at her sideways.

"Yeah, yeah. I love you, asshole, now go back to work and don't text me for at least two days," she said.

He was floundering around the room, picking up pieces of clothing he tore off in haste hours earlier, and noticed his silver Movado resting on top of one of his socks. Although the design was clean, efficiently minimalist and accidently sexy, it failed miserably at being an easy to read timepiece from even short distances.

*2:53.* Maybe.

"We've been here almost three hours, you realize that? I think you're starting to like me," he offered.

"Did you hear what I said? Just go, you big idiot, and stop making small talk like I'm that creepy guy at Dunkin Donuts you always talk about."

"Milton? I just saw him Sunday and he was pulling wads of hair tied in rubber bands out of a sandwich bag!"

"OMG, stop it," she said, straightening up against the flimsy backboard of the bed, making it slap against the wall.

"No, absolutely not, but he did ask me if I liked his *Magic: The Gathering* T-Shirt. Where do you think I might get one of those? It had some really pretty colors and I think it's twenty-five percent cotton," he said, stumbling as he moved his second leg into his pants and pulled them up.

"I almost feel bad for labeling him creepy because I swear every story you tell me about this guy just sounds silly and sad, but not dangerous," she said, as she reached for her phone on the nightstand.

"He's told me the story about how Vanna White, supposedly, told him he had beautiful skin tone at the airport like twelve times, hon. The guy's clearly a menace to society."

"What's *really* creepy is that you've mentioned that several times now knowing full well I had no fucking idea who Vanna White was until I finally Googled her. There's over a full decade plus separating us, you remember that, right?"

4

He slid the Movado over his wrist, then grabbed the black button-down shirt from the weathered walnut-brown chair against the wall.

"Listen, I may be forty...somethingish, but, I made this very clear when we met that I feel my intellectual development stopped in the fifth grade and the only chance I've ever had to survive romantically was to date you youngsters. Truthfully, I should just stay home and watch porn while eating boneless hot wings but, luckily, I found you with your complete lack of desire to evolve or mature. Plus, you have the most delicious ass," he said raising his eyebrows gently and moving towards the bed.

"Fuuuck no, Stephen," she said, laughing at the end, "Get that shirt buttoned up and get your own cute ass out of here. You brushed off my last advance so it's home to wings and *Spankbox.com* for you."

He let his head sink to his chest then slinked to the bed, leaned down and kissed her right beneath her left eye.

"You're the brightest spot in my day every time I see you, baby. I hope you know that," he whispered, as he pulled back from her.

She let a sly smirk creep across her face, then kicked up at him with her feet, "Ya know, that would've almost been sweet coming from anyone else. Get out of here you jerk, and I'm serious don't text me for a while. I need a mental *and* physical breather."

"Just send more dick pics then? Seriously, you must have two hundred shots of the Lil' guy, but I'll send more."

She came up from the bed towards him, reached her arms around his shoulder and turned him to face her, "Stephen, I can't keep showing up here when you want a couple hours of distraction from your guilt or 'confusion' or whatever else goes on in that head of yours. We both know how this ends for me."

He took a deep breath, accentuating the exhale, then leaned his head into hers.

"Remember that line in *Steve Jobs* where he says, 'I'm poorly made'?" he asked.

"Of course, " she answered.

"Eh, you know I'm not going to try to bundle this up in some pseudo-clever monologue. You're right. You're always right about me and this but I don't wanna tear into that wound right now. I know what needs to be done though. Promise."

"Plus, you told me you'd elaborate on the book you started about your childhood, your mom and dad, et cetera but you forgot. I've never heard you go into so much detail about when you were a kid. I want to hear more."

"Ah, Henry and Lillian-the *Frankie and Johnnie* of their day, at least for a veeeery short time. It's not a biography though babe, it's a novel. OK, so one that's based almost exactly on my life to the point where I haven't bothered to even change the names of the characters yet, but, a novel, still," he said, then laughing and reaching down next to the chair where the typed pages of *The Alexander Circus* rested, waving it in front of her.

"You brought it?" she shouted. "Why didn't you read some?"

"I was too busy disappointing you sexually. Shit, that would make you hornier than anything I could do to you in the sack anyway. I should've read it."

She poked at his stomach a couple times, then, "OMG, I should've never told you how turned on I get from listening to your voice. Huge mistake."

"Giving me your number was the huge mistake, I think."

"You may be right, but either way I do want to hear you read that to me, even after I've dumped you. Now, just go back to work, think about me and what we did all afternoon. Let that be all that swirls around in that screwed up brain of yours today," she said, crossing her wrists around his neck. "I love you, and shame the fuck on me for letting that happen but I do, and I'll deal with it…but you do owe me a real conversation soon."

"Absolutely," he replied, then smiled at her as he held her eyes for a moment.

He kissed her on the lips, letting his own linger, then let his hands drift down her side and over the edges of her hip bones. He rested them there as they kissed-him drawing his head away from her as he bit her bottom lip playfully, her tongue finding its way back into his mouth. With careful and deliberate motion, he rolled his wrists outward, causing his hands to slide downward on her legs. He leaned into her and pushed his hands back and around the top of her ass, kissing her fervidly.

She cupped her hands around his neck, pulled back and gave him one last little peck on the lips. His roaming hands spilled down a few more millimeters, resting firmly on her ample backside cheeks.

"It's just an ass, Stephen. Everyone has them and I know mine is pretty rockin' but you don't have to employ the cloak and dagger shit to put your hands on it, just make your move, chump," she said.

"If I recall I 'made a move' there once and it was harshly denied so, excuse me if I maintain a modicum of decency instead of utilizing the frat boy grab," he replied.

"*That* move only works with proper lubrication. Meaning the kind that allows a platinum band to slide across this finger," she countered, wagging her ring finger. "In the meantime, you should familiarize yourself with this finger."

He smirked, watching her middle finger snap up, then smacked her butt as he went over to the sink and took a couple gulps of water right out of the tap, then scooped his keys off the counter next to it.

"Ugh, why do you do that? This room cost less than a meal at *Arbys*, do you honestly think they ever clean the filters on these things. Gross," she said, wincing.

"And yet you never seem to have a problem making out with me, Heather, sooo, either you have a bacteria fetish or not even disease can dampen my sex appeal," he said.

She rolled her eyes and hopped back onto the bed.

"You don't totally disgust me, yet," she answered, "but I have a high tolerance for all kinds of shit, obviously. Now get out of here, I need to call my other boyfriend," she shot back.

"Please just tell me it's not some guy with a sixteen-ounce beer can between his legs. I'm fort-, I'm older hon, and no matter how much I stretch this thing it won't crack six-ish inches. I can live with someone with more money and of course they're a better lay but please let me feel like I win the dick war," he said.

"Seriously if you're not out of here in ten seconds I'm going to unfollow you on Twitter."

"Noooooo!" he begged, his eyes widening. "I only have ten followers, that would put me back in single digits. You wouldn't."

"Ten…nine…eight…"

He smiled and blew her a kiss, then scurried out the door.

"You know…I like you considerably, meaning kind of a lot, wherein some people would call it love sorta even, riiight?" he said, his voice trailing off as he made his way down the hall, away from the room.

She smiled and picked up her iPhone and logged onto Twitter and his page came up immediately, as it was the last one-the only one-she ever looked at.

"*Stephen Alexander*. Stupid cute idiot with two first names, I should unfollow you. If I knew how the hell to do it," she mumbled.

She stared as his profile picture for twenty seconds, then jumped into her Camera Roll, scanning through the others she had of him. Most were from motel rooms, though a select few were sent by Stephen from work functions, happy hours with friends or the aforementioned dick shots that had grown into an art form of late. The most recent included his penis, semi erect, sporting a tiny Santa Claus Christmas ornament and peeking out of purposely chosen fir-green boxers.

The picture she landed on most often was Stephen leaning up against the bedroom closet of his apartment, clean shaven head, warm blue eyes, an amber-grey chin goatee, wearing a black Henley shirt and a little scruff, two silver hoop earrings in his left ear and a pair of jeans that "made his ass look like a Running Back" in her words. His eyes were slightly squinted-which she asked him several times if was by design though he never gave her a straight answer-and a smile that was equal parts devious and sexy; the smile was the drug.

She looked at the picture and started rubbing her inner thighs together and let the fingers of her left hand start massaging her exposed nipple, tickling it, then adding more pressure as it hardened. Her right hand slid across the sheets of the bed and into her purse where she fetched her battery powered Bullet vibrator and let it rest on her bare stomach for a moment. She took a deep breath, tossed the phone down on the bed next to her, and exhaled with far more force than necessary.

"Fuck."

Stephen made his way to his car, a black BMW 335xi, that he bought months earlier and was too expensive for what his income afforded but satiated his voracious appetite for the German saloons. His iPhone rested in his front right pants pocket, and he expected the familiar buzz of a text message to reach his leg before he opened the driver's door but it was late. Heather was consistent in her post-romp texts, usually arriving seconds after he departed and colored with subtle jabs while still making it apparent she'd relished their time together. The fact that it hadn't come yet meant she was either serious about wanting a break or that she was showering or masturbating, with both the latter scenarios being enticing enough that he stood at the threshold of the car contemplating a return to the room.

"Tom listen, I wanted to try and make it back in but I blew a hole in one of the tires on my new car, can you fucking believe it?" he said aloud. "I'll be in first thing tomorrow after I sort this out."

*Never going to buy it. Plus, the prick will inspect the tires.*

"Hey Tom, no way I'm going to get back there today. I need to head back to Magnatech and go over the changes with them again in person, " he said to no one.

*No chance he'll buy me going there Today because it's their inventory day and he'd call to verify.*

"Tom, how are ya? Hey I don't think-" his excuse contemplation was interrupted as an older woman walking a Yorkie through the motel parking lot stared at him disapprovingly, then sneered as her eyes surveyed his waistline. He glanced down and saw his unfastened belt and part of his right pant leg caught up in his sock. He waved enthusiastically at her and she quickened her pace, whispering something to the dog.

"Everything's alright M'am, I promise. Just making up lies to tell my boss, same thing I'm sure you did to get out of making gun barrels during the Civil War. Cute cat, by the way, how old, about thirty-eight? You can groom cats by the way, they like it!" he said, shouting at the end. He was aware it was a Yorkie and not a feline, and normally wasn't sarcastically combative to the elderly but there was a subtext in her unspoken judgment that was more sinister than only her initial disdain for his appearance and proximity to a seedy motel.

"Canadian Club sipping, Mahjong-at-the-Senior-Center playing, geriatric terrorizer. How dare she look at me like that," he mumbled in a nondescript, ridiculous accent as he strapped into his car and dug into his pocket for his phone.

Still no text from Heather, though upon inspecting his phone he noticed a couple from Chyanna, a woman he met at a friend's poker game a month earlier. In less than seven words and with a clever use of emojis, she explained how she hoped to be underneath or on top of him soon. He smirked and considered replying, but then ignored it.

10

*Hey Tom, it's Steve. So, I just got way laid, then was non-verbally assaulted by an elderly lady with a mangled Ewok-Cat so I'm thinking that qualifies for time off under FMLA, right?* he said to himself, looking in the rearview mirror. He noticed one eye was bloodshot and that his amber-silver goatee had begun to creep too far to the right due to his lackadaisical, rushed shower shaving. Surely Heather *had* to notice this recent development, yet she wasn't telling him. She was either so blinded in her lust, he imagined, or was so tired of his shit that her silence was a calculated plan to allow for his humiliation when someone finally called him out after the patch of hair migrated to his cheek.

He glanced back down at his phone, hit the Home button and watched the backlight illuminate his wallpaper, revealing no new text message. "You be as cool as you like, sweetheart, I see how it is. There's plenty of chicks out there who'd love a guy with a BMW and a cheek goatee," he said as he hit the Start button in the car and clicked the lever into reverse and backed out.

The late April Connecticut roads were still sandy and dotted with small heaps of snow, clinging to life in their rings of melting ice. The car's thermometer had the outside temperature at 58 degrees but that was optimistic and likely a product of parking for several hours in direct sunlight. Winter had arrived in anger somewhere in early February and unleashed a merciless assault on New England until the third week of March when the skies relented and longer days allowed the ground to warm again. With several feet of snow dumped in central Connecticut, the roadside piles were certain to remain through the end of the month at minimum.

Stephen reached his right hand down to the *iDrive* wheel in his car, spinning it between his thumb and middle finger, until the navigation screen on the dashboard read 102.1. The familiar sound of Paul Rodgers voice filled the speakers of his car. At least thirty percent of the time-Steven reasoned-you'd hear Bad Company on 102.1 if you switched it on. There was no way that math could be accurate, he knew, but "Shooting Star", "Feel Like Making Love" and their self-titled staple, "Bad Company" played incessantly, lead only by Clapton's "Cocaine" which was every tenth song, he often joked. He thought about switching the channel to Satellite radio, catch up on *Motormouth,* a syndicated talk show hosted by Gary Morse, one of the pioneers of "shock radio". He'd softened up over the years, and the current format was more about the interplay between the personalities and playful skewering of political figures and celebrities vs. all out buffoonery but it was always entertaining. The radio show was another family-a group of virtual friends-often comforting Stephen on long drives or moments of distress where he needed to escape his own reality. If he switched the show on now though, he decided, he'd be engaged in whatever they were discussing for an hour and become too distracted.

As he finished belting out the chorus to "Seagull", a lesser known though exceptional Bad Company song-strumming chords against the side of his steering wheel with his right fingers-he noticed up ahead on the left side of the road that *Willie's Place* was open. Willie's was a popular diner and seasonal ice cream spot which appeared to have started full service, as the lot was packed. He had to take a leak, and passing up the opportunity for a Vanilla shake was as unlikely as 102.1 not playing Bad Company again by the time he got back in the car so he signaled left and rolled his foot onto the brake.

Working the counter some days was Kirsten, a mid-twenties recent college grad with a tribal lower-back tattoo and "more daddy issues than *Parenting* magazine" he reported to his friend Chris after getting to know her early last year. She wore black Yoga pants and bent, contorted and stretched all over the restaurant with a backside that would stop ninety-year-old men in their tracks. She leaned over one day to fetch some dishes from the floor and caught Stephen letting his eyes roam from her hamstring straight up and over to the tattoo. She peered back at him with a smile, and a week later wrote her number on the back of a guest check and handed it to him. They exchanged numerous playful and graphic texts and days later she was at his apartment grinding on top of him until he tapped out at 1:30am, dehydrated and ears ringing from her comical, over-the-top screaming. She started dating a local attorney shortly after and they hadn't revisited their bedroom activities since but he always appreciated the view.

The place was mobbed, with apparently every Connecticut resident within forty miles deciding low to mid-fifties meant it was time for T-shirts and Banana Splits. He pulled his car into an open spot in the back corner near a green and brown, rusting, seventies era woody-type station wagon with a dented roof and damaged paneling- the passenger's side rear door cracked open. Typically, he'd walk around and ask if anyone owned the car, suggesting their battery may be dying or thieves may grab what's inside but as he surveyed the vehicle he decided neither of those situations would impair the owner's life any more than owning the car already had.

Stephen glanced at his phone resting on the passenger's seat before shutting the car off, contemplated pushing the Home button to see if he'd missed a text while singing along with Bad Company, but then chose not to.

For six seconds.

His index finger depressed the concave circle at the bottom of the phone and the familiar rectangle with Heather's number appeared. He considered not reading it before he took a leak, bought his frozen dairy treat and ogled young Kirsten but his curiosity was eclipsed only by his ego.

*<Just so you know, I absolutely didn't think of your crooked goatee chaffing my inner thighs as you were going down on me while I was just using my vibrator and orgasming uncontrollably. Was thinking about "Who's the Boss" era Tony Danza. #TotesFirstCrush>*

He chuckled, staring at the phone, wondering how they'd allowed themselves to use "clever" hashtags in virtually every text they sent one another when both had claimed their bitter disgust for the

13

repurposed pound sign. He started typing back, *Baby you know Alyssa Milano was on that show and that I bumped into her once at LAX and she called me "dummy", so are you trying to hurt me now #SpankBankTop5*. He left the words in the box without sending, tossing the phone back onto the seat, his need to pee exceeding his desire to see her reply, as witty and ridiculous as he was sure it'd be.

Most of the patrons of Willie's were inside, he observed, as they likely discovered upon arrival that a temperature in the fifties wasn't ice cream weather after all and sitting outside when there's a ten mile an hour breeze across un-thawed ground is uncomfortable. He pushed the center button on his key and heard the beep, confirming it locked, as he walked toward the building. The lot was almost full, with only the corner where he'd parked next to the dilapidated station wagon against the edge of a bordering tree line offering any significant open space. It was his go-to area, as there was no pavement, and customers only drove into the worn grass and dirt if every paved spot was filled, providing a reasonably safe locale for his new car, isolated from door dings and overzealous children barreling out of minivans *en route* to towering cups of Gummy Bear-infused soft serve.

He glanced back over his shoulder and peeked at the station wagon again, wondering if it was the owner's choice to park it so far out due to embarrassment or because it'd been abandoned, as a car looking as it did may be. The latter was a likelihood considering it was backed in with the rear door ajar, but perhaps it was instead one of the cooks and Willie asked them to park it out there in fear of frightening patrons.

The *thwack* sound of one of the Port-O-Potty doors on the lot smacking shut whipped Stephen's head around and he looked in that direction but saw no one exiting. As he began to turn his head back towards the front entrance, he saw a man slide into his right eyeline and scoop up a little girl, playfully.

"Wooooo Amanda, you like that?" the man asked, holding her out in front of him as he passed Steven fifteen or so feet away, zipping

14

through parked cars and away from the building. "You love to swing, don't you?"

Stephen turned to watch the man playing with the girl, and, noticing he was heading towards the station wagon, for a moment felt guilty for trashing the poor guy's car. The man's pace quickened as Stephen edged closer to the restaurant's front door, his bladder throbbing from neglect. The door was less than three feet away when he first heard the girl speak.

"Where is my daddy?" she yelled, "Who are you? I wanna get down."

Stephen stopped dead.

# Chapter 3

"*Hey*, buddy," Stephen shouted as he turned back around, walking towards the man holding the girl. "Little girl, are you OK?"

The girl writhed around in the man's arms and one of her shoes came loose as it rubbed against the man's wrist, falling onto the pavement. Stephen heard her say something muffled and inaudible.

"Hey! Put her down," Stephen yelled, quickening his pace, weaving between the parked cars. "Stop!"

The man grabbed the shoe and ran, letting the girl fall, dragging her for the last thirty or so feet to the station wagon.

*The unlocked passenger's side door.*

The girl was trying to yell but her words lacked breath. Steven cleared the last parked car and sprinted towards the two of them as they reached the car.

"What the fuck are you doing with her?" Stephen screamed as he approached them, running.

The man ignored him and swung open the unlocked door of the car, pulling the girl up from the ground by her shirt and tossing her like a wet towel onto the rear bench seat of the car. As he started to close the door Stephen lunged at his midsection, tackling him.

As they fell, the man's head bumped the side of the car, slicing his lower lip. They hit the landscape hard, and Stephen wound his legs around the man's midsection, sliding his body around to apply a choke hold but didn't have the angle. The resistance he felt was greater than the man's late-fifties, five-foot-nine frame would've suggested possible, so Stephen began rolling to his right and tried to use the leverage of the car's rear corner to his advantage.

The little girl sprung up from the car seat and pulled the mushroom style locking mechanism skyward and started pawing at the inside of the door but the handle was missing, and there was no wheel crank to lower the window. Outside, the two men were wrestling and then bumped into the car, knocking her into the rear of the front seat. She slid her butt on the bench-seat closer to the door, flopped down onto her back and began kicking at the inside of the door as hard as she could.

Stephen pressed his forearm firm against the man's neck, leaning his full body weight against him, pinning him to the rear of the car. "Stop resisting, " he said, as he applied more pressure and the man's face vibrated in resistance while glowing with redness.

The sweat from the man's head lubricated the spot it was pinned, so it slipped downward. Against his torso, Stephen felt the man reach his hand towards his own midsection so he shifted left and tried to wrap his arms around his neck to apply the choke hold again, but the angle still wasn't there and the man was now on his stomach, rolling away from him.

Inside the car, the little girl's feet grew numb as she continued kicking the plastic paneling on the door. She shuffled her torso closer and started kicking the window instead. *Foomp. Foomp. Foomp.* She pounded with both feet simultaneously, re-adjusting as the vinyl seat made her slide away from the window after every few kicks.

The man stood near the back corner of the station wagon and started running for the driver's door. Stephen chased him, slamming his body into the inside of the driver's door as it opened. He saw the girl kicking wildly at the window in the corner of his eye as he attempted to restrain the man, then threw two quick punches at his stomach as he tried to pull him to the ground.

"Come out this door! Run to the restaurant", Stephen shouted to the girl as he felt the man's arm grab at the back of his neck, trying to break free of the front choke he was applying.

Stephen hopped up off the man, having position and leverage, and pulled him straight up and then let his own body fall, sending the man up over him and down onto the sandy outskirts of the parking lot. He realigned himself, made his way towards the man, still on the ground, then jumped on top of him to apply a pin that would allow enough time for the girl to summon help inside of Willie's. As Stephen wrapped his legs around the man's body and began to position his hands, he felt his left side catch fire.

The little girl pulled herself up over the back of the front seat of the car, grazing her head on the steering wheel before landing on the cluttered cushions. She grabbed onto the side of the vinyl, kicking her legs furiously, sliding herself forward, dragging coins, food wrappers and paper debris with her and finally spilling out onto the grassy dirt where the two men were still fighting.

The man pushed Stephen off himself and watched the little girl, shoeless and sprinting, head towards the restaurant. Dazed, and in horrific pain near his lower rib cage where the man applied the stun gun, Stephen cautiously rolled sideways before crouching forward and attempting to get up. He watched the man reach into his car, digging on the floor, hearing the faint clink of something colliding with metal.

*The fucker has a gun.*

Stephen forced his torso up towards his knees and began standing when the man spun around and swung downward at Steven's head with the wooden baton. Stephen fell backwards, blood from his temple area jumping from his skin and down into the dirt as his head hit the Earth. The man tossed the weapon onto his front seat, started the car and sped out onto the main road, leaving billowing clouds of dirt, gravel and sand hovering around the entire parking lot, right as the bell that rested over the door at Willie's chimed with the arrival of the girl.

18

Stephen's body lay still, bleeding for several minutes before a late model Honda Accord with an exaggerated rear wing pulled in. The silver car buzzed like a weed whacker at idle waiting to tear through Crabgrass as it crept over to where Stephen's body lay. The young driver killed the ignition and stepped out of the car with his passenger, immediately noticing the body.

"Whoa, hey dude, you OK?" the kid asked, looking down over Stephen, who'd started bleeding profusely from the temple.

"Idiot, just call 911, he's dead I think. Fuck," the other kid said as several other patrons from Willie's rushed over to where Stephen lay.

A heavyset man with a stained *Uconn* sweatshirt pushed his way between the two boys, "Holy shit," he said. "Don't touch him, someone just called 911 inside. Oh, my God."

"Is he alive?" the Honda driver asked the man.

"I told you he's dead, dude. Look at his head," the other kid replied.

The overweight man knelt and put his hand an inch above Stephen's mouth and rested the other hand softly on his chest. "He's breathing, someone get me a towel, a shirt-something, need to try and stop this bleeding."

Several other restaurant patrons had filed around Stephen's body in a half circle, and one pulled his light blue T-shirt off over his head and walked it over to the man.

"Is he the girl's father? What happened? Oh Jesus, he looks pale," a woman standing with the others mentioned.

"Her dad's inside with her-Bev, you out here?" the heavyset man yelled. "Can someone see if Beverly knows how long before they'll be here?"

"Sure," said the kid driving the Honda, then ran back towards the restaurant.

The man on the ground with Steven wiped up some of the blood, pressing the T-shirt against his temple, careful to not jostle his neck. As he repositioned himself, several more patrons came barreling out towards the others.

"Oh no," a middle-aged woman in a Red Sox cap exclaimed as she cupped her hand around her mouth when she saw his body. "How'd this happen?"

"Did this guy attack the girl? Did she do this to him? Good for her," said an early-thirties man with a shaved head and face full of piercings, his black tribal tattoo creeping up from out of his white *Affliction* T-shirt.

"Somebody said a car ran him over, then took off, but how'd he get way over here?" a woman in the back blurted out.

The man holding the T-shirt against Stephen's head took his left hand from his chest and fished out his cell phone from his left front pocket. It slipped through the ends of his fingers, then hit the ground. "Shit, hey could someone grab that," he asked.

The woman in the baseball hat walked over, scooped it up and handed it to him.

"Thanks. Hey, did that kid find Bev? We need that Ambulance, this thing is bleeding at a good clip here and I need more than a T-shirt to stop it," said the fat man. He thumbed his passcode into his smartphone, dialing 911, leaving moisture on the keypad from his sweaty digit.

"Holy shit!" a younger man yelled, arriving at the circle of people surrounding Stephen's body. "What the hell happened, is this what the girl was yelling about?"

"Hello-hey is this Joe? Joe it's Darren Barlow down at Willie's, you guys get a call from Bev?" the man tending to Stephen asked. "Pulse feels like it's fading and-" he cut himself short, hearing the faint sound of an ambulance siren in the distance. "Never mind Joe, they're almost here."

Beverly McGuiness, the restaurant owner's longtime girlfriend, broke through the pack of people standing around, "Darren, I called them. I think-"

"Yeah they're coming. Thanks. OK, people back up a little bit so they can get the bus out here, alright?" Darren interrupted, motioning with one hand to clear the area.

The thick crowd slid back against the edge of the woods, some lining up against the front edge of Stephen's BMW. A new car pulled into the lot, ahead of the ambulance, and one of the patrons waved at it to move closer to the building and out of the way. The young driver of the Honda hopped into his car and turned the ignition-startling those standing nearby-then backed it out and moved to an open spot on the asphalt, just as the ambulance was pulling in. Two local police cars trailed, making their way to the back corner where Stephen lay, still motionless.

Darren fished through Stephen's pocket and found the keys to his BMW. "Hey Bev, can you move his car, at least I assume it's his, give them a little more room here. See if these keys work," he said, tossing them to her.

The ambulance backed in right as the officers got out of their cars. The entire restaurant had now gathered around the scene except for two of the cooks and Willie himself who was on the phone inside. Bev looked around for a place to insert the plastic key in the BMW before realizing it was a push-button start. She depressed the brake, pushed the Start button but had no idea how to change gears. She left it running as she hopped out and over to where everyone stood.

"Uh, does anyone know how to drive that car," she asked. The passenger from the Honda nodded his head and walked around to the driver's door, jumped in and clicked it into drive before pulling it about fifteen feet closer to the tree line, which dispersed some of the onlookers.

The EMT's made their way to Stephen's body, kneeling on each side of him. The two officers surveyed the area and one made some notes on small pads they held.

"Thanks, you can let that go now," one of the EMT's said to Darren, as he took some sterile bandages from his kit. "Did you see what happened to him?

"No, I...I'm not sure anyone did. The little girl, she, she just came running in and-"

"It's OK. Bryan, you getting a pulse? Feels thready here."

The second EMT was maneuvering his stethoscope into several positions searching for a heartbeat. Darren stood up, moving back several feet, and spied a man carrying the little girl approach the crowd.

"Is that him?" he asked.

"Do you know him?" Darren inquired.

"No, but...he may have saved my daughter. She said there was a man, right baby, this man here?" the man asked the girl in his arms, her face still buried in his shoulder. "Is that the man that helped you?"

She pulled her face away from her father's body and looked down at Stephen, then tucked her head back against her dad. She mumbled something, and then her father cautiously placed her on her feet.

"Amanda, you don't have to look again but, baby, tell me if that's the man that fought with the other man who picked you up?" he asked her.

"Sir, are you the child's father?" one of the officers inquired.

"Yes, I am, Bill Shander. This is Amanda," he replied.

"OK, can you just step over here for a moment, and can you tell me if you know the identity of the victim here?"

He leaned in and took a long look at his face. "No, I don't, not at all. I, well, my daughter came running back inside-she likes to use the Port-O-Potty when we come here, makes her feel like a big girl instead of having to use the one inside, so we usually let her do that and she wasn't gone much longer than normal, or, I don't know, maybe I didn't notice because I was dicking around on my phone and texting my wife, and-"

22

"Sir, it's OK," said the officer. "Just tell me what she said when she came in, if you can remember."

"I didn't hear her at first, there were a couple others closer to the door-do you remember what you said baby, when you ran inside?" he asked Amanda who was still tight up against him.

"We'll talk with her when things settle down and we'll be interviewing others but do you recall what you heard her say, if anything."

"She was crying and yelling and, all I remember is her saying 'a man picked me up' and then a few moments later she said something about another guy-this one I'm sure-that 'told me to run inside when he was fighting the bad man'. She was sobbing so hard I didn't want to make her keep talking so I went up to the front of the restaurant-"

"Terry," the other officer shouted over to the policeman interviewing the father. "Something over here maybe, take a look."

"Excuse me," Officer Terry said.

Bill watched the cop walk away, then kissed Amanda on the head, cradling her against himself. "You're so brave baby, I love you. Daddy's never going to let anything happen to you OK? You hear me? Such a brave little girl," he said, as she started to cry.

The EMT's had secured Stephen to the stretcher and were loading him in the ambulance. Darren felt dizzy and had propped himself up against a nearby car as Bev returned from inside with some water, this time with Willie trailing her, still wearing his soiled white cooking apron.

"You doing OK, Darren?" Willie asked.

"Better than that poor fuck they're loading up, I think," he replied.

"Jesus. So do we know anything at all about this guy or what the hell happened? He tried to save the girl from some other guy? Wait, is he still alive?" Willie asked, motioning towards the ambulance.

"Barely, from what I could tell. May not survive the ride to Northwest General," Darren said, wiping his forehead with the towel Bev had brought out.

"This whole thing, fuck man, it happened in what, a minute or two? Anyone get a plate number of the guy who drove off?" Willie said, reaching down to into the dirt to pick up a shabby Half Dollar that rested amongst other scattered coins.

"I don't know, the cops are here, they'll sort it out I guess. Just makes me sick that some scumbag would try to nab one of our kids like that, right in broad fucking daylight. Could have been Hannah or Zachary," Darren said, thinking of his own children.

The driver of the ambulance slammed the rear door, jumped up front and activated the sirens before driving away-the onlookers pulling in tighter to the spot where Stephen was. The young kids in the Honda were pecking away at their phones texting as the rest of the crowd spoke in hushed and worried tones, still unsure of what had transpired. The two police officers were discussing a discarded, crumpled bag from a grocery store located in the next town over until one of the patrons interrupted them and took ownership, blaming her "bonehead" son for the careless deed. Bev was fiddling with the BMW key fob that hung among the keychain the kid from the Honda had handed back to her a few minutes earlier.

"Well, if anything I'm just glad that fuck is gone. No way he comes back here after this. Sad that another man had to take a beating, maybe give his life even, for that piece of shit but...no way he comes anywhere near here again," Willie said.

"I wish that made me feel better but it doesn't," Bev countered, sliding the keys into her back pocket.

"Willie, you have a camera up on that corner of the place, don't you? Right there" Darren said, pointing over to the silver apparatus jutting out from the right front corner of the roof. "Maybe it caught a plate number or something."

"It's a fake. Got it off Ebay when the place in Barkhamsted got robbed. Don't go blabbing that around, though," Willie said, searching for a cigarette in the front of his apron.

"How many is that today?" Bev asked.

"Oh Christ, you're gonna get on me about smoking when we had a lunatic kill some poor fuck here at the restaurant? Come on, babe. Not now," Willie groaned.

One of the officers started walking back towards Willie and the others, and Darren got up off the ground, wiping away more sweat and brushing off the back of his pants.

"So, Officer...Jackson," Willie said, reading the nameplate on his chest. "Was telling Darren here that my camera is a fake but, any chance a patron saw the license plate of the prick's car?"

"The license plate's dead. Woman in the restaurant remembered it as she saw it pulling in because it was a North Dakota plate and was ironic being a messy car I guess. *841 MUD.* Officer Marbern called it in, came back stolen from a junk yard in New Jersey weeks ago. We have folks checking into the that location too," said the officer.

"Ugh, shit man. That's too bad," Willie said, bringing both his hands across the top of his head, lit cigarette in his left.

"You're going to burn yourself Will, put that thing out," Bev said, moving her hand up and down.

Willie looked at the cop and rolled his eyes and the officer grinned.

"We need to talk with everyone who was here, and the state boys will be coming shortly so do me a favor and see if you can get everyone who may still be inside-employees, any other patrons, etc., to gather over by those picnic tables on the side of the building and we'll move these folks over there after we tape this area off, " Officer Jackson directed.

"Sure sure, of course, whatever you need," Willie said, dropping his cigarette to the ground and digging the heel of his black work boot into it several times. "Can't believe there's no plate though, shit. Something must be up though if this guy is carrying a stolen marker. Not just random, ya know."

The officer ignored him and started walking back towards his partner. Willie reached into the front left breast pocket of his apron and pulled out the Half Dollar he found earlier, flipping it up in the air using his thumb to make it spin. It hit one of his knuckles and bounced down into the dirt, disappearing.

"Oh, come on," Willie moaned, crouching down to see if he could spot it. A foot and a half away he saw the glimmer of the coin, resting up against a tuft of worn grass amongst the sand and dirt. He stepped over and reached down to pick it up and noticed a small piece of paper, folded several times, near some other loose paper. He picked up the folded item, along with the coin which he slid back into his pocket, and unfolded it.

"Bev, babe, give me your glasses," Willie said.

"What are you doing, the cop wants you to-"

"Honey, please, just give me your glasses, OK?"

"I don't even have them out here with me they're-"

"Babe, for fuck's sake they're on your head, in your hair."

Beverly pulled the glasses from her head, her face grown flush, and walked them over to Willie.

"Thanks doll," Willie said, mussing up her hair as she turned away from him.

He stretched the temples of the glasses around his wide face and positioned them onto the bridge of his nose with his left hand as he held the piece of paper in his right. When they rested comfortably he used both hands to unfold the paper so he could see the writing inside. He pulled each layer back, then moved his face closer to the four by seven-inch document.

*Dillers Propane - Breddleton, PA 17031 (412) 583-6719*
*-indecipherable smudged handwriting-*

Willie brought the paper as close to his eyes as he could before it blurred but, other than the printed business name and address on the top there was nothing anyone would be able to make out. He stood there for a second, pulling the paper back away from his face.

"What you got there, Will?" Darren asked, approaching him.

"I don't know. Maybe nothing but, who do we know around here that spends any time in Western Pennsylvania?" Willie said.

"Uh, I don't know-you'd know the people that come here better than I would but-nobody off the top of my head, why?"

Willie folded the paper over one time and tucked it inside his front apron pocket where the coin was, then fished another cigarette out of the pack and pushed it into his mouth.

"Like I said, it's probably nothing. "

# Chapter 4

*It* sounded like her grandmother making popcorn, kernels exploding from the heated oil and hitting the glass top that covered the sauce pan. Random pops and clicks coming from around the corner from where she rested on the floor. Grandma always told her it was "better this way" even though the method her mom used was quicker and easier to eat right out the bag. Whatever was making the popcorn noise wasn't delivering the same pleasant smell either, as all that filled her nostrils was the scent of urine and something recently cleaned, like a bathroom toilet.

She tried to pull herself up by pushing against the thin mattress she was sitting on, her back leaning against cement, but the bottom slid against the slick floor and she was weak-her arms like spaghetti. Down her leg, she felt something wet and cold and all around her was pitch black except for a faint light in the distance where the popping sound originated. The surface underneath the mattress was hard and slippery and felt cold as she moved her left hand around on the floor, bumping into a pile of wrapped treats-granola bars and dried fruit.

"Hello," she said, her voice cracking-a phlegmy whisper-though she was trying to yell. "Hello, it's me Emily.

The crackling pops were getting quieter, though the light coming from that direction was still the same, flickering somewhat, she noticed as she scooted her body off the mattress and onto the chilly floor.

"Mom? Mommy can you hear me? I can't see you," she said, rubbing her hands across her jeans.

28

She felt wetness on the inside of her right leg and realized she'd peed her pants. It wasn't soaked or warm so it must have been a while ago, before she fell asleep, she assumed.

"Mom, where are you? I'm in the basement I think," she cried out, her consciousness gaining momentum, giving rise to anxiety. "Can you turn on the light? Mom!"

The popping sound increased, as the smell of the cleanser intensified in her nose. Her mother rarely went down into the basement never mind clean it so Emily assumed she'd awoken near a spilled bottle of bleach. Her thoughts and memories played hide and seek, as quick flashes of her mom's face crept in, then her dad, a laugh from her older sister as she plopped down off the slide in the Mall Playscape, then nothing.

She stood up, teetering at first, stretching her hands out in front of her, unable to see a foot in front of her. She slid her socks over the hard floor and towards the light, an intense, paralyzing need for water invading her senses. She tried to build up saliva in her mouth but it was parched-cottony and chapped-and she needed to cough. As the air left her lungs in choppy hacks, she slid her feet several inches across the floor towards the flickering and intermittent crackles, noticing a bottle of Spring water sitting on the floor, partially illuminated by the weak and distant light. She crouched down and spun the cap off, tipped her head back and downed five large gulps before spitting some of it up and nearly falling over. She wiped the bottom of her mouth, placed the bottle back on the floor and stood up.

"I'm sorry Mommy, if I peed my pants or broke something. I didn't mean to. Can you please let me out now? I don't like it down here and I'm hungry," she said, moving forward again.

She remembered wild laughter. A crowd of people. Falling.

Her eyes focused on the dimly lit substance several feet in front of her, looking almost like giant rings of cobwebs hanging down from the ceiling. She squinted her eyes and reached her right hand out, shuffling her feet closer. She was still thirsty and almost stopped to

29

grab the water bottle again but kept inching forward. Across the top of her head she felt something slide, startling her, fearing it may be a gigantic spider web she was moving around in. She reached her arm up and felt around and caught hold of a string with a small metal cap on the end.

*A light switch.*

She yanked down on the string and heard the familiar *click clack* of a light operated by pulling string yet there was no light. Still only darkness, spoiled somewhat by the unknown source in the back corner of the room. She tried again but nothing.

"Mom! Daddy! Please, are you down here?" she screamed, letting go of the string and rushing forward.

A man was singing to her. She was lying on her back in a car. He called her Emily.

She stopped moving and tried to recall the image but they were coming in and out as fuzzy pictures across the back of her eyelids in random blinks. She turned and reached up for the cord one last time, pulling down hard over and over, but darkness remained. She turned back around and ran towards the faint light again, arms outstretched, her momentum stopped by the metal that pressed back against her little fingers as she hit it. She could feel the breath in her lungs-hurried and uneven-tightening the inside of her chest as it entered and almost whistling as it left. She curled her hands around the chicken wire that restricted her path and looked from side to side, the soft light from the faraway and unknown source revealing what looked like large beams of wood or metal on each outer edge. She ran to the left side and felt her hands slam into a solid surface, so she felt around and it was smooth and metallic with no openings. Frantically, she turned around, stepping towards the opposite direction, kicking over the water bottle, then felt her hands hit more of the wire, so she stretched her arms up as high as she could, feeling around for an end to the metal but her fifty-five inches and outstretched limbs found nothing but the same. The little girl let go and backed away from the wire, turning her head towards the distant light.

She was in a cage.

# Chapter 5

*Heather* watched the tiny bubbles showing that Stephen was responding to her iMessage disappear, as they'd do with lengthy replies. She stared at the small screen and wondered what ridiculous, clever hashtag he'd reply with, as his were always a couple degrees cagier than her own. In past relationships, she'd always felt a need to compete, even dominate and outshine her partner, whether in social settings or with one another. Her dialogue was usually more inventive, cunning and profound than her lover's but with Stephen it wasn't always the case. She'd read back texts and recall conversations, and even in those examples where she *knew* she had eclipsed him in substance and vocabulary, he somehow found a way to appear more charming and witty. A month and a half earlier she'd texted him an eloquent, well-versed summary of a documentary on morality and religion in modern culture, ending with "Do you think any Religion-any society or culture with their rules and constructs-has found the whole of what's meant to be man's true morality?" He texted back, *I'm going to find your 'whole' later, and it's definitely gonna be a religious experience for you ;)* Even the ridiculous old school winky face versus the emoji version was by design, and the response arrived in seconds after she sent her own text. She was in awe of the quickness in which he could formulate his keen and deviant replies.

The iMessage bubbles vanished minutes earlier, so she let out a little "humpf," and tossed the phone onto the bed then grabbed the vibrator off the comforter and dropped it into her pocketbook. As she made her way towards the bathroom to start the shower her phone started playing the theme to *Friends.*

*Brianna.* Her best friend of twenty years that insisted on the theme-song ringtone after they binge watched every episode on Netflix over three Pinot Noir-drenched weekends.

"Bree, what's shaking honey?" Heather asked, putting the call on speakerphone.

*"Do you have me on speaker you bitch? Is he there right now? Hiii Stephen,"* Brianna replied.

"No, I sent him away. You think I'd put you on speakerphone if he was here? The way you trash him? Please."

*"Oh, this coming from the woman that says incessantly, 'a real friend tells you the truth even when you don't want to hear it', that's perfect."*

Heather made the raspberry sound into the phone before replying, "Yeah well that's only relevant if I'm the one truth telling, dummy."

The tiny speakers crackled with Brianna's laughter.

"Why are you calling, aren't we getting together tonight or are you blowing me off for another *Here Fishie* date?" Heather asked.

*"Oh, fuck no, I'm so done with that site. By done I mean I'm literally checking my messages right now while I'm talking to you but yeah, I'm done and no I'm not going on a date tonight, we're absolutely hanging out. Plus, you know why I'm calling, don't be a pain in my ass,"* Brianna said.

The night before Heather assured Brianna that she'd request-or rather demand-Stephen sit and have a conversation about where things were going, his intentions and so on, before he left. For weeks, she'd complained that she was growing uneasy with the relationship and Brianna had given her somewhat of an ultimatum, one that Heather promised her she'd adhere to.

Heather sighed.

"Hey, go ahead and sigh all you want," Brianna jabbed, "but I'm going to be the one scraping you up off my newly tiled bathroom floor while you're coming apart and I have to keep pausing our Sons of Anarchy marathon."

"Shit, you did the tiles in the downstairs bathroom? Which ones did you end up going with, the cinnamon cream ones or the slate gray?" Heather asked.

"Seriously, the cinnamon cream ones are, like, so much better looking than the sample we saw in the store. Unreal!"

"I knew you'd pick those, didn't even understand why the gray ones were in the running."

"Hey, stop trying to play on my love for my new tiles, jerk. So, what happened today?"

Heather rolled her eyes, knowing Brianna could never know. "Ugh, Bri listen, it's not always that easy to just-"

"It is always that easy if you make it. Stop patronizing me and don't pretend this guy isn't keeping you up at night. So what if he's a great lay and funny and all that, he's not-"

"Bri, I know, OK, I know. I told him today that this needs to happen and it will but I'm dragging my feet on it and I'm not oblivious to the damage that's causing but, be patient with me. I'm not exactly getting nothing out of the situation, you know? I'm not a victim here, he didn't suck me in with some giant web of lies-I knew what was up."

"Yeah yeah, I didn't say you were a victim but-wait how many times did you cum today you little tramp? How long was here there?"

"A few hours."

"A few hours!? Ooohh you dirty little thing. What, like four times? You make me sick, getting off all morning and afternoon as I sit here and watch this French-Canadian monstrosity put my tiles in, sweating all over the place, ass crack up to his neck."

"OMG, you totally wanted to fuck him!"

"I would have let that giant Canook roll his perspiring self all over me but he never even gave me the time of day, I'm not kidding.

*Was more interested in making sure the seams were lined up perfectly than my obviously delicious breasts that were conveniently exposed almost to the nipples."*

Heather laughed and dropped the phone back down on the bed. "You say I have problems. You haven't met a contractor or repairman that you didn't want to hump."

*"I may know what constitutes a bad relationship, sweetheart,"* Brianna replied, *"but there's no rules for lust."*

"Hey, I need to get in the shower and get a few things done before I head over there later, my love," Heather said, hearing wailing in the background of Brianna's end of the call. "What's that noise, you leave a joint burning on the rug again?"

The sound of the emergency vehicles roared in the background, distorted in the speakers.

"Cops or something going by. Shit, imagine if that store got robbed again? Or could be that couple down the road, remember? Twice last fall I told you the husband chased her out of the house swearing, then Christmas Eve I drive by and she's pummeling him with her fists on the front porch as the neighbors watched. See, that's the kind of dysfunctional shit I need in my life. Someone that makes me so sick with love that I want to punch them. Someday."

"It's the dream, absolutely," Heather said, the background noise having ended. "I'll be there at seven. Don't have more than half the bottle finished before I get there."

"I'll be passed out, just let yourself in and go look at my tiles, then toss a blanket on me. Love you."

"Love you too," Heather said, reaching down and tapping the end button on her phone. As she did, she spotted the paper-clipped pages of Stephen's book resting on the tattered motel chair.

"Hmmm," she said as she hopped up from the bed and made her way to it.

<#>

*There was his father, and a fire in the background. Now he's gone, but there's fire everywhere. On top of something cold now, maybe ice. Far off in the distance it's green like New England spring, but they aren't really trees. Something pushing down on his head, his neck twisting. There are others jumping near him, but no sound when they hit the ground. The night sky is all encompassing immediately, stars dot the black canvas in heavy concentrations in the middle but less so at the sides. Someone whispers "try harder". The smell of ocean salt is dense. He's riding his bike and falls onto the grass, a voice behind him laughing. In a car driving fast at night, Trance music pulsating. A Pug dog on his chest. There are fifty people in a stairwell screaming. The ocean smell is gone and it's only tangerine or another citrus. Bells chime, something intense flashes several times. Nothing.*

# *Chapter 6*

*Emily* stood motionless, listening to the *fa dump fa dump fa dump* of her heart in her chest. She couldn't hear the crackling anymore, only the thumping inside her. She felt her legs buckling, though she remained standing, and there was no breath in her lungs, or there was too much; she couldn't tell if she needed to inhale or exhale.

The unknown light and sound in the distance offered no heat but she decided it was fire and imagined it spreading to the walls and burning the cellar where she stood, trapped in her cage. The smoke rushing up into her face and through her nose-invisible because of the darkness-stinging her nostrils and the insides of her mouth then making her cough wildly. She could almost feel the warmth of the flames approaching, as it was at her uncle Pete's bonfires, the flames thriving and multiplying as he'd toss wooden pallets on the pile and she'd feel her skin roast.

Soon the flames would scatter onto the ceiling and be racing overhead, catching onto the wood framing her enclosure. They'd latch on the beams, dig their red-orange claws in as they spiraled down towards the floor looking for more fuel. Across the room, some of the flames would encircle a bottle of the cleaning solution she smelled earlier and explode, knocking other items stacked around to the ground where they'd ignite as well. The intensity of the heat would grow to be so torrid and sweltering that she'd melt, standing right there in her socks.

Her legs gave out and she crumbled to the floor, letting all the air from her lungs rush out in a pained exhale. She drew a deep, heavy breath-as a gasp at first-then let it out, before sucking in more air and doing the same over and over for what seemed like minutes but was only seconds. Her mother told her she was "hyperventilating" once when a Huntsman spider landed on her arm at the age of seven. She remembered feeling dizzy before mom made her breathe into a brown lunch bag as she was stroking her chestnut hair on the edge of the bed. Her breathing was so loud, she recalled, as though she was wheezing the way her Grandad did when he had Pneumonia. She wondered if the paper bag was a trick, with the feel of her mother's hands on her head and neck as she moved over and through her locks being the real cure, as her breathing settled so quickly then.

There were no paper bags or mother's soft fingers now, only a cold cement floor and isolation. The intense hunger she felt earlier had devolved into nausea, and, as thirsty as she was still, she feared the liquid may come back up as soon as it hit her stomach. She took slow, deliberate breaths through her nose, holding them for a moment and then releasing though her mouth-another trick mom taught her years back. She did this for about a minute until her heart calmed and the visions of fire and burning relented, though somewhere not far from her there *was* something burning, she was sure of it.

Emily reached for the bottle of water, deciding to take two small sips and risk the consequences as her throat was scratchy and her lips felt torn and cracked. She touched an index finger to them before drawing on the water and could feel the splits and callouses. Two sips turned into three gulps and then she slammed the water bottle back down onto the hard floor, wiping her mouth before trying to stand back up, then bracing herself against one side of the enclosure.

"Hello," she uttered, her voice strained. "Hello, it's Emily and I don't know why I'm here and I'm scared. Can someone answer me? I need to get out of here, please. I'm sorry for whatever I did or if I'm in trouble, please, just let me out. "

Her words gained strength as she spoke, but she didn't want to start screaming. She feared any slip into panic may cause her to pass out and the only thing that terrified her more than being where she was now was being unconscious for whatever was next.

She grabbed tight to the chicken wire, pulling at it back and forth, with all the force that she had, rattling the wooden door against the frame. Then she pushed her face up against it tight, making it feel like it may cut her skin if she went any harder, to see if she could identify where the source of the fire was.

"Hello, please will somebody help me, it's Emily and I think something's burning and I want to get out now," she yelled. "I don't want to be here."

She was fighting back a wellspring of tears, byproducts of terror and confusion, but she took control of her breathing again, remembering something her dad said when she was younger. "*If you get lost and can't find your mom or myself, and no one else is around, just stay where you are. We'll find you.*"

*We will find you.*

She pulled away from the metal wire in the door, took a breath through her nose and decided that whatever was burning couldn't harm her-at least right now-as there was no smoke, or even the faintest odor of anything burning. She turned her body forty-five degrees and sat down, resting her back against the side wall of the cage, picking up the water bottle and placing it between her knees. She had no idea how long she'd been here-whether hours or even days-but she assumed hours as her hunger wasn't so all consuming that days would make sense.

*The man that was singing.*

She tried to remember the words or tune of the song. His voice was scratchy. His face was familiar but not one she saw every day, and he was smiling while-

"It's not really fire, you know. It's fake," the unknown voice said from somewhere behind her, causing her to jump forward, knocking the water bottle over and spilling its contents across the floor. "Made me crazy at first."

Emily shot up and pushed up against the wire mesh and looked towards her right, "Who is that? Who are you, are you in here? Hello?" she questioned, whimpering at the end.

"I'm right on the other side of you, not far. Same setup as you," the voice said.

Emily felt her heart start racing again, elated to hear she was not alone yet nervous the voice may be the one who put her there.

"You, you're in here, same as me you mean? In a cage," Emily asked.

"I don't think you can call this much of a cage, really, more like a shitty chicken coop is all," the voice said. "Doesn't matter though because you're probably, what, nine or ten? I don't think you're strong enough to bust out and even if you are it won't matter. I broke free once and there's nowhere to go anyway. Just an iron door down the other end here with a big ass lock on it and another door over around the corner closer to you, locked as well."

"How do you know that? I mean it's so dark in here and, where's that fire? I can't see where it's coming from but it sounds close and I can see-"

"It's fake I told ya," the voice interrupted. "It's a fireplace on a TV screen that' running all the time. It'll go for about an hour, winding down as the time passes, then start right back up again. It's some twisted shit, for sure."

Emily figured she was a girl about fifteen or sixteen and she swore a lot, just like her neighbor Cassidy who was about the same age. Every time other kids were around she was saying "shit" and the F word but when her mom came home she was a perfect angel. Emily tried to swear a few times but it sounded silly in her head.

"How do you know about the rest of the room, are there lights in here? I have a string here but I pulled it and nothing happened. I don't even know if it's morning or night time, do you know? Do you know where we are," Emily said, growing manic as she spoke.

"Emily-that what you said your name was when you woke me up yelling?" the girl asked.

"Yes," she replied, sheepishly.

"So, Emily, where do you *think* you are? Do you have any idea?"

"Well...in a basement, somewhere. I remember someone looking at me, singing, I was in a car but lots of it is fuzzy. I think I was with my parents at the Mall. I just want to go home," Emily said, as she started to cry and put her hands back on the metal in the door, viciously tugging at it.

"Emily!" the girl yelled. "Emily, stop it, you'll only hurt your hands and start bleeding OK? Can you hear me?"

The was no sound other than the very faint crackling twenty feet away.

"Emily, listen to me, please" she pleaded.

"OK, I'm sorry. I'm scared and don't know what to do," Emily answered.

"First of all, I know this room because I fucking escaped once, from this stupid coop I mean. I got out into the main area surrounding us here and I touched and looked at every damn thing in here, as dark as it was. I could probably paint a picture of it blindfolded I remember it so good. The thing is though, like I said, there isn't any way out of here that I can tell from the time I had scouring every inch after I busted out. That's why the dumb shit put me back in here, same as before 'cause he knows it doesn't matter if I break out every day, I'm still just gonna be stuck in this big ass room with nowhere to go. Unless you're not really a tiny little girl and instead you're the Hulk or something."

Emily didn't respond.

"Hey, I know this is scary and I hate this shithole too but the only thing I can tell you is that, well he doesn't do anything *too* bad to you, or at least he didn't to me. Other than, you know," the girl said.

Emily recalled another conversation she had with her father that wasn't long after the talk about what to do if she was ever lost or in unfamiliar places, that one being far more uncomfortable.

"What man, who's the man and how did he get us here, I don't understand," Emily questioned.

The girl was sitting, knees bent, facing the opposite direction Emily had been when she first spoke to her. The tattered, off white summer dress with floral patterns was a size too small and didn't go far below her knees, and it smelled of horrible perspiration. She pushed herself up and made her way over to the chicken wire door of her own enclosure, resting both hands on the mesh and letting out a small sigh.

"Emily, you sound like a little girl, under ten maybe, right?" she asked.

"I'm nine," Emily answered.

"OK, listen. This is a world of shit we're in here, I'm not going to lie to you, it's not a happy place and it's not gonna be easy for a while. This sick fuck-I call him Stan 'cause it kinda sounds like Satan, you know? Well, this twisted asshole took us here and he's taken others, I think, well I know 'cause I've seen at least one other and maybe heard more but...So, he likes young girls and takes them into the room through the big heavy door over closer to my side-where he's taken me before-and he, you know, does stuff. Do you understand what I mean Emily?"

Emily listened to her own breath go in and out, in and out, in and out three times, then moved back closer to the chicken wire. "Kinda, I guess."

"Yeah, well, it's nothing a little girl like you, or me, should have to think about but it has nothing to do with us at all, you understand? This scumbag is just some pervo freak and I let him do his thing and pretend I'm somewhere else and then when he puts me back in here I take my hands and I squeeze the skin above my knee-really hard-over and over until my fingers get so tired and sore I can't stand it. I dig into my skin so deep that it's all I can feel-nothing else. Not gonna let that old prick make me feel anything I don't want to," the girl said, her voice amplified at the end.

"What's in that room, the one he takes you too?" Emily questioned.

"Ehh, a shitty shag pad is all. Crappy old bed, some other little cots, a refrigerator, a TV and a there's a bathroom with a shower but no door. You have a bucket and some paper there behind you, for your business, did you know that?" she asked Emily.

"No, I didn't see it," Emily answered, shuffling away from the door and towards the back, bumping what appeared to be a bucket with her right foot. "Here it is, I think."

"OK good, because he'll take you in that room to go to the bathroom sometimes so it's kinda like for emergencies but it's there if you need it," the girl said. "Feel on yours and see if there's a piece of metal, like a handle to pick it up."

Emily reached around the lip of the bucket and onto the sides but couldn't feel anything other than the plastic of the container itself.

"I don't feel any metal, or a handle," Emily said.

"Ha, see I knew it," the girl shouted. "He screwed up when he changed mine out a while back and left this metal piece on here. So, what I've been doing is bending it a little, then pulling it off and using it as a tool to mess with the hinges on this door here, loosen it up again."

"But I thought you said it doesn't matter if you get out cause there's nowhere to go?" Emily questioned.

"That's true, Em, and that's because we don't have any keys to those doors, but I know he has them on him all the time, a big set like a janitor at your school or something, you know what I mean? Those big ass key things hanging from their belts and whatnot," she said.

"Yeah, I've seen them," Emily replied.

43

"Well, what I'm going to do is loosen the door hinges good, then one of these times when he gets really close I'm going rush right at the door and break it off and pin him underneath, and use the end of the metal handle piece I've been filing down on the floor here to stab the fucker right in the neck, then take his keys. He's not that big so I figure if I pin him under the wire of the door he won't be able to get up real easy and I'll be able make it happen quickly. It's all gotta be right though. I need to get this end real sharp and make sure the door is loose enough and then he's gotta be right near the door and looking away for only a second. It's gonna work, I know it is."

Emily listened to her describe the plan and violent end of the man that had put her here. The same man that was singing to her.

"He is small, the man? I think the man who had me in the car was big."

"He seemed big to me at first, too. But he's skinny, maybe fifty and is usually wearing glasses and stupid fucking shirts that look too small for him."

"Are there more like him?"

"I...I don't know, but sometimes I hear noises when I'm in the other room and it could be another voice, or voices, it's hard to tell. Shit I can't imagine if there was another one of these assholes. Well, anyway, you and I have to come up with a plan 'cause I don't want to miss an opportunity if one comes to get this guy, OK?"

"I just want to get out of here, I'll do whatever you want. I need to see my mom and dad and-"

"Emily," the girl interjected. "Hey, so my name is Amber, by the way. Aint no way I wanna spend any more time in this shithole myself so don't get too fired up or you'll lose your breath and start panicking and we'll both be screwed. It may not be tomorrow or even next week but we're getting the fuck out of here."

"You swear a lot," Emily said.

Amber laughed emphatically, then, "Shit kid, I gave up all sense of decency a long time ago when I found myself in this nightmare. I figure when I get out I can go back to being all sweet and proper."

"I didn't mean that I thought it was bad or…"

"I know, it's OK. The last thing we need to be worrying about here is hurting someone's feelings, right? We have enough damn problems."

Emily giggled, then moved back to the side where Amber was and sat down with her back resting against the wall, then said, "Amber, can I ask you something?"

"Sure kiddo, what is it?"

"Do you know how long I've been here?"

"Uh, well I think he brought you down early yesterday, like real early, when it was still dark out. Heard a little commotion outside, some voices, then half woke up when he was dicking around down here but I almost block it all out now. Never heard a peep out of you though so didn't think he had anyone with him, and maybe he was just talking to himself outside."

"Oh OK. Well, can I ask another question?"

"Yeeessss."

"Well, you said you gave up being decent or not swearing-I forgot exactly, but I mean you said *a long time ago*, so I was just wondering, how long have you been here, locked up like this?"

Amber heard the question move into her airspace and spiral down into her ears. They were words she knew were coming and dreaded hearing.

She could tell Emily about the days that eventually drifted into weeks which then folded into months and about how she stopped counting when it had grown close to a year. She could tell her the way she counted those days-unable to see sunlight or nightfall other than ever so slightly through cracks in either of the rooms but instead used the number of TV Fireplace cycles and how she'd estimated it to be about an hour long. She could inform Emily that, even though the man wasn't violent with her that he did have a temper, and too much

45

resistance would mean she'd feel pain. Pain that may be too much for her tiny body and inexperienced years to bear. She could elude to the fact that she not only heard other voices sometimes when she was in the other room but often they were screaming, in the distance, behind another door she'd never seen or in some other part of the building she was never taken. She could tell her that, in the last few months alone there'd been at least five other girls in that same cage she was in right now, a couple a little younger, some older, and all of which Amber never saw again but one for certain she knew left not moving, slung over the man's shoulder as he carried her out the door near the fake fireplace, Amber screaming and cursing at him as he took her away.

She could tell Emily that, as much as she loved the idea of her little plan with the metal handle on the bucket and the rush she'd get out of jamming that thing deep into his neck, that the horrible, brutal truth of their situation was that this was likely their final stop on the road of life. They were going to die here and it was going to be a tortuous and excruciating trip most of the way. She could tell her that the real reason she started sharpening that metal bucket handle end was so that she could slice her own neck wide open and be done with this fucked up place.

She told her none of that.

"You know, Emily, I don't know exactly because there's no way really to count. No calendars or clocks or shit like that but if I was to guess, I'd say a few weeks," she lied. "But don't worry, 'cause my plan is going to work and we're going to get this asshole then get ourselves the fuck outta here and back home, OK? Does that sound good?"

Emily felt the first sense of calm she had since she awoke, and felt her breathing begin to normalize. She was hungry, tired, confused and still scared, but she was no longer alone.

# *Chapter 7*

*As* Heather drove home from the motel where she'd been with Stephen, she pulled down her sun visor and saw the familiar 3x5 card she'd taped to the back. "No More Unavailable Men", it said, making her laugh out loud in the car. The Bluetooth wouldn't connect the music on her phone to the car stereo-as usual-so she poked at the presets on her dash to see what was on. While searching, she glanced at her phone on the passenger's seat and it was still black-no reply. That wasn't unusual, as there were stretches when he was working and couldn't text, or driving, which he was good about being cautious of, but it wasn't those instances that concerned her.

Heather had boys sniffing around from the age of fourteen when her breasts made their first appearance. She was awkward, somewhat clumsy and was still clinging to the tomboy side of her that living with two brothers fostered, but it was then that her eyes began to hold onto the curve in young man's butt or the strong shape of his jawline or that vein in their forearm longer than it had previously. Being raised in an Evangelical Christian household until she broke free in her early twenties, having boyfriends in the traditional sense wasn't allowed and she hadn't even kissed anyone until her seventeenth birthday. The "birthday kiss", as it would be remembered, was from a fellow parishioner, Daniel, who'd left the church a year earlier and caught Heather post-celebration outside a local convenience store. He told her she looked "prettier than usual" and that she had frosting in her hair, in doing so moving himself up close to her and pulling it from her amber strands as she stood against the brick-walled face of the shop. Heather watched as Daniel's hand reached up towards her face and into her hair, removing the confection, his brown eyes looking deep into her own. She recalled thanking him before he said, *"I hope just because I'm not there anymore I'll still see you around?"* She was never able to recollect what, if anything she replied, though vividly remembers that she smiled at him and let her hand reach into his, and then he kissed her for about five seconds, cradling her face with his free hand. He said goodbye and she only saw him one other time after that, several months later, while passing in a local shopping center, and she learned the following year that he'd moved to California to go to San Diego State University.

The kiss not only ignited elements of Heather's womanhood she was unaware she possessed, but was also the catalyst for her leaving her religion and embarking on the personal journey of determining who she was as a woman and human being. The church had taught her about sacrifice, selfless love and suppression of desire. It taught her to shun personal growth vs spiritual and to accept that very little in her life was of her own control, as God had a plan for her. When she decided to leave, it was with the belief that God had still existed but that if He truly loved her He'd support her curious and evolving nature. It wasn't until she began losing friends and one of her brothers before she decided that God was in fact a concept-a man-made construct-and not a mystical, all knowing, powerful being. The only Deity she worshipped at this point in her life was her freedom from oppressive ideologies, and that was one of the reasons she was so drawn to Stephen.

They met at a book discussion for *The Art of Racing in the Rain* by Garth Stein. Stephen was hosting at a local library, as it was his favorite work of modern fiction and he relished the opportunity to discuss it with others. She'd discovered the book from a Community College professor that taught creative writing and made no secret that he'd like to get creative with Heather on endeavors more personal than writing short stories. She ignored his advances but was somewhat turned on by his persistence and fearless nature.

Heather was five-seven, brunette, buxom with chestnut brown eyes so big that a "moose could fall inside them" Stephen once said. They were deep and vast-the envy of most who knew her-but it was her smile that first captivated anyone who's own eyes found her. A piercing white smile-a row of perfect teeth snuggled in plump full lips-that was impossible to not fall in love with. When someone smiled with a mouth like hers-formed with genuine sincerity-the joy was infectious and those in the vicinity yearned to know her. Of course, there were always detractors. The pessimists and cynics who felt anyone who would smile at a stranger that way, and willing to engage the unknown, must be insincere or have ulterior motives, so those types would grow icy in her presence; the origins of their misguided perceptions surely rooted in their own fears and insecurities.

Heather went to the book signing with her friend Stephanie and Stephen drew both their eyes. The age gap was more pronounced with Stephanie, so she let her eye wander to others whereas Heather's gaze fixed on him. The shaved head, goateed look was a recent fixation for her as she'd preferred longer haired men-rock and roll types-looking more Jesus than Mr. Clean. Stephen was tall, in shape and had enough wannabe rocker with his two hoop earrings in his left ear. He was wearing a white long-sleeved sweater and dark jeans and had been setting up the table with copies of the book and some Q&A pages to help start conversations. Their eyes met briefly but he continued with his prep, not engaging her until the finish of the event where she asked him how many times he read the book, to which he replied, *"Five, which I am assuming is five more than you."* She admitted she hadn't yet finished it but loved the narrative and how it was told from a dog's perspective, mentioning that *"If there was a book I wish I'd written, I'd say it'd be this one."* The post-event conversation lasted far too long between them considering she hadn't finished the book and Stephanie grew ansty-a fact Stephen picked up on-so they exchanged numbers and he said, *"If you want to talk more about the thirty pages you read, call me."* He smiled at her and finished packing up and she was already picturing him shirtless and on top of her in her new Memory Foam bed-in-box she bought on QVC. Another impulse purchase after too much wine and a recently ended fling with a dude that made bagels at the mall and thought the Magna Carta was an album by Pink Floyd.

"Where the hell are you," Heather said looking down at her phone, tapping the Home button, revealing nothing but the wallpaper picture of her and Brianna. She doubted he was *engaged elsewhere* because they'd spent most of the day together and although he was young in spirit he wasn't a nineteen-year-old kid snorting Viagra. The places the mind will go when you allow yourself to fall for someone who's made no secret there's someone else can be all-consuming, she often experienced; for a girl that had long abandoned faith, she was placing an enormous amount in Steven.

Heather picked up the phone and called Brianna.

"Hey girl. You better have a couple Industrial sized bottles of Pinot on hand because I'm having a bit of day," Heather said, keeping an eye out for police officers who may frown on her holding the phone in her hand while driving. "Oh, and did you ever find out what the hell was going on with all those cops, by your place? Was it the neighbors?"

She listened to Brianna inform her that there'd been some type of serious event at *Willie's Place*, the restaurant not far from where she and Stephen had spent much of the day. Occasionally he'd stop there and get a milkshake, as he claimed it was in his "Top Five". Stephen had numerous Top Five lists and 'Best Ofs', she was beginning to realize, which only enamored her more to the man, especially since the math rarely worked as there appeared to often be seven, ten or even fifteen on a list of five.

Heather pulled her car into a gas station on the right and swung the car around, deciding to take a ride by Willie's to ease her mind. The amount she worried about Stephen was irrational, often overwhelming-a byproduct of being "the other woman"-and feeling like any moment her connection to him could be severed by not only him or her, but a circumstantial event that left interlopers out on the fringe. Brianna once spoke about a married man she dated who, after a serious car accident, ended up in ICU for three days. Brianna, forlorn, overwhelmed and distraught rushed to the hospital only to see the woman she knew was his wife, their kids, the in-laws and others huddled around waiting room chairs sharing sorrows, fears, condolences and offering support to one another concerning this man she barely knew. Her concern was real, but her place at the table didn't exist. She was a distraction, an intruder, a liar. Although it was the man himself who courted *her*, pursued her with vigor even-no secret to much of the family that gathered around each other there in that Hospital-her presence would be unwelcomed.

Heather looped her Jetta around again, headed back in the other direction, deciding instead to drive home and take a deeper peek into the mind of her absent lover through his words, which lay on the passenger seat next to her.

## Chapter 8

"*Yeah*, I'm familiar with the place, over in Breddleton. Bob Diller's not a guy you forget so easy," said Sheriff McCabe, looking across the room at one of his Deputies tapping something into the keypad of his smartphone. "Well, meaning he's a charismatic fella, big guy too, that's all. You need me to pick him up, or-"

Deputy Jeffrey Curtis, sitting several feet away, leaned back too far in his rickety swivel chair and almost fell over, bobbling his phone but recovering the device as well as his balance. Sheriff McCabe dead stared him as he continued listening to the man on the phone.

"Well, unless you call the occasional domestic incident between him and his wife 'out of the ordinary', then no, I wouldn't say I've seen anything noteworthy coming out of Bob's place. What is it you folks up Connecticut way are looking into?" asked the Sheriff, as he tapped his index finger against his thumb.

Deputy Curtis was inching backwards in his chair again so Sheriff McCabe covered the mouthpiece of the landline phone with his right hand, "Jeff, will you put that damn phone down and finish that report for God's sake."

Deputy Curtis looked over at him then grimaced as he pushed himself straight up in the chair, resting his phone on the metal desk, buried in old coffee cups, scattered paperwork and manila folders. He grabbed the ballpoint pen that lay next to the Incident Report he'd started fifteen minutes earlier before allowing a Facebook notification to pull him away again.

"One four seven, got it. No problem, Officer Aniello was it? I'll take a ride over there and I'll give you a call later either way. Right. Take care now," Sheriff McCabe said, dropping the handset into the cradle.

"So, what did the Connecticut boys want with Diller the Killer? I told you we used to call him that in High School, right? Fucking guy was like King Kong he was so big, hairy as hell too, but somehow, he was great at getting chicks so it was, like, one of those double meaning things, you know? A real killer *and* a lady killer," said Deputy Curtis, grinning and nodding his head at the Sheriff.

"The pride of Potter County, Pennsylvania they should call you, Curtis," the Sheriff said. "So, I need to head over to his shop because his name came up in some attempted kidnapping they had in Connecticut, sounds like indirectly so it's probably nothing but see if we have anything in his file at all other than him smacking his wife around. I recall there was something about a dispute with a delivery guy out there a year or so ago."

Deputy Curtis stood up and walked towards Sheriff McCabe, the ballpoint pen dropping to the floor. "Yeah, you know that jackass has always had a thing with people delivering shit to his place. He scared that UPS driver half to death a couple Christmases ago, you remember?"

"Vaguely, but that's not the incident I'm talking about. Thought he roughed some poor bastard up about half his size that was delivering car parts or something. Check into it, and finish up that paperwork and clean that abomination of a desk because I have a feeling those Connecticut boys are going to end up here before long," the Sheriff said, grabbing his hat from the window sill near his desk.

"Sure, no problem, but, you sure you don't want me to head out there with you? If he's a few hits into a bottle and the old lady is getting lippy he's liable to make a run at you, uniform, gun and all,"

Deputy Curtis said, imitating an angry gorilla, complete with ridiculous vocalizations.

The Sheriff stared at Curtis, and for the umpteenth time in his recorded memories of working alongside him the last nine years, decided he hadn't regretted not having children.

"I'm good. I'll be back in an hour or so," the Sheriff replied, making his way to the door and out to his car.

Charles McCabe had been a Sheriff in Potter County for twenty-two years. Over that time span he'd come to know a good portion of the residents, transients that weaved in and out of town, law enforcement officers in surrounding areas and of course the Deputies that worked alongside him. Jeffrey Curtis was as forgettable a human being as one could be yet for a variety of reasons-some arguably petty-Sheriff McCabe was annoyed by almost everything he did, and that discontent resonated and took its time to dissipate. There was the obvious sloppiness and lack of focus, but there were other intangibles he couldn't explain, and, while listening to him talk, he often wanted to walk out of the room, which on many occasions he did. Watching him diddle with his phone with his ridiculous grin, as though he was penning something seductive to a woman on the other end, made him vomitus. He found a way to procrastinate on everything until the last possible second yet somehow completed it-though usually half ass-offering his smug, self-assured explanation every time. Curtis hadn't made a pot of coffee for the entire duration he'd been there, though was a ravenous consumer of the beverage so the pot was always ninety-five percent empty and searing the brown remains in the bottom, leaving a crusty black Arabica pancake for someone else to scrape out. Curtis was moronic and disinterested in the law, from the way the Sheriff saw it, and that was the epicenter of what bothered him most.

Sheriff McCabe pulled the car off Route 6, onto 449, making his way up from West Pike towards Breddleton. The skyline was gray and patchy, with the tops of the surrounding trees bending, the leaves fluttering, as high pressure fought to make a comeback, his sinuses forewarned. The mid-nineties Ford Crown Victoria was in desperate need of a tune up, as it knocked and pinged its way into fourth gear under acceleration and the front end began to shimmy at 60MPH. The radio was a wasteland of modern country music, news talk and Christian discussion but he managed to land on an FM station lower in the dial that was playing "Dark Star" by Crosby, Stills & Nash so he left it there. Forty years earlier, the song was a staple of his small but eclectic vinyl collection which was heavier in Haight Ashbury and Folk Rock than one might imagine from a twenty-five-year-old transplant from Savannah, Georgia. The hippie rebellion led him to the Northeast years prior, tired of watching his cousins come home in pieces from Vietnam, though he was drafted shortly after and served until the back of his calf was tore off in a friendly fire event during Operation Apache Snow. The evolution into police work came after his best friend got pinched on a distribution charge for selling Marijuana outside an Allman Brothers concert in the late seventies and he vowed to "make a difference", to be a force for change from within the system instead of looking in from the outside. Like so many before him, however, the years, experiences, mental remnants of the war and the dark underside of the pedestrian world eroded his altruistic intentions. He found himself in Pennsylvania after following his ex-wife to her new career as a Director for a telecommunications company in the late eighties. She'd moved up the ladder with long hours and intense focus while he stagnated as a patrol officer outside of Philadelphia, rarely crossing paths with one another at home, initially by circumstance, eventually by design. They had no kids, and she left him in 1993 in the middle of the night, leaving everything except one of their two cats. In the years since, he could never put it together why she took the one-eyed, ornery, mangy tabby cat and left him the docile Maine Coon but he relished the twelve years he had with the feline before it died on a rainy Monday after the Super Bowl, which he'd always heard was one of the year's most depressing days.

55

Even cats hated that all that was left was golf for a couple months, he assumed.

Sheriff McCabe saw the Diller Propane lot up ahead on the right and began to slow the car down right as he heard the Deputy chime in over the CB Radio.

"Sheriff, Curtis here," the voice said, fuzzy and chewing. "I finished up that report. Thinking of going over to Maggie's for some Wings. You want some of those Parmesan Garlic ones you like? Over."

Ordinarily, he may have welcomed the gesture as thoughtful, but he'd told him several times in the last week that he was attempting to eat healthier and dial back the salt.

"Just because there's a hole in your face doesn't mean you need to keep putting stuff in it, you understand that, right?" declared the Sheriff. "I'm all set. Over."

"I hear ya boss. You make it to Diller's place yet? Over." the Deputy asked.

For a moment, Sheriff McCabe felt guilty for snapping at him but then remembered this was the same man that once applied super glue to several of the Port-O-Let seats outside the town fair two years earlier while in uniform.

"I'm here, I'll check back when I'm ready to head back. Over and out," said the Sheriff, hanging the Microphone onto the hook under the dash.

He pulled his hat from the passenger's side seat and aligned it in the mirror, checking his teeth for anything that shouldn't be there-a byproduct of working with Curtis so long, who was often an oral clothesline for food particles. As he exited the car, stepping into the dirt and gravel lot of Diller's Propane, he noticed a torn and dingy American flag that was resting at about three quarters mast up the rusted metal pole. His year and a half in Vietnam and time amongst the counterculture had opened his eyes to some of the misdeeds of the United States, but, in his eyes, it was still his family, and letting one of your asshole siblings go outside with mismatched socks and shit all over their shirt may be what they deserved sometimes, but it was still disrespectful.

"What brings you down this way, Sheriff?" the voice said from behind a box truck off to his right side.

"Is that you Bob?" the Sheriff asked.

"Yeah, I'm pulling some of the tape off the side of this truck. The damn kids are always taking Duct tape and spelling out messages and shit on here. Nobody can just normal the fuck out anymore, know what I mean?" Diller spouted, wiping his hands on a maroon colored rag as he emerged from behind the truck. "You have any kids, Charlie? I can't recall but don't think I ever saw you with any."

"No kids, just that mental midget Curtis to contend with, which is unquestionably worse."

"That shithead could get lost in a closet. I don't understand why the county still has him on the payroll. He got an Uncle in the Governor's office or something?"

"I've asked myself that question for years, Bob," McCabe said, surveying the area around the truck and then looking down at Diller's hands. "You looking to change careers, because I'm certain I could get him bounced with a couple phone calls and you look like you could handle yourself in a squabble far better than Jeff."

Bob laughed and then dropped the wipe rag to the ground and stepped closer to the Sheriff. "So, anyway, what is it I can help you with?"

"Well," he replied, turning back to look at the abused flag on the pole, its metal rings slapping against the steel in the breeze, "I got this call from the Connecticut State Police, and apparently they came up with something that had your name on it, may have fallen out of a vehicle at a crime scene they suspect. Was an invoice with something written on it but unreadable I guess. They're going to fax a copy of it but there was a partial number on the upper right side, 147. Any chance you have-"

"One four seven?" Diller interrupted. "Hate to burst your bubble Sheriff but that's the first three digits of every Invoice I've given out in the last three years or so. The pack had like a thousand in them and they all start with 'one-four-seven'. I probably fill one hundred-fifty cans a year, make another hundred or so deliveries, give or take. This last order of Invoices started with those numbers and I'm still a hundred plus from running out."

The Sheriff nodded, then looked over at the front door of the shabby office where Diller's wife had been peeking out. She had a tall glass of something in her hand she sipped in between hits off a cigarette, and scooted away as she noticed the Sheriff's gaze.

"Yeah, I figured it may be a longshot, with partial digits and nothing legible on the slip but I suppose the Connecticut fellas were hoping I'd either get lucky or roll up here with you loading Russian sex slaves into this truck or something," the Sheriff joked.

Bob Diller roared, laughing and smacking his hand on the side of the truck. The Sheriff watched as his wife ran to the door of the office and pushed it open a few inches, angling her head so her ear was filling the gap.

"Holy shit, now that's a good one, Chuck. You think if I had my hands on some young whores I'd be sending them *away*? Get the fuck outta here! Have you seen my wife? Woman could stop a clock with that face. All she does is tear into my ass all day long, can't even have a drink or two even though she's nearly shitfaced every day by four in the afternoon." He noticed the Sheriff's eyes darting back and forth to the front of his building. "That crazy broad is listening out the front door, isn't she? Mind your damn business, woman, you hear me!?"

His screaming startled his wife, and the door snapped shut as she disappeared back into the shadows of the office.

"Go easy on her, Bob. You're not all backrubs and bouquets and I'm sure she could say a thing or two about you," quipped the Sheriff.

The much larger man stared at McCabe and gave him one of those looks assuring him that he knew-they both knew-who the tougher man was.

"Listen Sheriff, I'm not saying I'm fucking Don Juan over here but you don't have to live with her. It's always the man's fault in this Goddamn P.C. world, everyone's a feminist nowadays, even these bearded Hipster fucks that come by on weekends and buy Propane for their camping trips as they drive on through. I told one of these little shits last fall that the girl he's with was 'smoking hot' and you know what he says?"

"What's that?"

"Fucking punk says, 'Hey thanks for objectifying my girlfriend. She lives to be desired by men like you,' then calls me a Neanderthal. I have little tolerance for the people I don't hate so it took everything I had not to sock that little bitch."

Sheriff McCabe locked eyes with Diller for a few seconds until Bob turned away, then glanced back where his wife had been peeking out.

"It's a different world, Bob, I'll give you that, " the Sheriff suggested, angling his Campaign hat slightly to the left on his head. "So, maybe take a couple days and think about if you had anyone stop here that was a little 'off' or may have had a young girl with them and anything seemed peculiar. I can't promise you won't see or hear from the Connecticut fellas, or the FBI for that matter, but would imagine if I can relay any information you can recall to them it may decrease those chances. At least for now."

"Fuck man, that's the last thing I want is a bunch of cops poking around here, getting in my shit. And don't start thinking that's 'cause I have things to hide, I don't, but still don't want nosy assholes combing through my business."

"I understand, and right now I don't think that's a high probability. I'm guessing the prevailing theory is that this guy was some drifter type, maybe just trying to nab this girl on a whim. Most of the time when you see something more organized the suspect is driving a van or vehicle more conspicuous than a beat to piss woody station wagon with a damaged roof that sticks out like a sore thumb."

Bob Diller was reaching down to pick up the rags he'd used to wipe his hands off earlier when he heard the Sheriff mention the station wagon. He stopped for a second, scooped them up and stuffed them into his back pocket, then looked back at the front of the building to see if his wife was being nosey again.

"A station wagon? What did it look like, other than being a 'beat to piss woody'?"

"Well, they only gave me a brief description-and my guess is the guy may have ditched the car unless he really is just some reckless one timer-but it was described as Seventies era, brownish green in color, that wood-type paneling, banged-up roof they mentioned, especially the rear left I guess."

Bob listened to the Sheriff describe the car, one he'd seen at least once a week as it passed by the shop, and a few times a year when he made deliveries to the old farm where it was usually parked in back, several miles up the main road. The car wouldn't have left an impression on him but the man driving it, going on about two years ago, stopped at Bob's lot one afternoon looking to have tanks filled in a rush, also inquiring about rates for filling a larger set up at his home. When Bob began carrying one of the tanks back towards the rear of the car the man grabbed it from him and said, "I got this", then slipped it into the side door of the car. Owning a business meant sometimes you needed to let wiry little assholes do things that might result in another man losing his teeth, but the moment had etched itself into Diller's memory and the man nor the car had stopped back at the lot since, instead only paying for deliveries out to the farm.

"Hey so, this could be nothing but, salty prick that lives a few miles up the road on an old farm has a car like that. He rubbed me the wrong way first time I met him and hasn't been back since but I fill his larger tank at the farm a few times a year. Has a huge barn and a gone to shit house on the lot," Diller said.

"What spooked you about him?" the Sheriff asked.

"Spooked? Do I look like a man that gets 'spooked' Sheriff? Come on. The skinny fuck irked me is all, didn't want me loading a tank in his car and was a weird dude. I get that when you're out in the sticks like this you're going to run into some characters but this guy was tweaked about something. Or maybe he's just an asshole. Either way, he's got a car that matches that description."

"You mind grabbing me the address, Bob?"

"Sure, no problem."

"Good deal," the Sheriff said, staring over at the flagpole again.

"Will give me a chance to see what the wife is up to. Can't have a solid hour in my life alone and not have her rifling through my shit. You're a lucky bastard, Chuck, being single and all. Unless you're still hosing that broad from the Urgent Care?"

Diller stumbled into an all-night convenience store after a day-long drunk, seven months earlier, as Sheriff McCabe was leaving with Karen Marchand, the office Manager at a local Walk-In Clinic. He fired off a couple incoherent sexual innuendos, then mimicked penetration by inserting his index finger into a hole made with fingers from his other hand. McCabe escorted him outside, asked how much he'd drank and received slurred, inconsistent answers so he opened the rear door of Bob's car, told him to lie down for an hour and that he was going to have Stella, the cashier inside, hold his keys. That was his only option otherwise he'd have to bring him in for DUI. Bob flopped down on the back seat without much prodding and the Sheriff closed the door, tucking the keys onto the rear passenger's side wheel and under the fender, letting Stella know when he wakes up where they were. The fact that Bob recalled the incident surprised the Sheriff, unless his probing came as the result of the perpetual gossiping that went on at most of the area establishments.

"She's a good girl," McCabe offered, tapping his index finger against his thumb at his side. "Been close friends for some time, that's all. So, if you could kindly get me that address, Bob."

"Sure, of course. Didn't mean to pry," he lied, looking down at the Sheriff's tapping fingers. "Anyway, I can write down the address if you want but it's easier if I just tell you. If you take a right out of here and turn where that farm stand used to be, remember, up until like ten years ago?"

"Yeah, the one with the two carts, always had hand painted signs in red."

"Exactly. Well, take a right on that road-no sign but it's *Middle Farms Rd*-take a right and then as it starts to turn to gravel, another eighth of a mile or so it splits, head right and the guy's place is down the end around a sharp turn to the left. White house, dilapidated but has a halfway decent looking barn, newer, some other sheds just in need of a little upkeep. It's a shame the asshole let it go 'cause the family who owned it, might have even been *his* family, they kept it nice. Gone to shit now."

"Thanks Bob, I'll check in with Curtis, then I'll take a ride by there. I appreciate your help," said the Sheriff, pulling down on the corner of his hat. "Oh, and maybe take a look at that flag and put her out of her misery or shoot another one up the pole or something? Looks like it's seen better days."

Diller knew he was being jabbed at but left it alone. Quid Pro Quo for the comment about the woman.

"Sure thing, Chuck. Be careful out there, I doubt the guy is dangerous but I've been fooled before. I'd say have Curtis meet you out there but that numb nuts would only shoot himself or shit his pants."

"You're probably right, and I'm sure this is going to be a waste of time but a quick drive out there and we can keep the big shots out of our airspace. Have a good afternoon, Bob."

"You too. Oh, and Chuck, you need a cigarette or something? Seem a little twitchy," Bob suggested, nodding his head at the Sheriff's fingers.

"Quit years ago. Take care," the Sheriff answered, sliding his right hand into his pocket.

Sheriff McCabe walked back towards his car, letting his eyes drift enough to spy Mrs. Diller clutching her drink and watching him walk away, until she saw her husband move towards the front door, then she vanished in a blink. He figured the odds Curtis would end up having to come out on a Domestic was fifty-fifty after Diller got inside and lit into the wife about minding her own business. He almost wanted to leave, park a half mile down the road and wait, but the sooner he could check the farm out and give an all clear the better. Nine years earlier there was a string of unsolved murders at gas stations in the Northeast that stretched into the Midwest and, when one went down nearby, the whole area was crawling with law enforcement, Federal and three other states. His office became a waystation for all of them, and when the murder was ruled unrelated and they packed up and left-leaving the place trashed-several weeks' worth of other vital work went neglected. With how lazy and incompetent the Deputy had become, the last thing he could afford was to get sidetracked if this lead evolved into something it wasn't solely by going unchecked.

As he buckled himself into the car he pondered skipping the obligatory call to Curtis, but he couldn't shirk his duty because he loathed talking to him. He pulled the mic from the hook and depressed the button.

"Jeff, it's Charlie. I'm just leaving here now and headed up to Middle Farms Rd., run down one more lead. Shouldn't be there long. Over."

"How was Diller's place, you find any dead bodies? Over," the Deputy needled.

"Nothing out of the ordinary. Talk soon. Over and out," the Sheriff replied.

"OK Sheriff. Over and out."

Sheriff McCabe slid the tangled, corded mic back onto the hook and started the car. After slamming the transmission into reverse and cranking the wheel hard right, he rolled the wheel over to the other side and dropped it into Drive and sped off, heading up the road towards the old farm.

## Chapter 9

*Heather* walked into her condo, reaching back and pulling the keys from the lock, then kicking the door closed with her right leg. She tossed the clipped white pages of Stephen's book onto the small, round wooden coffee table that filled most of her breakfast nook, then slipped off her mid-heeled shoes. Part of her felt uneasy about delving into a deeply personal area of Stephen's life without asking but he was MIA and he *had* offered to read some of it to her soon, she rationalized. She slid her purse off her shoulder, then rummaged through it to find her phone, and when she had it in hand, opened the Home screen and went into the text chat between her and Stephen from earlier. There was still no reply, so she dropped the phone back down into her purse and made her way to the living room couch to plop down with the manuscript.

As she nuzzled herself into the plush cushions of the dark gray fabric couch, she paused, again wondering if he'd be upset if he knew she was reading his work, and, would she feel guilty after whether he knew or not.

"Fuck it," she said aloud. "I love 'em but if he had my journals he'd be reading voraciously then posting commentary on Twitter."

She opened the pages and rubbed her bare feet against the cloth of the couch as she began reading.

{*****}

Stephen Alexander was born on December 5th, Nineteen Seventy-Four at a couple seconds past 2am. He came into the world with a bright red, misshapen, soaking wet head that looked like it had been "bumped on the table" on the way out, his old man always joked. He went on to say that if the head and face didn't start to look right in a week he was going to give Stephen up for medical research. Although the doctors found his father's wit amusing, his mother struggled to see humor while three men and two women stared into her vagina and made fun of her seemingly deformed child. The night, nine months earlier, when Stephen's father assured his mother that smoking marijuana would have, "little effect on her", because it was her first time, proved to be a catastrophic mistruth, eventually resulting in Stephen's conception.

Henry Alexander drove Lillian Kelly out into a cornfield in the Northwest corner of Connecticut that evening, armed with an eighth of an ounce of weed, a few warm Budweiser bottles and a condom that had slipped out of his denim jeans and under the seat of his Chevelle. He and Lillian laughed at the absurdity of the two of them being together-he from the next town over in the "renter's" section, poor and waist deep in dysfunction-she from the affluent section of her hometown in a stable, white collar family. Henry told tales of a drunk father hitting him so hard that his shoes would come off, but that Henry could never determine if that was due to the sheer force or that the shoes were hand me downs from his older brother who had larger feet. Lillian laughed because Henry's storytelling was masterful, poignant and hysterical but the content was often so alarming and brutal that she wanted to cry as well, which she often did, disguised keenly in an uncontrolled belly laugh.

Henry poked fun at Lillian's crush on a local basketball hero named Tommy Triazzo that was about seven feet tall and had every father in New England ready to sell his daughter to if he even looked at her.

"You're what, a B cup at best Lill, come on. Plus, what do you know about Italian cooking? What was that we had the other night, Ragu on English Muffins with shake cheese? The kid's grandmother would slit your throat in your sleep. Better off you hang with me and we kill your old man and live off the Insurance."

He'd go on that night making her laugh, sliding up against her and letting the index and middle finger of his hand tickle the outside of her exposed thigh, peeking out of her lemon-yellow summer dress. She'd giggle and swoon, eventually lying back on the front seat as he moved his hand inside her thighs and up her leg until the Catholicism kicked in.

"Wait, didn't you say you had some grass? Let's smoke it," she said, straightening herself up in the seat and pulling her dress back into place.

Henry understood the intricate dance involved in taking the relationship with Lillian to the most intimate of physical realms so he was patient, respectful and happy to oblige her request, mentioning only that, "This probably won't affect you much, meaning you won't really feel high the first time, but I can't guarantee you won't want to bang me inside of ten minutes. It tends to do that." She smiled and watched him light the joint he'd rolled earlier and kept in the bag with the rest of the loose weed.

Henry was about five-foot-ten, strong jaw and chin, soft blue eyes and a mess of brown hair that was often too out of sorts for Lillian's tastes, if she was being honest. He had a poor man's Paul Newman thing happening, and his hands were working man's, yet softer to the touch than expected. He laughed in stuttered, abrupt-yet wildly infectious-spurts. His smile was effortless and honest, and was the first thing Lillian noticed when she saw him outside her school with a couple of her older brothers' friends, smoking a cigarette.

Lillian Kelly was a shapely five-four, with chestnut hair tickling her shoulders and pouty full lips. Her skin was milky Irish but absent of freckles like many other Irish girls. She wasn't big-chested, but was well proportioned, offering the boys more on her lower end than up top. Her eyes were a green-blue hybrid, iridescent and radiant, and when she smiled she usually tilted her head to her right which seemed to illuminate them more than usual. It had been almost two months since the afternoon when those eyes first met Henry's and they found themselves in that Connecticut Cornfield on a rare, tepid mid-March night.

"OK, listen, don't suck in too hard, alright? Just take a long slow pull on it and try to hold it for a few seconds if you can..." was the last thing Henry Alexander said before the night veered into pandemonium. She had, of course, sucked way too hard, coughed some out, but then taken a couple more drags off the joint, the last one lasting several seconds, held for at least ten. She sat motionless, then started slapping at Henry's chest and screaming, then diving right out the side window of his car and into the mud on the outskirts of the cornfield they parked against. She slipped getting up, then ran full steam into the rows of corn, howling and screaming like a lunatic, knocking much of the vegetation down as she dashed wildly about with no apparent direction. Henry couldn't help laughing but knew it must be terrifying to be in her head in that moment so he chased her for almost twenty minutes, then wrestling her to the ground and tearing her yellow dress at the waist. He sat there with her, deep amongst the rows of corn, and assured her that her chest wasn't going to explode and that time hadn't actually stopped. He moved his body into an Indian Style position, pulling her between his legs and resting her back up against his chest, letting his hands rest on her shoulders. He massaged her, tenderly, as he whispered all the reassurances he could

68

think of into her ears, then sliding his hands onto the back of her neck and into her hair. For a solid hour, he ran his fingers through her amber strands, massaging her scalp, thumbing at her neck, rubbing her earlobes, until she fell asleep in his arms. He moved her head down to rest on his thigh, letting her sleep as he stroked the side of her face, continuing to rub her ears. The sound of a falling tree branch startled them both, waking her, and they made their way back to the car, cracking up at how the night had unfolded. When they got back to the car, Lillian pulled herself up tight to Henry, kissing him with passion and intensity, allowing her hands to explore down the front of his chest and stomach, pushing him into the side of the car. Henry fumbled to find the condom in his back pocket but it was gone and, less than an hour later, in the glow of a late winter New England moon, microscopic Stephen Alexander was brought into existence in the back seat of a Chevy Chevelle.

Henry and Lillian, though very much in love and unable to keep their hands off one another for the next couple months, weren't prepared for Stephen's arrival. The fact that neither set of parents were embracing the idea, coupled with an increase in Henry's drinking, made the days that followed their romance in the corn arduous. So, they did what many other couples under tremendous pressure-lacking family support, income, reasonable prospects or sensibility do when they're pregnant-they got married.

Twenty months of anything but bliss passed, and Stephen's little sister Jessica was born into what had devolved into a tumultuous situation on a good day. Incessant fighting, alcohol fueled rage, financial strife and the occasional moment of unhinged hilarity was the norm and by the age of four Stephen and his little sister had already moved six times, a result of Lillian's recurring claim that she wanted a "fresh start". This usually meant they were also running from a previous fresh start that had not only failed to take root, but left someone with unpaid rent and several piles of dog shit in the living room. Henry would surface every few weeks in the first year after she left, show up at one of the new houses claiming to be sober and ready to take on the responsibility of fatherhood, then Lillian would throw him out because he passed out on the front porch with his pants off. By Stephen's fifth birthday, Lillian finally had enough and divorced Henry, but the cycle of fresh starts and running from town to town continued, and there were always animals.

Stephen tried to count the number of dogs they had up through his eighteenth birthday once, settling on thirty-nine. Thirty-nine dogs, sometimes as many as three at a time, and always living in an apartment or meager rented house. The dogs covered every end of the canine spectrum, with a focus on the retriever breeds, however, and most dumber than a bag of stones. There was Casey, the Yellow Lab, who'd stare you right in the face wagging his tail, panting and brimming with enthusiasm to do absolutely anything you wanted, ready with boundless energy. There was Chip, the Basset Hound, who'd chew everything that its stubby legs would give it access to and no home remedy or vet sanctioned tactic to curtail this habit could deter him. Lillian gave him to a co-worker that said she wanted a dog and didn't care about the chewing if it was housebroken. Stephen learned years later that Chip had eaten the woman's favorite pocketbook. Not just chewed it up but eaten the whole thing-strap, metal clasp, contents and all. There was Ox, the Newfoundland, a massive, black beast of a critter with unkempt mounds of fur that smelled like dead rodents, but with such a loving disposition you'd ignore the stench while you let him chase you in circles, eventually knocking you down, slobbering you with a canine car wash. Buttons, a mix breed that Lillian scooped up at a local pound, was either ingesting massive quantities of fiber or had IBS, as all it did was crap in the house. In every corner, every space, near furniture, on furniture and-against all logic and rules of physics-*on* the stove at one point. Buttons would greet you at the door with exuberance as you walked in, tail wagging maniacally, a soft whimper building to a full-fledged wail, surrounded in piles of shit, then, after you'd take him outside to do his business-which he would-he'd come back inside and crap on your rug. Buttons lost a battle with a car one afternoon while darting off after a squirrel into the road. He seemed fine for a day or two, then collapsed dead next to his water bowl while Stephen was putting socks on to go play outside.

Of all the pups Stephen grew up among, it was the one Lillian brought home shortly after his fourteenth birthday, Oscar, that had the most lasting impact. Oscar was a Golden Retriever that had an IQ somewhere between an Amoeba and an Aardvark, according to Lillian, but was affectionate to a fault, and enamored with Stephen far beyond other human companions. He'd follow him from room to room, stare at him from yards away as he lay on his side, thumping his tail on the ground if Stephen maintained eye contact, and would become agitated if anyone appeared to be upsetting Stephen. Oscar, like many retrievers, had a penchant for adventure and a knack for slipping his collar so he often embarked on journeys of the surrounding areas near their home, usually returning with burrs and pieces of shrubbery in his thick, matted gold-amber fur. Sometimes he'd show up with a cut on his paw or deep into his abdomen-war wounds sustained in the battles with neighborhood dogs and cats or from a nearby female pooch that, though in heat, wasn't liking the cut of Oscar's jib. Oscar was the comfort and solace for Stephen's failures with pretty, adolescent girls and the sanctuary he ran to when bullies' words became actions. Oscar listened to Stephen's grand plans of revenge, romance and success as well as his unbridled tears and labored breathing as he'd anxiously pace his room trying to make sense of events in his life. Oscar was the counterbalance to the turbulence in his head and the impartial friend that every teenage boy needed as they clumsily made their way through their awkward, pathetic existence.

Oscar died at thirteen, somewhere on a mountain in New Hampshire where Lillian was living several years after Stephen had moved out on his own. He wasn't speaking to his mother so he found out through a letter she mailed him, along with pictures of the dog and the two of them together. For years, Stephen said that whenever he got a dog again he'd name it Oscar in honor of the pup that had been such an instrumental part of his young adult life, but later abandoned the decision, thinking it was best to let the name live on in respectful remembrance.

Other than the dogs, there were often cats, birds, hamsters and fish. Lillian crammed each tiny living space she settled into with abundant critters, her children and a mountain of tag sale sourced knick-knacks and oddities that usually ended up destroyed by something non-human. She carted her kids off to seventeen different towns in Connecticut and Massachusetts between the years of 1975 and 1992, always with a carload full of trinkets and at least one dog. Year after year, sometimes twice in the same year, Stephen and his sister would have to walk into a new classroom in some town where everyone was a stranger and listen as the teacher would announce, "Class, we have a new student today. Their name is Stephen/Jessica and they're sitting right over there..." as they'd point them out. For Jessica, an adorable brunette with huge doe eyes, it was a less excruciating experience, other than the occasional jealous blonde who was formerly the object of the schoolboys' affection. For Stephen, however, sporting a fiery red near-afro that Lillian refused to cut, being skinny as a rail and having massive feet, being thrust into the spotlight as the "new guy" presented far greater challenges.

Immediately the torment would begin, usually starting with his hair. "Hey Ronald McDonald, where's Grimace?" The big feet only exacerbated the situation, promoting jabs like, "Holy cow, do you ski on those things?" In the earlier years after Kindergarten, Stephen employed the tactic of stoic silence in the face of bullying, though it still often resulted in a punch, trip or *Kick Me!* sign taped to his back. Around grade six he decided to shake things up when the resident tough guy, Reggie Harrington, sat down in an adjacent seat on the school bus and declared he had issues with Stephen. Reggie was a year older, lanky, dirty blonde hair with a fair complexion and lots of freckles. His eyes were often squinted, as though he was staring at the sun through clouds and he was missing a quarter of one of his top teeth, right next to the incisor on his left side.

"Listen, spaghetti headed freak, I don't want you waiting at my bus stop anymore, or getting off here either. You wait at the stop over at the fat kids house down the road, you understand?"

Stephen became a constant target of Reggie's insults ever since he moved to Stafford, CT months earlier. Up until that day, Stephen never said a word or made eye contact with him, but he couldn't avoid noticing the oversize and out of season winter coat the boy wore every day. It was Navy blue, had patches in places, numerous food stains and a tear down the left arm revealing white insulation that was always catching on something as Reggie walked down the aisle of the bus, leaving a strewn mess of fibers floating all over. The coat was ridiculous, a reality amplified by the fact that Reggie seemed to have no idea how goofy he looked wearing it.

"Did your mom get that coat at a yard sale for retarded Eskimos or did you steal it from a Dumpster," Stephen shot back at Reggie that day on the bus.

"What the hell did you say, freak?" Reggie yelled in Stephen's face, sprinkling him with saliva and bits of the Cheese-n-Crackers he was always shoveling into his freckled face.

"I'm just wondering where you got that coat because it's stupid and you look dumb in it, " Stephen opined. A hushed gasp from the surrounding kids was heard faintly.

"That's it, shithead, you're getting your ass kicked when I get off this bus, you hear me?" Reggie said, as he grabbed at the front of Stephen's T-Shirt. Most of the other passengers on the bus had moved closer to the middle where the two boys sat to listen. "You hear me, freak? You're gonna fight me when we get off the bus, so you better not wuss out!"

"Sure, I'll fight you, but win or lose you have to burn that dumb coat. Promise." Stephen answered.

73

"Win or lose, look at this jerk," said Reggie, summoning the adolescent onlookers to survey his battle companion. "You couldn't take me if you had fists made of metal, kid." The lingering kids roared with laughter, as the driver shot back a glance and told everyone to settle down.

Minutes later, the two boys exited the bus, with several kids not on that stop in tow. The bus pulled away and the remaining passengers were all crammed up against the rear window, hands and faces pressed tight, hoping to catch a glimpse of the first and likely only punch thrown.

"I have to give you credit kid. Most people chicken out when I want to fight them but at least you didn't run," Reggie said. The six other children formed a half circle, watching anxiously as Reggie dropped the books he had with him on the ground and crept towards Stephen. Reggie left the coat on, and locked in stare with Stephen who was standing motionless, saying nothing. "OK, I'm gonna beat your ass now, freak. It's your own fault."

"As long as none of us have to see that coat again, then I'm ready," Stephen countered.

Reggie's face turned red and he clenched his teeth, lunging at Stephen, who put his hands up in front of his face, offering no counter, then fell backwards onto the ground with the force of the attack knocking him over. Reggie punched Stephens face and the side of his head, his accuracy weakened by the defensive posture, arms fully shielding his neck and head. "What have you got to say about my coat now, huh? You red-headed little pussy. Say something now," Reggie yelled, the onlookers moving in closer to see if there was any blood or if Stephen was crying. After a couple minutes Reggie stopped raining blows on him and stood up.

"So, I kicked your ass, just like I said I would," Reggie declared, looking down at Stephen on the ground, frozen, still covering his face. He scanned the crowd that had backed up as Reggie stood and they were all staring at him. Their looks spoke less of admiration or fear but instead pity, and Reggie scooped up his books and made off up the road, not looking back.

"Hey, that was pretty cool you fought him. I mean, you didn't win but at least you didn't chicken out like he said," a neighborhood kid Stephen didn't know suggested. "You need help up?"

Stephen shook his head no and stood, brushing himself off and watching Reggie walk away towards his house that was just over the hill. When he first got to town, he heard a conversation on the bus between another victim of Reggie and a little girl where they discussed the frequent beatings from someone referred to as a "step father" that Reggie would often endure. Stephen wasn't sure what kind of father a Step was but was certain that beatings coming from any adult couldn't be fun. The dilapidated house he lived in had junk all over the lawn and when Reggie wasn't around the other kids were always making fun of it. They called him "Wedgie" Harrington because one time this Stepfather threw him out onto the porch by his pants because he didn't knock before coming into his parents' room and one of the neighborhood kids saw it happen, leaving Reggie to fish his underwear out of his butt crack. Other kids mentioned that the police were at his place sometimes as well. Stephen watched Reggie sluggishly ascend the hill and disappear into the horizon, feeling bad for picking on his coat. It was torn, in shambles, an absolute wreck and was an easy target for ridicule but Reggie wore it every day without fail. Maybe in the chaos of his pre-teen life the jacket was the one item that was *his*, that felt uniquely his own and provided some symbolic sense of protection from unknown terrors that existed inside the walls of *717 Brickman Rd.*

Stephen was only in Stafford for another month after the incident with Reggie, and most times that they were on the bus together Reggie avoided him, never engaging, though there were moments where he bumped against him or told him to shut up. He never addressed the fight they had again, however, not once. In none of those remaining days, without one exception, did Reggie ever wear the tattered coat again either.

The years with Lillian and Jessica continued, much like the brief time in Stafford and places before it, in cyclical patterns. They'd find a home in a new town and Lillian would list all the reasons it would be better than the last, they'd hunker down in only to be uprooted in several months, sometimes close to a year, then off to the next. Stephen would do his best to blend in, assimilate, avoid confrontation, only making his presence known if imperative or feeling a rare moment of bravado as he did on the bus with Reggie. He'd absorb the insults and jabs, sometimes clever, though more often recycled and unimaginative, and every so often he'd discover another loner lurking in the shadows that he'd attempt friendship with. His intentions were always sincere-desiring companionship and camaraderie-though he couldn't deny that the benefits of having other objects of ridicule around him sometimes diffused or lessened the attacks.

To and from towns of Southern New England the three of them traveled, like Caucasian gypsies, with no plan or ultimate destination. Intermittently, Lillian's mother Ruthie would make appearances to help turn the lights back on or fortify Christmas gifts that year but she was often tangled in her own mess of domestic insanity. Lillian's father had died not long after Jessica was born, as his battle with the bottle had intensified when Lillian's brother committed suicide in California. Lillian wasn't close with her brother William, but the event rattled the family and soon after Lillian's mother lost her son and husband she took in another Irish alcoholic with a temper and rarely had a moment to break away and tend to anything other than her own turbulent life. Ruthie was kind-as generous as a mother could be to her own daughter and grandchildren-but her capacity for love and empathy had been whittled down in her grief.

Somewhere around Stephens tenth birthday he remembered seeing a familiar looking man show up outside the school he was

76

attending, waiting on the sidewalk wearing Jeans and a black button up shirt, wide-lensed sunglasses on his face. The man smiled at him as he made his way out of the school in Vernon, Connecticut and towards the line of yellow buses. Stephen slowed his pace, watching the man approach him, still grinning, and immediately Stephen knew it was his father. He hadn't seen him since he was around five years old and Lillian rarely ever spoke of him so the lack of instant recognition made sense.

"Hey kiddo, you know who I am?" Henry asked him.

Stephen stared at his dark sunglasses and the curly brown hair, much like his own only missing the intense red hue, and answered, "Dad?"

"I told your mom you'd recognize me, but she thought you'd walk right past. You look great, Stephen. Getting tall, gonna be a lot taller than me I think," he said, taking his sunglasses off.

Stephen stood silent, staring at him for a moment then looking down at the gray, cracked sidewalk and tucking both his hands into his front pockets. He wouldn't see him again for almost two years.

{*****}

Heather finished the chapter and folded the pages back over, letting the manuscript rest on her chest. She was watery-eyed and swooning and no longer cared about her "rules" so she jumped up and fetched her phone from her purse.

*<I love you. Like, way too much. XOXO>*

She sent the text and let herself fall back on the couch, hopeful for a quick reply, but as she glanced down at the pages of Stephen's book on the floor she placed the phone on the carpet and picked it up again, unable to stop herself from continuing.

# Chapter 10

Sheriff McCabe pulled his Crown Vic around the last turn in the gravel road and saw the old farm house come into view. It was as Bob Diller described it-run down, poorly cared for but a newer barn and a few weathered sheds. The grass that lined the dirt driveway intersecting the gravel road was massively overgrown, with rusty and blemished pieces of farm equipment littered about with no apparent order. As he brought the car to a stop near the front entrance, he saw a mangy gray cat hop down from a ledge on the front porch and get lost in the brownish-green weeds that covered most of the landscape. One of the pillars at the top of the porch steps had black numbers, "44", nailed to it, though one of the fours was drooping.

"Curtis, it's Charlie. I just pulled up here. Do me a favor and see if you can pull the tax record on this place. I'm going to send you the address to your phone, which I know you're screwing with right now so you should have it in a few seconds. Over and out," the Sheriff spoke into the CB radio. He pecked the letters and numbers into his phone and hit send, then tossed it down onto the seat next to him.

The farmhouse was weather worn, neglected and appeared deserted but there was a Hunter green, new door at the front-out of place with the rest of the structure-that had two different locksets above the handle. The Sheriff made his way up to the front steps, watching another cat come scurrying off the porch, this one a dark black with snow white paws and a dab of white under its chin. It hissed after stopping about fifteen feet off the porch, then bolted as it noticed the man wasn't deterred in his movement by the warning.

At the top of the steps, the Sheriff looked closer at the door, then left and right down both sides of the porch, spotting random piles of debris, some chicken bones and garbage and what appeared to be a stack of old shoes in one of the corners on the left side. He walked down towards them, passing one of the front windows that was boarded up and painted black, the glass pane cracked several inches at the top. When he stood before the shoe pile he realized they were a combination of old sneakers, some mangled loafers and pairs of suede moccasins, all faded from the elements. They were stacked by hand meticulously, though, placed in the corner to allow for the large pile not to topple over.

As he walked back towards the front door, the Sheriff spotted a tiny black object protruding from up above the right corner of the threshold the door was mounted in. It appeared to be a little hook, reversed, as it angled downward. As he got right underneath it and stretched himself up towards the unknown item he noticed a convex glass cover at the end of something resembling a pen sized flashlight. He peered around the side of it and noticed the device itself was attached to a small metal frame with a very thin wire exiting from the house connected to it.

*A camera.*

*What the hell does some okey doke living in a gone-to-shit farmhouse need a camera and fancy new door for?*

The Sheriff walked to the other end of the porch as he contemplated the question, seeing another cat running through the yard, this time a hundred yards away or more and over near the side of the large, burnt-wood style barn. He stared at the oversized brown structure for a moment, then back behind it where there was one of the smaller sheds and what appeared to be a Bobcat excavator tucked in behind it. The front yard was in shambles, with feral cats running all over, no sign of life-other than the felines-yet there was a camera on the front porch and a thick, recently-installed door, and the massive barn was likely constructed within the last couple years. He rubbed his right hand over the back of his neck, massaging it for a moment, then walked back towards the front door.

"Hello, it's Sheriff McCabe. Anyone home," he asked, thumping on the formidable green door, as he glanced up at the camera. "Hello?"

He knocked a few more times, each rap with more force, then thought he heard something move inside so he backed a step away. As he waited to see if someone came to the door, he looked over at the pile of shoes and felt an unfamiliar chill snake its way up his spine.

He pounded on the door a few more times, "Hello. It's Sheriff Charlie McCabe, just need to speak with you a moment if you're in there." Nobody answered, and inside remained silent.

"Well, if there's anyone home I'm giving you a heads up that I'm going to take a quick peek around back, then be on my way," the Sheriff announced. "Fuck, I hope there's no damned dog back there."

McCabe walked back to his car and slid onto the seat and called Curtis on the CB again. "Curtis, it's Charlie. Did you find out who's on the Deed for this place? Over."

A solid thirty seconds passed before Deputy Curtis answered back with, "Sorry Sheriff, was taking a leak. Hey, you know it's weird cause I ran the address through the town database and it looks like the property was sold to some company a few years back, 'Juan PL Holdings' it's called and I Googled it and found almost nothing except a PO Box out of Florida. You want me to keep digging into it? Over."

"Yeah, or, give Shirley a call over at the Town Hall, see if she recollects anything. Over."

"Roger that, Sheriff. I finished the report too and I'm just going to eat those wings then stop down at the Library because Gordon says the kids broke that back window again. Maybe I'll stop in and see Shirley when I'm out. Over."

"Sounds good, and if you get any relevant info please text me. I'm going to poke around here for another few minutes then head on back. Over and out."

"Wait, Sheriff, is anyone there? I mean, did you talk to anyone? Over."

"No, looks like no one's here but there's a few notes I'm going to put down for the Connecticut fellas. The place is a shithole for the most part but there's a camera near the front door and a barn that looks new. Few things seem out of sorts. Over."

"A camera? Huh. Sheriff, you sure you don't want me to make a drive out there, or at least call Worthington at the Trooper station and have him meet you down there? Over."

"No, I'm fine here. I'll poke around back a sec, then take off. Let me know if you dig anything else up. Over and out."

"Gotcha, boss. Over and Out."

He hung the CB mic back on the hook and grabbed his phone in case he wanted to snap some pictures. Then, scanning the distance between where he'd parked and the rear of the property, he positioned himself into the seat and started the car, electing to drive around the other side.

As he drove past the barn he noticed what appeared to be another black camera resting atop the left front corner of the roof. It was conspicuous but certainly a camera he determined as he got closer. He moved the car past the barn and towards the shed where he saw the Bobcat, tucking his cruiser in behind it and killing the engine. For a moment, he contemplated calling Worthington, the State Trooper Curtis mentioned, but decided he'd nose around for a few minutes solo then head out. He went to the rear of his car and grabbed a pair of leather work gloves, tucking them into his back pocket, as there were rusted and unsafe looking pieces of equipment littering the entire area.

He made his way to the backside of the barn looking for an entrance, and as he walked passed the Bobcat he noticed another camera on the right, rear roof corner, same model as the one out front.

He continued walking the perimeter of the barn, slipping his gloves on, then intermittently tapping his hand on the wood frame, knocking almost. About halfway down the side, he saw one of the large white propane tanks that Bob Diller was likely filling while he was here. It looked newer, was large enough to heat a structure of this size, if that's what it was doing. As he got to the front of the barn he saw the large double doors, secured with a hefty metal chain fastened with two oversized padlocks. He stopped and looked up towards the camera, wondering if anyone was watching him as he stood there, surveying his actions and allowing his curiosity, until such time curiosity turned to discovery. He put both hands on the chain and pulled with moderate force, ratting the links against the metal brace bolted to the wooden doors.

"Hello. Anyone in there? It's Sheriff Charlie McCabe," he yelled, half expecting to hear some frightened voice scream back to him. There was nothing but silence and a staggered wind moving some of the long grass around near the edge of the barn. The sun was beginning to sear the back of his neck even though the air was still crisp, offering some relief as it whipped over and around the skin behind his head.

He let go of the chain and looked back up at the camera, removing his hat and waving it in back and forth, for no reason other than to signal to anyone watching that he knew they were. There was an ominous and inexplicable vibe to this place, though no evidence existed of any illegalities, yet who knew what lay inside the walls of that reinforced front door or the barn, he wondered.

The Sheriff pulled off the gloves, tucked them into his back pocket again and made his way back around to the car, this time on the opposite side of the barn. Inspecting the rear of the broken down, formerly white Farmhouse, he noticed yet another camera-a different model-installed right underneath one of the gutters that was hanging down at a thirty-degree angle or so. Four cameras, huge locks and chains, reinforced doors, and no sign of life anywhere, other than those malnourished cats. Every "something just aint right" meter he had was buzzing, though there was still nothing suggesting criminal activity.

He fished his cell phone from his pocket and called Deputy Curtis instead of ringing him on the CB again. "Hey, it's me. So, I know you probably haven't left to head to the Town Hall but were you able to find anything else on the company that owns this place? A few things seem off to me but nothing concrete. I'm going to head back in a minute but just thought I'd check."

The Sheriff listened to Deputy Curtis tell him that he *had* found some additional information and one was that the "Juan PL Holdings" was a parent company of another one called "Kinetic Detonation Systems" and there was a website that mentioned how their specialty was creative demolition services for specialized construction, excavation and engineering projects.

"Huh, well, I suppose that would explain why someone would want to keep things locked up tight and have cameras around. Wouldn't want to blow some poor asshole up that got nosey, like me. OK, well I'm going to pack it in here then, but can you get me a phone number of the business and text it back? Thanks. See you in a little bit," he said, ending the call with the Deputy and sliding the phone into his front pocket.

As he walked back to the rear of his car to toss the gloves into the trunk, he saw what appeared to be another large propane tank sticking out from a corner of the back of the Farmhouse where there was apparently a recess, a courtyard maybe. He held onto the gloves, then hustled over to the back of the house, looking up at the recently discovered camera and tipping his hat for any potential onlookers. The rear of the place was well groomed up close to the structure itself, but forty or so feet away the grass turned into uncontrolled weeds. When he made his way around the corner into the recessed area where the Propane tank rested, a smaller model than the one near the barn, he saw a push mower tucked up against the house, resting near a bulkhead door, presumably leading into the cellar. Across the area in the back and attached to the house itself he saw another camera affixed to the top of a window, resembling the one on the corner he'd passed, and looking back at the cellar door he spied one more video device, this one smaller, and positioned right over the top of the bulkhead entrance. Resting near the red lawnmower was also an axe and a roll of what looked to be metal fencing or chicken wire banded together with twine.

On both sides of the cellar door, bookending the ground level entrance, were small double pane windows that appeared blacked out from where he was standing, so he moved closer to inspect them. Hunching down, then onto his knees, the Sheriff looked through the first window and saw that it was completely covered from behind with a piece of wood that looked painted black from where he was standing. He walked over past the bulkhead, which had a smaller chain than the barn doors though also secured with dual padlocks. The doors themselves were not standard issue, instead constructed of dense, reinforced steel and hinged onto the concrete bulkhead entrance with Industrial grade fasteners. It would be understandable that a company manufacturing or housing explosive materials would need to secure the supplies and watch the area closely, but would they be storing the items in the basement of a Farmhouse, he questioned.

Kneeling again, the Sheriff inspected the second window on the other side, this time touching one of the cracked panes of glass. The crack was almost across the entire surface, so he pulled one of the gloves from his back pocket and put on his right hand, then pressed firmly onto the glass, cracking it across the entire width, separating it by a few millimeters from the other piece. He wiggled his fingers into the space, alternately applying pressure and vibrating his hand back and forth, but the two separate pieces remained fixed, so he took his fingers and started tapping at the top of the piece on the right trying to loosen it from the corroded off-white molding. It started tearing away from it enough so he could jiggle it free from the frame, revealing a cut-to-size section of Particle board behind it that was spray-painted black. He reached his hand in, jabbing at the time-weakened substance, poking a hole into it, then using the hole to wrap his fingers inside and pull a chunk of the board out, then grabbed onto the leftover section and removed it. Behind the glass and board was a custom-made metal grill, like a prison window, though with smaller gauge iron bars. He stuck his gloved hand through the opening of two of the bars, revealing that layer was the final one between the outside world and the basement itself.

From where the Sheriff was kneeling, and with only the bars impeding his view, he could see a flickering light that looked as though it was originating from a television or monitor of some sort, resting on a small table. There was a structure blocking his ability to see down any further but he pulled himself up as close to the metal bars as he could, peered inside, and still saw only the TV/monitor and the corner of a wooden shelf, holding what looked to be cleaning supplies.

The monitor could be to view the cameras from that location, if there was a guard or someone there, and there's nothing extraordinary about cleaning supplies in a basement, he thought. Installing metal bars in a secure space where there may be dangerous materials was nothing to question either, but there was one thing he couldn't get past. Why would anyone put so much effort into securing the dilapidated home on the property as well as the barn? It would make perfect sense that if the company was manufacturing or housing combustible materials that the massive barn might be a place to do it, although still not the most practical solution. Why not build a metal hanger type set up, with oversize garage bay doors to let trucks in and out, why a barn? The Sheriff was no engineer and had little knowledge of what the requirements of the company were, but, even if he could let the barn go, with the house locked up this way something felt off.

He stood up and brushed the front of his khaki pant legs, took off his hat and placed it on the ground near the now open window, save for the bars, and reached for his cellphone to call Curtis. The call went to voicemail so he left a brief message as he headed back to his car.

"Curtis, it's Charlie again. Hey, do me a favor and send Worthington down here if he's free, nothing pressing, no trouble, but I think I may want another set of eyes on this. In fact, if you can break away from what you're doing why don't you take a ride down as well. Nothing urgent but, I'll see ya when you get here," he said, arriving back at the car and then ending the call and sliding the phone back into his front pocket.

He opened the trunk of the cruiser and fished out a flashlight and crow bar, then slammed the lid down, making his way back towards the rear corner of the house, his index finger and thumb tapping against one another as his free arm dangled. He wasn't sure what his intentions were but between the chicken wire, the metal bars and the eerie pile of shoes on the porch, Sheriff McCabe was having one of those moments so many cops do where evidence or probable cause is overshadowed by instinct and gut feeling. At this point, he had no viable reason to break into the cellar, which he wasn't even sure he would consider, but something told him this dingy farmhouse peppered with cameras and heavy-duty security measures had stories to tell beyond just hazardous materials.

Or maybe it didn't, and he was venturing into Deputy Curtis territory by making poor assumptions and taking rogue actions that may cost him his job or even a lawsuit. He stopped halfway back to the cellar door, took another long look around the property, then slowly drew in a deep breath, dropping the crow bar to the ground as he exhaled.

He stood there for about thirty seconds, then decided to take one last look in the open window, this time with the flashlight. Peeking inside, then replacing the damaged particleboard and panes of glass, would be less likely to cause a firestorm than prying open the cellar door and having a look to quell a hunch. Of course, the cameras at every corner had likely recorded his snooping and destruction of property at the basement window but he could always chalk that up to probable cause. *I know I heard something,* he learned years earlier.

Crouching back down onto his knees, the Sheriff shined the flashlight he had clicked on into the window space, pressing it up against the metal bars. He angled it in several directions, illuminating the backside of what was a TV set and the rear portion of a cement wall that seemed to be the divide between either a heating unit or water tanks or both, and the rest of the basement. He cranked his neck as far left as he could get it near the bars, moving the flashlight all the way right, but could only see the piping that lead to that dark, obstructed corner, but was reasonable enough to assume housed the boiler, etc.

He readjusted his position, then attempted to light the shelf where the cleaning supplies were, and just as the beam ran from down on the concrete floor then up to the shelf, he heard what sounded like a loud gasp, then a "Shhhhh". He dropped the flashlight onto the ground and paused a moment, then, "Hello, is somebody down there?"

"Help! Yes, we're down here!" the girl's voice shouted back.

Sheriff McCabe shot up from his crouched position and, as he did, heard what sounded like another voice yelling at the one that just called out to him. He ran back for the crowbar he'd dropped and, after grabbing it from the dusty ground, sprinted back towards the bulkhead door and inserted it underneath the chain and padlocks, using all his arm and upper body strength, trying to pry it apart. He had no leverage, and the crowbar was shorter and less efficient than the larger types most would carry in a profession like his, but he continued to push and pull and find a sweet spot to allow enough tension and a solid fulcrum to break the chains. The metal doors began to show signs of indentation as the crowbar dug into it, but the links on the chain didn't seem to be weakening. He needed a longer handle and something that gave more leverage.

*The axe.*

The Sheriff pulled the crowbar from the tangled chain and dropped it, then ran for the ax, grabbing it by the hickory handle and sprinting back to the cellar doors. He jostled the chain around, slipped the head of the axe into the links and started moving the handle circularly until it caught and he felt tension with the handle at a forty-degree angle to the metal door. With brutal and immediate force, he slammed down the axe with both hands held tight, following with all his body weight. The axe broke loose from the chain but it remained in place as the Sheriff toppled over sideways. Immediately he reinserted the axe into the chain links again, swiveling and adjusting until it locked in place, this time at approximately thirty degrees to the ground. He wrapped his gloved hands back onto the wooden handle and plowed forward with all his force once more, hurling forward, hitting the ground next to the black cellar doors, but this time hearing a clear *Pa-WINK!* signaling that one of the links had broken. He got up and yanked the chain from the door handles, pulled one of them open, then reached back for the flashlight and shined it down to the bottom of the stairs.

Another door, secured with a padlock.

He grabbed the crowbar and axe, then dashed down the wooden steps in the entryway to the cellar. The door was mahogany brown wood-sturdy, and likely contained metal reinforcements from initial inspection, but the padlock was only average size so he slipped the flat claw of the crowbar underneath the metal buckle and started pulling furiously towards himself. The metal plate was loosening but not enough based on the force applied so he dropped the crowbar, picked up the axe and turned it backwards so the butt was facing away from him. He looked overhead, determining he had to choke up on the handle based on the clearance, then began to hammer down onto the lock as forcefully as he could, given the tight quarters. One, two, three solid hits and then the fourth struck more of the door itself. Inside he heard garbled voices shouting. He adjusted his body position, then took several more whacks at the lock, a few of the hits producing noticeable sparks. He laid the axe against the sidewall and used his side to slam against the door but it was thick and formidable, unlikely to move with the force of one man. He picked up the axe again, spun it butt facing away, then smacked down onto the padlock, two, three times and then with the fourth it broke free and fell to the ground with a thud against the concrete base.

He unclipped his gun with his right hand, then depressed the lever on the basement door with his left, hearing a *click* as it pulled the latch bolt through the faceplate. He eased the door open, hand on his weapon, then pulled himself up against the wall where he stood as he pushed the door all the way open, almost hitting the TV that was resting on the stand.

"This is Sheriff McCabe. I'm entering the basement, weapon ready. Who's down here?" he inquired.

There were a couple seconds of silence, then both voices starting yelling over one another, allowing him to only hear "Help", "Please," and "Get out," clearly. The voices continued, shouting at full volume, and he cautiously leaned himself in through the doorway and over to the corner of the cement wall that separated the area with the TV, which showed a fake fire on the screen. He stopped at the wall, drew his weapon from its holster, brought it up near to his chest then rolled around the back edge of the wall.

Standing inside two homemade cages, constructed of wood and metal-chicken wire, and screaming over one another in terror, confusion and anxious optimism with their little fingers pulling at the meshed enclosures, were Emily Roberts and Amber Barstow.

# Chapter 11

*Henry* Alexander knew he was an alcoholic the moment the Blackberry Brandy hit his stomach and the warm rush cascaded back up through his chest and into his face, leaving it flushed and tingling. The boy that handed him the flask was also on the JV Football team at Northwestern High School in Connecticut, but had taken only a sip before passing it to Henry. The hesitation stemmed from the same place it did with the other two boys in the circle-fear and a lack of palate for what they were slinging down their throats. At thirteen going on fourteen, it was the age where kids like Henry and others would experiment, test the limits of what their bodies could handle in drink or smoke, challenge adults who questioned them and let their eyes fix on a girl's figure longer than a year earlier. The testosterone surged, guiding most decisions, though the concept of consequence had come into clearer focus with adolescence. Where some young men could withstand the rejection from pretty girls and keep moving on to the next or jump right in the face of an older kid that had something to say about a ripped pair of jeans or not cower in the corner of the bathroom in terror when a drunk father came looking for you with a belt because you bothered to be there where he got home, Henry could not. He was perpetually seeking an antidote for his angst-filled existence and any elixir that might provide him the courage to step outside of himself and be the young man he desired, and found it when the booze reached him that day.

Later that afternoon, after his first drink, he went up to Jonathan Perry, a perpetual asshole and bully, and smacked him four times in the head right in front of the girl he was talking to. Three other kids standing outside the corner store watched as Henry relentlessly attacked him until he went down, then climbing on top of his five-foot-nine frame, pummeling him again with his fists, hitting his face, neck and chest until he was finally pulled from the boy by the other kids. Jon Perry was bloodied, sobbing and scurried home completely bewildered by the random attack that he may have deserved yet was unwarranted in *that* moment.

That evening, Henry went into the cabinet beneath the record player in the living room and snatched a bottle of something called "Vodka", then retreated to the bathroom and drank four large gulps before almost vomiting. The burn was overwhelming, so he ran his mouth underneath the bathroom faucet which only made it worse. After several minutes, and with his younger sister banging on the door to get in, he hid the bottle underneath the sink behind stacked rolls of toilet paper and a spray can of Lysol.

Walking out of that bathroom he felt like a giant. He bolted into the living room and looked out the window, hoping to see his father's Chevrolet pull in the driveway. The familiar thud of the car door slamming as his dad would sling his gray or black suit jacket over his shoulder, head to the mailbox and remove the contents, then come inside the house and ask, "What are we eating?" His mother would answer something from her place at the sink, then James Alexander would head for the doors underneath the record player. As thirty minutes would pass, then roll into an hour, dinner was served and James would be half a bottle deep into one of the liquids he'd pulled from the shelves. He'd start with the staring, first at Henry's mother, glaring almost, then ask a question like, "What do you do all day?" and then slam his fork down on the plate, chewing what he had in his mouth deliberately unhurried, whether he got an answer or not, which was rarely. He'd move his eyes to Henry's sister Annette and tell her to get him one of the bottles he'd left in the living room or fetch another, sometimes both. She'd oblige, avoiding making eye contact but if she did, or didn't move quick enough, he'd scream until the little girl erupted in tears, running from the table, prompting the standard response where he berated her mother then smacked her on the side of her head for "raising such an insubordinate and troublesome daughter". Sometimes the blow would be so hard it would knock Louanne Alexander from her chair and onto the linoleum floor and James would stand up and dump her plate all over her, then retire to the living room with his bottle. Sometimes he'd keep staring at her as her lips quivered and he'd beg her to cry, taunt her, hoping she'd come apart so he could explode at her "irrational emotions." One August night, James struck her so hard that her wig was knocked loose and lay crooked on her scalp and he erupted into laughter, which started Annette bawling, then infuriated him so he pushed his wife from the chair with all the force of his six-foot-one, well-built frame and knocked her into the refrigerator, cutting her head on the handle, leaving her unconscious for five minutes. When Henry stood up to tend to her James slammed his fist down on the table and shot him a look daring him to keep moving towards his mom, so he sat back down and turned away, hoping his mother wasn't dying as she bled all over the kitchen floor.

As Henry stood in the picture window that afternoon after football practice, Vodka and Brandy infused blood coursing through his veins, he knew today was not going to be one of those days. He paced back and forth waiting to see the car make the turn down his street towards the house, his mother at one point coming into the living room, glancing at him, but never saying a word. He ran back to the bathroom and slammed the door, then reached underneath the sink to grab the bottle of Vodka. He spun the cap off and downed two more large gulps, wiped his mouth on his sleeve, then put it back where he'd hidden it earlier. He looked at himself in the mirror and brought his chin up a couple times, then heard the familiar rumble of his father's Chevy making its way down the street so he ran back into the living room and watched the car pull in. His father got out, slung his black suit jacket over his shoulder and walked towards the mailbox. When he got there, Henry banged on the picture window with his left hand, smiling out at his father. James Alexander stopped at the curb and looked back at his son, watching him beat on the window, grinning, then stormed towards the house, ignoring the mail.

Henry watched at the window as his father moved up the driveway, then sped through the living room into the kitchen, stopping dead in the middle of the textile floor, startling his mother. A moment later his father walked through the mud room door and into the threshold of the kitchen, pausing, staring at Henry.

"You have something to say, boy?"

Henry stared at him and started smiling again, then, "Who's it gonna be fiirs tonight, Pop. Who gets punched firs you asshole," Henry said, his words slurring.

Louanne froze at the sink as she was washing a plate, letting the water run.

"Oh, I see, so this is how is starts. Have yourself a little drink today, son? Think now you have the guts to stand up to your old man? Well good for you, about time you toughened up. But, I'm still the King of this castle and if you-"

"You're a goddumn pussy is wat you are, and the nex time you put your hanse on my motha or anyone I'm gonna fucking kill you, ya understand. And if I don't get you the firs time I'll fuckin stab you in your sleep you goddamn coward, you hear me?" Henry screamed at his father, standing six feet away.

The smirk left his father's face and he started to remove his belt, about to start talking when Henry said, "I fucking mean it you prick, you bettah kill all of us tonight cause if you don't I am going to slit your throat the firs chance I get". Henry was wobbling and braced himself on one of the kitchen chairs, never letting his gaze leave his father's eyes. His mother said nothing, remaining motionless until James took his hands off his belt, made a sound like, "Pffft", and brushed past Henry and into the living room to open a bottle.

Henry's father drank less than normal that night, and there was no shouting or violence, but the incident hadn't ended those days forever. For the next couple years, James continued to get blackout drunk, as Henry imbibed almost daily himself while going through high school. Some nights the two of them would catch each other in a fit of booze fueled rage and come to blows, knocking furniture over, breaking lamps and tables, and sometimes they'd pass each other in the hallway or kitchen, not saying a word. The attacks at the table, and most importantly on his mother, ended, however. For all the years Henry could remember prior-though much of it he'd blocked out-the anger, violence, rage and terror was incalculable and constant. There were very few moments where anything resembling peace existed. It was so bad a year before Henry first got drunk that his older brother Peter had left the house and moved in with a friend who lived with his single mother twenty miles away, rarely ever coming back home. The solace that alcohol provided Henry from the brutalization and abuse at the hands of his father-the origin of which came from the very same liquid-was immeasurable. The irony of the situation was not lost on young Henry, who understood the hypocrisy, though was unfazed by it completely. When James Alexander got drunk he became a violent, crazed dictator hell-bent on tormenting his victims, where Henry became a jovial, self-assured, fearless jester. There was no woman he couldn't approach, no teenage boy that would give him pause if their words grew combative and no grown man with sinister stares and angry fists that could unnerve him when the juice hit his blood. Henry would call it the "click"-when the buzz first reached his senses and he felt the instant change from sobriety to liberation. That click powered the engines of his confidence, motivation and resolve until the day it became all that was left.

Henry was already known as one of the local drunks when he met Lillian his Senior Year. He was usually hammered by shortly after noon but managed to keep it together well enough in the first few months they were dating, sticking with weed most of the time, until the night in the corn field where Stephen was conceived. That evening took a charming turn but the events got him off marijuana for a spell and he was right back into the sauce after Stephen was born. Infidelity, crashed cars, lost jobs and too many nights passed out in places other than home had Lillian at her wits end, understandably, and those early years, up until after Stephen's tenth birthday, Henry rarely saw his son or his daughter. He bounced back and forth between drunk tanks, AA sponsors' couches, hospitals and his mother's place in West Hartford, Connecticut. During one stretch at his mom's, Henry became adept at repairing motorcycles, doing so in Louanne's basement for a few months, until he tried to ride a Triumph Bonneville up out of the cellar on a wooden plank and destroyed the bike, almost killing himself. Louanne stood off to the side watching her son, only a couple Scotch's deep at that point, set up the two by four, laying it on the wooden steps up the cellar hatchway, then revving the twin four-stroke engine repeatedly while clutching the hand brake. As he let go of the front brake and went hard on the throttle, the bike leapt forward and shot up the wooden plank sending Henry's head right into a crossbeam on the cciling, the motorcycle flipping up backwards and smashing onto the cement floor, just inches from landing on him. Louanne screamed manically and ran to her son who was bleeding from his forehead and face, unconscious. He ended up with a concussion, a few stitches in his head and a bum knee that ended his appearances at the local touch football games on Saturday mornings.

Henry waited that day outside the school for his son years later, recognizing him immediately by the gait he had, not by appearance, as it was the same walk he had as a boy that age. It spoke of trepidation, inferiority and disconnection from those around him and was a magnet for the wrong kind of attention. Henry mentioned that to Stephen before seeing his little sister, Jessica, and picking her up, swinging her in two full circles. Jessica didn't recognize him at first but was happy to oblige anyone picking her up and swinging her around. Henry left his kids that afternoon with the intention of getting sober in a facility up near Albany New York, and made it more than halfway there, until a quick pit stop off the Massachusetts Turnpike found him sitting at the counter of a Diner, eating eggs in the afternoon and taking the nineteen-year-old waitress back to *The Highstone Inn* a mile back down the road. She brought a bottle of Irish Whiskey, he brought a tsunami on a paper leash.

Henry drank his way through much of the Northeast and Eastern Canada in those days, not seeing his children for a couple years until one morning he woke up under a Christmas tree in New Hampshire with a towering, stoic Native American man staring at him, his wife holding their child against her, as his eyes saw daylight.

He flew out of that house that morning, making it back to Connecticut that evening, immediately seeking out Lillian at her mother's which was always a safe bet on a Sunday no matter where the current domicile was. He told Lillian about his plan to head west to California to a rehab that had worked for some of his sponsors, and that his brother had already migrated that way, getting a job as a prison counselor. He promised money for support, finally, and regular phone calls once he got his head together and most importantly he assured Lillian that there'd be no more drinking once he hit the West Coast.

She agreed to allow him to see the kids the next day after school at their apartment before he left, and he showed up in a dingy white Oldsmobile Cutlass with broken power windows and four different wheels. He was wearing a light blue button up shirt, jeans, sunglasses pulled up and resting in his mess of curly brown hair, and a pair of walnut brown sandals on. Stephen watched as he got out of the car in front of their house, taking his sister's hand and leading her out to where Henry was waiting up against the car.

"Whoa, look at this kid. I go away for a little while and you shoot up another six inches. You playin' any B Ball, kiddo?" he asked Stephen, walking over towards Jessica.

"Yeah, well kinda a little maybe," Stephen answered, modestly.

"Not sure what that means but it sounds like you must be good," Henry jabbed, laughing into a snort, then picking up Jessica, placing her on the hood of his car like he'd done it a thousand times before. "I'm just kidding, son. I don't care if you play basketball or not, whatever makes you happy, you know? You were always better at football from what I heard anyway."

"Yeah," Stephen replied, his eyes down at his size eleven sneakers.

"What about you, cutie? You playing any sports or just making little boys go crazy with those big eyes? I better not hear you've kissed any of them, they're gross you know!" Henry said, tickling Jessica's tummy as he spoke.

"I only like one boy but three like me," Jessica countered, after giggling from the tickles.

"Three!?" Henry questioned. "I might have to take you with me, I can't have my little girl getting chased around by three boys already. You should be making sandcastles and braiding Barbie's hair or            something,            not            fighting            off            boys."

"Where are you going?" Jessica asked.

Henry pulled her down from the car and placed her next to her brother, then slid his dark glasses down over his eyes as the afternoon sun intensified. He leaned against the Oldsmobile and folded his arms, looking off into the distance opposite the sun as he spoke, drawing in a couple long breaths as the kids stood there in front of him.

"You know, guys, your old man's got a sickness. I..I'm not the best at doing much of anything other than drinking and when I drink I'm not a good guy to be around. Some people drink and they hurt people with their hands or their words, but when I drink I hurt people with my choices. I know that doesn't make a lot of sense to you right now but someday it will."

"What if you just don't drink too much anymore, Daddy? Take smaller sips," Jessica suggested. Henry would hear those words in his head for the remainder of his lifetime, each moment he reached for a bottle or a line of crushed Vicodin on a coffee table before he snorted it; her naive, precious solution to his complex and all-consuming problem was often the antidote to his poison.

"Baby, ya know, I'm going to try that. I promise you," Henry said, rubbing his hand across the left side of her face. "Right now, though, before I can even try that kiddo, I have to go away for a while. I need to head West and see my brother, get some help with grownup problems. It doesn't mean I don't want to see you, it means I want to see you more, which I know probably makes no sense because I haven't seen you in a long time or much of your whole life. Your dad is screwed up and I need to get that fixed so I can be there for you two, and, well, not be a screw up anymore...or-"

"Mom says we shouldn't expect to see you again," Stephen interjected.

"I've hurt your mother a lot, Stephen, and she's right to be upset with me and she has every reason to believe I may not come back. I've been gone most of your lives and the pain that I feel in that is not something I can convey to you, which means I can't make you understand right now. But, I'm going to try and find a path to healing this disease I have, that much I know, and I promise you I'm gonna try and come back someday...or maybe you guys can come out there."

"I'm not leaving mom," Stephen shot back.

"I don't expect you to, and I know you're pissed off kiddo and you have every right to be, I've been a shitty father your entire lives. It's not even fair to call myself a 'father' 'cause I wasn't present enough to deserve the title but I know that I love the two of you and you're both so deeply rooted in my heart that there's not a day that goes by that I don't hate myself for what I am and how I've hurt you," Henry said, reaching his fingers underneath the lens of his sunglasses to pull away tears. "But if you could understand the place I came from, the world that I knew at your age and what my life was you'd know that my indifference to you guys-my being gone-was never due to lack of love or desire to have you with me every moment. Instead it was my inability to let go of my fears and to face the fact that I'm an alcoholic."

"What's an al-cho-callic?" Jessica asked.

Henry wiped more tears from each of his eyes and pulled his sunglasses back up into his bushy brown hair. "Ha, babe well you know, that's actually the first time I've ever used that word to describe myself and honestly I've just started to figure that out. But what it means most importantly is that daddy is sick, he has a problem, and he needs to get better, and while he does that he needs to not be around for a while, and I'm so sorry for that," Henry answered, while turning around and reaching in through the open window of his car. "Here, I want you guys to have this. I've been saving it for a long time and it's for the two of you and it's not for your mom, you understand? I'm not saying that to be mean, but I want this to be for you both, OK?"

Henry slung the baby blue pillowcase full of coins over his shoulder after he pulled it out and then laid it down at both their feet, making a slushy clink as it hit the earth.

"This is eleven hundred and ninety-two dollars. It's all the change I've ever had since the two of you were born. I saved every penny I had my hands on, every coin I ever found on the street and it's always been for the two of you. It doesn't cover the cost of what I've done to you both, in being absent, or the lack of responsibility I showed to your mom in caring for you on her own for so long but I've started to fix that too. Like I said, this money is for you and you do with it what you wish. If I were you I'd give it to your Gramma Ruthie and have her divide it up and keep some for you aside, dish it out here and there. I almost stopped over to see her and ask her to do that before I got here but she's not my biggest fan."

"That's going to take a long time to count. You couldn't stop at the bank and cash it in for like, bills and stuff," Stephen asked.

"Wait till see you see how fucking heavy it is, the two of you will be out here counting it in your PJ's with flashlights at midnight," Henry answered, pushing at Stephens shoulder playfully.

Henry latched onto to the pillowcase of coins and slung it over his shoulder and walked inside up to Stephen's room, reminding him again that this was their money and should be divided equally and that he'd also be sending their mother money. Jessica asked several questions regarding the number of dolls she'd be able to buy with her share and Henry just kept replying "Eeewwww, dolls?" which made her giggle every time. Stephen sat down Indian style near the sack of loot with the two of them and started counting some out, setting the paper coin wrappers Henry had slipped in the pillow case off to the side. They started stacking piles of the change on the wood floor of Stephens room, individually at first, then on top of one another's, making a game out of it where the one who's coins made the pile topple was the loser. At one point the stack was almost ten inches high as Stephen cautiously added a small handful of dimes when Henry passed gas, sending everyone into a fit of laughter, shaking his concentration, and destroying the tower in the process.

The three of them played their game for about an hour until Henry got up, hugged them both and told them he loved them but that he better go, as their mom had said she'd be back soon. Jessica stayed with the pillowcase full of treasure, pulling bits out, stacking them on her own, singing a happy song to herself with nonsensical lyrics about the sky, fairies and sunshine. Stephen made his way over to the window and stood up against it watching his father get into the car, adjusting his sun visor, then sliding his glasses back onto his face. He heard the car start and watched as Henry sat there motionless for a while, then bring his hands to his face, rubbing it in circles, then across the top of his head and through his hair. He remained there, doing that for another minute, then turned out into the street and drove away.

It was almost five months until Henry called the house the kids were living in at the time, in a different town, telling them he'd made it to California. His voice sounded younger, brighter, Stephen observed. Henry said he hadn't drank in almost two months and that he was going to "meetings" every day. Stephen asked if they were work meetings and Henry answered that nobody was punching a clock or wearing suits but that it was the hardest work he'd ever done. They talked for twenty minutes, then Stephen put his sister on the phone. His mother followed, and kept asking about when there'd be more checks. The phone calls became semi-regular from that point onward, with little gaps in between as Henry changed jobs or moved somewhere new, but it was almost three years to the day when Stephen and Jessica saw him again.

A day that altered the course of Stephen's life forever.

{*****}

# Chapter 12

*Sheriff* McCabe stood on the basement floor, gun raised to his chest, clad in all khaki colors and hat, cherry brown belt with an oversized silver buckle with the obligatory star on it, and matte black, steel toed work boots. His chin was strong, but some would say protruded a little too much, and his eyes were deep set and round, suggesting Asian ancestry, though he had no blood from that part of the world that he was aware of. His frame was solid for a man of sixty-seven, and he managed to squeeze in at least forty pushups a day, coupled with as many sit ups when the mood struck. It was the belly that was the trouble spot, like all men in his family before him. His body fat percentage was low, he didn't consume an obnoxious amount of beer, and junk food was occasional at best, but he couldn't shake the gut. With his latest blood work revealing a rise in cholesterol and blood pressure, along with his advancing years, he wanted to make a concerted effort to eat wholesome food and less of it.

As he remained standing-paralyzed and watching a slideshow of his life, mortality and snapshots of his youth and former marriage-he heard an unfamiliar sound circle around from the sides of his head and into his ears. Ringing and resonating, digging its way through his skull.

*They were screaming.*

Sheriff McCabe ascended from his brief stupor, tucking his weapon back into its holster, and sprinted towards the screaming girls in cages. There were two of them next to each other, separated by a wooden wall, one maybe nine or ten and the other in her later teens, looking emaciated and time worn, the other as though she'd fallen out of a birthday party and landed in the cage an hour earlier.

"Girls, I'm going to get you out, I promise! I need you to stop screaming and pulling at the cages, please," the Sheriff implored.

"I need to get out, my mommy doesn't know where I am. I can't be here, please!" Emily screamed, as the other girl silenced herself and stopped rattling the door of the prison that contained her.

"I know, and I'm going to get you out, I promise. But before I can pop the locks off I need you to tell me if there's anyone else inside here, in the house, or in through that door. Have you seen anyone today?" asked the Sheriff.

"Please just-"

"Emily it's OK, we're going to get out. Hang on babe, let me talk to him," Amber said, pushing herself up close to the chicken wire, angling her face sideways. "Sir, this crazy fuck is down here at least once a day, sometimes twice but I haven't seen him at all today, but that doesn't mean he's not here. Please just get us out, he could be back any minute or be hiding somewhere, I don't know. Please help us!"

Amber's voice was strained and the Sheriff ran back over to where he'd dropped the crow bar outside the threshold of the basement and picked it up, running back towards Emily's enclosure and inserting the flat end underneath the metal brace that was secured with a padlock through the loop and attached to the door.

"I need you to back away from the door because I need to break this off and I don't want any sparks or little pieces of metal to hit you in the face," the Sheriff instructed Emily. "That's good honey, just another foot or so. Great."

He had a tight fit underneath the metal plate and yanked down with full force, cracking the wooden door, and pulling the lock off, sending it to the floor. Emily came bursting through the entryway with the door still closed, pushing it into the Sheriff, whimpering as she fled.

"Honey, hang on, hang on," said the Sheriff, grabbing onto her arm as gently as he could, hoping not to further traumatize her. "I know you're scared and we're going to get out of here, I promise, but I need you-just for now-to try to be as calm and quiet as you can and sit down for me, over against the wall there. Can you do that for me?"

Emily stopped as he latched onto her arm, spinning halfway back towards him, her heart racing and thoughts in a frantic, jumbled mess.

"Can you do that hon, please, for a minute while I open the other door and get her out too?" he urged her.

"OK," Emily answered, shivering.

"Thank you," he said, leading her over towards the cement wall. "Sit here a minute and I'll be right back, I promise. I'll be right over here."

The Sheriff left her, then hurried towards Amber inside the other cage. He could hear Emily begin to cry again but he wanted to crack the lock on the other enclosure and get the girls out, then off the property as soon as possible so he had no choice but to let her sit for now. He picked up the crowbar, slid the flat clawed end underneath the metal bracket as he did with Emily's, then wedged it in snug against the wood. He motioned with his head to Amber to back up, which she did, and he yanked down hard on the bar with his full upper body strength, but the claw of the bar wasn't inserted far enough behind the metal plate so it popped out, digging some slivers of wood from the door and up into his face. He started to align the flat side of the crowbar again when the bullet caught the top side of his right shoulder, then grazed the rear left side of his neck, sending him sideways and forward into the cage and down onto the cement floor. He grabbed at the wire fencing that covered the top of the door with his right hand as he went down, but didn't have the grip strength and his weight carried him backwards.

The man with the gun walked towards the Sheriff, weapon pointed at a forty-five-degree angle down towards the floor, as screaming erupted from Amber inside her cage. Emily jumped up from her spot on the floor and flailed her arms out at the man, hitting him in the side of his torso and on his back, but he pushed her away with his free hand, staring down at her as she hit the basement floor.

"Stay there or I'll shoot you," he demanded, eyes wide and fixed on her.

He kept walking towards the Sheriff who was writhing in pain, trying to roll over as blood gushed from his shoulder. Emily stuck her fingers in her ears and screamed the words to an indecipherable song as loud as she could, looking down at her legs that she'd pulled up tight against her. He was wearing dark blue dress pants and a light blue denim shirt that was a too small and tucked into the pants. The top couple buttons were unfastened, revealing a tuft of dark chest hair and a medallion on a silver chain. Amber watched him move closer to the Sheriff, then rushed the door of the cage, crashing into it.

"You sick motherfucker! I swear I'll kill you if you touch her. Come get me! I'll give you what you want, leave them alone, you hear me!" Amber shouted at him, face pressed into the fencing.

"You'll have your time, baby. Be patient," the man said, keeping his eyes locked on the Sheriff, handgun pointed down at him. "I know you have a gun, so if you move suddenly I'm going to unload my weapon into you. The only reason you're not dead yet is because I need you to tell me if anyone else is coming and who knows about me. If I don't get those answers, or if I don't get them as quickly as I'd like, I'm going to put slugs in both your ankles and knees and you can fucking bleed out as you watch me kill these girls in front of you. You understand?"

After the last sentence came out, Amber erupted into a barrage of swears and started banging violently on the walls of her prison. Emily was still sitting, rocking herself back and forth, her hands still in her ears and singing an out of key melody. The Sheriff lay on his side, the exposed wound in his shoulder bleeding down onto his back and out through the hole in his khaki shirt.

106

"Just let-let them go. They're babies for Christ sake, let them go. You wanna shoot me after, fine, but let them go," the Sheriff choked out, through labored breath.

"I asked you questions, and I'll give you another chance to answer, then I'm going to start firing so let me try this again. Who knows you're here, are they coming and who else knows about me?" he asked, his voice wispy and thin, devoid of depth or weight.

The Sheriff wiggled against the cement floor, edging himself up towards another door that was at the other end of the room not far from Amber's enclosure.

"Careful officer, I see that hand get any closer to that weapon of yours and I'm going to blow your goddamn fingers off," the man said, letting the pitch of his voice rise at the end. "Here, you trying to make your way out that door, let me help you."

The man moved to the door near Amber's cage, sliding one of his keys from the carabiner into the primary lock and opening it as his eyes remained fixed on the Sheriff, gun angled down at his face. "There you go, and feel free to crawl inside if you like, though I can assure you there's nothing in there that can save you. So, about those questions I asked…how about I count back from three and then start firing?"

"I'm sure you're not stupid…you know I'd check in with my station and let them know where I was. I asked them to make their way out here...but assured them it was non-emergency, so, knowing my Deputy he may or may not show. I was asked to check this place out based on something that came over a fax from another state. Can't say what their business with you is," Sheriff McCabe answered, wincing in pain as he spoke.

Amber had moved away from the front of her cage and grown quiet but Emily abruptly jumped up, no longer singing to distract herself but crying at full volume.

"Sit the fuck down!" the man yelled in her direction, scaring her back down.

107

"Mister, I answered your questions, and like I said I'm sure at some point folks will be showing up here so whatever you have going on is going to get found out. The only question is, do you want to be here when it happens and with murder charges added on to whatever else you did?" the Sheriff queried.

The man made a loud exclamation of disgust with his mouth before speaking. "I know cops, you hypocrite. I know fucking cops and lawyers, politicians, doctors and you're no better than I am. You just dress your sickness in uniforms. You think this is all about me, that I invented this? I was born into it, and people like me are on every continent on Earth, some a lot uglier than me. I'm sure you've seen it, Sheriff. You know what I'm talking about. The blight that lives in the crevices of the sanitized world. The darkness inside fancy, well-lit homes. The disease that flows through the veins of the same ones you probably pulled out of a hole somewhere twenty years earlier. You're all a bunch of fucking hypocrites. Now move yours hands away from your sides, so I can come slide that gun out. Then you're gonna go inside the door you're leaning up against and if you're lucky you'll live a few hours before this entire place burns to the ground. Sodom and Gomorrah, right? Sometimes things need to burn."

Emily was rocking back and forth, hands still in her ears, but now with her head up and watching the man move closer to the Sheriff, humming but no longer singing. She heard the man saying something but didn't want to know. There was a good possibility she was going to die here, in only a few minutes, or worse-later, after watching the others killed and then enduring unspeakable horrors.

"You know, it was fortuitous timing for us here," the man said, staring down at the Sheriff. "I pulled in maybe ten minutes before you showed up and started nosing around the place, and if I'd gone down here first instead of the house I may not have seen you on the cameras, putting your hands all over everything. You may have had a chance to come up behind me, as I leave the hatchway to the cellar open usually, and sometimes put the gun by the top of the stairs. Stupid, I know, but

108

what are these little bitches going to do, right? I don't need a gun to have my way with these two, but you-big time lawman, probably been in a tussle or two with your hands, shot a few people, well…you I may need the gun for."

"Let me ask you something. What are all those shoes on the porch for? Little trophies, just a fucked-up hobby of yours, what," the Sheriff prodded.

"Are we in your office, Doc? You're the one on the ground, ya dumb fuck and I'm the one with the gun. I'll ask the questions. Not to mention, psychoanalyzing me isn't going to help because I've no intentions of bettering myself as I've accepted what I am. Have you?"

The Sheriff moved his hands away from his body about ten inches on each side as the man stopped speaking. He only needed him to look away for even another second so he could reach for the hunting knife he'd wrapped down into his work boot and lodge it deep into his torso or neck, depending on how close he got.

"I don't pretend to be without my demons, asshole. The difference is I don't unleash them on the innocent. I suffer with them alone," the Sheriff answered back, darting his eyes from the man and back to the shelving behind him several times by design, in hopes that curiosity lead him to make a quick mistake and look away.

Emily continued to rock back and forth, humming, attempting to drown out the dialogue between the two men, but then as she watched the man move closer to the Sheriff she grew silent.

"Enough of your bullshit, shut the fuck up and slooowly turn over and lie flat on your gut, keeping those hands and arms out away from your body so I can see them," the man instructed, peeking in at Amber who was now silent and sitting in her cage, halfway back from the front.

The Sheriff started turning over, and right as he got up into a push-up position, he heard a whooshing sound and turned his head backwards, catching a glimpse of the man with the gun as he whipped himself around just in time to feel the full force of Emily slam into him at waist level. The blow knocked the man down onto the Sheriff, but his reflex action kept him holding onto the gun as he toppled over. Emily bounced off him, backwards into Amber's door, her shirt catching on one of the loose pieces of wire, tearing it about four inches up her side.

The pain in the Sheriff's shoulder and neck exploded as the man came to rest, half on top of him, his other half slamming into the cement wall. He jammed his knee into the man's rib cage while also elbowing his jaw from the position, then grabbed onto the arm with the gun, right above the wrist, and pulled himself up, using his legs and back against the wall as leverage. The Sheriff's wounds further ignited, but he wrestled with the girls' captor, both arms now locked onto the wrist with the gun, and slammed another knee into his abdomen, sending his own gun out of its unclipped holster and onto the floor. Behind him, Emily wiggled at the lock on the cage door trying to pry it open but her tiny fingers and adolescent strength were unable to break it apart.

The Sheriff pulled down the man's hand with the gun, following his momentum, then pivoting his body back around in a half circle, quickly reversing direction again, cranking the man's wrist over backwards at an angle; a technique called *Kote-gaeshi* that he'd learned years earlier while studying Aikido but, until this moment, never had a practical use for. The gun fell from the man's hands, hitting the basement floor as the Sheriff attempted to realign his aching frame in a more leveraged position so he could apply a pin to his arm, a choke hold, or at least wrestle him to the ground and use his body weight to an advantage. The man was thinner than him, but had formidable body strength-more than one might assume looking at his form-and he was not without some of his own combat training as repeated attempts to drag him to the ground or wrap him up were met with strong evasive counter moves. As they were grappling, the Sheriff noticed a short knife that was dangling from a loop on a carabiner the man had hooked to his pants. It wasn't holding a blade much longer

110

than two inches but if he could break free of the Sheriff's grasp and grab hold of it-easier than it would be for the Sheriff to get ahold of his-then it may be game over. As much as he wanted to untangle from the man and lunge back for his own gun, it would be a battle of timing as to who might recapture theirs and fire first and if it was the assailant and not him, three people may die in that cellar instead of one. So, he held on, continuing to try and gain an edge.

Fearing his grip may diminish, the Sheriff used his lower body to turn the man around about twenty degrees, hoping to make a forceful push into the cellar wall and cause the man to lose his breath, enabling him to take control. As he turned, he saw Amber standing near the front of her cage, motioning to him the way someone would to a car, asking them to back up. He feared getting the attacker too close to the girls but it was further away from where the guns rest on the floor so it was a risk worth considering in the seconds he had to contemplate it.

The Sheriff spun the man around, putting his back towards the enclosure, then lowered his center of gravity by crouching and exerted every bit of strength he had in his legs to drive the man backwards into the cage. He hit the wooden cross brace hard and his neck snapped back into the metal wire. The sheriff headbutted him but just missed his nose. From behind, in several furious and deliberate strokes, Amber plunged the shining silver, homemade weapon made of metal from the bucket into the back and side of the man's neck as the Sheriff held him there. The man gasped, trying to reach up to clutch at his throat, but the Sheriff held him in place, watching the blood spray from his neck, some catching his face and chest. Amber jammed the shank into him over and over while screaming, until the Sheriff pulled the man away from the cage and let his body drop to the floor. He was gasping for air, gurgling as the blood poured from his jagged wounds. Emily was crying and ran towards the door but the Sheriff gave chase, stopping her before she made it out.

"I know, I know, don't look at it. I know you want to run and we're all going to get out of here, I promise. I need you to be brave for me a little longer. I need to get her out, then my friends will be here and we're going to leave together," the Sheriff said to a trembling Emily.

She didn't answer but offered a timid nod, still traumatized from the brutality of the sudden, violent events.

The Sheriff scurried back towards Amber's cage, noticing the bleeding man crawling into the back room through the door he'd just unlocked.

"Hey, stay down!" the Sheriff screamed, as the man's body slumped across the cement floor, pulling himself with one arm, the other at his gushing neck.

Sheriff McCabe stood frozen-unsure of the best move-then shot forward towards the two handguns on the floor, kicking them back and away from the rear door the man was pulling himself through, leaving a red streak beside himself. He grabbed the crowbar that was a couple feet from Amber's enclosure, hearing he man choking and hacking as his legs dragged through the end of the doorway.

The Sheriff dug the crowbar back in behind the metal plate, wiggling it to get a good fit, watching the man's feet disappear as he lumbered forward into the back room. His shoulder was in searing pain, though bleeding less, likely from the hot projectile acting as a cauterizer to the wounds. He had little time-he assumed-before the man may get access to another weapon in the room he was moving into, though he was certain his vocalizations spoke of imminent death. He secured the bar, then pulled down with all the force he had left, popping the lockset from the door. He opened it and went over to Amber who was standing against the cage wall, looking down at the floor, muttering something to herself, soaked in blood on her neck, face and the front of her dress.

"Honey, listen to me. We're getting out of here because you stopped that monster, but now I need to secure him, then call for back

112

up. Run and go sit with her, OK?" the Sheriff instructed, nodding towards Emily.

Amber shook her head as the Sheriff led her out of the cage and over towards Emily. The Sheriff ran towards his weapon on the floor, scooping it up and heading to the doorway, carpeted in blood. He paused, looking back at Amber who was just crouching down next to a sitting Emily, then through the doorway and at the man still crawling across the dark floor. Sheriff McCabe reached his hand around the corner of the threshold, latching onto a light switch on the wall of the room the man entered. He flipped it up and a soft, yellow light fell over the injured man and the contents of the room. He saw no gun or weapons in the direction he moved, so he sprinted over to the shelves that lined the walls of the girl's room, seeking out anything that might provide warmth to the trembling children on the floor. As he combed through the shelves, he spotted something resembling a fabric cover for a piece of furniture so he grabbed it and brought over to the girls.

"Here kids. Cover yourselves and warm up," he said, laying the fabric across their legs. "We won't be here much longer. Listen, I know you're dealing with a lot in this moment but I need to know, as best you can answer, if you think there may be anyone else in here. Back in that room?"

Amber was disengaged, detached from the moment, but Emily spoke as she lifted her head up, "Is that man dead? Where did he go?"

"I'm going to put my handcuffs on him right now, but he's not a threat anymore. Listen," the Sheriff pleaded, looking down at Amber who was pulled up tight against Emily. "Is there any chance there may be more people in here? The basement or the house upstairs?"

"I-I don't think so but I can't be certain. I heard voices sometimes in that other room, back there," Amber answered, motioning with her head to the door the man pulled himself through.

"Ok. Well, I'm going back there and to call again for help, but I think they're on their way here already. Can you sit here with each

113

other for a minute while I do that, I won't be far away?" the Sheriff asked.

"Yeah," Amber replied.

"Good. Thanks, just sit tight," he asked, reaching into his front pocket to grab his cellphone.

He redialed Deputy Curtis's number and waited as it rang three times before he answered.

"Jeff, you on your way? Great, Worthington too? Listen, I need you to call an ambulance and get on the horn with Barry Sills over in Ulysses. Tell him to get every able body with a badge out here, as well as a forensics team. Or call Worthy and have him get the state team here ASAP...I'll explain when you get here, and I think the site is secure but be vigilant as I can't guarantee that...Yes, please get on it now, I'm OK, just make the calls and I'll see you here. Park in the back of the house, you'll see my car, then enter in through the hatchway in back. There will be a couple kids, girls, down here so don't startle them, and bring some blankets from the car or take mine if you don't have any" he said, tapping the end button and sliding the phone back into his pocket.

He rushed over to the open doorway, peeking his head around the corner and towards the back left of the room. In the right corner, shrouded in shadows the recently illuminated light couldn't reach, was the man leaning up against the wall, a thick trail of dark blood leading to his side. The Sheriff crept towards his body, scanning the room around him as he moved. There was a dingy bed with black sheets pushed against the wall close to the man, an unfolded cot at the other end and a small bathroom and shower with the door open directly across from him. The walls were barren, and on the floor lay only a small oval shaped green and brown area rug, a sliver of which was stained red from the man's wounds.

The man in the corner uttered something, and the Sheriff rested his hand on his gun that he'd slipped back into its holster. As he moved closer, the man pulled his legs up close against his body, revealing a large blood stain across his pant leg.

"Fucking got me good, that one," the man choked out, some red streaks oozing from his mouth onto his bottom lip as he continued bleeding from his neck. "She was always feisty."

The Sheriff drew his Glock from its holster, angling it down at the dying man.

"This is the par...the part where you, you decide if you wanna be the one...that gets credit for the kill or that little bitch in there, right?" the man spoke, his words muddy and stuttered. "Sure, she deserves it but...but it was never in her nature, where with you it is. You can kill as easy as me. Probably enjoy it more, too."

"Just tell me if there are any more," the Sheriff instructed, moving himself and the gun inches closer.

"Like me? I already tol...I told you we're everywhere. You can kill me right here and now but there's ten thousand more you'll never find," the man answered, then pulling his right hand up to his gushing neck.

"I mean anymore girls in here. Tell me now or I'll make these last minutes of your life so fucking painful you'll carry the pain into the next life you scumbag," the Sheriff said, moving closer, his eyes fixed down over the barrel of the weapon.

The man stutter-laughed, choking on the blood that was now seeping out his mouth at a steadier pace. "You cops, always with the bravado, swinging your dicks. Not as easy without the gun though."

The Sheriff lifted his foot, moving his steel toed boot towards the man's neck, ready to press down.

"It's just me here, and those two girls. They were for my...my amusement. Not good for much else, little tramps like that," the man said, prompting the Sheriff to press the ball of his boot into the left side of the man's neck, eliciting a growl.

"Fuck you, you coward! Shoot me and get it over with," the man yelled. The intensity of his scream and partial rise off the floor got his heart pumping and the fatal wounds leaked more heavily onto his soaked, blue shirt.

"I'm content to just sit here and watch you die," the Sheriff said, stepping back several feet, lowering his weapon, staring straight at him.

The man's eyelids drooped as his wounds gushed, and his head sagged down towards his chest before he spoke his final words, "I took them all, every one. My girls and their pretty feet."

The Sheriff took his foot and pushed it into the man's chest, rocking his body. There was no response, so he knelt, placed his hand on the side of the neck that hadn't sustained the trauma and felt for a pulse, leaving his fingers on the skin for twenty seconds, feeling nothing. As he knelt, he reached at the man's waist and detached the carabiner that held the keys, then stood up and went to the heavy steel door that stood off to his left in the back of the room, secured with a massive padlock.

"Girls, I'll be right there, OK? My partner will be here any minute, with some other folks and they're going to help you and then we're all getting out of here," the Sheriff yelled back to the girls from just inside the room.

The Sheriff jammed several keys that looked as though they'd fit into the lock, and on the fifth try, one popped it. He flung the door open, tucking himself up against the wall next to it, then, hearing nothing, jumped into the threshold. As he stared into the dark abyss, he saw tiny slivers of light reaching in from the two cracked windows that rested at the top of the cellar walls, illuminating what appeared to be a small table with something resting on it. As he stepped inside, he thought he heard movement towards the back of the room, so he stretched his arms and weapon outward, yelling, "Who's there? Don't move, I don't want to have to shoot you."

He slid sideways and back up against the wall, feeling something jab into his back. It was another light switch like the previous room had. He reached behind himself and flipped it on, but

116

this time the electricity sparked several fluorescent type bulbs that hung from the ceiling versus the traditional variety in the room behind. As the purple-ish light filled the area, it revealed a table with a laptop sitting on it. The walls had hooks that held S & M gear-whips, various shackles and chains and two medical grade scales against the wall on the right. The laptop was plugged in to a cord stretched in from the outside, and its fan had kicked on, which was likely the sound he'd heard, he surmised. He crawled through the middle of the room, letting his eyes dart around, taking in the macabre spectacle of the surroundings. His wounds were throbbing, still leaking blood and fluid, and he'd need to drink copious amounts of water as well as have the gashes tended to soon.

"Amber, Emily, can you hear me? Are you still sitting there against the wall as I asked you to?" The Sheriff yelled at the end, cranking his neck backwards.

He heard Amber answer back that they were OK but were coming in the room with him.

"Please stay where you are. I'll be right out," he shouted back.

"I fucking hate this room, but I need to see it again before I leave," Amber declared in the threshold of the first doorway, holding Emily's hand, ignoring the Sheriff's request.

"I don't want to go in here," Emily said, trembling as she surveyed the area.

"It's OK Emily, just squeeze my hand and don't be afraid. Close your eyes if you want, " she told her.

"Hey, I asked you to stay put," the Sheriff said, walking back towards the two of them.

"I've stood still long enough, I need to get out," Amber fired back.

He looked at her, then over at a shivering Emily. "I understand. You're right, let's get you out."

The Sheriff moved into the center of the room where the girls stood, trying to block the dead man in the dark corner from the girls eyeline. He looked around one last time before asking Amber to help him on the journey out.

"OK, do me a favor, and line the two of yourselves up behind me, like a little train? Put your hands on my hips and the other on the one in front of you, alright?"

Amber nodded and she put Emily right behind the Sheriff, helping her place her little fingers on his hips, then slid in behind her and rested her own hands on Emily's shoulders, prompting her to look backwards and up at her.

"It's just me, kid," she said, then smiled at her.

Sheriff McCabe looked over his shoulder and saw the girls positioned behind him so he began to ease forward towards the doorway into the main room. With cautious and deliberate motion, he slithered across the floor, his weapon now back against his chest, and so far, the girls were moving rhythmically behind him. There was no academy for this, no book one could read to prepare you for the horrors of witnessing young girls locked up like animals and then attempting to alleviate their fears as you tried to help them escape. Their trust had eroded to a measurement somewhere less than nothing, yet you had to somehow gain their confidence, as a stranger in a terrifying place, then walk them through the gauntlet of hell they'd existed in for who knows how long, all the while not knowing what terrors lay around the corner yourself.

His back was burning now, and the adrenaline-fueled strength he had in the last fifteen minutes had escaped him and he felt his legs falter as he continued moving towards the doorway into the main room.

As the Sheriff and his tiny train of freed prisoners arrived at the threshold of the last room, he paused, saying only, "Look straight ahead and don't stop until we get to the other door where the light is," and then proceeded to head straight on through. Of the three of them, only Amber looked back at the dead man on the floor as they walked, and letting one of her hands go, she moved backwards towards him and spit on the body.

Noise erupted outside the basement hatchway-voices-so Sheriff McCabe stopped in his tracks, whispering, "Shhh, be silent." They all froze in place, though he could feel the anxiety and agitation coursing through the human chain. He clutched his weapon, moving it several inches away from his chest, his heart rate climbing, which sent fiery waves of pain into his shoulder.

"Charlie, you down there, it's me and Worthy?" Deputy Curtis yelled from atop the cellar stairs.

In all the years working with Curtis he'd never once had a moment where the man showed up anywhere that'd given him even the slightest degree of pleasure. Until now.

"Down here, but come easy. No weapons," the Sheriff answered back.

Multiples sets of footsteps plunked down the wooden steps of the basement and the anxiety rose in the girls once again. For an unknown number of days, the Sheriff imagined, these poor, innocent children were subjected to horrors that no adult should ever know, whereas a child should never imagine. Any voice, any stranger coming towards them may be a threat, a peril, a tormentor. There was no way, yet, to ascertain if the man acted alone or not, but it was clear both girls were traumatized deeply, possibly for life, and even the voices of liberators might induce fear.

"The bus is pulling in right now, Sheriff and-holy shit," Deputy Curtis said, turning the corner by the cement wall, witnessing the sight before him. Both Curtis and Officer Worthington, who walked in behind him, froze where they stood.

"Listen, you get these kids looked at immediately, then get on the horn with every Goddamn agency from here to LA that has files open on missing kids, OK? And call the Connecticut folks if you haven't already," the Sheriff said, his legs buckling a bit.

"Whoa, Sheriff you OK? Hey, Worthy get these blankets on those girls, will ya?" the Deputy said, stepping fast over to the Sheriff and grabbing him under his arm as he wobbled.

"Don't worry about me, just get them outta here and tended to, then come back down with a kit. I took a shot in the back but it ain't gonna kill me," the Sheriff shot back, wincing.

As State Police officer Worthington was slinging the blankets over the girls, he peered back at Sheriff McCabe, who nodded back at him. A woman's voice yelled down the stairs announcing she was an EMT and both men called back to her to come down. Deputy Curtis led the Sheriff over towards the cement wall at the back, peeking into the room through the doorway and over at the dead man on the floor at the end of the blood trail.

"You kill him, Chuck?" Curtis asked.

"Wait," he replied.

Two EMT's, one a thin woman, the other a well-built man-both wearing dark blue shirts and slacks-walked into the basement with a gurney in tow and two medical kits. They paused a moment, confused as to the context of what they were witnessing so Sheriff McCabe chimed in.

"The girls are all you need to worry about right now, get them outside but keep in mind they haven't seen the sun in a while. The other is a stiff, and I have a through and through but Jeff can look at that for now. Leave a kit, will you?"

"Uhh OK, but I'm going to call county on this too, I think we need-"

"Fucking call them all-do it, but get these girls out of here," the Sheriff barked, interrupting the female EMT.

They led the girls out of the basement with Worthington's help, he in front, the gray blankets draped over them. Deputy Curtis continued to scour the room with his eyes until the Sheriff made a sound indicating he was in pain.

120

"Oh shit, let me get a look at this wound," Curtis said, jumping up and grabbing the Med Kit the EMT left as requested. "So, you shoot the guy or what? What the fuck even happened here, Chuck?"

"One of the girls got him, sliced his neck open from inside the cage. Don't know what kind of twisted shit went on here but I'm sure it's more than any goddamn kid should ever have to endure. Might be months before this one's untangled and who the hell knows if there's more of these sick fucks."

"Holy hell, I can't even imagine. You saw her cut the guy open, what, I mean, where were you?"

"You mean, why didn't I do the cutting instead of her? I was wrestling with the prick after he shot me and-hey, are you going to look at this wound or what?"

"Oh shit, sorry boss," Curtis said, opening the kit and pulling out scissors, gauze, antibacterial and saline solution. "No, I wasn't questioning what you were doing I was just, you know, trying to figure how she got at him is all."

Deputy Curtis worked the scissors around where the bullet had sliced through the rear of the Sheriff's shirt. The gash itself had clotted and stopped gushing, though the back-middle of his shirt was soaked through. The abrasion on the base of his neck was smaller and not oozing, so the Deputy wiped it with gauze and saline, then applied some antibacterial and bandaged it before starting to clean the larger one on the rear of his shoulder.

"Eh, it's alright. I'm-ya know I don't know what I am. I wasn't prepared for coming out to this rundown shithole and finding two little kids who will be fucked up forever from this. I can't remember half of what even happened it went by so fast...what I said to them, if it was the right thing or if I made it worse. How the hell do you know what to say when you stumble into this?"

"I don't think you can start second guessing and what not, not now, not ever. You got them out, Chuck. They're going to sleep in a bed tonight and hopefully see their family, who've had no damn idea where they've been and probably thought they were dead, because you showed up here and did everything *right*, not by doing anything wrong."

The Sheriff leaned forward as his wound was being cleaned and dressed, looking down at the floor with a heavy exhale.

"Thanks Jeff. I'm a stone prick to you most of the time, I know that, and likely will be again tomorrow but...thanks," the Sheriff said.

Deputy Curtis laughed, digging too deep into the Sheriff's back near the wound but he decided not to mention it.

"You know, one of those Connecticut cops told me that some guy there ran up on this Perp here, at least I'd think it's him" the Deputy said, motioning towards the dead man on the floor, "Trying to nab that girl they mentioned when they called you and he took a bat to the head or something. Now he's in a coma. I guess the scuffle knocked a bunch of shit loose from his car and that's how they found the address of Diller's place. Imagine he hadn't went after that dude or the guy gets away, maybe nobody finds this place today or ever and these girls are stuck here. Fucking crazy how shit like that works. The moth theory or something, I think it is."

"Something like that," the Sheriff replied, not correcting him.

Outside they heard additional vehicles pulling up and several voices talking, then a loud metallic pop, as if someone had dropped a steel can full of carbonated water onto asphalt.

"The whole goddamn world is gonna show up at this place, right?" Deputy Curtis questioned. "This will be all over TV and there'll be interviews and whatnot. You think that whole thing with the explosives company was a front or something, or maybe it's legit but the dude was just some twisted fuck too?"

"I couldn't say at this point but that barn could certainly hold some bombs, and the Enola Gay with 'em," the Sheriff answered, right as someone made their way down the cellar stairs.

"Holy shit," the Coroner said as he turned the corner. "He back there?"

"Yeah, bled out from a cut to the neck after he dragged himself in there" the Sheriff replied.

"Nice job," the man said.

The Sheriff didn't bother to mention Amber was the cutter.

As the Coroner made his way to the dead man in back, officer Worthington came pounding down the stairs then leapt around the corner, facing the Sheriff and Deputy, his face pale, glistening with sweat.

"Charlie, if you can move I need you to come out here now," Worthington insisted.

Deputy Curtis pulled away from the Sheriff, stood up and extended his hand, which the Sheriff took, pulling himself onto his feet.

"Thanks. What's going on, Worthy? What was that pop I heard a minute ago?" Sheriff asked.

"Just come out here," Worthington responded, zipping back up the cellar stairs and outside. The Coroner looked at the two other men, shrugged his shoulders and then went to the dead man's body.

Curtis and McCabe walked out of the basement, into the diminishing light of day. The wind had settled, and there was an Ambulance and three other police cars pulled up right outside the hatchway door behind the house. Amber was sitting in the open rear section of the Ambulance as the female tech examined her, while Emily sat on a blanket nearby, each shrouded in dark towels and holding a bottle of water. Officer Worthington had started running back out around the house and towards the barn.

"Sheriff, I called social services and someone I know at the Hospital. I'm not even sure what protocol is here but we're going to get them looked at then hopefully someone up the chain can offer some guidance," the female EMT said, noticing the Sheriff emerge from the basement.

"That's fine, it will get sorted out. Please get them hydrated, cared for, do whatever you need to for now, and I'm sorry I snapped at you down there. That was uncalled for," he replied.

"It's alright, I understand. And thank you," she said, offering a quick smile.

He saw Amber sitting on the edge of the ambulance, so he walked over to her before following officer Worthington to wherever he was headed.

"How you doing?" he asked, looking down at her.

"I could use a cigarette, and I don't even smoke," Amber replied a few seconds later.

He grinned at her. "You and me both. So, whatever amount of time it takes to unwind the hell you endured here I don't want you to give a second's thought about what happened at the end. That prick got off easy, and you did the right thing. You saved my life, really, you know that right?"

"I'm happy I killed him. Just wish I got him sooner, before..." Amber said, squinting as she looked up into the fuzzy light of early dusk.

"Will my parents be here soon?" Emily blurted out from the blanket below.

"Hopefully soon. Did you get anything to eat, cause-"

"I feel like I'll never be hungry again, but at the same time I could eat and never stop, if that even makes sense," Amber interrupted.

"I'm sure a lot of things won't make sense for a while. I'm going to let these folks look after you and I'll be back to check on you in a minute," the Sheriff promised, smiling and walking over towards Deputy Curtis who was waiting anxiously.

"Did Worthy call you Charlie down there?" Curtis inquired, as the Sheriff approached him.

"He does that sometimes. Where did he run off to?" the Sheriff asked.

"Freaking took off around the corner like a bat outta hell. What ya think he stumbled on?"

"Who knows, but I don't think I'm ready to see a dead little kid right now."

The two of them made their way out around the rear of the house, where officer Worthington was sprinting back towards them. "There you are," he shouted, catching his breath. "I don't know who we need to call for this. Nobody does."

The Sheriff and Deputy looked at one another and picked up their pace until they passed the corner of the barn where several other officers on scene were gathered in front of the now wide-open doors. They stood there, arms on their sides, one on his phone, and as the two of them got to the threshold, they saw another inside the barn looking upwards, standing behind an older silver van with a Montana plate. Off to the right side, Sheriff McCabe saw a heavy plastic curtain affixed to a metal rod, hanging between two posts just inside the barn doors, that was pushed to the side. He stepped into the dimly lit area behind the other officer who was alternating his head back and forth, left and right, at about thirty degrees skywards. As he got up right next to the man and looked up to the left where he was staring, he saw it. A long glass wall that stretched from the front of the barn and all the way back to the end. On the other side, the exact same thing running the entire length of the barn as well. Behind both transparent walls were two rows, stacked on top of each other, of small enclosures, maybe six to ten in each row. In all but a few of the enclosures behind the glass, on each side, were girls trapped inside, banging on the doors of their cages, screaming, with voices muted by the heavy see through substance that lay a few feet away from their prison doors. Sheriff McCabe stepped in a little deeper, then Deputy Curtis rushed up next to him and scanned each side of the interior as well, letting out a sudden gasp.

The Sheriff took his hat off, moving around closer to the middle of the structure, then letting the arm that held it fall to his side, his fingers tapping together against the fabric. He looked to the left again, then the right, counting at least twenty-three girls begging to be set free.

"Good God," the Sheriff whispered.

# Chapter 13

𝐵𝑟𝑖𝑎𝑛𝑛𝑎 sat next to Heather, three days after the last time they spoke, fearing that if she didn't come by her Condo she may be guilty of being the worst friend in history, despite Heather asking for space. She placed her ring-clad right hand above Heather's knee and squeezed it, saying nothing.

Brianna was equal parts Jersey Shore and Jessica Simpson. A beautiful blonde with a svelte, hourglass figure, a penchant for tacky jewelry and spray tanning, but a country gal at heart that would rather be on a horse than a dance floor. She was brimming with attitude and vigor but if you opened a door for her or told her that she smelled nice she'd love you for a lifetime. Her professional expertise was Real Estate-having sold Heather the Condo she was currently sitting in-and her wits, street savvy and tenacious work ethic helped her ascend to one of the most successful agents in Northwestern Connecticut. As much as she adored Heather, loving her like part of the family, she was ill-equipped to provide her the requisite support in the current situation, however, though she could empathize. Brianna preferred humor and profanity as a means of escapism in tragedies, versus warm hugs and endless sobbing.

"Babe, I…you know I wish there was something I could do, anything, of course but…I think you have to leave it alone right now. I mean, I can't believe the similarities to me and that fucking prick Will, it's uncanny it really is, but anyway, I think you have to wait it out, you know, with his family all there now," she said to Heather, her head in her right hand, crying.

Heather felt the hand on her leg and heard her words, then placed her left hand on top of hers, the contact only serving to exacerbate her tears.

"You poor thing," Brianna consoled her.

"He could be dead, right now, as I sit here bawling and coming apart and I wouldn't even know. I wouldn't get a call, a note, anything-he'd just be gone. I don't know if I can handle this," Heather choked out through tears.

"I know babe, I know," Brianna replied, squeezing her hand tighter.

The news got to Brianna first, two days prior, that the incident at Willie's place involved someone being attacked and that a BMW owner was thought to be the victim. Brianna made her way to the restaurant and asked to see the rear of the car by coming inside the police tape and, upon reaching it, spotted the small black and white magnet affixed to the spot on the right of the license plate. It was psychedelic looking tree, a logo for *Tree House Brewing Co*, a popular Massachusetts brewery Stephen was enamored with, so much so that he put the magnet on the car. When Brianna confirmed it was, in fact, Stephen's car, she asked an officer on scene if the name of the victim was also Stephen, to which he asked if she was a family member. She told him no but his reaction-and the car parked there without him and Heather mentioning she'd received no replies via text-suggested she was correct in her assumption.

Brianna had sold a home to a Doctor at Northwest Memorial Hospital-where Stephen was likely taken-so she called him that day asking about the situation, and even though it was against protocol, he volunteered information that in fact, yes, Stephen Alexander was a patient there, currently in the Head Trauma unit, in a coma. Brianna struggled with how to share the news with Heather, deciding, after careful deliberation, to wait until she arrived at her place that night for their get together. Immediately Heather suspected something was wrong-already anxious with not hearing back from Stephen-so she pressed Brianna for answers, why she looked so distraught, and Brianna folded. Heather bolted from the house, demanding that Brianna not follow her home, which she obliged, reluctantly, choosing to call and text her the next morning instead.

The days that followed, for Heather, were long and arduous. She texted Stephen countless messages the first night after hearing the news, hoping by some off chance the information she received wasn't accurate, then realizing somewhere after 2:00am that others may be with him, have his possessions, and that her incessant contact attempts may be met with confusion and disdain. She drove to the Hospital the next day, walked into the main lobby, then turned around and got back in her car and drove a mile down the road, turned back, went into the lobby again, then sat in a chair for forty minutes. Before she left she went into the gift shop and bought a card and a small stuffed duckling toy, electing to throw them both out as she sat back in the lobby; she was forlorn, and without direction in how to proceed.

That evening she went home and began pouring through old texts from Stephen, his pictures, his posts on Twitter and a handwritten note he'd left on her car once that said only, *"Aren't you just something?"*, with a little smiley face underneath it. The tears consumed her that night and the following day, sending her twice to the shower, and once to the toilet when the nausea became too much to bear. It wasn't until the second day after learning of what happened that Heather responded back to Brianna's frequent calls and messages, fearing if she didn't there'd be police at her door. She agreed to let her come visit the next day, and Brianna's presence was more calming and therapeutic than she assumed it would be.

Brianna sat next to Heather, holding her hand, letting her continue to cry, while her eyes followed the ticker scrolling underneath the pictures displayed on a twenty-four-hour cable news station that Heather put on as background noise earlier.

129

*...Connecticut restaurant was where police got first tip about Pennsylvania captor. Local man in coma may have been key element of investigation...*

There was a picture that left the screen moments after she looked that appeared to be *Willie's Place*, surrounded in police tape, then the screen turned to a parking lot with a woman standing in front of a station wagon and a man wearing overalls, waiting to speak with her.

"Honey, can we turn this up for a second? I think this is about what happened at the restaurant," Brianna mentioned, reaching for the remote on the edge of the couch.

*"So, you saw him fight the man off, help the girl escape?"*

*"No, I came out of the restaurant after the fight. Just tried to help stop the bleeding. He saved that little girl, though. Brave and selfless soul."*

*"That was Darren Barlow, a local resident who tended to the victim after being struck by the perpetrator, Martin Sherback. Sherback, who died in upstate Pennsylvania after a skirmish with police inside his house, was in Connecticut when he stopped at 'Willies Place', a local restaurant, apparently trying to kidnap a young girl. Now, another local man, Stephen Alexander, lies in a coma at an area hospital for trying to intervene in the botched abduction."*

*"He saved my daughter's life. She may not be here if it wasn't for him. The man is a hero to me and my family, should be to anyone with kids."*

Heather had started listening but now sat up straight, leaning in towards the television.

*"And now, Stephen Alexander may be a hero to far more than just Bill Shander, the father of that little girl, as we join Marcus Templeton out in Breddleton, Pennsylvania."*

*"Jennifer, that is likely to be true, based on the scene here out at this property in Pennsylvania. Long-time law enforcement officers*

130

*tell me that, when the scene was first discovered, they were almost immobilized-having never seen anything like it their whole career."*

*"It's disturbing, there's no other way to put it. It's not something you ever expect to see out here, or anywhere. The only thing that makes you feel better is that there are so many lives that were saved that may not have been. Girls that will see their families again."*

*"That was Officer Michael Worthington from the Pennsylvania State Police who was one of the first on the scene. Another officer-Charles McCabe-said to be responsible for killing the alleged perpetrator and captor here-has been unavailable to reach for comment and apparently sustained gunshot wounds in the melee with the suspect. However, that fight and eventual death of the suspect resulted in what is sure to be a story that will be talked about for quite some time. These images are the first to be shown of the scene here, exclusive to this network, and of course because of the ages of the victims, their faces are being blurred and their names withheld, but this is very intense video Jennifer."*

Heather and Brianna listened to the voiceover as the images showed girls, some escorted out of a barn like structure, some put into the back of ambulances and one striking image of multiple police officers walking past a row of what appeared to be jail cells. The voice said the girls, aged as young as seven and one as old as seventeen, were 'locked up like animals' in various cage-like structures for an indeterminate amount of time with one reported missing as long as four years earlier. Both Brianna and Heather cringed watching the footage, imagining the conditions the children endured, removed momentarily from the connection the experience had with Stephen.

*"Twenty-five girls, Jenn. Twenty-five children that will hopefully soon be reunited with parents and loved ones. A truly incredible scene here in Pennsylvania, all thanks to a brave Sheriff and a man sadly resting in a coma back in Connecticut. Let's hope he comes out of this soon and can be given the lavish praise and thanks I know so many people likely want to give him. Jennifer, back to you."*

131

The two of them remained motionless, staring at the TV, trying to absorb what they'd heard, disseminate it, comprehend. Brianna looked at Heather, her eyes still on the screen even though another news story was on. Brianna grabbed the remote and lowered the volume about fifty percent and as it diminished a vibration began humming underneath her left leg. It was Heather's cell phone ringing. Within five seconds, Brianna's phone chimed that she'd received a text message, then another. Heather was still comatose, oblivious to the noises around her.

"Babe, your phone was ringing I think. You want me to grab it? Are you Ok?" Brianna asked.

Heather stood up and walked into her kitchen, poured herself a glass of water in a red plastic cup, then returned to the couch, drinking it all as she made her way back. She plopped down, dropping the cup to the floor and looking back at the screen.

"Heather, honey, this is big, I mean, crazy news here on top of everything going on. I don't even know what to say, but, I'm worried about you," she told Heather, clutching her left hand. "Obviously, the priority is that Stephen get well and come out of this thing but, holy shit, this is going to be huge if he does. I mean, *when* he does, of course."

"Did he save all those girls?" Heather asked, staring off to her right, away from Brianna.

"Uh, well I guess what it said was that he, I don't know, did indirectly because somehow they found the guys address after he was fighting with him. I think that's what they said, but, yeah, he may have," Brianna answered.

Brianna's phone continued to chime as Heather's phone vibrated intermittently.

"I need to see him," Heather blurted out, jumping up from the couch.

"Babe, hang on a second, " Brianna said, grabbing Heather's wrist. "It was hard trying to go in there *before*, it's going to be a shit

132

show now, you know that. And he's still unconscious, you need to give it time. Your phone, and mine, are blowing up. I'm sure it's your mom calling, why don't you call her back?"

Heather walked over the carpet at the base of the couch where her phone rested, checking the screen and seeing that it was in fact her mother who called, as well as a coworker.

Brianna pulled her phone from her purse and saw three different text messages, all related to the story that had evolved from a local, isolated event into a massive national storyline.

"I can't call my mother right now, it's too much. Can you call her for me, and maybe check in at the hospital again, just in case, you know?" Heather asked, her eyes at the floor.

"Of course, hon, absolutely. You want me to stick around awhile or do you want to be alone?"

"You can go. I'll be alright," she answered, her eyes reengaging Brianna. "I just have to...I don't know. I suppose I don't have to do anything except wait. I need to wait like everyone else. All those girls though, so many of them. They might have died in those cages if nobody found them, right? I mean, Stephen, he's..." Heather's words trailed off as she lay back down on the couch.

"A hero, Heather. Absolutely."

Brianna brushed Heather's hair away from her face as she lay on her back, then stroked the side of her head several times before bending down to kiss her forehead and scoop up her purse.

"I'll say even more prayers for him tonight than I did last night, even though I know you think it doesn't help," Brianna said, then laughing. "Hey, listen, if there's a time to think about God it's right the fuck now. Something put Stephen at that place at the right time and, Jesus, look what the hell happened."

"I appreciate you, hon, and say all the prayers you want, and thanks for caring so much. I love you," Heather said, reaching her hand up to squeeze Brianna's.

"Call me if you need absolutely anything, alright?"

Heather nodded her head, and Brianna let go of her arm and went out the door.

## Chapter 14

*Stephen* was five and a half years old, living in Hartford, Connecticut, when he first learned the lesson of consequence. His father Henry, in a rare appearance at that time in his life, had agreed to help a neighbor across the street remove a nest of Yellow Jackets that had stung many of the local children and become a nuisance to the residents. He explained to Stephen on the porch that day that he and Mr. Potter were going to poison and then burn the hole they lived in next to a small tree right off the sidewalk later that night. He also explained, in explicit detail and with stern warnings, the ramifications of not adhering to the rules he was setting forth regarding the endeavor.

*"Listen kiddo, and don't forget what I'm going to tell you now, OK? These little yellow fuckers are nasty, angry little buggers that just want to sting your face off. If I get stung, because I'm allergic, I'd have to go to the hospital and get shots because my face and hands would blow up and I'd look like one of those lumpy Gourd things your mom always has on the window sill. But if you get stung, there's not going to be any hospital trips, but you're gonna feel pain like you've never felt, like wherever the little shit got you is going to burn and sting and feel like a Grizzly Bear bit you, ya understand?"* he asked little Stephen.

*"Uh huh,"* Stephen replied.

*"OK, so later tonight I'm heading over there, when it's dark, and burn up that hole and kill them. But here's the thing, they might not all die on the first try so we need to put a big heavy brick over the*

*hole and leave it there for a day or so, alright? What that means is, and I mean it, DON'T take that brick off the hole, you understand? Cause if there's any left alive they're going to be pissed off and want to sting the shit out of the first dummy that lets them out. Got it?"*

That night, around nine thirty, Stephen watched as his father and Mr. Potter poured some type of liquid down the hole where the Yellow Jackets lived and then Henry inserted a blow torch into the crevice for almost a minute before yanking it out. Immediately, Mr. Potter covered the hole with a brick, pushed some dirt up around it, then they both walked back across the street, so Stephen leapt from the couch and back into bed where he was supposed to be.

The next morning, right after eating two Blueberry pancakes, most still on his face, Stephen made his way to the porch of their first-floor home in Hartford. He leisurely walked down the steps, wearing white gym socks pulled as high as they'd go, a pair of dark blue cotton shorts and white polo shirt, stained with blueberry around the neck and collar. He walked up the sidewalk in front of his house to the left, looking over his shoulder and at the brick where he'd witnessed his father and the other man perform their mesmerizing acts after dark last night, then turned around and did the same thing, this time over the other shoulder. He noticed a neighborhood kid, Micah Berringer, who was younger than him, sitting on the curb across the street about ten feet from where the brick was. Micah looked back at Stephen, saying nothing, then over at the brick.

There was never any question he would cross the street and get closer to where the brick rested, but he extended his ritual of strutting up and down the sidewalk a few more times before abruptly jetting out into the road after scouting for oncoming cars. When he got to the other side, he sat down on the curb about seven feet from Micah, in front of where the brick lay in the dirt.

*"You're not going to take it off,"* Micah said.

*"Why, you dare me?"* Stephen replied.

*"You're too chicken and you'll get stung."*

*"I'm not chicken, and the bees are dead."*

*"My dad said they don't all die right away."*

*"No, my dad killed them."*

*"It wasn't your dad, it was Mr. Potter. He told me he was gonna do it."*

*"Nuh uh, it was my dad. Mr. Potter helped. The bees are all dead anyway."*

*"Don't take the brick off. I'll tell my dad."*

*"I didn't say I was taking it off, but they're dead."*

*"I told ya you're chicken."*

*"I'm not chicken, and why would I be scared of some dead bees?"*

*"They're Yellow Jackers. They sting worse than every bee on the planet."*

*"It's Yellow Jackets, not Jacksters. But they're like bees, they fly and sting you and make honey."*

*"They don't all make honey and my dad says they don't all sting, neither."*

*"Well your dad smells like Pizza and doesn't have a job."*

*"Your dad took his pants off in my back yard when my mom was hanging laundry."*

*"No sir, shut up."*

*"I'm leaving cause you're going to get stung if you pick up that brick."*

Micah got up from the curb and walked about thirty feet away, Stephen watching him go. He then turned his head back, stood up, looked down at the brick, then moved a couple feet forward.

*"Don't do it,"* Micah warned one last time.

Stephen edged closer, then let his body fall into the dirt on his knees, resting his hands a few inches in front of the brick covering the hole in the ground. Even if Micah hadn't goaded him, there was no way he wasn't picking up that brick. Every ounce of childhood curiosity Stephen had at that moment in his life was channeled and focused on it and what lay beneath. Could his father and the other man harness such power that they could destroy a thriving nest of bees with their tricks? Can insects survive fire and poison? Would any lone, surviving creatures inside that hole really be waiting right there, at the very top, ready to escape? And if there *were* any alive remaining, would they make it their first order of business to sting him immediately versus flying off somewhere, trying to find a new home?

He got his answer as he reached down and pulled the brick up from its spot on the ground, nestled in some loose dirt, inches from a small, blossoming Sugar Maple tree. It was as though five different needles with little fans on them, whooshing and buzzing around his head and neck, had decided to set themselves on fire and stab him. Although he could never recall the actual dialogue, Micah and another local kid that happened upon the scene right as Stephen picked up the brick, told stories of how all he said as he was being stung and running towards his house was *Sting! Sting! Sting! Sting! Sting!* At least fifty times, finally crashing through the screen door and into the arms of his mother who, at first confused, soon tended to his numerous welts and then called Henry at work, laughing that he "was right about Stephen and the brick" and how she owed him "that thing he likes" now. At the time, he was sure it must be those extra big cans of beer he always had with him.

The memory of the Yellow Jackets was vivid and colorful-moving like a film running on the back of his eyes-but was only a recollection. As the images began cross-fading into something less surreal and seemingly tangible, Stephen experienced an unfamiliar sensation coursing through him.

*Consciousness.*

There were electronic sounds, repetitive beeps followed by others with varying syncopated rhythms. There was a low, dull whoosh, like a fan tipped on its side and covered in pillows. Muffled voices could be heard in the distance, some laughing, others speaking in a monotone, lifeless cadence. As the dim light began to pry its way

138

underneath his eyelids, Stephen noticed an array of colored lights off to his side-through blurry lenses, as though wiped with Vaseline. The space around him was cloudy, muddled and poorly illuminated but spying a couple chairs, a window covered in drab, generic curtains and with the device next to him making all the sounds and displaying a variety of digital visuals, he knew he was in a hospital room.

He felt no pain, or any sensation at all-other than those his eyes and ears picked up-in his body. He wasn't hungry, thirsty, though he had a dry mouth, and he didn't feel like he had to go to the bathroom, which was unfathomable as he peed more than a man in his eighties due to one of his many poor adolescent choices.

When he was thirteen, Stephen made the fateful mistake on Jessica's birthday to walk on a metal guard rail home from a video game arcade in Manchester, Connecticut. Right before he elected to jump down he slipped, hitting the metal crossbeam between his legs and severing his urethra. At first it felt like nothing more than an annoying pain that would fade over time, but on the walk home Jessica noticed the front of his light blue shorts growing dark and when Stephen inspected inside the front of his underwear he discovered he was bleeding from the tip of his penis. This revelation sent Stephen into a panicked run home, with Jessica trailing, screaming and bawling, attracting the attention of onlookers, one of which followed them home and ended up calling Lillian at work. It was her first day at a new job and she left early when a neighbor she barely knew told her that her son was, "Bleeding out of his dick, Ma'am."

That summer of his fourteenth year was spent in a hospital bed with a full-time catheter installed and the fear of what the days ahead would look like. The wound itself healed on its own without surgery, surprising everyone, and had no effect on his sexual performance, which was the one question Henry kept asking Lillian over the phone from California. The permanent damage was a build-up of scar tissue that continued to grow and decrease the size of his urethra, causing symptoms not dissimilar to BPH, and sending him to the bathroom far more than an average guy his age. Every time Stephen awoke, which was usually twice in a night's sleep, he had to pee. Except this time.

He was lying somewhere, feeling paralyzed, as he recounted the story from his youth, and one of the early sections of *The Alexander Circus* he'd written. The room was coming into focus, rinsing off the murky sheen it had over it, and resolving itself into a clear snapshot of a large, darkened hospital room. The last time he woke up in a similar scenario was following an appendectomy-bathed in sun and artificial light-and with an ex-girlfriend, doctors and his mother nearby. He recalled questioning them if something had gone wrong because it was peculiar to have so many loved ones and a doctor surrounding your bed following such a routine procedure. The question was meant to be playful and humorous, but later that day he regretted that he mocked the kindness and support they'd shown.

Lying next to him, entwined in its own wire and wrapped on the metal railing of the bed, was a call button for a nurse. Stephen felt as though he was moving his arm to reach up towards it, though nothing happened. He looked down at his arm, then to the fingers of his hand. He wiggled and they complied. He then attempted to lift his arm up again, this time feeling the strap against his forearm resisting. He rotated it in small circles with only mild force at first, increasing it as he continued, and felt the Velcro restraint begin to give way somewhat. A moment later he realized it was not loosening but instead his arm was being pulled back towards his head so the thinner part of his arm was now in the strap, though still unable to break free.

The fact that he was in restraints troubled him, more so because he had no recollection of why he was in the hospital. An event that would require him to be strapped down would likely be mental health related-suicide attempt or total breakdown-and although he was certain he was overflowing with issues, he wasn't clinically depressed. Having no memory of why he lay there, however, made it at least plausible that he'd snapped or done something drastic, he reasoned.

The door swung open and a man wearing white and blue, carrying a clipboard, walked in, soon to alleviate his attempted suicide concerns.

"Mr. Alexander, good evening. How are you feeling? Can you hear me OK?" the tall, slender Asian man asked him. "Don't try to speak if you don't think you can, just nod for me."

Stephen tried to speak but had either forgotten how or had wads of cotton in his mouth, so he nodded gently.

"Good, thank you, and yes the speaking may take just a little while longer, which is normal, with the medication and just coming back into regular consciousness," the doctor explained.

Stephen tried to move his left arm again, disturbing the sheet that covered part of it, which the doctor noticed.

"Ah yes, and we had you restrained somewhat, mainly your arms, as it's not uncommon upon waking that you may flail them, involuntarily or from simple confusion, but let me take that off for you," the Doc said, walking to the left side of the bed and removing the Velcro restraint from his arm with a loud *Shhhrrrrrrrrriiiiiiippp.* "There you are. Why don't you see if you can lift that arm off the bed for me now, a few inches is fine."

Stephen pulled his arm skyward, leaving the bed about three inches, then letting it fall back to the mattress.

"Excellent, thank you. I'm going to go take the other strap off and then if you can do the same for me there, " asked the doctor.

Stephen did so as the doctor removed the strap, this time bringing his arm up about four inches.

"Perfect. Now I'm going to reach under the covers here," the doctor said, standing at the foot of the bed, and run a cold, metal instrument up under your foot and I want you to let me know if you feel it."

The chilly metal hit the underside of his foot, then slid upwards towards his toes, and Stephen's knee bent without effort, sending his leg towards the ceiling.

"No question on that one, so let's try the other."

The cold steel produced the same result, this time causing unexpected flatulence that he never felt leave his body.

"Hey, you know, it wouldn't be an overnight shift if a patient didn't fart on me so don't sweat that," the doctor joked, "and it's good to know things are getting moving again down there."

Stephen rarely felt embarrassment, much to the chagrin of every woman he'd ever dated, but in that moment, being so vulnerable-exposed and helpless-he felt his face grow warm.

The doctor continued poking and prodding in different areas, testing nerves, reactions- seeing if Stephen felt pain or other sensations-which he began to at a breakneck pace from where he was when he first awoke. The doctor's badge said "Watanabe" and he was a solid six-foot-four, strikingly thin, with dark, tightly cropped hair. He was wearing glasses, readers only-odd for a man who looked no older than thirty-but his demeanor was genuine and pleasant, and he appeared to know what he was doing, though how would he know if he did or didn't, Stephen wondered.

The doctor wore standard issue hospital blue scrubs with the obligatory white coat, and had a large round pen-type device in his left breast pocket that, as Stephen was noticing, was then pulled from that pocket revealing a bright light shined down into each of his eyes.

"Seeing that light well, are you? Nice and bright?" he asked Stephen, to which he nodded. "OK fantastic. Now, I'd like you to follow the light, only with your eyes, keeping your head as still as possible please. Here we go."

His eyes followed the light, back and forth, then suddenly he felt as though he had to sneeze but it vanished, as they often do when one is aware of its arrival.

"OK, Mr. Alexander, so a couple of the nurses will be in shortly to do some vitals, draw some blood, et cetera. Right now, things look excellent, though there are still tests to follow and we're going to have you here a few more days for observation and rest. I'd like to ask you, though, before I see you again in the morning-and again only speak if you feel like you can-otherwise just nod as I'll put these in yes and no questions. First, do you know why you're here?"

Stephen turned his head left and then right on the pillow.

"Alright, that's to be expected, with what transpired, which I'll get to in a moment. Secondly, do you feel any significant pain anywhere on your body?"

Stephen moved his head left then right again.

"OK good to hear. So, how about other strange sensations, pain elsewhere, anything not feeling 'right', if you know what I mean?"

"Caaa peee," Stephen forced out, trying to say he can't pee.

"Oh, yes, feeling like you can't pee you mean? I looked at your history and I'm aware of the trauma to the urethra so one of the things we did to make this experience more comfortable is put a catheter in. These pain meds can wreak havoc on urination so was the sensible thing to do. So, for now, don't worry if you aren't feeling the need to go as it's all flowing right into this little bag here, which I'm sure you've dealt with in the past. Also, did it hurt to speak?"

Stephen shook his head no, electing not to speak out of laziness.

"Awesome. Well let me give you a little insight here into what's happened with you and transpired since you've been here, as well as what to expect. First, I'm Doctor Naoki Watanabe and I'm a Resident here-your Primary physician while staying with us if you will. Your family Doctor, Cagna I think it was, was notified of the situation and will be getting all your records. You already had a Urologist, a Dr. Harberg, and he knows you're here, then there's Dr. McDonald, your Neurologist, who I can assure you without any embellishment, is one of the finest brain doctors in the country. You'll be speaking with him tomorrow as well.

As for your family, they've been notified. Your mother's been here, rather frequently, as well as a sister, Jessica maybe?"

Stephen nodded.

"So, let me explain why you're in here, though I've no doubt some of these memories will begin to ease their way back to you. A few things," the doctor said, turning as a nurse came in with the vitals cart. "Good evening, Gwen. Stephen here is awake, cognizant and doing great, so would you just give us five more minutes?"

"Absolutely," said the petite, round nurse dressed in a vibrant pastel explosion, her vitals cart smacking into the door as she moved, one of its wheels turned screwy.

"Thank you, Gwen," the doctor said.

"So, you received quite a smack on the left front of your head, in an altercation. You were struck right here," the doctor showed him, pointing to the left, frontal lobe section of his skull, "with a club, and it put you right out. There was some initial swelling that looked worse than it turned out to be but, to put it simply, you were in comatose state these last four and a half days. You woke up for the first time late last night, opening your eyes a bit and showing signs of movement but then went back out. We dialed the medication down somewhat and we were hopeful we'd see you again today, and it was a little later than expected but, here you are."

The doctor laughed, and patted his hand on Stephens shin as he stood over the bed.

"Traumatic brain injuries can often be perplexing, daunting, difficult to assess and work around because the human body, although having incredible powers to heal itself, also often finds ways to baffle us at every turn and work on its own timeline so we're at the mercy of you, the patient, and not what science and medicine can do. However, so far, I'd have to say that your specific case has me very optimistic, Stephen."

He watched the doctor as he spoke, searching his mind for anything connected to what he was being told. A strike, pain, falling, an altercation-anything, but although he could remember his mother's face, his sister, he could recall the car he recently bought, where he worked, and "who he was", he couldn't recollect any incident that

144

would result in head trauma. He couldn't even remember the last couple weeks, currently.

"So, as I mentioned, I feel many of the memories will come back to you, and often they arrive quickly and it may even become overwhelming so I'd also like you to speak with a mental health professional, either of your choosing, or we have a few exceptional ones here at Northwest. I've already asked Dr. Marjorie Weiss, a Psychologist here on staff, to visit with you before you're released. Of course, we're going to let your mom and others know you're awake now, so, although I'd prefer you get as much rest as possible and don't have too many distractions, I'm sure they're going to want to see you.

There's something else as well," Dr. Watanabe said, letting his voice diminish.

Stephen stared at him, lucid now, expecting to hear one of those stories like the one in his favorite movie *29th Street* where Anthony Lapaglia gets stabbed but then they find cancer. In the film, the cancer is removed and he's saved by the random series of events and his lifelong lucky streak, but Stephen didn't believe in luck, and this wasn't a movie.

"You were struck outside a restaurant, Willie's something or other, by a man trying to kidnap a little girl," the doctor continued. "You intervened and saved her. However, that courageous act led to something far greater and…you know, what might make more sense is for you to pop on the TV, when you're feeling up to it-tomorrow maybe, and let that be your guide instead of me ramble on about it. You did something incredible. It's all anyone's talking about."

Stephen stared at Dr. Watanabe, his words reviving no memories.

"I'm going to let you get some rest, and I'm sure Dr. Weiss will want to punch me when she hears I laid all this on you just after you woke but sometimes non-traditional scenarios require non-traditional measures. Plus, if it was me and I came back to the world with so many adoring me, I'd appreciate a heads up. In any event, I'm glad you're awake, as will your family and many others be, but for now let me get Gwen in here to look you over. This will all make sense to you soon enough.

Have a good night. I'll see you tomorrow."

Stephen watched the doctor smile at him, then attempted to smile back, feeling only part of his mouth and lip move upwards, so he lifted a few of the fingers of his left hand up, signaling goodbye.

Dr. Watanabe exited the room, calling for Gwen to return. Stephen watched the door ease its way back closed, giving a mild click at the end.

He looked up at the ceiling, racking his damaged brain trying to latch on to a moment, a snapshot, a noise, a smell, a feeling-anything-that could bring him to the incident and eventual injury. He knew *Willie's Place*, as he frequented it often, and there was a slight amount of pressure and pain-less than a one on the scale-emerging from the left front side of his head. He imagined himself pulling in to Willie's, getting the vanilla milkshake he often stopped for, walking out to his car and something happening to him, but no memory of a little girl or altercation came.

He thought about the days prior, getting the new car months earlier, driving it at a good clip up winding roads in Western Massachusetts, his "Alexander Tunes" *Spotify* playlist blaring from the cars sixteen speakers. He thought of his boss giving him shit because "BMW's don't handle like they used to" and how he replied, "Well the good news is, your minivan handles the same way it always has. Awful." He remembered his boss laughing but then avoiding him the rest of that afternoon. There was a discussion about a road trip to a new brewery after work one night, with several people from the office and…Heather was there. Heather came later that night at his request. He texted her and she came right down, sitting by herself at the end of the bar at *Sam Diamonds,* a sports bar with just enough pretentious, wannabe craft beers to get Stephen through the door. Heather waited there for him and they left together that night.

*Heather.*

Heather was sitting on the bed in a motel telling him not to call for a while, but she was laughing. They were in an embrace, then he left.

The nurse made her way into the room to check the vitals, announcing herself with vigor-pleasant, yet too boisterous for such a situation.

He saw Heather again, and the motel door as he looked back at it, saying something to her before leaving. She didn't text him but then she did. An old woman.

"Ma'am, 'scuse me. Heeey do you know where my pho is?" Stephen asked, with dry and weary vocal chords.

# Chapter 15

"*Oh*, my God, he's moving." Lillian Alexander exclaimed, standing up from her chair. "Baby, it's mom, can you see me?"

Stephen's eyelids rose as his arms and legs moved-a gentle stretch as the arrival of consciousness greeted him. He heard the voice, knowing immediately it was his mother, but hadn't focused on anyone as the light began spilling in.

He saw the face clearer now, a couple yards away from him on the left side. It was Lillian and she was wearing all black, crouched down and smiling at him.

"Can you hear me, Stephen?" Lillian asked, leaning in closer.

"Hey Ma," he answered, in a hushed, raspy tone.

Lillian grabbed ahold of Stephen's forearm, then leaned her head down to the metal railing on the edge of his bed and started sobbing. In the distance, he saw his sister Jessica sitting in a chair against the wall, then rise to make her way towards the bed. She was wearing a body-length gray dress, her mahogany-brown hair in a ponytail and the ever-present silver Crucifix dangling from her neck on a chain.

"Hey big brother," Jessica said, standing behind their mother, placing her hand on her back to console her as she continued to weep.

"Hey sis," Stephen answered, his voice crackling.

"I've been praying for you, every day. Luke and Madeline as well," Jessica said, referring to her six-year-old twins.

The deep Christian beliefs Jessica held and Stephen shunned were not something he'd discuss as he lay there, watching these two women that loved him show their affection and concern. Instead, he'd thank her and be grateful, learning lessons from the last time he was in a hospital bed.

"Thanks sis. Where are the little cuties?" Stephen asked, some weight coming back to his voice.

"They're with their dad. It's Sunday, so..."

"Ah, yes, I understand. Well, I thank you for being here. I know it's not something you'd usually miss yourself."

"I wanted to be here," she said, smiling, then reaching her hand out to squeeze his, leaning against their mother.

"Stephen, this is all so incredible," his mother interjected, standing straight up next to the bed, wiping under her eyes with a tissue she pulled from the box on the nightstand. "We didn't know if you'd come out of this thing, if you'd even survive and then to hear what happened...the doctor said he didn't tell you everything yet?"

"He started to, said something about helping a little girl, and the TV being a better place to hear it. I don't have any memories of what happened yet, but some started creeping in last night."

"Well, it's amazing, it really is," his mother said, grabbing hold of his hand again, squeezing it tight. "Not only is my baby boy alive and talking but he's a hero, a celebrity."

"It's truly a miracle, all of it," Jessica added.

As clarity of consciousness returned, and Stephen listened to his mother and sister speak, reminders of where their personalities and opinions diverged from his began illuminating like fireflies in his awakening mind.

"Whatever it was, I don't have any recollection," Stephen said.

The door opened again and it was Dr. Watanabe, followed in by a woman in casual clothes.

"Well, this is where the party is," the doctor said, the women in the room giggling collectively. "Stephen, you're looking well. Feeling alert, enjoying the visits I hope?"

"Sure. Beginning to feel like this isn't a dream," Stephen replied.

"Right. I know it's going to all be a little strange for a while but I'm glad you're getting clearer. Any memories coming back?"

"Some last night that I think are more recent but...not of the incident though."

"It may be awhile so no need to worry, just give it time. So, I'd mentioned Dr. Weiss, one of the Psychologists here, and I wanted to introduce the two of you."

"Hello, Stephen, nice to meet you," the woman in the yellow top and glasses said. "I'm Marjorie Weiss and I hope we'll have a chance to talk before you're discharged. A lot going on with you, I hear."

"That's what they tell me," Stephen said, eliciting laughs from his mom and sister.

"Well, I'm going to leave my card on the table by the bed. You call me anytime you like but let's try to speak at least once before you go home."

"Sounds good," Stephen said, letting his eyes fall to her chest.

The woman thanked Dr. Watanabe for the introduction, said goodbye to everyone then left the room.

"Well, Stephen, I'm going to let you get back to your family but, as I mentioned to you yesterday, there are other doctors that are going to want to see you and most of that will start happening tomorrow. My best guess-and this may certainly change after Dr. McDonald does his evaluation, is that we may have you out of here by Friday, which will also give us more time for the swelling to go down. How does that sound?" Dr. Watanabe asked.

"Better than Saturday, I guess," he answered, causing them all to laugh again. Stephen figured everyone in the room was high on

150

anxiety because nothing said in the last five minutes, by him or anyone, was funny yet laughter was coming easier than it did for an infant tickled by their mother.

"Have you turned on the TV? Peered into the rearview of your recent events?", the Doctor questioned.

"No, not yet but I will shortly," Stephen replied.

"Fine, no worries. I'll stop in and see you again before the end of my shift, and, try to take all that in small pieces. No 'binge watching', as they say," Watanabe said, eliciting a snort from Lillian. "Have a pleasant rest of your day, and take care ladies."

"Wow, nice guy, and cute too. Why can't he be ten years older?" Lillian said, watching him exit the room.

"Ten? Jesus Ma, maybe start a little closer to someone born before the Internet," Stephen shot back.

Jessica shuffled around, rubbing her hands together, heading back to her chair near the door. Taking the Lord's name in vain and discussing her mother dating was always enough to make her uneasy. At one point during a past Thanksgiving dinner, Stephen had found a book about four or five deep in a stack she had on her coffee table called, "I Love Female Orgasm". He brought it over to the table, showing it to everyone, including Jessica's husband, who reacted with extreme displeasure even though Lillian and the rest of the table were in hysterics.

"Oh, you hush up. I don't need to date anyone," Lillian fired back, "I have my dogs and now I have my son back. We need to get you out of here because there's a mountain of things to deal with, Jessica will tell you. We've been getting calls nonstop, and we both have had several people stop by the house, mainly news people, and Jessica doesn't even have the same last name but they found her."

Stephen stared at her as he tried to absorb the information she'd shared. "Hey, I'm sorry about that sis, really. I know you like to live a private life, so-"

"It's alright Stephen, we'll manage. You did a wonderful thing and we're proud of you. It's an inconvenience that will go away, don't worry about it, " Jessica interjected.

"Oh, I almost forgot, I have your phone and your iPad and some other stuff that was left in your car," Lillian said, picking up a leather bag that lay next to the bed and pulling them out. I'll plug the phone and iPad in to charge so you should be all set if you want to check them. You must be going nuts, not being able to check Twitter. Imagine how many followers you have *now*?"

"Thanks Ma, I appreciate it. Any idea where my car is?" Stephen asked.

"It's at my house. Officer Jackson was nice enough to have it towed there. I know how much you love that thing," his mom replied, rolling her eyes. "So, as soon as you get out of here I'm going to have a party at the house, Stephen. There's so many people that want to see you, not to mention all the TV folks and so on. Now, I know you're only now getting out of this thing and have a lot on your plate but we're going to have to talk about that soon. I mean, I had some agent, publicist-whatever it was-call me yesterday and said you're going to need to have a Manager to handle all these interview requests and what have you. Then I got a call from that news magazine program, *Nightly Roundup*. They're offering you a lot of money to speak with them," Lillian said, reaching into her pocketbook as she finished speaking.

"Ma, ya know, not sure I'm up for- "

"I know, I know," Lillian said, still fishing through her pocketbook, "but this isn't going to just go away. We need to come up with a plan to deal with it before it gets overwhelming. We should discuss it, tomorrow night after dinner, I'll be here in the morning and then come back after the doctors finish up with you and we can go over a strategy."

"Ma, I understand what you're saying but, as I was telling the doc before, I don't remember anything about what put me in this position in the first place. I don't remember the incident itself or even

152

arriving where it happened. I think I need to take some time to heal and sit with things a few days before any of that, OK?" He told Lillian.

"Well sure, fine, it's your business but you know we're all impacted by this too. I can't stop these people from calling, trying to set up interviews. People want to hear your story and-"

"I don't know what that story *is*, Ma." Stephen said, cutting her off. "Let me at least sort that out first."

"Alright, I understand," Lillian said, moving back towards the bed and leaning down to kiss Stephen's forehead. "Oh, and you know Sophia has been calling and I told her you're OK but-"

"I'm sure. I've yet to go through anything on my phone but I'll call her, Ma," Stephen interrupted.

"Well alright. Get some rest and I'll see you in the morning, sweetheart. I'm so happy we have you back. I love you."

"Thanks. Love you, too," he said.

Jessica made her way to the bedside, then reached down and clutched Stephen's hand, "So happy to have you back. I love you and I'm so proud of you. As soon as you're well enough I know Christopher and the twins will be delighted to see you."

"Thanks, sis, me too," he answered, smiling up at her as he squeezed her hand.

His mother and sister walked out of the room, stopping before the door to offer one last smile and wave, and then they were gone, just as the lids on Stephen's eyes began increasing their weight.


<#>


*The tiles felt cold on his feet. An empty room, outside only sand. A phone won't stop ringing. A mouth screaming, no sound. A hand slips through fingers. Words on a piece of paper. Driving across Nebraska, the corn bends into the road. Children crying his name. A body under a sheet. Stuttered laughter. A swing under moonlight. Nothing.*

&lt;#&gt;

Stephen awoke later that night to a bedside monitor cycling through its odd rhythmic tones, his face and neck wet from perspiration. His eyes opened and it was dark, the clock to his left on the nightstand reading 11:17. His mind went to Heather, who, as his memory and cognition strengthened he realized must be a nervous wreck. She likely wouldn't come to the hospital, in fear of the result that may produce, and she had no ally that could provide her an avenue to him. He looked to his right and saw the phone and iPad on the table, with the phone being closest and likely reachable, still connected to the charger. He slid himself up against the right edge of the bed as close as he could get, then pulled his arm up over the railing, stretching for the phone. The tips of his fingers touched the white charger cord so he pushed down against the fake wood of the end table and tried to drag the phone towards him, using the cord. It rested on a magazine, and if he pulled too hard it might slip and crash to the floor so he dug his fingertips into the cord-inching it closer to his right side, until he could grip the entire thing with his digits. He then rolled his body onto its right side, lifting the phone up, dangling from the charger, and used his left hand to cradle it underneath, keeping it from falling. He placed the phone on his stomach after he straightened back out and pulled the charger cord out of it.

The phone was on, so he placed his thumb on the concave Home button and unlocked it. The tiny green and white Messages tab said "789". Seven hundred, eighty-nine text messages. There was a stretch, a couple years back, where he'd almost cracked into one hundred text notifications but that was due to laziness and dating several women at once, two of which texted an entire sentence, one or

154

two words at a time, like maniacs. Seven hundred and eighty-nine though-that was something altogether different.

He didn't have the mental fortitude to take that on now but he needed to reach out to Heather and let her know he was alive-if she hadn't heard already. He hit the Messages icon and saw countless rows of unread texts, some from numbers he didn't recognize, one from a co-worker, another from an ex-girlfriend-each row being pushed down a space as new ones came in. He avoided clicking on any of them, instead hitting the "create" box to type in Heather's number, except he'd forgotten it.

He'd never saved her as a contact-a pathetic attempt to be discreet considering his most recent situation-and now had no idea what her number was. As he racked his brain trying to think of the digits, a new text notification popped up on his screen from *860-874-5415*. He clicked on it and saw the newest text that came in, as well as one other from two days earlier and then several from last Tuesday. He read the latest one.

*<I heard you may be awake. I only know about you through the TV news. I can't stand this but I can't do anything either. I hate you and love you more than ever. #DontTryToFigureItOut>*

He felt the wells in his eyes begin working as he scrolled up to the next message, dated two days prior.

*<I don't know what to do. I'm lost and the only person that knows where to find me is gone. Or maybe gone, or just lost himself somewhere. Or someplace else. I just can't think about it. I love you.>*

He didn't read the others, instead opting to send back a reply.

*{Babe, I think the alarm app on my phone must be busted cause I just had a reeealllllly long nap. Like, crazy long. Are you still cute and sexy and in love with a BMW driving shithead or did I sleep too long?}*

About half a minute passed before he saw the reply bubbles, squeezing the liquid from his eyes and out onto his cheeks.

## *Chapter 16*

*Heather* tossed the phone down onto the couch after sending the text, causing it to turn onto its other side, concealing the Home screen. For a moment, she considered leaving it until morning, too anxious to know if she may hear back from him, too terrified she wouldn't. She stared down at the pink cover that wrapped the back of her Phone, half expecting that if she stared long enough she could will a reply text from Stephen. As twenty, thirty then sixty seconds passed, she picked up the phone from its place on the couch, keeping it face down, and held it up against her chest. She contemplated returning it to the spot it landed and going to bed-a final attempt at restoring control to her life-but then flipped the phone around, revealing a text message from him.

She fumbled around the phone, opening the Home Screen with her passcode as the device bobbled in her hands, and saw the reply about his supposed nap, questioning if she was still in love with him, and she immediately began pounding her fingers into the digital keypad as adrenaline surged through her.

*<YOU'RE AWAKE!!!!!!!!!! OMG babe, I've been a wreck here, hoping I'd hear from you. Are you OK? I miss you like crazy and have been going out of my mind worrying!! Can I call you??>*

She had her face glued to the iPhone's screen, waiting to see that he was replying, and five seconds later the tiny bubbles appeared. She watched as they hovered there, underneath the text she'd sent, signaling he was typing something back. He was engaged in a conversation, albeit a digital one, but it was *him*, talking back to her after days of not knowing if he was even alive. She felt herself grow lightheaded as her heartbeat picked up, so she took a few slow, steady breaths, hoping to stave off a panic attack.

*{I want to hear you but think I need at least another day before I can do much talking. Plus, you get so turned on by my voice that I don't want to ruin it by sounding like a phlegmy senior citizen ;)}*

She quietly giggled, her eyes wet, and lay back against the pillow on the left side of the couch before responding.

*<I understand hon!! Just happy to know you're awake talking to me. I'd say these last few days have been a nightmare for me, but, that would be ridiculous considering what you've endured.>*

*{Me? Just a nice nap is all. Hey, any cool news stories since I went to sleep?}*

*<Not really. That moronic President we elected Tweeted that he thinks there's a conspiracy to have him committed, but that's about it.>*

*{I don't know if that's a conspiracy. Hasn't most of his staff told him they recommend it?}*

*<You might be right. Oh, and apparently, some guy that I used to shag is famous now. He, like, saved a girl by hitting a bat with his face or something #SoWrongButIKnowYouLaughed>*

The second she sent the text she felt queasy, wondering if it was in poor taste and too soon to dig at the details of what had transpired. Her fears were squashed when she read his reply.

*{Huh, hadn't heard that. But if he used to bang you I'd think he was famous anyway, having survived #BecauseYoureAnEpicLayNotCauseOfAllTheDiseases}*

She belly-laughed out loud, her misty eyes leaking some of their contents onto her maroon sweatshirt.

*<I love you. I need to see you. When? Sorry if I'm being selfish>*

157

*{Couple more days in here I guess then I'm out babe. I hear I'll be walking into a shit storm. Is it as bad as they say? Have you been watching the news?}*

*<Babe, it's all anyone has been doing. This thing you did, this crazy, brave thing led to massive consequences, very positive ones. Have you not seen anything yet, on TV I mean?>*

*{I haven't even turned it on lol. Should I?}*

She stared back into the phone and wondered if he was being facetious, then tapped out a reply.

*<Are you serious? Hon, you're more popular than funny cat videos! Have you looked at your Twitter, anything??>*

*{Not a thing. Just kinda in and out of this dream like state since I woke up and hoping I get some memories back. Still have no clue lol. I did recall seeing you though, I think? Motel?}*

She felt guilty now, asking him about everything, knowing what he endured and how difficult it must be trying to work that out in his head and assimilate back into daily life. There may be cognition losses, physical pain, lost memories and distance to travel before he'd be "him" again, and attempting to accelerate that process could be dangerous, she assumed. Selfishly, she was elated to hear her recalled their most recent visit, however.

*<OMG hon, yes!! I feel like such a jerk because I went all heavy drama on you that day and now I wish I just kissed you and told you I loved you five thousand times before you left!>*

*{You realize I'm not actually dead now, right? ;)}*

*<C-UP! Don't say that!!>*

C-UP was her invented acronym for "Cracking Up" that she often used in text communications with Brianna, Stephen and random others, they often assuming it was simply an autocorrect mistake and ignoring it.

*{It takes more than some idiot with a crowbar or whatever the fuck it was hitting me in the head to put my lights out, babe. Well I*

*guess he sorta did put them out but they are back on, woo hoo! #KindaIshMaybe}*

She looked at the words on the screen, her dewy eyes saturated beyond capacity, imagining he hadn't survived. There was a stretch in the days since he was attacked that it was all she thought about. Never seeing his baby blue eyes or hearing that warm, just-enough-baritone voice, watching his subtle grin grow into the smile that made her legs wobbly and kissing those pillow-like lips of his. Reading the passages of his book, the moments describing his parents and his tumultuous adolescence along with the beauty of his innocence and comedy of his charisma, brought her closer to him even as he lay unconscious. The ominous and heartbreaking thoughts of his end could be released now, but they'd soon be followed closely by daunting thoughts of another origin.

*<I love you. I know there must be so much going on and your family will be around and, maybe "others" and I don't want to be needy, disrespectful and too emotional but I just love you and I need to see you but most importantly I'm just so happy you are OK. I can't imagine if I'd lost you.>*

*{Listen cutie, I live in another woman's house and I stole soap and towels from like the last three places we got naked together in. I don't think you need to worry about being "disrespectful" with me, I'm a classic shithead xo}*

*<All of us are damaged but I like to think you're a work in progress. And, at the moment at least, the world adores you XO>*

*{Well speaking of, I better let you go and see how popular I am or if I'm actually caught in a Black Mirror episode. I love you too kiddo and I'll check in with you tom. See you soon I hope as well xoxo}*

*<Goodnight and sleep well, but not for too long! ;) xoxo>*

*{Promise xoxo}*

Heather stared down at the phone, picturing Stephen lying in his hospital bed, likely bandaged and wearing only the standard-issue gown, and how pathetic and adorable he must be. She also thought

159

about how frightened he must feel without his most recent memories, and how anxious he may become as they began flooding back, and especially after he started opening the literal and virtual doors to the outside world.

Stephen already had at least two people competing for his affection, and numerous others for his time. That number had now grown exponentially by an amount she was unable to contemplate. She tossed her phone down on the couch and got up to pour herself one last glass of Pinot Noir to accompany her elation and deaden her fear.


<#>


Stephen exited out of the text string with Heather, then stared down into the phone, seeing the long list of unread messages, and decided it was too daunting to tackle right then. Twitter, however, was something he could handle, thinking commentary and follows from unfamiliar people would be less mentally taxing than sifting through texts, which would require more time and personalized effort.

He swiped the iPhone's Home screen over three times to the left, landing on the page with the Twitter app in the upper left corner. On the icon, in the upper right corner of the blue and white logo, appeared the number "19,279". Almost twenty-thousand notifications in five days. The highest number he'd seen in that spot previously was thirty-eight, following an exchange he had with a B-list actor about a little-known film he starred in that Stephen was fond of. The final number of notifications that exchange resulted in ended up around seventy, and that was while he was actively involved. This was almost twenty-thousand notifications and he hadn't logged into the App in almost a week. He could feel a small bead of sweat forming on his forehead and his heart rate begin to climb, almost causing him to abandon his plan, but then he tapped the App button with a sharp poke and waited for it to load.

Looking down at the Notifications Tab inside the app, he noticed it capped out at "1287" for some reason, a figure that seemed less impressive but was likely incorrect. Instead of scroll through the notices, he decided to go to his Home page and see how many Followers he had. The previous number was eleven, where the current number had ballooned to 114,083. Over a hundred thousand people he didn't know that wanted to be in his space, hear what he had to say, peek through the window of his life and add commentary or "likes". As he was logged into the App, notifications lit up in a blue banner across the bottom of the screen showing he had additional new followers and Tweets directed at him, inflating the number. The Notifications count inside or out of the App couldn't be trusted, he decided.

Although he didn't have the energy to engage with even a handful of his new Followers, his curiosity led him to at least peer into what some of those who'd reached out to him were saying, so he tapped the Notifications tab on the bottom of his phone and started reading.

*Barry Tomkins and nine other followed you.*

*@GreatTweets4All "You are the MAN dude! Stephen Alexander for President!!!*

*@TheSniffydoodle "I can't stop watching those girls come out of that place. Incredible. Thank you for saving them."*

*Carolyn Heller and twelve others followed you.*

*@DarleneSchrepka "Mr. Alexander you're a gift from God. Bless you."*

*@RamblingAbare "You define 'hero', Stephen. Can't wait to hear your story!"*

*Linda Dempsey and five others followed you.*

*@FireballCake @POTUS "If this guy doesn't get a couple nights in the Lincoln bedroom, nobody should! Bravo, my friend!"*

As he scrolled through the notifications, the blue ticker below continued to light up, announcing more Tweets at him and additional followers. He took a long, slow breath through his nose and then let it seep out through his mouth, then exited the Twitter App, resting the phone on the night table to his right.

Resting nearby was the Television remote, which he picked up and pointed at the flat screen TV mounted in the upper rear corner of the Hospital room, letting his finger hover over the power button. He hadn't seen or heard anything on Television since he'd regained consciousness, and part of him wanted to avoid that world at least until memories of that day returned, but as always, curiosity-hand in hand with ego-made the final decision.

The screen lit up with a Hospital landing page as his index finger depressed the bright green button on the remote control. It mentioned deals in the gift shop as well as visiting hours. He looked down at the remote for the Channel adjustment, then thumbed the arrow upward, hitting a blank channel and then an Episode of *Home Improvement*. The next channel was an advertisement for a bathroom cleaner-one with a toilet that sat in an exploding garden, based on the hundreds of pastel flowers showering the can. He realigned his thumb and hit the button one last time and an all-day news channel filled the screen. It was *Topics With Tanya,* an hour long panel discussion show hosted by Tanya Jones, a former Lawyer and professor at UCLA that had been hosting the show-discussing true crime and political stories-for seven years. She was pasty white, with an almost mullet of light brown hair, spiky on top, long on the sides and back, and usually interrupted her guests more than any other host on television-a habit she regularly defended-claiming it was necessary to "move the show along." The screen was alternating with her in center frame then switching to three other guests joined by video. He slid his thumb over to the volume and pushed it up.

*"...because we aren't talking about someone in Law Enforcement here, this is a civilian. Right place at the right time-or wrong place if we're talking about the poor guy's injuries but-"*

*"Oh Tom, come on, we're talking twenty-five girls here, I don't think we can ever say it was the 'wrong place or time', especially considering that his injuries weren't life threatening and he's apparently awake now."*

*"Yes, but Tanya this is someone very likely ill-prepared for a scenario like this-instant fame, adulation, being recognized everywhere. He's going to have challenges with-"*

*"What difference would it make if he was in Law Enforcement, Tom? Most officers aren't celebrities, they would face the-"*

*"My point was that this was not someone normally associated with performing such acts, making heroic moves, and the spotlight is really going to be on this fella and I wonder how or if he may be able to handle it."*

*"Tom, Tanya, I mean, aren't we all asking ourselves, at least a little bit, why all the focus is on this Mr. Alexander-as much as I and everyone respects his brave efforts-and not on the individual that found the lead, the receipt or whatever it was that lead them to the place? Or certainly this officer McCabe who got shot at the scene, who, yes I know has received a ton of praise but-"*

*"Linda, I have to say that sounds ridiculous, frankly. I know from your blog and Facebook page that you're a religious woman and you believe everything that comes to be has an origin, a "creator" if you will, and this guy in Connecticut, Mr. Alexander is the genesis, to use a biblical word, of this entire liberation of these girls."*

*"What are we doing assessing 'points' or 'credit' to any of this, anyway? There were many hands in this situ-"*

*"OK, OK, Phil, Linda, Tom we need to break away from this because we have some new video from the scene in Pennsylvania where the girls were released a few days ago, apparently shot from a first responder on the scene who wasn't sure it could be shared at the*

*time but has now been cleared. It's a different angle, a little closer from the right, of a stream of the captive girls being lead out from the barn enclosure. As with the previous videos, the faces and any identifying markings have been blurred out, and some of the audio has been scrubbed, with the victims all being under age. Here it is."*

The screen filled with a man walking next to three girls, all appearing between nine and twelve based on their size in comparison to him, emerging from a barn-like structure. Then, another two men, in police uniforms, escorting four others out, one clinging tight to one of the men and likely crying, as she kept bringing one of her hands to her face. Immediately, a female police officer, another woman in civilian clothing and a female EMT walked from the location, this time holding the hands of seven girls, whose own hands were all in each another's. All the girls had on plain looking dresses, most stretching to inches above the ground and white or light blue in appearance, some with floral patterns, some solid colors. Several of the girls looked as though they'd prefer to be running while others were shuffling their feet across the ground with no urgency.

A video box appeared on the right bottom of the screen, overlapping the primary shot of the girls being freed, with Tanya filling the entire area, shaking her head and looking distraught. In the main shot behind her, two other girls exited the barn, one on a stretcher with an IV in tow and several EMT's walking alongside her.

*"You know, we've seen similar video so many times already in the last few days but they never get any easier to watch. The striking images of these little girls, these babies, being led from where they were imprisoned and harmed in who knows what manner, as we still await so many answers...just incredible. Hard to watch but impossible to look away. The sadness and empathy you feel for what they've experienced mixed with jubilation and relief that they're now free. Just incredible."*

Stephen felt his stomach turn upside down-a nauseous sensation coupled with the tumbling flip one gets when startled-then felt the length of his body shiver. He worked his thumb onto the channel arrows and went to the following station. It was another Cable News program, this one showing other videos from the scene in Pennsylvania. A long stretch of yellow police tape, a multitude of Ambulances, a few men wearing jackets emblazoned with "F.B.I.", numerous state troopers, assorted media and random cut-in shots of some of the girls being pulled out of the barn again.

He went to the next channel and it was a commercial. The one after that showing a weather forecast, then landed on another where a panel of guests were discussing how Stephens's altercation led to the Invoice being found, and soon after, the other girls. Underneath them on the screen, a banner labeled, *"Prisoners No More"* scrolled by.

He placed the remote on his chest, hit the power button with his thumb and watched the TV go dark.

He closed his eyes, took several deep breaths-drawing them in full and slow-pausing before he exhaled with the same deliberate and relaxed motion. His heart rate was climbing but the structured breathing helped soothe the increase. The room was silent, other than the slight background noise outside in the hallway and the usual beeps from the monitors. As his eyes closed, he could hear the *Thwoosh Thwoosh Thwoosh* of his pulse, more than he heard the other sounds around him, so he reached for his phone and went into his music library, looking for one of his playlists full of New Age music. After finding it, he pushed "shuffle" and adjusted the phone's volume to about halfway, right as the mellow keyboard sounds, layered over rain water, began flowing from the tiny speakers.

He closed his eyes and recalled the video images of the girls being led out into the light. Something, somehow, he was apparently responsible for. His eyes slipped open, but he forced them closed again. As his lids fell, immediately he saw it.

*The station wagon.*

His eyes snapped back open.

# Chapter 17

*The* next thirty-six hours, for Stephen, were saturated with doctor visits-between Dr. Watanabe checking in, the neurologist, Dr. McDonald, following up after a new CT scan and MRI, his own Primary Care Physician making an appearance-and what seemed to be every nurse on staff checking his vitals on the hour. As the shadows decreased in his bland, off-white and gray hospital room and the evening spilled over its contents, stealing the light, Stephen sat up in his bed trying to sort through the mental pictures that had made sudden, brief appearances of late.

The station wagon lead off the barrage two days earlier. He could see it parked near trees and remembered his body up against it. He recalled a slamming door while standing outside. There was an image of a small girl running. There was a physical altercation, though he could see no opponent. There were flashes again of Heather, lying on a bed, standing before him, her arms draped over his shoulders. There was a figure of a man but no face or identifying marks. Then only darkness.

In the last four hours, the images-the wilted and incomplete memories-would cycle though his conscious mind in the same basic order, revealing only the minutest new detail as the loop played. When it first began, the morning after the station wagon appeared, there were a couple flashes, all centered on the car, but then others crept in. It wasn't until today, in those last hours, where the tape playing in his head slowed down and let him see a little more, though still only fragments of a much larger picture.

As Stephen closed his eyes and started sifting through the snapshots again, Dr. Watanabe opened the door of his room and strolled in, smiling and carrying a manila folder and clipboard.

"Hello, Stephen. How you feeling? Not like you need to stay in here another ten days after all the poking and prodding you've had to suffer through, I hope?"

The doctor laughed, sliding into an odd vocal see-saw noise at the finish.

"I'm good. I understand why it all needs to be done," Stephen answered.

"I figured you would. You seem like a reasonable guy, and I must say the nurses and myself are going to miss you. We've had a rash of cranky patients of late and you've been a treat for us."

"Wow, if I'm a treat I'd hate to see the shitheads."

Dr. Watanabe chuckled, causing him to drop the chart right next to the bed and making a loud pop on the hard floor.

"Sorry about that," he said, picking it up and placing it on the chair with the clipboard next to Stephen's bed. "I'm very happy to see your coming back into your own, with your voice sounding strong, good tone and inflection, what about the memory? Anything new since this morning?"

"Last few hours there have been more pieces filling in. It's like they're coming back at a quicker pace. I'm just sitting back and watching the show that started since I turned on the TV."

"Ah, yes. I figured that may have greased the wheels. No need, now, to push yourself, force anything, it'll all return when it's ready to. That applies to the police officers that will want to speak with you, which is one of the reasons I wanted to see you before I left. There's one here now, a gentleman from the FBI, and he's hoping to talk a few minutes if you're feeling up to it? I can absolutely put him off if you aren't ready or don't have the energy."

Stephen hadn't turned on the television for two days, had only shared a couple texts with his boss, his mother-who'd also been visiting-and Heather, and had stayed completely away from social media. He felt strange engaging with anyone else while his memories of the event were only a feeble outline.

"I don't remember anything whole, really, at this point but if he wants to speak to me I might as well get it over with." Stephen said.

"OK, I'll let him know when I head back out. The other thing I wanted to share with you is that, in that folder I just placed on the chair, is your after-care file, which is still being updated with follow-up visit dates and such, but, I'm releasing you tomorrow. Both Dr. McDonald and Cagna feel it's fine to do so. How do *you* feel about that?" the Doctor asked.

"Well if I said I wanted to stay here for another week, somehow I think my Managed Care plan would tell me to go fuck myself, and just lie down on my couch so I guess I'm ready to roll," Stephen replied.

The doctor howled with enthusiasm. "I'm going to miss that wit, but, yes, I think it's time we send you on your way. I know you mentioned you'd watched a little television and absorbed some of what your events have led to and what that likely means once you leave here, but, are you feeling alright about that? There's going to be a lot happening, Stephen."

"My mother tells me I already have an 'agent' or something," he said, shaking his head and adjusting himself more upright against the pillow. "I'm going the AA route, doc-one day at a time. Not sure what else I can do."

"That sounds like a great idea," the Doctor replied, nodding his head as he looked at him. "So, I'm going to get out of here, and I'll let that gentleman know you're OK to talk but I'll advise him no more than ten minutes if he can keep it at that."

"Thanks. Oh, and hey Doc, I was wondering, you know, because I'm such a big celebrity and all, why haven't there been more people coming in to my room here? Figured I'd be inundated with people trying to get me to cure their leprosy, marry their daughter, et cetera."

"Hmmm, well I suppose I forgot to mention that little detail and I know if you were on the wing facing to the Southwest you wouldn't be needing to ask this question. So, there are two guards down at the elevators in the lobby, one at the main stairwell entrance, two positioned down at the nurse's station and one just a few feet outside your door here-all on rotational shifts. Had we not had a setup like that then, absolutely, you'd be mobbed in here. There's routinely a group of at least one hundred people a day, more likely two hundred, that try to come see you every day since you've been here, and as I mentioned, were you in the other wing, you'd see the throngs of people outside, many carrying signs, praising you, etc., but most just wanting you to know they're here. Don't even get me started on the phones! If we didn't have a block on your room you'd have to keep it off the hook. I can't believe no one's shared this with you yet."

There was a moment a day or so ago when Lillian had mentioned "all the people out there waiting to see you", as he woke and was still foggy but he assumed she meant way outside-the country-or even just figuratively. A couple of the nurses joked that they hadn't seen a patient this popular since some professional golfer was here years earlier, but Stephen assumed they were only being polite.

"They may have and I sort of blocked it out. I'm a master of that skill, just ask anyone I've dated."

The Doctor snorted, then re adjusted his clipboard and file folder.

"I'll see you in the morning, and my best guess is that we'll have you out of here by 1PM or a little after that. Have a pleasant night, Stephen," Dr. Watanabe said, smiling long and full, then walking out the door, almost dropping the clipboard again, its smooth and slick surface too slippery to be held against the folder without constant pressure.

"Have a good one, Doc," Stephen replied.

Stephen thought about picking up his phone from the end table next to him, see how inflated his Twitter follows had gotten but then decided against it. There was a sense of pressure, a feeling of responsibility to these unknown citizens of the world, to respond to them and say thank you but it would be impossible to do that at this point, the numbers too vast. As that thought came and went from his mind, immediately he realized there *was* a way to do just that without occupying the next five years of his life. He reached over for the phone, almost dropping it in his haste, and lay it down on his stomach, angling it forty-five degrees so he could see it clearly. He placed his thumb in the depressed Home screen circle and it unlocked, revealing the first page of his apps, which he swiped at with the index finger of his left hand as he stabilized the phone with his right. When the Twitter app appeared in the corner he poked at it to open, then went to his page.

He stared at the tiny thumbnail picture of himself on the left-a selfie he took standing on the edge of dock near the Rhode Island shoreline. The background picture was of a Sea Turtle moving through cerulean waters, much like the tattoo he had on his upper left arm near the shoulder. His last Tweet was a link to a video by the band *The Slow Show*, from England, over ten days ago. It had two likes the last time he recalled looking at it but now was up to four hundred and ninety-seven, with over three hundred Retweets. Either the little-known band had been signed to perform at the next Super Bowl or they'd become unknown passengers on his sudden popularity train. Certainly, it was the latter, as excellent a band as they were.

He hit the "New Tweet" button in the upper right corner of the screen and, after a minute or so of thought, composed one that he sent out to the universe.

170

*Alive, awake, and grateful to be. Thankful for all the follows and well wishes, but mostly that so many lives were saved. Peace, folks.* 😊

In less than a second, likes appeared in his notifications, with commentary soon following, none of which he read as the door to his room swung open and a man wearing a dark blue suit walked in.

"Good evening, Mr. Alexander. Dr. Watanabe mentioned he let you know I'd be coming in," the man said, heading right to Stephen's left bedside.

"The FBI guy, I presume?" Stephen answered.

"Yes, agent Steven Duplas, out of the Hartford field office. How you feeling?" the agent asked, pulling a small notepad from inside his suit jacket.

Stephen watched him prepare to ask questions, readying his pen and pad, looking down expressionless at him-his dark, tightly cropped hair parted in the right middle, a strong jawline and pronounced chin. He wondered if the similarity in looks and demeanor to the FBI agents portrayed in movies so often was a result of Hollywood getting it right, or the FBI assimilating after years of being portrayed this way. Regardless, it was amusing to see first-hand, he thought.

"I'm alive, so can't complain too much. Still a little pain, and the memories aren't all back, not even close, so, still a way to go. I told the Doc about that-the memories-and that I don't imagine I can be of much help, but feel free to ask me anything you like."

"Right, he explained that you don't remember more than fragments in this last week or so and I completely understand, and although there will be additional questions down the road, I think for now we can just focus on a couple specific areas that are not as recent-memory-dependent, if that's OK?"

"Sure, of course. Ask away."

"Great," said agent Duplas, thumbing a couple small pages of his notepad out of the way and pushing the ball point pen into the paper. "So, can you tell me if the name Martin Sherback, who was the suspect here, the man that attacked you and was subsequently killed in Pennsylvania, does that name sound familiar at all?"

"No, not at all. The only thing I know or care about, which is the bane of my existence, in Pennsylvania, is the Philadelphia Eagles. I'm sorry."

"A tough team to love, agreed. But then again, I'm a Raiders fan, so..."

"Jesus, so you're miserable *and* an asshole. Tough one."

Agent Duplas cracked a smile but didn't laugh, then pulled the chair next to the bed closer and sat down. "I hope you don't mind, just more comfortable, and I was out there in the lobby for a while today, standing. Anyway, you're right on both accounts with the Raiders thing. So, no connection to Pennsylvania and the name doesn't ring a bell. Would you mind if I showed you a picture of the suspect?"

"Sure, but as I mentioned I don't have any images in my head of the man's face at this point but who knows, maybe it stirs something up," Stephen replied, sitting up straighter in his bed.

The agent pulled a small picture from his outside suit jacket pocket and handed it to Stephen. The man he was looking at had wire rimmed glasses, dark hair, non-threatening, and not noteworthy in stature or appearance. Although he looked like many other men that one might bump into in everyday life-ordinary and nondescript- Stephen had no more specific knowledge or recollection of him. He held onto the picture for about thirty seconds and then handed it back to the agent.

"No idea who he is, I'm sorry," Stephen said.

"I'll have you take another look in a week or so, see if anything pops up, but the prevailing theory is that this guy was not a regular visitor to the area and had no regular ties here. Unlikely that you'd know or even recognize him but always want to cover every base, look from every angle and such," Agent Duplas replied.

"I understand, and I wish I could be of more help, at least about the incident itself but it's foggy still. Part of me hopes it doesn't get any clearer, because maybe I don't want to recall what happened, ya know? But then part of me *needs* to remember, see his face, connect with the moment so it doesn't remain this mystery that I can't ever be a part of, if that makes sense."

"Absolutely. If this had happened to me and I had the amount of press and the public all over me I'd at least want to remember it, tell my story, share in the experience that so many are discussing. You'll get there."

"So, what *is* the current theory with this guy? Was he just some sicko asshole kidnapping girls for his own pleasure? Sex trafficking, what?"

"Honestly, we aren't entirely sure yet, and may not know for some time. We have a laptop of his and some of the best hackers in Quantico tearing through it as we speak but this guy was careful, calculated-extremely cautious. High-level encryption, no cell phone or email trails so far, no obvious connections to anyone else. In our preliminary interviews with some of the girls we haven't heard anything that leads us to believe he was working with anyone."

"Fuck. The whole thing is so diabolical. I haven't even dug into it all yet, really, but what I've seen and what you're telling me...I don't understand the evil one needs to possesses to do something like this. Take someone's fucking kid, lock them up, and..."

"My 'off the record' guess from examining the crime scene and reviewing initial evidence is that he was probably meeting his own twisted needs with these girls but that he was also selling some to a network of others like him. There are several known out there, but we generally see these originating overseas and the kids we find are usually Eastern European, Asian and never with volume like this. It was a staggering number of girls to find in one location which makes me think this must be a part of a larger operation. Very early on into the investigation, though, so difficult to speculate. Do the business

173

names *Juan P.L. Holdings* or *Kinetic Detonation Systems* mean anything to you?"

Stephen politely mimicked someone racking their brain, though he no recollection of the names. "No, can't say that they do."

"OK, well, there's no obvious ties to anyone locally but with a case like this we need to draw a very large circle around things, then slowly reduce that diameter. Plus, two of the more recent victims were from Connecticut and Massachusetts-both within a thirty-mile radius of where this latest botched attempt occurred-so, just peeking inside every door, looking for patterns, connections. "

"So, what about these girls? Are they alright? I mean, as well as one could be after enduring what they have. Were they badly hurt? Have they all been reunited with their families?"

Agent Duplas placed his pen and paper on the nightstand before answering, "It's an evolving situation, of course. Many have been reunited with family, some have splintered families now-a result of longstanding trauma from their child initially disappearing and in one case the girl was an only child and her mother had taken her own life almost a year ago, very tragic. These girls-these children as that's what they are-they're going to be facing a multitude of battles going forward but for the most part they're all in general good physical health. The mental health concerns will be larger issues but-and I can't stress this enough-none of what they face is more daunting than what you helped liberate them from. You taking action with Amanda at that restaurant made all this happen, Stephen, and a lot of lives are better for it."

"I appreciate the kind words, thanks, but I guess I wish it had happened a lot sooner. Poor kid and her mother...fuck. Just awful."

"I hear ya, but just remember what I said. What you helped facilitate is a far better reality for all these kids. Don't forget that."

Stephen smiled and nodded as his eyelids began to droop.

"Hey, let me get out of your hair so you can get some sleep," Agent Duplas offered. "I appreciate your time and I'm going to leave one of my cards on your nightstand here, in case you remember anything you think may be relevant. I'd also like to check in again, couple days, if that works for you?"

"Of course, sure," Stephen replied, his words dragging.

"Sleep well, and I'll speak with you soon," the agent said, standing up from the chair and sliding it back next to the end table, then turning and heading for the door.

Before the sentence was finished Stephen was asleep. He'd get six and a half hours before a nurse and his mother would wake him up from a dream where he was unclothed, and trying to jump in a car that was rolling backwards down an incline after he parked it.

<#>

*A familiar voice. Orange and yellow leaves at his feet. A phone call, then running. Walking on train tracks over water. A box of photos and notebook. A car rolling away. Her voice.*

## Chapter 18

"*I'm* much obliged, M'am, sincerely I am but that's not necessary," said Sheriff McCabe, sitting in his recliner, looking over at the muted television across the room. "I will, and thanks again. Have a good afternoon."

"So, it's been like this the whole time, then," Deputy Curtis asked, sitting in a weathered wooden chair across from the Sherriff.

"That damn phone will ring again in less than ten seconds, mark my word," the Sheriff replied, and three seconds later it did. "Hello, Chuck McCabe. Yes, and thank you so much but I'm not providing any comment at this time. Take care."

The Sheriff hung up the phone, then took the handset and placed it on his end table and unplugged the wire connecting it to the base so he wouldn't have to hear the annoying sound that followed when left off the hook.

"Wow Chuck, that's something. I've had some calls and you know they've been hammering the station house but…you said the cell too?" Deputy Curtis asked.

"I turned that damn thing off. I can't delete the voice mail box fast enough to keep it free and was getting texts from people I don't even know-no damn idea how they got my number," McCabe said.

Deputy Curtis looked around the room, as the back of his neck began to perspire. The Sheriff noticed his intentional disconnection and frowned, then got up and went to the kitchen.

"Come on, Jeffrey, are you kidding me? Why would you give out my cell number, honestly?" asked the Sheriff, taking a glass from the cabinet over the sink and filling it with tap water from the nozzle below.

"I...I didn't think I was doing anything I shouldn't have because this producer from *Newsource* called the station and said she had an interview with you and was trying to finalize some details but had forgotten where she wrote down your number, but that you gave it to her."

"Jeff, you can't possibly be that boneheaded. We've dealt with news people before-not like this I grant you-but we have. You know the tactics they use to get information. Why the hell didn't you check with me first instead of just give it out?"

Deputy Curtis tugged at his hat that was resting in his lap, spinning it around and looking down towards the floor.

Sheriff McCabe's home was a modest, sparsely-appointed farm house ten miles from his office. The walls were mostly bare, the only exceptions being a painting of the Grand Canyon over the couch in the living room and an actual photo of the landmark above one of the light switches in the same room. The carpet at Deputy Cutis's feet was a worn Hunter green, and the few decorative pieces scattered around-a couple candles and a figurine of a jungle cat-were either another shade of green or black. In one of the corners rested a natural wood bodied Ovation acoustic guitar, coated in dust, not played in years. Sitting nearby was small glass table with two rocks glasses and a bottle of Scotch Whiskey.

"I'm really sorry, Sheriff. I didn't mean to make headaches for you," Curtis said, still looking down at the floor.

Sheriff McCabe walked back into the living room where they'd started talking and sat down on the couch, tipping back the water glass and finishing it all in three quick gulps, then placing it on the time worn, walnut coffee table as his index finger and thumb began their routine.

"Jeff, listen, I know this has been a pain in the ass for all of us-not just me-but it's not going to last forever and if we manage things right it won't be awful. I'm only asking you to be careful, be smart, OK?" the Sheriff said, causing the deputy to look up at him.

"I know, and you're right. I'm sorry. I guess all this activity, with the Feds and everything, being at our place and the phone calls, well, I got stupid for a minute. It won't happen again, I promise."

"I appreciate that, and I don't mean to sound pissy but, it would be nice to get back to work and not have every schmo from here to LA in my business."

"I hear you, Chuck. Hey, but, can I ask you something?"

The Sheriff nodded.

"Well, you feel good about what you did though, right? I mean, all these girls being saved and some of them already reunited with their families. All that crying and joy between them, you've seen the video of it, I know you have. *You* did that, Chuck. Or you sure as hell did most of it, anyway. I know you're being bothered a lot but, you can understand why though, right?"

Sheriff McCabe leaned back against the rear of the couch and exhaled.

"I don't mean to pry into this right now," Deputy Curtis assured him, "But I just wonder if you *are* gonna talk to any of these news folks because you did something amazing and should be proud of that."

"I know what you're trying to do and I appreciate the effort, Jeff. I understand the magnitude of this, and I'm delighted to have helped those girls, reunited them with their families and all that but, I'm not someone accustomed to or comfortable with a lot of fuss. I don't crave attention, nor do I enjoy it. Maybe that makes me a cantankerous bastard, a curmudgeon or whatever you wanna call me but it's just who I am. Plus, I already talked to the news a few times, and you were there for two of them, so it's not like I'm in seclusion."

"I know, I didn't say that but, I heard you were offered a chance-a couple maybe-to go on TV and talk about it, maybe offered a lot of money and I wonder why you wouldn't want to do that?"

"Curtis, I did my *job*, that's what I did. I didn't do something I wouldn't do on any other day. Yes, it was a day unlike any previous but I can't go on fucking TV and take money from people to talk about a job I did that I'm already paid for. Maybe that's just me, I don't know. You were there so I am sure at some point if not already you're going to be offered money to talk about things, but if so you better be damn sure it's been cleared by those Feds and you don't go getting yourself or our office in trouble, you understand?"

"Yes boss," the Deputy replied, spinning his hat in his hand again, then standing up. "Well, I don't want to keep you, I know you have the day off and wanted to check in with you and see how you were doing."

"I appreciate that, and thanks for coming out," said the Sheriff, getting up from the couch and heading over to shake the Deputy's hand.

"Oh, hey, did you hear that Tanya woman on that TV show offered the kid in Connecticut who just came out of the coma a hundred grand to come on her show? Can you believe that? Just heard on the way over," the Deputy asked, walking into the kitchen and towards the side door exit.

"Holy shit, no," the Sheriff answered.

"Can't imagine he wouldn't take it cause, you know, I get what you're saying about it being our job and all but, this was just some guy that saved a girl then gets beat up and put in a coma. How could you turn that down? Fucking deserves it as far as I'm concerned."

"Maybe he does, but, I don't know if having a pile of money is going to make it any easier to be in his shoes. Could make it worse."

"You might be right about that, Chuck. Be some nice God damn shoes though, right?"

The Sheriff laughed and opened the door, walking outside behind Curtis.

"Thanks for coming out. I'm going to get a new cell number, I think I can call for that, so I'll check in with you later if I get it done and either way I'll see you tomorrow. If you need to reach me try the CB or call Eleanor down the road and she'll pop over and get me."

"Sounds good, Sheriff. Enjoy the rest of your day, looks to be a fine evening" the Deputy said, removing his hat and sliding into his cruiser.

"Good deal."

The Sheriff walked back into his house, towards the living room, staring at the house phone on the table by the couch. He needed to call the cell company and have his number changed but if he plugged the phone in it would likely start ringing again immediately. He stood in the threshold of the kitchen and living room for a few seconds, then rushed over to the phone, plugging the handset in, dropping it back into the cradle, hoping his quickness would decrease the chance of it ringing once the line was active and he could pick it back up and dial out.

As soon as the handset depressed the buttons in the cradle, the phone began ringing in its familiar *Ring-Ring, Ring-Ring* pattern. He let it go three times, then unplugged the primary cord from the wall and grabbed his cell phone from the coffee table, powering it up.

"Hey. You coming by here, or am I driving your way?" the Sheriff spoke into the phone. "Bring the cruiser, not your own car. I know, just...for me, please?"

# Chapter 19

*The* morning of his discharge was bedlam.

The staff and police officers did all they could to keep onlookers, news media and well-wishers from blocking the hallways and exits he was traveling by wheelchair, but were outnumbered and overburdened.

With the final observations, vitals and checklists completed, the only remaining task he needed to do before leaving was to stop and see Dr. Weiss, the Psychologist, three floors down from his room. The orderly pushing his wheelchair informed him that his mother was waiting in a car in the Physicians garage. He then explained he could get Stephen out there in less than seven minutes by using a clandestine route on that doctor's floor if he wanted to stop there and see her. Stephen, squinting his eyes though trying to keep a smile on his face, watched the crowd taking pictures and attempting to break through the human barriers, decided it might be wise to stop in and see the shrink for a moment, then make a hushed exit.

"Yeah, so, can you get me to her office and then out of here?" he asked looking up over his right shoulder at the orderly.

"Absolutely," the man replied.

The orderly signaled for one of the officers to clear an opening so he could get Stephen to the main elevators, then signaled to the cop the number five with his fingers. The officer spoke into his walkie talkie that "he'll be exiting on five in thirty seconds", causing several of those gathered in the crowd to head for the stairway nearby.

"Bet it was way worse when that golfer was here, huh?" Stephen said, eliciting a smirk from the orderly.

From the crowd, Stephen heard things like "We love you", "You're a hero" and "God Bless you," as pictures continued to snap, reminding him that he'd left his phone in the room.

"Shit, buddy, I forgot my phone. Could you maybe-"

"It's taken care of, Mr. Alexander. All your personal belongings are in a bag headed out to the car for you," the orderly interrupted.

"Awesome, thank you," Stephen replied, as he was loaded into the elevator. The doors closed, with just the two of them and one member of hospital security inside.

When the doors to the fifth floor opened, it was to an awaiting crowd, smaller than the one he came from, though still shouting many of the same statements. The orderly and hospital security guard cleared a path and right as Stephen was being pushed down the hall, someone among the onlookers dropped a red envelope into his lap.

"Ma'm, please be respectful, alright?" the orderly snapped. "Mr. Alexander, would you like me to take that?"

"No, it's alright," he answered, only able to see the face of the blonde woman who dropped it as he turned backwards in his chair. A face that was tan, vibrant, awestruck and smiling.

The rest of the hallway was clear, and in thirty seconds they arrived at Dr. Weiss's office and the security guard knocked on the door. There was no answer, so he rapped harder on the glass-pane.

"Come in," the voice inside asked.

"Thanks Tim," the orderly told the guard, who'd opened the door for them. He pulled Stephen in backwards, then turned him around to face the desk at the back of the room where the Doctor was sitting sideways, reviewing notes.

"I'll be down the hall, Mr. Alexander, when you're ready. I'll radio down to your family that you're going to be a little longer," said the orderly.

"What's your name, bud?" Stephen asked.

"John, sir," he replied.

"Well, I'm Stephen, John, so enough with the formalities. You probably saw my dick when I was getting dressed so a first name basis makes sense."

John the orderly smirked again, then said, "OK, thanks," and left the room as the Doctor began speaking.

"Good afternoon, Stephen-and I'll venture a guess it's alright that I call you that after your little comment? No pun intended," the Doctor said.

"Of course," he answered, surprised by her wit.

"So, he mentioned your family is waiting. Is this you saying goodbye or did you want to have a talk? I know we haven't spoken much but I think it would be beneficial to spend some time chatting, don't you?"

He looked at the doctor, a woman of late thirties, highlighted blonde hair, wavy at the ends, understated features accentuated with little makeup, and no wedding ring although there was a picture of children on the back corner of her teak desk.

"I'll be the first to admit this whole thing is a bit of a mind fuck but, I don't know if there's anything you can do about it, or that us talking can help. I'm just checking in to let you know I'm leaving and that I feel good, overall, so you're not afraid I'll wheel myself into traffic or something." Stephen said, adjusting his wheelchair to a more convenient angle with his hands.

"I think wheeling yourself around this hospital is the greater threat, from the looks of what I saw out there." she quipped.

"Wait, you haven't heard? They all adore me, why would they want to hurt me? And look," he said, picking up the red envelope in his lap, "Got my first love letter, not even two minutes ago. The safest place I could be is out there with my sycophants, uh, I mean friends."

"You're going to have a lot of adulation directed your way, Stephen, no question. Would you say that's something you're comfortable with?"

"Where was this worship when I was in my twenties? If anything, everyone's late. Sure, this was a big deal but a few years back I finished a *Rubiks Cube* in just under three hours and I haven't even shown you my cart wheel."

The doctor looked at him with a sly smile, then leaned back in her chair, making it squeak.

"In talking with you in the brief time since you arrived it's very clear that you're intelligent and self-aware, so I don't want to attempt to condescend to you, but, do you feel that you often use humor as a deflective mechanism?"

Stephen deflated his posture in the chair. "Ohhhh boy, here we go. Should I get a copy of the *DSM V* so I can follow along with you?"

"Is there something about Psychoanalysis that bothers you?"

"What? No, of course not, I'm not a fucking Scientologist. I'm-I didn't mean to be a ball buster I just don't know what you want me to say. I'm being myself," he answered, shifting around in his chair.

"Which I want you to be, of course. I was only asking a question, one that-if you're familiar with this process-I'm sure you've been asked before."

Stephen moved his hands across the sides of the card the woman dropped in his lap. Feeling the sharp edges, depressing his thumb into one of the pointed corners over and over. Opening his hand, he stretched his fingers across the height of it, then bent it inwards.

"I'm sure in all the history, charts and shit you get access to you must have seen that I'd visited a shrink before, after my dad died, so you know that," Stephen suggested. "And yes, I'm familiar with the basic principles as well as my own pathetic and obvious tactics to deal with elements of my life but that's not why I stopped here."

"Ok then, so, why did you?"

Stephen let his eyes wander around the office as he answered. "I know this whole thing is going to get nuts, it already has, and, I don't remember much of anything yet so I'd like to know what you think I should do? I don't want to disappear forever because then I look like an asshole but because I lack any real memory I can't really start talking, ya know?"

"Well, I don't know if that's an answer I can provide you. I mean, certainly if the memories aren't there you can't start filling in the blanks yourself just to say *something*, but many people are going to want to hear from you, outside of what you recall of these events even. Who you are, what you like, what you don't, where you were born, your childhood and so on. You helped facilitate an incredible, life-altering event and people want to share in that, but mostly they're just going to want a little piece of you. Do you think you're prepared for that?"

He picked up the card in his lap and tapped it down against his leg a few times, then slid it next to his right thigh tight up against the edge of the wheelchair seat.

"Fuck, I mean how can anyone be prepared for something like this? I went to sleep and was just some idiot from Connecticut and I wake up and I'm told I'm apparently a hero, but I don't remember any of it, and I don't want to talk to all these people I don't even know about my life, and why the hell would they want to know that anyway? That doesn't have anything to do with what happened. My history didn't make me do what I did any more than it would have caused me to not do it, had I not responded."

Right as he finished speaking he realized the absurdity of what he spoke, as he was penning a novel inspired by, and fortified with, his childhood.

*The book.* He remembered he had no idea where he'd put it after he left the hotel.

"Well, that could be debatable but I do feel strongly that the public is going to want to know everything about you, Stephen. It's not going to be confined to the events of last week. That kind of invasive and constant scrutiny can be overwhelming for many people and I'm concerned about how you'll handle it. I think we should plan to meet again tomorrow, for a full session, maybe a couple hours. I can come to you."

Stephen looked at her face, which in most scenarios he'd find alluring but at that moment only induced feelings of annoyance, then he sighed intentionally.

"Ugh, see that? I did one of those intentional sigh things and I hate people who do that", he said, fidgeting in his wheelchair. "OK listen, I understand what you're saying and maybe we should talk again soon but I have too much going on right now and I can assure you I'm not going to let it overwhelm me-I can control it. I already have a shitload of people texting me, tweeting me, leaving messages and emails and I'm not even responding right now. This is going to go at my pace, not theirs."

"You may be able to control how much you take in, Stephen, but you can't control the volume, and your indifference may only serve to increase the intensity anyway," the doctor replied, spinning back in her chair, pulling something from the library behind her. "Here, why don't you take this. It's a paper written by a colleague of mine about-"

"Doc, listen, I better go before my mother has my story sold off to Geraldo or some idiot in my absence, no offense," he interrupted. "This is going to be a much bigger deal in her life than mine, that I can assure you," Stephen said, wheeling himself back away from the desk.

"That sounds like something we should be talking about as well, then," the Doctor replied, tucking the papers she had pulled out away.

"I know, I know, it's always the mother that fucks us up, I watched *The Sopranos*. The difference here is that my mom doesn't want to have me whacked because if she does she can't hit me up for a C note every few weeks."

She looked at him with a measured stare. "You have my number, Stephen. Please give me a call and if you'd like me to come out and see you tomorrow, or any day, just let me know."

"Will do, Doc, thanks."

"Have a good day," she said, picking up her phone and dialing as she nodded to him.

Stephen pulled the door open and yelled down the hall for the orderly, who returned in fifteen seconds, then taking him out to the garage where his mother was on the phone, waiting in a car.

<#>

There were three news trucks at the end of the long driveway as they pulled in, one that crept down the asphalt driveway behind them. Stephen hopped out of the car, motioning with his hands to back up, which they did, and then he returned to the passenger's seat.

"I put three signs up, one huge one on the oak tree, two in the ground saying, "Private Property" and "No Trespassing" and still these assholes pull into my yard. The cops have stopped coming by because they say there's nothing they can do if they're out there on the street and not breaking any laws, but, I'm going to set up a camera myself or something, catch them when they pull in like that, cause that's not right," Lillian said, pulling the car up against the garage.

"It's just what they do, Ma. They'll be on to something else soon," Stephen said, reaching for the canvas bag of his personal effects on the floor.

"Honey, don't carry all that yourself, let me help you," Lillian offered.

"I'm good. Let's just get in the house because I need to take a leak."

"Yeah yeah, I'm going. I'm an old woman, you can't rush me."

"You get around just fine, Ma. No way most women your age could deal with those two hulking monstrosities you call dogs."

"They're not even here, so you can hush. I brought them to your sisters so they could watch them while I was shuttling back and forth between here and the hospital. Can't leave them alone all day."

"Mom, you know Jessica can't handle those things, come on," Stephen said, watching his mother walk up the wooden steps of her rented house, fiddling with her keys. "Why didn't you kennel them or something? Plus, she was at the hospital sometimes too, so it has to be an imposition on them."

"Oh, they're fine, you've seen that house they live in, with the huge yard and the cleaning lady they can afford. A few days watching some dogs isn't going to kill them. Geez."

Lillian turned the key and opened the front door, immediately greeted by a gray and black cat in the entryway.

"Pookah, baby. You miss your big brothers huh?" she asked the cat, who was meowing and weaving in between Lillian's legs.

"Welcome to the fucking Zoo," Stephen whispered, walking inside carrying the bag.

Lillian's house, as they'd all been for as long as he could remember, was a rustic country cabin look, consisting of wicker baskets, wreaths and dried flowers, an abundance of worn, wooden furniture and the taint of smoke and piss. The urine and smoke became so prevalent in his later years that he stopped noticing it, only reminded when new friends came into the house and had that look people get when something smells odd or unpleasant. She was a master decorator on a budget, however, and could turn each rented space into a cozy, livable world that even the pungent vapors of ash and canine waste couldn't tarnish.

"Place looks cute, as always Ma. Can't say I mind not being slopped to death by those beasts, though. And who's this little critter?" Stephen asked, squatting down to pet the cat.

"How can you claim to be such a dog lover when you always have such a problem with mine? They're sweet animals, Stephen, and they love you, even though you don't give them the time of day when you're here," Lillian jabbed. "The cat is Pookah. Picked her up at a yard sale in Torrington. Poor old woman was selling everything before her kids sent off to the home, as she told it, including the damn cat. How do you not let an old woman take her cat to the Nursing Home? They've done studies where they say it's very therapeutic."

"I do love dogs-all animals-Ma, we've gone over this. Yours are always a little, ya know, manic-for lack of a better word."

"Hey well they say animals pick up on the emotions of those around them and they're really only like that when you're here so, maybe it's *you* that's the crazy one. Ever think of that?"

Stephen stopped petting the cat and stood up, leaving the bag on a chestnut brown rocking chair by the front entrance and making his way to the bathroom, past the plaid, upholstered couch in Lillian's living room.

"I never said I wasn't crazy, Ma. But those dogs are fucking lunatics, and it's not just when I'm here," Stephen said, uttering the last sentence a hint above a whisper.

"What did you say?" Lillian shot back, playfully eyeballing him. "Your Mom here isn't deaf yet, son."

He smiled as he peed, half on the seat, which he wiped up with a fistful of wadded toilet paper before walking back into the living room.

"So, I'm alive, I'm here-but I have about eight trillion things to do as you can imagine so what is it that was so important you needed to talk to me about right away?"

Lillian started a pot of coffee in the kitchen and grabbed a package of pinwheel shaped marshmallow cookies from the cupboard, a staple of all their homes growing up, and returned to the living room, plopping down into a maroon velvet covered recliner in the opposite corner to Stephen.

"Well," she said, sliding one of the chocolate marshmallow cookies into her mouth, "While all this has been happening, you in the hospital, there have been lots of people calling me, stopping by here and wanting to know about you and speak with me annf, it's beeh-"

"Jesus, Ma, those things are like fucking dry, chocolate glass cookies, don't try to talk while you're eating them," Stephen interrupted, sending his mother into a fit of laughter, spitting out some of what she was chewing.

"Staaarp," she said, mouth still full, and heading to the kitchen to check on the coffee.

"What is it with you and those damn things anyway? I get the chocolate and marshmallow but the sharp edges and that chalky biscuit board cookie layer, seriously, it's like they're trying to inflict damage," Stephen shouted to Lillian, out in the kitchen.

He listened as she opened the fridge, then searched for glasses, returning to the living room a minute later with two small glasses of milk.

"Well I can see the head wound didn't dull your sense of humor. Next time maybe wait until I swallow the damn thing, though," she suggested, handing a glass to Stephen, who placed it on the table in front of him.

"Are you OK?" he asked her.

"Yeah. You think that's the first time I've choked on one of those things? It's like an every-other-cookie trauma here," she replied, then taking a long sip of milk.

"Well don't go dying on me Ma. Unless you taught one of those Kodiak bears you call dogs to do CPR."

"Those dogs do more for me than you know, Stephen. It's not easy being alone as much as I am and they make me feel good. Happy. Is that alright with you, oh son that I barely ever see?"

Stephen felt the familiar constriction in his chest as the acid worked its way up from his stomach, into his esophagus. "I know, I know, your first born is a shithead, you've told me this on many occasions, so, let's accept that as a given and get back to what I was asking about before. What's so urgent that we had to talk right now?"

Lillian fidgeted in her seat, then leaned forward, "Well, you're my son and I love you and I'm, of course, just happy you're alive and well, that's most important…"

Stephen's father Henry used to have an expression, "Everything before the 'but' is bullshit." He was certain it was about to apply in this situation.

"But, there's a multitude of business related items that need to be dealt with before it makes everyone crazy."

*Ding! Ding! Ding!*

"OK Ma, well *who*, exactly, is it making crazy? I mean, most of it's all focused on me and I'm doing alright. I'm leaving it alone, letting it settle down. What exactly is going on that's so tough for you?"

"It's not just me, Stephen, it's your sister too. We've been getting endless calls and requests to speak to the media and release information about you and we've had very little privacy in all this," Lillian said, her volume elevated.

"I know, and I'm sorry about that, honestly I am, but you know I didn't choose for this to happen. I didn't volunteer to have my head bashed in and be knocked into a coma, then have a million people I don't know want to get in my business, for fuck's sake," he shot back, chuckling at the end.

"I'm not saying you did, honey, that's not what I mean. My point is just that it did happen. This is your life, *our* life now, and there's items that need to be addressed related to that life. That's all I'm saying."

"Like what, getting the agent you mentioned?" I don't know, Ma-"

"Stephen, I don't think you fully understand the complexities of all this, what it involves, and how far reaching it is. I mean, the hospital gave me a sack full of mail for you the size of a sleeping bag, and I'm sure there's more at your house. This is a big deal."

"I get it, I do, but I...I'm not ready to dive head first into it all right now, which I think is fair and warranted considering I just got out of the fucking hospital," Stephen exclaimed, his voice noticeably louder, and sweat forming across his brow as he imagined the mountain of letters.

Lillian put her glass down on the end table and leaned back against the rear of the chair, then reached for her phone that she'd placed on a small table on the opposite side.

"I want you to call this guy in the morning, OK? Talk to him, he's an agent that's worked with many high-profile clients who've become suddenly famous and he can help you, when you're ready. I'm texting you his number."

"Great, it'll be buried in the other ten trillion texts I haven't read," Stephen said, taking his feet off the coffee table and sitting up straight on the couch.

"You can't pretend this isn't all around you, Stephen. It needs to be dealt with, that's all I'm saying, when you're ready, sure. In the meantime, though, I wanted you to know that I've agreed to talk to that Tanya woman on TV, on video I guess it's going to be. They offered me a lot of money and you know I'm struggling here and it's-"

"Oh, for fuck's sake, mom, is that what this is all about, money?"

"It's not 'what it's all about' but yes, if someone wants to pay me money to talk about how you were a freckle faced little pain in the ass but now you're a hero then I have no problem taking it, and neither should you."

He looked over at her, then down at a picture on the coffee table. It was Lillian, Stephen and Jessica about twenty-five years earlier in one of the most contrived and uncomfortable looking shots ever put on film. Stephen was wearing a multi colored sweater, pastel stripes set over a black background, and sporting hair that looked like a fiery orange bird's nest laid on top of a red mullet and in mid-frown. Jessica was wearing a beige blouse with shoulder pads that made her look like she played Defensive End for the Giants, and an expression that suggested imminent diarrhea, while Lillian was done up like Tammy Faye Baker in a wind tunnel. For years, both Jessica and Stephen had complained about the ridiculous picture but she refused to put it away, claiming it was her "favorite". Stephen once said she must be a psychopath if she liked that picture and when he came back a couple weeks later it was an 8x10 in a larger frame in the middle of the coffee table, vs the 5x7 it was previously, resting on an end table near one of the bathrooms.

"I don't give a fuck what you do, OK, I really don't. If you can get ten billion for spilling the beans about me or whatever they're willing to pay you then have at it, but leave me out of it. I'm not going on TV and pretending that life hasn't been fucked up and that this situation brought us all together."

"Oh, right, because that would be a lie, and you're too moral a man and too ethical to contemplate such things, right?"

"It's the truth, that's what it is. And what the hell is that supposed to mean? I never claimed to be morally superior to anyone in this family. Jessica's probably texting the Pope right now as we speak."

"No, but you speak a lot about truth, and for a guy that does a fair amount of lying that's pretty damn hypocritical, I'd say."

Stephen shot up from the couch, bumping the coffee table, knocking the family picture down and sending the cat bolting into one of the bedrooms.

"I'm so fucking tired of hearing this bullshit, I really am," he said, storming into the kitchen to take a slurp off the faucet. "There's an expression, 'Just because you believe something doesn't make it true'. You and Jessica have been saddling me with this crap for years. You create a narrative about me then fill in the pieces to satisfy your own confirmation bias. You've had so much shit to say about the guy in the White House, well what the fuck do you think *you* are doing? It's the same damn thing!"

"Yes, Stephen, I know you're smarter than I am-or at least you think you are-and you're a tough guy to fight with because you know what a 'Straw Man Argument' is and all the logical fallacies, and always have a clever quotation to throw at someone or explain how they're arguing from ignorance or whatever it is. I don't care how much of that deflection you want to employ, kiddo, cause you're my son and I know when my son is lying."

"Of course you do," Stephen said, charging back into the living room," because it's just like I said, you're deciding something's true about me without any evidence. Using that logic, there's no argument you can present that's unwinnable because the answer is always simply, "It's what I believe." How the fuck do you claim you've become an atheist yet can't see the insanity of using that tactic?"

"First of all, I never said I was an atheist. I denounced Catholicism, for a number of reasons, but I never said I didn't believe in God. Talk about creating your own narrative, you're doing the same thing right now."

Stephen walked towards the front door and went to fish out his phone from the canvas bag.

"So, what, you're just going to run out the door?" Lillian shouted in his direction.

"I'm looking for my phone," he yelled back. When he found it, he turned it on, wanting to show her a text she'd sent just weeks earlier stating something like, "As an Atheist..." he recalled. As the phone booted up he realized it would be buried among a thousand other messages and that he'd likely start getting phone calls so he immediately shut it back down.

"Never mind," he said, placing it on the coffee table and flopping back on the couch.

"What, so you can show me some text where I said in jest that I'm an atheist? Not everything is so damn literal, Stephen, and I know you know that."

"Maybe, but calling me a fucking liar all the time isn't meant in 'jest', Ma, right? There's no sarcasm in that. You say that because you believe it's true and you want it to hurt me, even though it's garbage."

Lillian sighed, then got up and went to her purse to fetch a cigarette. Stephen watched her, the delicate yellow fibers of her oversized V-neck sweater just covering the mustard stain on the front left of her off white, long-sleeved undershirt. Her light brown, thinning hair styled impeccably, as it always was, and she'd lost weight in the last month, he noticed. Her hands had begun to show signs of arthritis, and as she reached into her purse looking for the smokes she pulled the hand back out and massaged it with the other before going back in and returning with a cigarette.

"Do you remember that time I neglected to tell Jessica that her ex-boyfriend showed up here, crazy and distraught, maybe ten years ago?" Lillian asked, lighting her cigarette and sitting back down in the chair.

"Yeah, why?" Stephen answered.

"Well, when I said I was thinking of not telling her, even though I knew she'd want to know, you said, "There's two types of lies. A Sin of Commission-where you make a statement that's untrue, an outright lie. Then there's the Sin of Omission, where your silence is the lie. I may be paraphrasing a bit but that was the essence of it, no?"

"Sure, what's your point?"

"Well, just because I've never asked you straight out, 'How many times have you cheated on blank'-whomever you were dating at

195

the time-and you've never volunteered that information, doesn't mean you're not actually doing it right?"

Stephen felt a drop in his stomach and the fingers on his hands balled up, clenched tight against his palm. He sat there for ten seconds, then stood up, grabbing his phone and heading to the entryway where he saw the keys to his BMW hanging by the door.

"Stephen, you can't run away from everything you don't like to hear," Lillian said, making him run back into the living room.

"I'm fucking **done** with you," he yelled back at her. "I don't need to listen to this shit. My whole God damned life I've been dragged around as you ran away from every motherfucking calamity your bad choices created and heard you hang up phones because you didn't want to deal with the truth of your own failures, but you have no problem pointing the finger at me or anyone else. Listen, you're the parent. You! You chose to bring us into this life, we didn't. You're supposed to prepare us for adulthood, mentor us, educate us, not suck us into all your drama and drag us all over hell and gone, broke as shit, because that felt better than being responsible."

"I know, that's your go to Stephen, the 'horrible mother' card. I was such a terrible mom that kept a roof over your head, food on the table, clothes on your back and trauma out of our house. I never had your drunk father over, scaring the shit out of you or anyone I dated around the house so don't try and paint a picture like you had some emotionally abusive childhood because you didn't. It could have been much worse."

"I understand the 'Perspective' argument, thanks. I know it could've been worse, for fucks sake it could be like what these poor girls went through-I get it. That doesn't mean it was normal. That doesn't mean it wasn't fucked up and scary as shit. Always walking into a new school, getting my ass kicked, wondering how long the cable would stay on, would it be that one day I happen to have a friend come over, or if there'd be seven piles of shit on the floor in the dining room. We could have lived in a hut in Nairobi, sure, but the only experience I can speak on is the fucked up one I lived with my sister that you orchestrated and dad tried to tear us away from but that you nixed every time. I know the truth, Ma, I've heard it enough times."

Lillian went to her purse to fish out another cigarette.

"I need to go, and thanks so much for sending my blood pressure into orbit. I'm sure that was at the top of the list of items my Docs wanted," Stephen jabbed.

"Is that what you think? That Henry was fighting the good fight every day to bring you guys out to California with him, live out the rest of your teen years in San Diego?"

"Don't even try to spin that because I talked to him about it numerous times when he was alive and I remember the phone calls, hearing you talking to him late at night and telling him, 'No, I can't let them go out there.' That *did* happen. I never claimed he was perfect, either, but at least he tried, and succeeded, in fixing his life. What the fuck have you done?"

Lillian took a long draw on the cigarette she'd lit, then exhaled it in one continuous stream. Her eyes started welling up as she leaned back in her chair and then she started to say something, but stopped.

"I need to go. Like I said, do whatever you want when it comes to the money, knock yourself out, but just leave me out of it," Stephen exclaimed, scooping his bag from the chair and heading out to his car, slamming the door on the way out.

# *Chapter 20*

*Stephen* depressed the Start button in his car and the engine fired up in a melodious symphony. He rolled onto the accelerator several times, for no purpose other than frustration, as he remained parked in his mother's driveway. The noise prompted a News reporter to walk through the trees and down towards the house, stopping to stare at the idling vehicle. Stephen looked over in his direction, then turned back into the car, reaching into the bag to find his phone. When he pulled it out there was already a text from his mother, which was a common occurrence after they battled. When he looked, however, it turned out to be only the number of the agent she'd texted him earlier.

The phone was littered with messages and the voice mail was full, and the thought of sifting through any of it was still daunting, but he couldn't avoid the device forever.

*Change the number.*

The idea came, and he decided to take care of it immediately, before heading to his apartment he hadn't seen in days. Just as he lay the phone next to the bag on the passenger's seat, an unfamiliar number appeared on the screen, calling in. He ignored it, clicked the gear lever into reverse and backed the car out from its spot and spun it around, heading towards the street. Worried the phone may slide off the seat during his spirited drive, he picked it up and went to tuck it into the bag when he saw another incoming call, this time from his sister. He slid the virtual button to the right and picked it up, the Bluetooth activating and playing her voice over the car speakers.

*"Stephen?"*

"Hey Jess," he answered into the air, popping the car into Park and stopping in the middle of the driveway.

*"So, mom said you stormed out. You OK?"*

"Just the same old shit, always about freaking money, exacerbated by this latest situation. I had to leave."

*"Yeah she told me a little. Hey, why don't you stop by on your way out. Christopher has the kids and dogs for about an hour and I'd like to see you."*

"Well, I was going to go get my cell number changed but, sure I guess I can swing by. I can't do the whole rehash thing though, OK? Just a nice, peaceful visit, please."

*"Sure, sounds good. I'll see you shortly."*

Before his sister even finished her sentence, another unknown number was calling him. He ignored it, tossing the phone into the beige canvas bag.

He slid the car in "D" and crept out the last half of the driveway, but as soon as the car became visible to the awaiting News vans and assorted strangers hoping to get a glimpse of him, the crowd converged on the exit, blocking his path. He slowed the car to a crawl, opened his driver's side window and waved his hand to the people standing around, now in a flurry.

"Mr. Alexander, what does it feel like to be home? How is your health?" a woman asked, holding a microphone, trailed by a tall man with a camera.

"So many people want to hear your story, Stephen, do you have anything to say to them?", another voice yelled from behind the first questioner.

He smiled, waved and continued easing the car out of the last few feet of the driveway. On the edges, several people that weren't part of the news media stood, holding signs-two in particular holding a banner between them that read, "True American Hero – Stephen Alexander".

199

"Yeah, that's me. They guy who verbally assaulted an old woman in front of her dog in a motel parking lot is a role model for all, no doubt," he said aloud, pulling the car onto the road and speeding off.

As he reached for the radio, he realized the moment he was recalling was one of the memories from that day. A second later he could see a man walking away from him, holding a girl in his arms that was wiggling and kicking her feet. Then he saw someone on top of him, felt his body wrestling against his.

As the images came and went, the screen in his center console lit up with another unfamiliar number and impulsively he chose to answer.

"Hello," he said.

*"Uh, hello, Mr. Alexander?"* the woman's voice said over the speakers.

"That's me."

*"Um, yes hello, my name is Diane. Diane Linton. You don't know me, or I don't think you would unless you got my letter at the hospital, but I'm sure you received many letters."*

*The Red Envelope.*

"Oh, yes, the one you dropped in my lap as I was leaving, I presume? How'd you get my number?"

There was silence, though he could hear her still moving against the phone.

"Hello? Were you the one that gave me the red envelope at the hospital?" Stephen asked.

*"I'm sorry, I'm sitting in my car outside the grocery store and someone came by and, I shouldn't have bothered you."*

"It's OK. I was wondering how you got my number and…it was you at the hospital then?"

*"No, I never went over there, only mailed a letter. I wanted to go but…I'm sorry, I needed to call you and say thank you. What you*

200

*did, for me, for my family...I don't know how to begin to repay you. To explain what it's meant to us."*

Stephen pursed his lips and wrinkled his brow, checking the rearview mirror to see how ridiculous it looked, as usual.

"Thank me?"

*"For saving my daughter, Hannah. She was...she was taken from me almost two years ago, and now she's back, because of your bravery, and that sheriff. I always knew she was alive-I could feel it inside me somewhere, just like the parents of the lost always claim-but I was right, and it was real. You brought her back to me."*

He could hear her start sobbing after she finished speaking. Realizing he sounded almost flippant about questioning being thanked, he felt embarrassed, though still unable to embrace the idea that he needed to be.

"Ma'am, I'm sorry, I didn't mean to sound dismissive or callous, it's just that, I haven't spoken to anyone about this yet. Haven't even sorted out my own feelings about any of it, never mind how to be sensitive to others, if you follow me? I'm so happy you have your daughter back though, truly, I mean that," he told her, taking a left onto his sister's road.

*"Like I said, I'm sorry to bother you. I know you just came out of your own trauma and chaos,"* the voice said through sniffles, *"but, I had to reach out to you and tell you that, had it not been for you and my girl being found, I don't know if I would have made it through another Christmas. It was always her favorite holiday and when she was taken-a couple weeks after Thanksgiving-I was devastated, as any parent would be of course, but...I hung on because as much as I couldn't bear to be without her then, or any day, I couldn't imagine not being there for her if she ever came back to me. This last Christmas, though, it almost broke me and I wasn't sure if I could make it through another. So, you see, you saved another life here. Not just my daughter's."*

201

Stephen pulled the car over on the right side of the street, just a few houses before his sister's place, tapping the Park button on the gear shift, then taking a long slow inhale and looking out the passenger's side window at a budding cherry tree in one of his sister's neighbor's yard.

*"I'm sorry if I've gotten too personal. I shouldn't have called, excuse me for-"*

"No, it's fine, really," Stephen interrupted. "I'm in my car, too. Had an epic battle with my mom, speaking of mother and child relationships, and very well may have another one with my sister soon. Amazing how you can share the same DNA, many of the same characteristics, personality traits and yet want to gouge these people's eyes out sometimes, isn't it? A horribly insensitive thing to say, in this moment, after what you've shared-I know-but I'm not known for my tact."

*"It's alright, and I understand what you mean. My mother's been so supportive in all this, even amidst her own suffering in losing a granddaughter, yet there were days when I wished she was dead, and then I felt like an evil, despicable person no better than the man who took my little Hannah. I'm no shrink, I don't know why that is, but I can sympathize."*

"Well, it's as they say, 'Familiarity breeds contempt', I suppose. The qualities that most annoy me about them are those that most remind me of myself. Though, it's others that remind me of me that also endear me to them," Stephen said, laughing as he finished speaking. "You know, Christmas is always going to be fucked up for me too-I'm sorry, I've forgotten your name already, like an asshole."

*"That's OK. It's Diane,"* the voice in the speakers answered.

"Christmas was *it* for me, pretty much my whole life, Diane. This is coming from a kid who basically identified as an atheist at eleven, too-and I'm sorry if that weirds you out, as I know it does some. Anyway, growing up, Christmas was not a religious holiday for us as much as it was a time of year that none of the bullshit, the stress, the new town we moved to, the bullies that waited around every corner and the second-hand, Salvation Army clothes I wore to school every day mattered as much. The Rudolph and Frosty specials would be on, there'd be a lot of food and of course presents, but it was this feeling of hope that was most exciting. Like there was a chance that somehow, is some way, that giant fucking Christmas tree my mother bought that never fit in our apartment was the conduit to something better, something more peaceful and maybe something permanent. It never was, but, it was the high I'd get off that feeling every year-used to begin to feel it in October and its spell would carry me through until the first week in January when I'd be hanging from a coat rack by my underwear outside the gym."

The voice coming through the speakers laughed, then was muffled as though moving through cotton.

"Wedgies were definitely a guy issue. The girls either said 'eeww gross' or laughed in our faces. Kinda like you're doing now," Stephen suggested.

*"Oh, my Gosh, I'm so sorry. That was, unexpected and, I haven't had very much to laugh at in a while. Definitely laughing with you though, not at you."*

"Suuure, they all say that."

*"So, you didn't tell me what happened to Christmas though. Why has it been hard for you?"*

Stephen looked out the right corner of his windshield and saw that his sister was in her driveway a couple houses down, looking over at his car, wondering if it was him. He opened his driver's side window and stuck his hand out, putting his index finger up to signal "one minute", then drew in a deep, sustained breath before replying.

"My old man. He died on Christmas a few years back. Guy always hated the day himself-unlike me-but he had his reasons. He died, and it wasn't expected, or maybe it was-I've never really sorted that part out-but, it's been hard to manage and reconcile. How do you allow yourself to still love something that happens to fall on the same day your father dies? Am I disrespecting his memory if I try to let joy back in on that day instead of crawling into a blanket and bawling every time? Ugh, I'm sorry, little tangent here."

*"No, really, it's OK. Go on."*

"Hey, listen, I have to run and see my sister but I appreciate the kind words and the call, although I'd still love to know how you got my number."

*"Please, I hope you're not running off on my account, and I again I do apologize for being so invasive and just calling. As for your number...I found it on a voting record website, was pretty easy actually. You might want to think about changing it or you'll be inundated with more stalkers like me, if you're not already."*

"I plan on doing that today, yes; it's been a little overwhelming. I'm glad I spoke to you, though. No need to apologize and I'm so happy you have your daughter back, truly."

*"I am too, thanks to you, Stephen. I understand it may take a while for this to all sink in and such but, you really did something wonderful here and I'm not going to be the last that's going to want to thank you. I owe you my life, really."*

"Just have a great Christmas with your daughter, OK? Enjoy the shit out of everything she does and says and hold on to her even when she wants you to let go. Some deep stuff there, right?"

The voice laughed again, then, *"I have to say, even though your language is a little saltier than I would've imagined, it's been very soothing to talk to you. Your voice is naturally calming, and I think you shouldn't be afraid to get out there and tell your story. People want to hear from you and you're easy to talk with. I'm sure you've been told that before, though."*

"It's been said, sure. My voice has some off-beat charm that some women like, men usually want to throat punch me, but hey, I'll take the compliment, thanks. If I could only get the bullshit I'm spewing out to be as impactful-or even anything loftier than the rambling phrases of a moron-that would be an achievement."

She laughed again, this time louder, and one of the tiny speakers above the door crackled.

*"You've helped me in more ways than you'll ever know. So, I'll let you go and I'm sorry for the intrusion,"* the voice said as the phone line beeped with another unknown number trying to ring through, *"but it was great talking with you. I hope to see and hear you again soon. Don't hide away too long. You deserve some limelight."*

"Nice talking with you, too, Diane. Oh, and how is your little girl-Hannah you said? Is she doing alright, after..."

*"It's going to be a long road, but she's had good days. Today has been one of them, and she's sleeping now. She doesn't usually make it more than a couple hours before she wakes up, frightened and calling for me, but I'll take a million more nights like that, knowing I can finally be there to answer her,"* she replied, her voice trembling at the end.

Stephen searched for words to respond but found none.

*"Thanks so much for taking my call, Stephen, and I hope you have a nice visit with your sister,"* she said, breaking the silence.

"Thank you. I'm glad you called, and I wish you and Hannah-your whole family-a lifetime of peace. Take care," Stephen answered.

*"Goodbye,"* the voice said, the call disappearing from the center console.

Stephen pushed the power button on his phone and shut it down, then clicked the car into Drive and pulled up to his sister's house, parking on the street. She was waiting outside, holding several magazines and playing with her hair as it fluttered in the light breeze.

"Hey sis," he said, walking up to the house. "No reporters here? I was sure there'd be a few."

"There was, but I have to say Chris has done a wonderful job scaring them off. They circle back and sometimes park down in the cul-de-sac. It makes Elaine, in the brown house, batty but not much she can do. So, what were you doing parked over there?" Jessica asked.

"Quick phone call. Didn't want to just park in front of the house and act like I was ignoring you."

"I see. Well, come inside. Like I mentioned, the place is empty for at least an hour."

"I can't believe you offered to take the dogs. Wow, sis."

"Well mom has had a lot on her plate and she could use the break, plus they adore the kids and vice versa, even if they're a little too rambunctious for them."

"You know, that statement could work either way," Stephen joked, stepping into the house behind his sister.

"The kids are rarely ever wild until you show up, Stephen," Jessica fired back, closing the front door.

"Funny, ya know, mom said the same thing about me and her dogs. Apparently, I instill lunacy in living creatures I'm near, but only in this family."

Jessica looked back at him, rolling her eyes, then made her way to the living room couch. Stephen followed.

"So, what was the fight with her about this time? You know, she's been at the hospital every day, multiples times, and she's an old woman. You need to keep that in mind."

Stephen looked up above the couch where Jessica was sitting, where a large portrait of Jesus was hanging, his arms outstretched and a light shining down upon him.

"Is that a new picture," he asked, pointing to it. "Looks like one of the dudes from *Lynyrd Skynyrd*."

"You know who it is, Stephen. Please don't be disrespectful to what I believe. Can we get back to what happened with mom?"

"Sorry, yeah," he said, stretching his arms up over his head and yawning. "Well, it's the same shit as always but now there's more dollar signs. I got bashed over the head and all she can think about is getting paid to talk about it. Fucking lunacy."

Jessica took a deep breath and rubbed her hands across the tops of her thighs.

206

"Jess, I can't not be who I am, same as you. I speak the way I do and I can promise you it's not going to send you to Hell hearing me say the F word sometimes," he said, sensing her agitation.

"You know as well as I do it's not only 'sometimes', and lately it's been in front of the kids. Just try to think about the language you choose, please."

He was leaning against the wall, looking over at her, Christian figurines, several Crucifixes and two different Bibles splayed out in front of her on the wide coffee table.

"Jess, come on man, seriously. What happened to you? Where is all this bullshit coming from, really? You and I used to laugh our asses off about mom and her nuttiness and the dogs and, speaking of Religion, remember the time she was going to convert to Mormonism because she met that guy at the dump who helped her load that awful bird fountain in the car? That wasn't *that* long ago."

Jessica got up off the couch, rubbing her hands together, her eyes angled to the floor.

"You meet Chris, and yeah, he seems like a pretty great guy, I've never doubted that, " Stephen said, moving closer to her. "But because he's neck deep in-what is it again, some kind of Evangelical church with like three thousand members-you suddenly adopt all his beliefs? How does that happen?"

"You don't know what I went through, Stephen. You've no idea the torment I faced as a young woman, the struggles with my weight, the social anxiety and dealing with my own scars from childhood-it wasn't just you. You never wanted to be around us for more than ten minutes since you were old enough to be out on your own, so it was me that had to deal with mom and the house much of the time. Christopher helped me immensely when I met him, and with finding some clarity in my life. Don't you speak unkind words about him," Jessica shouted back to him from the kitchen.

Stephen stopped in the kitchen doorway, leaning his left arm against the wooden threshold.

"I told you, I like the guy. I'm not trashing him, I'm questioning the total indoctrination into this religion of his, it's out of character for you and I certainly don't think it's good for the kids. He told me last fall, sitting on your patio out back that if I didn't repent **and** join this particular faith he was part of that I was going to go to Hell, Jess. In front of the twins! You and mom were there too, and yeah, mom rolled her eyes but you didn't say a word. Is that really what you believe, Jess? That your brother-sure, a guy who's a colossal shithead at times, but that he's going to Hell because I don't believe *exactly* what he does? That's ludicrous, come on."

"I never said I believe every word that comes out of Chris's mouth, and I know he takes a more literal interpretation of the Bible than I do and that he's very devout, but his faith, **my** faith, has saved me, Stephen. I don't expect you to fully understand it, I just need you to respect it."

"I understand, and hear what you're saying, but, how can I take that seriously when it was with you, this woman standing right here in front of me, that I used to laugh at the absurdity of Religion with? You were the one that told me Jesus was based on Mithra and Horus and explained all the similarities to the early Sun Gods and Astrology, *The Pagan Mysteries*-all that-and then just a few years later you've accepted as gospel everything you railed against. I mean, you can at least see how that would be difficult for me to ignore, right?"

Jessica walked back into the living room and sat on the cream-colored love seat that rested perpendicular to the couch of the same color.

"You don't need to be responsible nor worry about my beliefs or convictions, alright? I only ask that you respect them. Is that so hard? Plus, I don't poke at you about why you *lost* your faith. You're supposed to be here to discuss mom, anyway, so can we get back to that? Chris and the kids will be back soon."

"Lost my faith? Oh, come on, not this again sis."

"When you found out that you couldn't-"

"Jess, please, OK? I can't add that to the mix of everything else right now, and you know as well as I do that I was an atheist before that. I didn't walk away from God to punish him for a medical problem, and you have your timelines way off here."

"I don't want to argue with you, I know you have a lot going on."

Stephen rubbed his face with both hands, then made his way over to the couch, flopping down like dead weight.

"I'm sorry sis. This whole thing with you, and the intensity of it all, it's, well, hard for me to manage sometimes but it's your thing and…"

"Thank you."

"Anyway, the mom situation will blow over like it always does but it's frustrating to hear her start up with the money, you know? The idea of cashing in on this fucking-excuse my language-this messed up situation I walked into."

"You didn't 'walk into it', Stephen, you jumped in. You reacted. Something most people may never have done. You put your own life on the line and saved that little girl and then-and here's where I know we diverge but-I believe God took the rest in his hands and all those other suffering children were saved. But it was *you*, Stephen, you that set the course in motion with your bravery, and that's what God saw that day."

"Well, Jess, you know, it would have been nice if JC had tossed me a helmet or something in that moment if he was watching, but, hey at least I'm alive."

Jessica grinned, which was an abnormality when a joke was pointed anywhere in the direction of her faith, so Stephen figured he'd leave on a high note.

"I'm gonna go, sis," he said, hopping up from the couch. "If you talk to mom, as a favor to me, maybe just see if you can dial back her enthusiasm for the windfall here, let me get my head together a bit?"

209

"Ok, I'll try. Have you talked to anyone at all yet? Mom said a few of the cable news shows had offered a lot of money to sit down with them. Regardless if it's about money or not, sooner or later you're going to have to say something, Stephen. Not to mention I think a lot of people want to hear what you have to say. I think your family does, too," she said, smiling.

"I haven't, no, but I know I can't duck and cover forever. I'll deal with it."

"I know you will; if anyone can figure this out it's you. Oh, and how is your head feeling, by the way? I'm relieved to see only the one small bandage on there."

He moved his hand up to the left side of his skull and ran his fingers over the skin-colored bandage, which looked like nothing more than an oversized Band-Aid.

"I'm feeling fine, thanks. Stings a little up there and it's still swollen and what not but it's doing alright. Still waiting for the rest of the memories to come back but they're creeping in so I'm sure it won't be long."

"That's good to hear," she replied, smiling at him and getting up to walk him out of the house.

"Say hello to Chris and the kids and, hey, I'm sorry for getting all riled up about the God thing."

"It's OK, both He and I forgive you," she jabbed back.

"Ah, yes, I've heard that about the fella. Big forgiver," he said, smirking, then turning and walking out to his car.

"Get some rest, Stephen. You look tired and you have a long road ahead of you with all this. I'm very proud of you though, and I love you," she said, raising her voice at the end as he got closer to the street.

"Love ya too, Jess. Have a good night," he shouted back, getting into the car.

He reached for his phone on the seat next to him, turning it on. When the screen illuminated, he noticed a couple texts from Heather had come in, some randoms, a voicemail from an unknown number-which was peculiar being that he hadn't erased his full box yet-and one from Sophia, who deserved a call back. He went into the text messages, reading the one he dreaded first, which said only, "Please call me when you can", then Heather's which read, "Love you, dummy. Want to kiss your head".

He took a few measured breaths, in through his mouth and out through his nose, before closing the Home screen and tossing it back down onto the seat. He then tapped the Start button, hammered the accelerator-inducing wheel spin in the sandy asphalt-and headed home to his apartment.

# Chapter 21

"I know, but I'm fine," he told her over the phone as he headed onto Route 44, back towards his apartment. A couple hours had passed as he drove aimlessly, the daylight now gone and the cabin illuminated in soft orange light.

"I'll call you in the morning. I need a long, hot shower, an uninterrupted night's sleep and some decompression time is all," he said, accelerating the car to pass a box truck that had decided to take the 35MPH speed limit literally.

"I know what he said, and if there was any fear about me being alone I promise you I'd stay with my sister or something, but I'll be alright, I swear. I'll text you before bed and call you first thing in the morning. Goodnight."

Sophia was beautiful and easy to be with. She wasn't laugh-out-loud funny-not finding humor in the same absurdities he did and often failed to understand the subtext of some of his jokes-but she loved to laugh. Her tastes in music extended no further than Pop radio and New Country, however, so how they ever made it past the first date was hard for Stephen to fathom. She had her quirks, her eccentricities and her charm, though. She was good person. If she hadn't gone to London for the translator job, letting him live in her condo while she did, he'd be looking forward to seeing her when he got through the front door.

*Maybe.*

"You're not going to talk yourself into loving her, asshole," he said, jamming his index finger into the radio knob, hoping distorted guitars would drown out the conversation he was having in his head. He'd turned his phone back on, and the home screen lit up with a text message as *Motley Crue* was telling the world they were too young to fall in love.

It was Heather.

"Fuck," he said, realizing he'd never checked in with her.

He was less than ten minutes from home, but pulled the car over and read the message. It was a picture of her wearing only a pair of red "cheeky shorts" as she called them and nothing else, the picture cut off just above the top of her smiling mouth. The worded part of the message said, "I bet I can help you with SOME of your memories."

He drew in a deep breath, letting it out too fast and laughing as he exhaled.

*<I'll be home in ten minutes if you'd like to come by and perform your memory-rekindling services in person ;)>*

The reply bubbles appeared immediately, then, *{Make it 15, I want to stretch first ;)>}*

*<I have no idea why that sounds so hot but it kinda is. Get that perfect body over there in 15 then>*

*{SYS}*

Stephen exited the text window, jumping into the main Messages panel with a row of blue dots indicating numerous unread texts. On the last one down he noticed a blurb about a sheriff in the preview so he opened it, thinking it may be the FBI agent he spoke to, or at least related to their conversation.

*<Hello Mr. Alexander, it's Sheriff Charlie McCabe from Potter County, PA. Glad to hear you're in the clear and hope you're feeling well. I know a lot of folks that want to shake your hand, myself included. Got your number from one of the CT officers, hope it's no bother. Take care now.>*

"McCabe, that was the guy's name," Stephen said, recalling the Sheriff's name from the TV.

He pulled the car back out onto the road, eager to see Heather back at his place, but figured in the ten minutes he had he could call the Sheriff, be courteous. He hit the call icon within the text window, the Bluetooth connected and in five rings he picked up.

*"Good evening,"* the voice said.

"Hello, is this Sheriff McCabe?" Stephen asked.

*"Yes, it is,"* the voice replied.

"Good evening, Sheriff. It's Stephen Alexander, over here in Connecticut, getting back to you."

*"I'll be darned, well this is the first call I've got on my new number here. Almost forgot it had a ringer. I'm sure yours must be nonstop."*

Stephen chuckled, "Yeah, well I leave it off most of the time, honestly. This is the longest I've had it on without an interruption."

*"Probably a good idea you change your number too, though from what my deputy tells me that might mean you'd miss some very lucrative opportunities. A hundred grand to talk to that woman on the cable show there, eh?"*

"Excuse me," he asked the Sheriff, feeling a drop in the center of his abdomen.

*"Maybe you better leave that phone on a little longer."*

"I'm not aware of such an offer, but, to be fair I haven't listened to one voicemail or even turned on the TV since I left the hospital."

*"I understand, believe me. Sort of a strange new reality, huh? You wake up one day and you're the same asshole you always are, then the next you feel like the same asshole but the world is calling you a hero. Would screw anyone up."*

Stephen liked this guy. No nonsense, said what he felt.

"Indeed, Sheriff. Totally agree, not a scenario I was prepared for. Though, to be honest, I feel like the hero label belongs to you here, exclusively."

"First of all, call me Chuck, or Charlie-whatever you like. Secondly, not a chance. Not saddling me with this alone. You did something a million others never would have, and you were unarmed. Be proud of that. You're also younger and can handle all the attention and bullshit that goes along with it, I'm too old and miserable. Better you take it."

"I like the cut of your jib, Chuck," Stephen said, turning right off Route 44 and down the last stretch before turning into his complex.

"Well, I can tell you that you're the first person who's ever said that to me in my entire life. Thanks, I guess."

"You remind me of my father. Opinionated, charismatic guy that never pulled any punches but infectious; everyone loved him."

"Oh well, shit, then that's where we differ. I'm the kind of infectious where most folks feel ill after spending too much time with me, but I appreciate what I know was a compliment."

"I don't know if I buy that, Chuck. Though, you may be on to something because I do need to go here in a sec," Stephen joked, knowing he was fast approaching his apartment.

"See what I mean?"

"I'm almost at my place, which I'm thinking may be a shit show, even though it's dark now, so didn't really mean to cut you short."

"Oh boy, good luck. And listen, you have yourself a great night and as I said, I'm glad to hear you're doing well and thanks for saving that little girl. I know you'll hear it a million times, but, it resulted in something wonderful out here."

"Yeah, and hey I'm sorry you had to take a bullet from that prick from what I hear. Hope you're doing OK on that front?"

"Oh, jeez yeah, was only a scratch, thanks. Was a harrowing scene, though. Maybe sometime the two of us will have a beer, talk about it."

"I'd love that, Chuck, and I appreciate you reaching out. I'll talk to you again soon. You have yourself a pleasant night."

215

*"You as well, kid. Good luck with the sycophants and vampires."*

"Ha, thank you. Take care," Stephen said, ending the call and turning onto his street.

As the car approached his complex he noticed several lights shining brighter than those that illuminated the entrance, as well as a massive truck parked on the street outside. He slowed the car to a crawl and pulled up within a few hundred feet, seeing through the trees that several trucks and reporters were gathered in the parking lot, along with dozens of people.

He did a K turn in the street and headed back in the opposite direction, picking up his phone with his right hand and dialing Heather.

*"I'm three minutes away. Settle down,"* her voice said over Bluetooth.

"Hey listen, let's go to your place, it's a fucking zoo over here," he told her.

*"Oh yeah, crap I wasn't even thinking. OK, I'll turn around and see you there."*

"See ya in a few."

He tapped the red End button and tossed the phone onto the passenger's seat, and immediately it began to ring with an unfamiliar number, which he ignored.

His stomach started gurgling, noticeable even over the road noise, reminding him he hadn't eaten anything all day. Heather was always good about keeping snacks in the house-chips, crackers cheese, sliced meat-so he figured he'd have something there versus make a stop and risk being spotted.

He rolled onto the accelerator and got the RPM's up, the BMW's turbo engine drowning out his bellowing tummy.

## *Chapter 22*

*Heather* answered the door wearing her bathrobe and a wide smile that devolved into a trembling upper lip and leaky eyes as soon as Stephen spoke.

"Hey beautiful," he said, followed by a sly grin.

She fell into him and squeezed his lower back with all the strength she had, then started crying.

"Hey, easy there babe, you'll put me back into the sick house with a broken spine," Stephen said playfully, returning the hug and kissing the side of her neck.

"Oh, my God, I can't believe you're here," she said through tears. "I've been, such a wreck, Stephen. I didn't know what to do, didn't know what I *could* do, if anything and I-"

"I know babe, I'm sorry. I'm here now though. You've got me for the night, not going anywhere," he interrupted, then taking his thumb and rubbing away some of the tears in her left eye.

She pulled herself up against him, then began kissing his lips, chin and cheeks.

"Oh, baby, does that still hurt a lot?" she asked, pointing up towards the large bandage on the left side of his head as she wiped tears away with her other hand.

"It's still swollen and sore, sometimes it stings. I'm sure it'll be an annoyance for a while but it'll get better."

She looked up at it, then moved her right hand gingerly against his forehead and let her fingers slide over the skin and onto the bandage, feeling the raised surface of the wound.

"You poor thing," she said, raising up on her toes and leaning in to kiss the spot several times.

Stephen took his hands and brought them up around her cheekbones, looking at her straight on, "I'm alright, hon. I love you for caring for me as you do, though, as much as it's undeserved."

"Stop it. I hate when you say stuff like that," Heather said, putting her hands on his forearms.

"Oh, so you wanna have our first fight already? I figured we'd wait until I peed all over the seat and forgot to wipe it up."

Heather grimaced and pulled herself away from him.

"I'm serious, Stephen. Don't make me feel bad for caring about you. This was a nightmare for me *too*, not just you," she said adamantly.

"I know that. Was only being my normal self-deprecating me is all. I also think that, considering the severe trauma, memory loss and stress I've endured, that I should be able to have a few freebies on the peeing on the seat thing. May take me a while to acclimate back to the rules," he replied, making a face where he grinned, rolling his bottom lip up over the top one and squinting his eyes.

"Seriously? You want to come over here, after the text I sent you, and think you're going to get lucky making that face? Sahara Desert time, pal," she said, turning and heading towards the living room.

Stephen grabbed onto her wrist and spun her around, her chiffon green bathrobe fluttering open, revealing a bare stomach and the underwear she had on in the picture. He looked down her body, starting at her eyes, then moving down her midsection.

"What have you got for me in there?" he asked.

"Nothing you haven't seen," she answered.

"Step back a little, open that up for me," he instructed, motioning towards the bathrobe with a nod of his head.

"Why?"

"You know why."

She took three steps backwards and brought her hands together on the fabric belt that bound the robe, yet had already loosened, moving her fingers inside the knot and pulling it apart. The belt fell to each side, hanging in the loops on the outside, and the bathrobe spilled open, revealing her naked chest and red underwear.

Stephen looked her over, smirked, then took off his shoes followed by his black jacket, tossing it on the chair near the front door.

"Slide it off your shoulders," he told her.

She reached her right hand over to her left shoulder and moved it across her skin, lifting the fabric of the bathrobe and causing it to slip off that side, the weight and motion taking the opposite side with it, landing in a pile at her feet.

Stephen looked at her full lips, then her eyes, then let his gaze travel down to her ample breasts-her amber nipples firm and centered-then falling to her stomach and the bright red undies he'd seen a preview of earlier. He felt himself getting aroused, his heart rate quickening, his stomach still growling, though no longer relevant.

He pulled his sweatshirt up over his head, revealing his bare chest, then unbuttoned his jeans and let them fall to the floor. He kicked them aside, his eyes still locked on her almost naked form.

"Looks like something still has a memory," Heather said, looking down at his boxers.

He reached his hand inside them and began to stroke himself, moving his eyes back to hers. "Go over to the couch, turn around and put your hands on the armrest."

She complied, then turning her head back over her shoulder and watching him play with himself. Stephen continued to touch himself, growing in his hand as he moved up and down, his eyes locked on hers. He took his left hand and reached down his side, sliding his left thumb into his boxers, edging them downward a couple inches.

Heather stood with her head still angled backwards, bent over and holding onto the couch. "I want to see that", she said, fixated on what his hand was doing.

"You will, but first I want you to slide those panties down for me so I can see that perfect ass while I'm playing, just a little bit."

Heather lifted her right arm, then took her index finger of her hand and curled it down and around into the waistband and methodically inched the panties down.

"A little further," Stephen pleaded.

She brought them down a little more, suspended right at the top of her thighs.

"Perfect. Now put your hand between your legs so I can watch you," he said, pulling his boxers all the way down until gravity grabbed hold and they fell to his ankles.

Heather looked back at him, massaging himself, fully aroused, and felt herself getting wet as her breathing quickened. A cycle of tingling sensations began, originating between her legs and up through her back and into her breasts. She moved her eyes up to his, then back down to his stroking hand, which was more than full.

Stephen increased the speed of his hand, noticing how it changed Heather's eyes, her longing and desire building alongside the intensity.

She reached her right hand between her legs, guiding one finger in between them, stroking in a downward motion several times, then leaving her middle finger on her clit and massaging it in a small circle, her breathing becoming stuttered.

Stephen edged closer to her, still stroking himself as he watched, wide eyed and eager. His neck and chest starting to perspire.

Heather continued to pleasure herself, spreading her legs further apart by a few inches and arching her back out, her lower back angled upward, a few feet from where Stephen stood. Hushed moans weaved into her labored breathing and she circled her finger around, then brought up her other hand from the couch and began to squeeze the nipple of her left breast.

Stephen's heart raced, and he could feel the initial sensation of a gathering orgasm so he slowed his pace and dropped to the floor, grabbing onto Heather's inner thighs, burying his face and mouth between her legs, lapping at her at first, then moving his hands up to her ass cheeks and squeezing, as his mouth began a more calculated, slow sucking with his tongue, applying pressure and rotation right where she wanted it.

Heather let her arms fall to the armrest of the couch, her breathing now deep and intense, the moans becoming a rhythmic, sustained whimper. She felt his mouth all over her and was so aroused she thought she may cum but get ahold of her breathing, trying to prolong the pleasure. The feel of his strong hands on her, his warm tongue and mouth moving over her with just enough pressure; she needed it to sustain for as long as possible.

Stephen reached down between his legs in his crouched position behind her, stroking himself again, which Heather could feel as they moved back and forth with his motion, as he continued to lick her. The thought of him touching himself while he pleased her that way sent a shooting jolt through her nipples and she let out a loud, breathy "Ohhhhh."

He reached with his free hand up between her legs and slid a finger inside her as he continued working her with his mouth. She made another sound, but was more of a lengthy hum. He circled his tongue on her, lapping up her wetness and stroking downward inside of her as he did.

"Oh fuck, baby," she said, her right knee trembling.

Heather felt the surge rise from the center of her abdomen, both legs shivered and buckled as the wave overtook her. Her orgasm built from the middle, then sent her nipples into a frenzy and immediately shot downward between her legs, pulsating and electrifying her. Stephen kept his mouth on her, squeezing her cheeks harder as she came, her vocalizations a combination of moans and staggered breaths. As she finished, Stephen stood up and slid himself inside her as he grabbed hold of the hair spilled across her bare back. She let out a loud "Uhhh" as he made his way inside her, hard and fast, pulling on her hair, which amplified her sounds.

He slowed his speed, watching himself go in and out of her from behind, letting go of her hair and placing both hands on the sides of her hips. He put long, deep, strokes into her, stopping for a second when he was inside then pulling back out. Heather moaned with each move inside her, breathing in choppy spurts. He amplified his pace again, feeling the tingle swirling around between his legs, the rapid onslaught of nerve endings firing.

Then he stopped.

He let his body slump down onto her back, resting his chin at the nape of her neck.

"What's the matter, hon?" She asked, turning to face him.

"That was just for you," he replied.

"Ohhh no, none of that. You get-"

"Hey," he said, bringing his hand up to her left cheek and letting the left side of his mouth curl upwards. "That was for *you*. We can worry about me later."

He went over and scooped up his boxers from the floor and slid them back on.

"Are you sure you're feeling alright? I mean, I'm all for the scales being tipped in my favor but..." Heather said, walking around to the couch and flopping down onto it.

"If you recall that weekend after New Year's, I think you'll agree that I'd need to bang one out per hour for a month to catch up to you," Stephen answered, winking at her.

"Ohhhh yeeeeeeah," she answered, stretching her hands up above her head as she filled up the couch with her body.

"You can be honest and I swear I won't be upset, but, that would be at least seventy-five percent better if I had a bigger meat pony, right?" Stephen questioned as he made his way over to her.

"Holy shit, are you serious right now? How can you ruin something so fucking hot by saying shit like that?" Heather replied, smacking his leg with her hand.

"I ate lead paint chips as a child," he said, then smirking.

"I bet. And that cute little grin you have isn't going to save you this time," she jabbed back.

"OK, well then how about my averaged size wiener?" He asked, wiggling it with his right hand inside the boxer shorts.

She tried not to laugh but it slipped out, then she pulled him onto her.

"How is it possible you can be such an idiot but still so God damn attractive? The only possible answer is that I have some serious mental defects."

"I don't think that was ever in doubt, babe."

"You make me crazy. It's all you."

"I did a few minutes ago, but the psychosis comes from your mother I think."

"Uh huh," she said, angling sideways and letting her head rest on his bare chest as she pulled up against him.

The two of them lay like that for another twenty minutes, he running his hands through her brunette locks, she almost falling asleep as he did so. Soon his appetite became too severe to ignore so Stephen got up and gorged himself on meats and cheeses from her fridge, following it with a "Haze" IPA from *Tree House Brewing Company*, his favorite, and one she tried to keep on hand for him.

Later they showered together, staring at one another in sustained gooeyness under the steamy water like love struck teens on their first night alone in their parents' house. He washed her hair, scrubbed her back, massaged her legs, then moving his hands all over her breasts as he stood behind her and they were both clean.

After the shower, they made their way to the bed and made love again, this time with soft caresses, long, deep kissing and more meaningful glances. She cried in the middle and he embraced her and let his eyes flow as well. For a while after they remained in bed and stroked one another's skin, saying nothing; the only sound around them in the King Size bed covered in pastel pillows and blankets being the *click click click* of the Wall clock that Heather's mother gave her when she moved in. Then, from nowhere, a memory of the attack at the restaurant shot into his thoughts and he edged upwards in the bed, startling Heather.

"Are you OK?" she asked.

"Yeah, I'm fine. Had a flashback or something, of the guy that whacked me I think. I could see his face clearly. The little girl too. Just popped right in like it was on a slide projector, switching over from another one," he told her.

"Well, you said they told you that's going to happen, right?"

"Yeah. Was just out of nowhere though," he answered, reaching for his shirt on the floor to wipe perspiration that clung to his forehead.

Heather sat up against the headboard then turned her naked body to face him. "Babe, how are you doing with all the other stuff, though? You know, your mom, the news and everything. Have you talked to anyone, set anything up? I know it's only been a day since you've been out but I have to imagine it's not going to dissipate anytime soon."

"Eh well, mom's trying to make this about her and find an angle but I'll deal with that. I suppose I'm going to have to talk at some point about all the rest though. Can't just stay in bed here with you and pretend there's not a world out there, as much as I'd prefer to."

She squeezed his hand and leaned in to kiss his cheek. "I love you, and if there's anything I can do to make this easier for you, let me know and I will."

"Listen, you don't worry about me, OK? You're too damn good to me as it is and I owe you so much more than I give you, and that's something else I wanted to talk to you about. It's time that I tell her-"

"Shhh," Heather said, putting her hand up against his mouth. "Not now, hon, OK? There is so much more going on and I appreciate you saying that and, yes, it's something to talk about but, not now. You need to navigate this situation first, come out on the other side before diving into our shit."

"I'm tired of saying I don't deserve you, because I'm a pretty cocky fuck, but, you're way above my paygrade, truthfully."

"Oh, shut up. You keep doing what you did to me up against that couch earlier and I'll keep you around for a couple more weeks at least," she said, sliding back against the headboard and then down onto her pillow.

Stephen mimicked the move, then brought her hand over onto his chest and laced his fingers into hers as she slid her head onto his chest.

"You know, when I was a young kid, probably around ten or eleven," Stephen spoke, after they lay in silence awhile. "I used to lie in bed at night, worried out about all the things that made my life at the time seem so daunting. Some nights it was because my mom worked late at a cocktail lounge or was on a date and the babysitter was downstairs making out with her boyfriend. Other nights it was because I knew in the morning I had to walk down a hallway where some pissed off kid was going to push me onto the floor and spill my books in front of a laughing crowd of other assholes. Most nights it was because I wasn't sure how I felt about my father, but all the nights were the building blocks to my subsequent acid reflux. Anyway, one night, after hearing a man on TV talk about counting sheep to relax and fall asleep I tried to do it, but gave up in five minutes, feeling ridiculous because it wasn't working."

Heather pulled up, facing him, using her open hand as a rest for her head as she listened.

"I started thinking about what made me feel relaxed, and honestly it wasn't much, but the first thing that popped into my head was a swing that we had behind one of the houses we'd rented when I was seven years old. It was just a board suspended between too knotty pieces of rope hanging from a huge Maple tree in the backyard, but when I climbed onto it and began to glide back and forth over the ground, looking up at the sky through the green leaves, I felt at ease. The only other place I felt as relaxed was the ocean, which luckily my mother loved so we got to go there frequently. So, I'm lying there in bed and thinking about swinging on that tree and the beach, and I imagine myself on a swing suspended from the sky over the ocean at night-the only light from a humungous moon in the background-and my body travels up and back, up and back, just soaring in both directions like a pendulum."

"Do your toes ever touch? You know, the water," Heather asked.

"No, but kind of incredible you'd ask, as that was the one thing I always wanted to happen in my little ritual but it never did," Stephen replied.

"Why not?"

"I think because I was too afraid. I wanted to let my legs stretch out and feel the warm water on my feet as I met the bottom of my arch but I never did when imagining it. I suppose the vision itself had accomplished the goal of relaxing me and even though I was so enticed by the idea of letting my feet hit the sea water I just took solace in knowing that my version of counting sheep had worked every morning I woke up, remembering I had thought about it the night before."

"Did you think a shark was going to bite your toes or something?" Heather playfully asked.

"It was the unknown, I guess. The fear of wanting something but being afraid of what might happen if I got it. So, I stuck with what

I knew worked, avoided the possibility of damaging what I'd created. I still think about it sometimes when I can't sleep. Pretty sappy, right?"

She sat up, looking directly at him, "I think it's beautiful, babe, and I'm sorry if I sounded like I was making light of it. So...I want to tell you something but you promise you won't be mad?"

He grimaced at her. "Is this where you tell me that size really does matter and you were dating a Longshoreman in my absence?"

"Cut it out," she said, poking at his belly. "No, it's about, well, you know how I've always wanted to know more about your childhood and your relationship with your dad? Cause you circle around some of that stuff but it never comes out all the way."

"OK..."

"Well that day you left the motel, you'd accidently left the pages of *The Alexander Circus* there and, well, I started reading some of it. Maybe *all* of it," she admitted, staring at him, her eyes wide and dopey.

"Huh, I see. Well at least now I know where it is. Thought maybe some orderly at the hospital stole it and was going to sell the movie rights."

"Are you mad?"

"Mad? Yes, I'm livid, and completely turned off by you as I'm sure you can tell by looking at the medium sized rod in my boxers right now."

She pulled herself up tight against him and squeezed, then kissed his forehead, careful not to press up against the bandage, or his erection. "I loved it, Stephen. Every part of it so far. It's made me belly laugh and cry, which you know is not that hard for me anyway but, was a joy to go through. I want to know more-all of it-and I know the loss of your dad was devastating and I want to hear more about your relationship with him but, from what I've read so far, it's clear you grew to love him immensely but that took some time. Can you tell me more so I don't have to wait for new pages?"

He looked back at her and saw in her eyes that all her words were genuine, honest and sincere and that scared him as much as it endeared her to him.

"OK, but not *now*, alright? You're not exactly known for your late nights, babe," he jabbed, poking fun at her inability to stay awake most nights past 9PM.

She dug her arm into his right armpit and wiggled her fingers, causing him to let out a high-pitched squeal and shoot upwards in bed.

"Holy crap. Incredible that it's the same man who took me like he did, bent over the couch, that can also make that noise," Heather said, rolling her eyes in mock disgust.

"Tickling is considered torture. You realize that, right? Same as listening to you talk about makeup and how one particular brand is worth ten times what the others cost," he jabbed back, referencing her love of ultra-expensive cosmetics.

"Are you looking for me to do the other pit now?" she asked, rolling over towards that side.

He wrestled her off and held her down, "Enough with the trying to get me to scream like a toddler that just ate a Jalapeno. You want to hear more about my fucked-up childhood or what?"

"Yes please," she answered, shooting up straight against the headboard and clapping.

He looked at her, opening his eyes wide. "Yikes, hon. Be a tough one for anyone looking in from the outside to figure out who the loser is in this relationship."

They both laughed, then Stephen lay his head back against the pillow and recounted the stories of his mother Lillian and the Cornfield, and Henry and his alcoholic father. He talked about dogs and bullies and new homesteads. He shared, in his own words, the tales of coins stacked on a floor, pulled out of a pillowcase and bee stings all over after bad choices. He touched on the origins of the deeper relationship he built with Henry, his father, in his later adolescent years but then reeled it back in, waiting for another day where he may not come apart so easily. He laughed about the absurdity of it all and he cried over the sadness of it as well, she often joining right in. Mostly, he just let the words seep out of him knowing there was a woman lying next to him that didn't want to judge, correct, insinuate or criticize, only listen and experience.

He talked for two hours, then they fell asleep with weary eyes and aching bellies.

<#>

*Can't catch his breath. Tumbling down a grassy hill. The rain pours on a box. Anguished screams around the corner. Candles that smell like Christmas. Dogs licking his face. A baby isn't breathing. Nothing.*

## Chapter 23

$Stephen$ slept seven hours, never waking once to pee, which was borderline miraculous. He scurried out of bed looking for his phone, then realized there was no reason to turn it on, as it would only be headaches that awaited. Heather remained sleeping, on her side, her hands folded and neatly tucked under her face as always. He smiled over at her, then head into the bathroom to take a leak.

He opened the medicine cabinet, fishing out an oversized bandage to put on his head after running some warm water and a fingerful of hand soap across the purple and red bump. As he finished securing it and stood over the toilet, his right arm outstretched and bracing himself on the Sea Foam Green wall, he thought of Sophia. What must be going through her head after all this, the two of them not speaking for more than ten days prior to his hospitalization, now he's all over the news. When she left, it was shortly after a botched engagement attempt-he trying to manufacture love and desire where it didn't exist-with the plan being, "Let's see what time and space does." She'd been gone ten months now and absence was only making the heart grow indifferent. Part of him knew that *she* knew he didn't love her, but that in some way she likely rationalized a scenario where they could co-exist and not be in love. Being pleasant, kind, and decent to one another, sharing a home, responsibilities and family, and hope that was enough to make for a good life.

It wasn't, and he needed to make that clear. Today.

He gathered his clothes and went to the sink for a slurp of water, gulping it down, and then back into the bedroom, crouching down at Heather's side.

"Babe," he whispered, then kissing her forehead. "Sleepyhead, I have to go."

Her eyes crept open, and she blinked a couple times, then flinched, not expecting him to be inches from her face as they opened.

"I need to go, hon. Some things I need to take care of," he said.

"What time is it?" she asked.

"Just about 7am. Go back to sleep and I'll check in with you later. Had a wonderful night. Thank you for that," he said, kissing her lips and rubbing her ear lobe with his fingers.

"Be careful. I love you. Call me later," she said, dopey and slurring.

"I love you too. See you soon," he said, standing up, then heading out to his car.

<#>

On the drive from Heather's place he ran through dialogue in his head. Conversations, comebacks and "what ifs". He imagined a variety of reactions, all plausible, though couldn't decide which was most likely. He could hear her gentle voice in his head speaking a variety of words, never raising its volume above soft conversation, as she was as mild mannered as they came. She may accuse him of acting irrationally, based on everything that had transpired of late, implore him to think about what he was saying-not take any drastic measures. She would ask that they go see a therapist when she returned in a few months, or talk to her sister, who was a shrink.

*Unrequited love is more painful than dying, because at least death is an end.*

231

It was the first line to a short story he wrote ten years earlier and it kept repeating in his head as he listened to the ring tones over the speakers in his car. Sophia spent close to a year with Stephen before she left for London, encouraging his dreams, massaging his ego, relenting in most arguments. She watched from the sides of her eyes as his interest drifted elsewhere as months passed-his gaze following the bodies of younger women passing them and prolonged conversations with waitresses as she anxiously sat across the table. She loved him, still, despite the obvious waning interest, when she left and hoped London-and prolonged separation-may offer clarity.

*"Hey there,"* Sophia said over the speakers in the car.

"Good afternoon. How's England treating you?" Stephen asked.

*"Things are fine here. I'm headed to one of my classes in an hour, hoping the rain will ease up by then. How are you feeling, get some sleep?"*

"You know, I did, thanks. Didn't even get up once to pee the whole time, which, of course, is incredible for me."

*"Wow, yeah that is. Must be nice to sleep all the way through, though."*

"Absolutely. I'll take those nights anytime I can get them," Stephen said, seeing a new call from an unknown number appear on his info screen in the car, which he ignored.

*"Is that a call coming in? I can let you go if you need to take it,"* Sophia offered.

"Oh, no worries, unknown number. They're coming in at a breakneck pace so I'm changing my number as soon as the wireless store opens. I'll text you the new one later."

The content and cadence of their conversation was so banal and lifeless, Stephen thought to himself as he turned left onto Route 44 and rolled heavier onto the accelerator. There were things to be said, but he struggled finding inspiration to continue.

*"OK, thanks. So, do you have a couple minutes before you do that then? I need to get ready for my class but if you have a few I wanted to say some things."*

Stephen felt the weight of the words and heard the change in her tone, so he pulled the car into a small craft store lot on the right side of the road.

"Of course, sure. There were some things I needed to say, too, so-"

*"I think this will be easier if you let me say what I need to and then we let that ruminate for a while, if that's OK? It's not that I don't want to give you an opportunity to speak-I do-but maybe another time. I need to get through this and see where that puts us. Fair enough?"*

Sophia was a very intelligent woman, with a Master's Degree in Education, a Minor in Mathematics, well versed, strong willed, reasonable and fair minded, though in most conversations with Stephen she deferred opinions to him, letting him dominate discussions. She was subservient, almost to an extreme, and rarely challenged his ideas or desires, and almost never began a conversation of her own accord. Her making this statement, and even going so far as to suggest he not even respond, was very out of character, Stephen thought. Though, if he was honest, he enjoyed it.

"I pulled over. You have my undivided attention. Well, at least until some other random calls me in forty-five seconds, which I'll ignore, of course," Stephen said.

*"When I went to London to take this job,"* she said, wasting no time. *"It was at a place in our relationship where I'd allowed my love and desire for you to cloud the realities of our day to day life. I'd convinced myself that I'd accepted your wandering eyes, your unexplained, frequent texts and your increasing indifference to me and that by simply, 'loving you through it', I could bring you back to me in a way that was satisfying and beneficial for me-hopefully for both of us. Part of the mistake I had, however, was assuming there was a place to bring you back to."*

"Wait, Soph-"

*"Please, let me finish,"* Sophia said, cutting him off. *"When we met at that work event you were with someone else. It was brutally obvious, and I think you may have even commented as such, that you weren't that into her and she was just there as a plus one, someone to tag along with. But I remember the way she looked at the end of the night, watching you go off into other circles, working your magic with conversation and charm, the little touches on the shoulder to this woman or the next, the leaning in to whisper something to the girl delivering the mini quiches to the guests. She was sullen, despondent and just embarrassed, Stephen. Maybe she was just a date and someone you had no intentions of seeing seriously but regardless, that night, in that room, she was with you and other than a brief introduction to a few people, no one would have ever guessed that."*

"Jennifer was only-"

*"So, when you started talking to me,"* Sophia continued, speaking right over him, *"I had already witnessed that for most of the night but somehow, with your infectious wit and that damn smile, you were able to suppress those judgements I'd already made about you. I fell right into you and when you gave me your-I'm now assuming-bullshit line about, 'Hey that's cool you speak all those languages. I'd love to learn Spanish, but would be a lot easier if my teacher looked like you and not an App on my phone.', I suppose I was just thrilled that someone was talking to me and it happened to also be an attractive male, because bullshit or not, the line sucked."*

Stephen fidgeted in his seat, then reached down to adjust the position, reclining about twenty degrees as he looked out the window and saw a Cardinal, plump and red, perched on the top of a sign advertising homemade jewelry outside the store where he parked. He'd heard stories of the significance of seeing Cardinals-the timing, location and proximity to where one was-but couldn't recall any of the specifics, though he suspected that whomever told him these tales left out the one warning you that you'll be getting eviscerated by a lover.

*"By the time we started seeing one another regularly, I'd forgotten about the woman you came with that night. More likely, I'd buried the memories of her sadness and her shame to spare myself from having the inevitable internal dialogue that would've caused me to question things and likely pull the plug; I loved you at that point, I was convinced. Then, of course, your behavior became so blatant and obvious I had to address it and I did that by suffocating you, something I don't say as an apology, because it's not warranted, but instead as just an explanation. My mistake was not reading the signs for what they were-that you're a womanizer and that you were clearly not in love with me, and I tried to combat that by giving you more of myself, when what I should have done was leave."*

"But you did leave," Stephen interjected, maneuvering in his seat, sending the Cardinal flying off into trees in front of him.

*"I did, you're right. But you were never there in the first place, Stephen."*

"That's not true, I was…"

*"You were what?"* She asked, getting no response. *"When I left, as you recall, it wasn't out of anger or after me having these revelations, it was with the understanding that some time apart may help us in the long run by giving us space. In the first couple weeks after I left I was homesick, terrified, miserable and lonely and we barely spoke even after I dropped hint after hint via text and phone messages. You told me once you 'just wanted to give this break a real chance' and that's why you were so cold and unavailable, but that wasn't it and you know it. You never loved me from the start and you were probably fucking some girl you met at the coffee shop or someone at work or an ex or how the fuck would I even know? You're so damn wrapped up in your own space, your own world that at this point, anything I discovered wouldn't shock me. I remember trying to convince myself that maybe you were gay, and that the reason you never looked at me the way I looked at you for so long was because it was something I'd never be able to give you that you desired. That idea*

*came crashing down when we stopped at the convenience store in Enfield, on the way to see my mother, and you nearly went into cardiac arrest watching the twentysomething with the lower back tattoo bending over and putting those cigarettes away. It was like you were in a fucking trance the rest of the day, withdrawn and absent in conversation. You stare at asses on other women like those videos of Pugs you always used to show me, their heads following every movement the little treat makes, back and forth, back and forth. It's embarrassing."*

Stephen sat there, listening to her tear him down, waiting for that moment where she was so off base that he could interject with righteous indignation, countering her accusations. It seemed unlikely that moment would arrive, however, as she was spot on with her assessments so far.

*"Stephen, listen,"* she said, clearing her throat and shuffling the phone around, making his car speakers crackle and whoosh. *"I know you went through something horrible and traumatic recently, something that's likely to cause a lot of attention to come your way and may result in a lot of stress if it hasn't already. I'm not trying to add to that, honestly, I'm not, as harsh as it may seem that I am right now. Instead, I'm just letting you off the hook, freeing you from having to deal with the inevitable burden of defining what we are, addressing it. I know that you feel, you're compassionate, have empathy and although sometimes I wonder how you reconcile some of your behaviors, I don't think you're a sociopath like Christine. I remember those stories you told about her and how cold and unkind she was and all the deceit and cheating and how it blindsided you, especially having grown so close to her kids. How you were so confounded by her inability to feel anything, show remorse or connect to reality and how that led to your understanding of her mental pathology, and that it helped-at least a little bit-knowing you may never get closure. I'm truly sorry for what that woman did to you but, it doesn't make it OK to hurt those that followed her because you were wounded. It's hard to*

236

*understand, knowing that you do feel remorse and regret, and have genuine compassion for other people, that you can behave the way you do, really. If it's not a psychological malady then where is your gut check, Stephen? Your barometer for causing pain, your integrity, especially knowing what it felt like to be on the other side?"*

Stephen changed his position in the car seat again, shifting closer to the window and leaning his head against the cold glass. Through the windshield, he spotted more birds. This time, a couple crows that landed on the gutter of the red barn the craft store was in. One was cawing and squawking while the other flinched and ruffled its feathers each time the other made the noise, while also inching further away each time it happened. Knowing crows were often an allegory for death, Stephen wondered if he should be extra careful when he drove off, or if their intended message related to his complete annihilation in the current conversation.

*"Well?"* she asked?

"I don't have any answers, Sophia, other than you're right. Your assessment of me, for the most part, is accurate, and the timing of this conversation is fortuitous, and almost spooky, because it addresses things I needed to talk with you about as well. I suppose I wouldn't have chosen the route of just calling myself a man whore and total asshole but it doesn't mean that's untrue."

*"I don't know if you're a 'man whore' and I didn't call you an asshole either, Stephen, though sure, I suppose that can be implied. What I do know is that you're not in love with me and I have questions about your ability to show meaningful love to any woman right now- not just because of the accident-but until you do some serious soul searching and figure out what it is that drives you to do what you do, and, also what would truly make you happy. There's a part of me that feels like you do want commitment and monogamy but that you just keep falling back on what you know."*

"Fuck, now you sound like your sister," Stephen jabbed.

*"I don't think one needs to be a shrink to observe some of these traits of yours, Stephen. You talk about truth a lot and how absent it is from society, and I agree, but how long are you going to keep being dishonest with yourself? You told me all those wonderful stories of your dad, counseling you through life in your teens to late thirties, and him always saying, 'If you wanna keep feeling like you're feeling, just keep doing what you're doing' when you had issues with relationships or your mother, whatever. Well, how are you feeling Stephen? Are you happy? Do you feel like life's where you want it to be? Another thing you always mentioned that Henry talked about was that part of AA, the 'Searching and Fearless Moral Inventory', where one writes down their fears, their flaws, their proclivities-the good and the bad-and does an honest assessment of what they mean. Did you ever do that? Do you want to?"*

"Holy fuck, Sophie. Don't be afraid to speak your mind or anything."

*"I know, and I'm sorry it's all coming out like this-right now. Like I said earlier though, you're going to be thrust into the spotlight with what happened recently, which-can I please just make sure you understand-I think was an amazing and courageous act. Any issues I have with you relating to your character are contained only in your relationships with women."*

"Oh, hey, thanks," he replied, rolling his eyes and moving his body to the other side of the seat.

*"Anyway, I don't want you to have to lie about us, or be dragged into uncomfortable conversations, and frankly, I don't want to be either. I'm going to be coming home, for good, in about six weeks as my assignment got cut short. I just want to come back to my quiet little life, having parted on decent terms, without animosity or discomfort."*

"I can be out of your place in a week, so there's no worry-"

*"This isn't about living at my place, Stephen-you can stay there up until the day before I arrive as far as I'm concerned. This is just me*

*speaking truth and telling you what my plan is. Let's not pretend this is, or that it really ever was, anything more than two people just existing with one another, sometimes uncomfortably, and occasionally getting naked, which I never minded, by the way. If I'm being honest, in those moments, you always made me feel like you were one hundred percent there and that I was beautiful, and I appreciate that. That hasn't always been the case in my past."*

Silence filled the cabin of the BMW, hanging there, then seeping into Stephen's ears, drowning out any external noise or internal dialogue.

*"So, hey, why don't I let you go,"* Sophia suggested, after about a minute of quiet.

"I feel like you did the work for me here, in some ways. Now, on top of the guilt I have for all the accusations-which, like I said, I agree are fair so don't get defensive-I feel bad you had to say all that when it should've been me. Should've been me a while ago, before today," he said, followed by a deep inhale.

*"Let's not get caught up in responsibilities here, OK? It doesn't matter, all that does is that we got it out in the open and we move on and stop living in an alternate reality. So many people over here, in England and most of Europe, are worried about what's going on at home. Our President inventing or distorting reality to suit his agenda and it's got the world twisted and nervous, understandably. I'd at least like to have control over my own reality, you know?"*

"I always knew you were smarter than me, but, jeez Soph, all of a sudden you're this machine of reason, rationality and truth. Fearless. I'm supposed to give a talk on Cognitive Dissonance at my Atheist group next month, maybe you want to sub in?" he joked.

*"Ha, I still have my faith, as you know, so-that's your arena. I love that you're passionate about those things you believe in and those you don't, though. That's something I did learn from you, to dive into things with everything you have and not tip toe around. Always has been one of my struggles. Anyway, I need to jump in the shower and*

239

get to this class so, please send me your new number when you get it and, I really hope that you're doing well and that this media circus doesn't make you crazy. You absolutely deserve an incredible amount of praise, though. Have you even met the girl you saved that day yet?"

"No. Haven't talked to anyone locally about it other than family. I'm sure eventually I'll meet her. Small town."

"OK, well, I'm glad we talked Stephen and I'll speak to you soon. I'm sorry things had to be so intense but, I just didn't want to wait too long knowing that you'd be inundated with other things."

"I understand, I do. For what it's worth I do care about you very much, and I appreciate you letting me stay in the condo before I buy my own place and I'm sorry for making you feel shitty all those times. I have no excuse, I really don't. Thanks for bringing it to light, Soph. I mean that."

"You'll find your way, Stephen, I have no doubt. I wish you nothing but happiness."

"Oh, and, because we are talking so much about honesty and truth, I'd be a liar if I didn't say that the doctor told me one last pic of you in the shower might be just the thing to help with any residual swelling in my cranium."

Sophia chuckled. "You're one of the funniest men I've ever known, there's some truth for you. Don't hold your breath on the pic, though, even though I know you have others, which sort of makes me cringe knowing they're out there."

"Do you want me to delete them? I will," he offered.

"Um, yeah would you mind? That one you showed me from my bedroom doorway months ago was actually pretty flattering, but, I honestly would feel better knowing you erased them."

"Done, absolutely."

"Thank you. Take care of yourself, Stephen."

"Be well, Soph."

Stephen clicked the red end button on his phone and watched the call details disappear from his navigation screen in the car. He then thumbed the phone's Photo app and began digging through pictures, of which there were over five thousand. Luckily, there were only three naked pics of Sophia among the masses so, by arranging by date, he could find and delete them within minutes, which he did. For a moment after he erased them-knowing the pics still existed in his "Recently Deleted" file-he contemplated letting them remain, in case the urge struck to view them again. Then he thought about how that was just another lie, and only a distraction from elements in his life that would never do such things to him.

He went into the deleted folder and erased the three pictures of Sophia, then tossed his phone onto the passenger's seat and drove off towards the wireless store to change his number.

## Chapter 24

𝓣𝓱𝓮 *Americell Wireless* location was uncharacteristically quiet when he visited for the number change-a process that was less painful than he'd imagined. The staff recognized him, several asking for pictures, which he obliged, yet-despite the distractions-the experience was expeditious and headache free.

Stephen sat in the car, scrolling through his recent calls and texts, remembering some had come in prior to walking into the store. One was from Kirsten at Willie's Place.

*<Hey stranger ;)When you coming by here to see me? Willie and the crew too. You're all over the news! I booted the lawyer so, maybe come see me at home instead lol>*

He looked at the words in his phone, and a familiar, intoxicating sensation coursed within him. He looked over into the bag of his personal belongings from the hospital, pulling the red envelope out and resting it in his lap. He could stop and see and Kirsten later, call the blonde who dropped the card in his lap tonight and nobody would be the wiser.

Sophia tore him to shreds. His mother was selling his soul. His sister didn't understand him. Heather will leave.

*Fire sale.*

Stephen ran his fingers around the edges of the envelope, staring out the driver's side window. Clumsily, he tapped out a message to Kirsten, "Hey sexy. How-" then, as his eyes moved to the windshield and up into a cottony cloud, resting stray in the blue background, he pulled his hand from the screen and abandoned it.

"Definition of insanity," he said aloud.

The other text was from the Sheriff in Pennsylvania.

*<Good Morning, Stephen, Sheriff McCabe. Just wanted to let you know I enjoyed our conversation and I hope this message finds you well. Take care. - CM>*

"Huh," he said, staring at the text, pondering an idea.

He looked at his silver Movado, tilting it towards his face, the reflective metal bending light from through his side window and into his eye. As he squinted, he dialed the Sheriff back but the Bluetooth wouldn't engage so he tapped the Speakerphone button.

*"This is Chuck,"* the voice announced.

"Good morning, it's Stephen Alexander over here in Connecticut," he said.

*"Well good morning to you Stephen, "* McCabe replied.

"Hey so, I know it's last minute and it's Saturday and all but…wondered what your plans were are later?"

*"Am I around, you mean?"*

"Yes. Was wondering if you're free this evening, say around seven?"

*"Well, can't say I had much lined up other than stopping by the office to check on my Deputy and maybe making myself a Club sandwich. Did you need something?"*

"Well, sure, now I definitely need one of those Club sandwiches. That's in my Top Five sandwiches ever."

*"You make a list of your sandwiches?"*

"The ones I like, sure. Not only sandwiches. Top five beers, desserts, movies, bands; it's important to have those compartmentalized for easy reference in conversation, etc."

*"Huh, I see. Might explain why I'm so goddamn boring. So, you're going to be out this way, that what you're saying? Need to see me?"*

"I'm thinking of heading that way now, that's why it couldn't be until later. Might be earlier if I don't get snagged in traffic too much, or have to stop and piss more than ten times."

*"Ten times? Pictures on the TV made me think you were under seventy-five."*

"Not in the taking-a-leak department. In that realm, I've already been dead for twelve years."

*"I'm sure that will make sense before you get here. Anyway, I'll be here but, it's a long trip just for a social visit, though I'd welcome the company, of course. Not trying to sell me a time share or something, right?"*

"No, but in the morning you'll wake up in your bathtub, surrounded by ice, your back hurting. I'll leave a phone by the tub. You'll need to call 911 immediately."

*"Eh, you know kid, these days I'm happy when I actually wake up so that would be fine."*

"My guess is you have a shitload of days still ahead of you, Chuck, but maybe I can take up half of one? Not a lot of people I feel real comfortable talking to about this situation but, I get the vibe from you-even if you hadn't been right there on the front lines-that you may be someone I can have a conversation with. Feel up to it?"

*"Ya know, I suspect I may. Especially if you bring that fancy beer you young fellas drink, too, the kind that looks like Orange Juice and knocks you on your ass. Goes great with my Club Sandwich."*

"I can absolutely hook you up, Sheriff."

*"Call me Chuck, and, I'll text you the address out here, and call me if you get lost, but it's pretty easy once you're out this way. You sure you're up for the drive? Not exactly around the block."*

"I drive a ridiculously overpriced German sedan and there's a shit ton of windy roads on the way out to that part of Pennsylvania from what I recall. I'll be grinning ear to ear."

*"OK then. You be safe, though. Lots of State boys hide out waiting to nail some out of towner in a fancy car even if you're just a*

*hair over the limit. Of course, they see that it's you and I can't imagine any of them writing you a ticket."*

Stephen laughed, then realized he needed to source those beers.

"OK, hey listen Chuck, I need to make a quick stop, pick up a few things, then I'm on my way. I'll update you when I'm about an hour out. Don't forget to text the address."

*"Absolutely. See you this evening."*

"See ya later," Stephen said, ending the call and starting the car.

<#>

Stephen pulled his car up to the curb in front of Chris Ravener's home-a close friend and co-worker. Chris was often awake at obscene hours to play Xbox in those few available moments when his three children and wife Carrie were still enjoying their slumber, though it was late enough now where they were likely all up. Chris was the kind of father and husband that any man might aspire to be and any woman would relish waking up to, and the only co-worker Stephen ever welcomed all the way inside his universe.

Stephen sat in the car, looking out the side glass, hoping to see motion inside the living room of Chris's yellow Colonial home through the front picture window. It was likely that he had a few *Tree House* beers, and he couldn't risk going back to his apartment yet. A body moved across the space in the window, stopping dead, then came up closer to the glass, then disappeared in a blink. A moment later Chris came barreling out the front door.

"Steviedoodle," he yelled, coming at Stephen in a near sprint and using one his affectionate nicknames.

"Hey buddy," Stephen replied, getting out of the car and then offering him a hug.

Chris picked him up from the ground, lifting him a couple feet in the air, then turned ninety degrees and let him back down. "Jesus Christ, man. I can't believe you're here, you look great!"

"Thanks bud, been on quite a ride" Stephen said, folding his hands together and stretching his arms over his head.

"Dude, you're all over the fucking news, like everywhere. I mean, what a thing you did though, seriously. I need to hug you again," he said, latching on to him from the front and bear hugging him. "Damn, so great to see you buddy."

Stephen smiled at him as he pulled back away. "Good to see you, too. Hey, but, I come with selfish motivations, to be honest. Was hoping I could snag a few Tree beers from you if you have a couple extras. Have a little road trip planned and promised someone I'd bring a couple along."

Chris's head tilted and a slow grin came over his face. "You sly, ass-tapping mother fucker. Right out of the hospital, bandage on your head, and you're off to get road pussy? I salute you, my friend. You're living the dream."

Stephen laughed, then leaned back against his car. "No, all set with that. Actually, going to see that cop in Pennsylvania, the one who found the girls."

"Holy shit, man, really? Wow. Another fucking hero, just like you, seriously. He invite you up there or how'd that come about?"

"He reached out to me, we talked a bit. Think I just need a conversation with someone who's living in the same sort of headspace, ya know? This whole thing is a mind fuck."

"Dude, I texted you, called a bunch of times, emailed and shit, you know you can talk to me anytime, right?"

"Of course, and I appreciate that, but I don't wanna lay a bunch of shit on you with all you have going on. I'm sure those messages and voice mails are in my phone, too. Sorry I never responded but I was buried in shit as soon as I first turned my phone on. Never got around to dealing with it all. I have a new number too, I'll text it to you."

246

Chris shook his head, grinning.

"You call me at 3am if you want to talk about toenail fungus, you understand me, Alexander? Now, I won't pick up but you go ahead and call me," Chris said, then laughing and smacking Stephen on the arm.

Stephen smiled and feigned block moves as Chris continued to utilize one of the most widely employed male bonding maneuvers.

"I'm serious though, OK? If you need to talk just call me. Day or night."

"I appreciate it, and I love you bud. I'm sure we will have lots of rambling discussions on your deck before too long, just need to get some things aligned is all."

Right as Stephen finished speaking, two little girls and a boy, all in pajamas, came flying out the front door of the house, headed for Stephen.

"Uncle Steeeeviie," one of the girls screamed, her brown hair in a ponytail and bouncing all around her shoulders.

"Waaaait a minute, do I know you people?" Stephen asked in a silly voice, getting a collective hug and laugh from the three of them. "You all look familiar but I don't know if I remember. Let me see-"

"I'm Morgan!" Chris's youngest, four years old, in pig tails, shouted.

"I'm Hannah, but you know my name," the six-year-old blonde, wearing pink jammies said.

"Hannah? Hmmm, no I'm positive your name is Banana, but it sounds the same so I could see how you'd get confused," Stephen countered.

"No it's Haaaannnaaah," she yelled back, trying not to laugh.

"OK Banana, you keep telling yourself that. And who's this little guy? Oh right, you're Eyore, almost forgot," Stephen said, looking over at Ethan.

"Nooooo! Eee-thun," he shot back, then slapping Stephen's leg.

247

"Hey, no hitting," Chris reminded Ethan, while rubbing his head.

"Jeez, you must be learning that from your old man because I'm sure your mom can hit harder than that," Stephen joked, getting a chortle from Chris and big smiles from the kids.

"She could destroy me. It's not even a question," Chris offered.

"One time, um, this one time when, mom was doing her workout in the basement and daddy was holding on to the bag that she punches, um, she knocked my daddy over because she hit it so hard," Morgan said, working through her words carefully.

"Is that so? Wow, well your momma is a tough cookie I know that. Plus, your daddy here, he's just a big ol' squishy baby, isn't he?" Stephen said, grabbing onto Chris's sides and squeezing him, sending the kids into a laughing fit as they watched their dad giggle and try to get away.

"OK, enough tomfoolery. I need some beers. You want me to run in and grab them, steal some of the kids' cookies while I'm there" Stephen offered, winking at Morgan.

"Oh no, sorry dude. I have specific instructions to not let you in, the-"

"The cat pooped in the house seven times! It smells like diarear!" Hannah shouted, interrupting her dad.

The other kids laughed and Chris rolled his eyes.

"New cat, and it's a sweet little thing but it shits like an infant with dysentery. Plus, we had some neighbors over last night and the place looks like hell. She told me to say hello, though," Chris said, rubbing his hand over Hannah's shoulders.

"Ah, no worries man, and tell her I said hello back," Stephen replied, assuming her reasons for being evasive may also be tied to his last visit to the house where, in a rare drunken stupor, he took off his pants and knocked on their neighbor's door, asking to borrow "as many fucking eggs as you have available". Carrie was not amused.

248

"Let me run and grab the beers, I'll be right back," Chris said, sprinting up towards the house.

Stephen watched him traverse the dew-soaked grass in his moccasins then pull them off on the concrete porch, a move offered out of courtesy as much as self-preservation.

"What's my daddy getting you? Hannah asked.

"He's getting me some beer. Very special yummy beers that you're not allowed to drink until you're forty years old," Stephen answered.

"You can have beer when you're twenty-one, " Ethan asserted, his hands on the sides of his Spider Man pajamas.

"Well, that may be the law, sure, but like I said these are special beers, aaaannd you guys are little troublemakers so you need to wait until you're forty. Uncle Stevie rule!" Stephen exclaimed.

"Mommy makes the rules at our house," Morgan chimed in.

"A truer statement has never been uttered, my tiny friend," Stephen said.

"Cows haver udd-uhs!" Morgan yelled back.

"Another very accurate statement, and there certainly are a lot of cows around here. I can smell them, can you?" Stephen asked the kids, they nodding their heads in unison. "They don't smell as bad as you guys do though, peeeeee uuuuuuuuuu."

Stephen grabbed his nose and began waving his hand in front of his face, pretending to push away unpleasant odors, sending the kids into a fit. They laughed for a few moments and then Ethan saw a squirrel chasing another into a pine tree in the yard and he tore off after them, the two girls following. They dashed around, yelling too loudly for a Saturday morning, oblivious to hungover neighbors or sleeping babies as they savored their frolic in PJ's.

He watched them playing, dancing around like gypsies one moment, then standing motionless the next, envious of their lack of structure and purpose. They had no agenda or plan, only boundless energy and an infinite landscape and time-in their minds-to expend it.

Hannah circled around her older brother, watching him and mimicking some of his gestures as Morgan rolled in the grass singing a song. Each would complete a series of playful movements and then-having lost interest-would move onto something else chosen at random. Then, collectively, for a moment, they'd unify in a common goal to roll a hula hoop across the wet lawn, only to abandon that plan and go their separate ways once again.

Stephen leaned back against the car and thought about Heather as he watched the kids jump, tumble and roll in youthful bliss. She made no secret that she loved children and embodied anything and everything one could hope for in a parent. She was kind, compassionate, honest, patient, affectionate and had a youthful soul while still being responsible. Her demeanor was pleasant, soft and approachable yet she could be firm and tough as needed. He watched her interact with a young girl outside an ice cream shop one afternoon, the little girl's scoop of chocolate rolling away down the side of her sugar cone. Heather saved it with a spoon she grabbed from the counter and then, crouched down next to her, recalled stories of her own ice cream mishaps while the tiny brunette stared at her, wide eyed and enamored. Some folks without children were, "Hey, you're really good with kids", while Heather was never questioned by parents that didn't know her-it was always just assumed she was a mom. Children are infallible seismographs-revealing the slightest hint of patronization by others to their parents in an unspoken language-though Heather never tripped the gauges.

Chris appeared in the front doorway, saying something back into the house, then pulling the blue front door closed and slipping his moccasins back on. He was carrying a yellow plastic bag, drooping in the middle, and resting inches above the top of the grass as he walked back down towards the street where Stephen stood against his car.

"OK buddy, here you go. Six of the best IPA's around, which, obviously, you already know," Chris said, handing the bag to him.

250

"You're the best, man. I appreciate it. I have ten or so left at my place which I'll definitely hook you up with when I find my way back there."

"Oh stop, you've given me plenty. You turned me on to this place anyway. I'd still be drinking that fifteen bucks a case swill if you hadn't brought some of these by last year."

Stephen grinned, then looked back over at the kids who were now all climbing on a backyard playset.

"Thanks again, and I'll be in touch soon. Going to be out of the office a bit, which you may have guessed, but I promise we'll talk more."

"Hey, are you going to be OK? I mean, straight up, you going to be alright? I'm worried that you're ducking everyone and everything a little, gotta be honest. Guy I know is a fucking tornado of charisma but he doesn't want to sit down with Matt Lauer or one of those guys and brag a little? What's going on there, buddy?"

Stephen walked around to the rear of the car and placed the beers in the trunk, then slammed down the lid with a solid *thhwunk*.

"You know, I didn't expect to wake up one day with the world, or part of it anyway, giving a shit about me," Stephen said, leaning back against the side of his car again. "I understand what happened, I'm thrilled that it did and those girls were saved-of course I am-but..."

Chris nodded his head, looking Stephen right in the eye and spoke. "Hey man, you do whatever it is that you have to. I can't even imagine the pressure and insanity that would accompany this situation, I get it. I love you, you know that, but at the end of the day I'm just as dumb as the next guy asking, 'So when is this guy going to fucking say something', ya know?" Chris replied, followed by wild, abrupt laughter-a trait Stephen had grown fond of the longer he knew him.

"You know me, I like to isolate sometimes, but never stay hidden forever so, it won't be long."

"Eh, just ignore me. I got so shitfaced last night I can't believe I'm even forming coherent sentences."

The both snort-laughed and then Chris looked back over his shoulder after hearing a pop from behind him. "Ethan, put that stick down," he yelled towards the kids, cupping his hands around his mouth. "I've told you not to whack sticks against the shed, now stop it."

"I'll tell you what, they might be rambunctious little stick wielding maniacs but you've some great kids. I'm not very fond of you but, the kids are epic," Stephen said, eliciting a chortle from Chris.

"Make sure you text me your new number, asshole, and drive safe in that German death sled. Holy crap, I'm still scrubbing skid marks out of my boxers from that ride to lunch the day you got it," Chris said, leaning in for a hug.

"I'm sorry your sphincter is set to Minivan," Stephen retorted.

Chris looked back at his bubble-like people mover parked in the driveway. "You know, I really did turn in my balls when I bought that thing. It drives nice and the kids love it, but-hey, does BMW make a Minivan?"

Stephen lowered his eyes as if he was peering over the top of reading glasses. "I'm going to pretend you never said that and hug you goodbye, shithead."

"Oh, you stop out at Willie's yet? I know they'd love to see you. The big guy was asking about you," Chris asked.

Stephen looked over the kids playing again. "No, not yet, but I suppose I'll have to soon. Shit, Willie's the reason this thing really got rolling, from what I hear."

"You know, I said that to him and I figure he's the type of guy who'd eat up the limelight whenever he can but he says, 'all I did was find a piece of paper'. He's been on TV quite a bit though so I'm sure they're paying him a few bucks. Maybe he can finally afford to paint the place," Chris said, looking back at the front door of the house.

"Indeed."

252

Chris opened his arms and latched onto Stephen and squeezed. "I love you buddy, and I'm so glad to see you. I'm sorry about Carrie, she's just-"

"Hey, don't, it's OK. You have a great woman, a great wife there. One of the most doting moms I've ever seen," Stephen interrupted, still wound up tight in the embrace. "She isn't wrong about her issues with me anyway, so, let her do her thing."

Chris let go, stepped back and looked over at his children, still playing in the yard behind him. "If it's any consolation, she thinks that video you posted on Twitter a few months back where you're having a conversation with a potato was hysterical."

"Well it was. I live under no illusions that I'm not a genius."

Chris grinned ear to ear, then patted him on the chest a couple times before calling out to his kids. "Guys, Steve is leaving so get over here and say goodbye."

The three of them froze where they stood for a second, then, franticly and at full volume, jetted back towards the front of the house, all stopping as though they hit an invisible gate, four feet from where Stephen rested against the car.

"OK, so Uncle Stevie's on a tight schedule here," he explained, moving his head from left to right and then back as he addressed the wide-eyed children. "As much as I'd like to hug all of you I think I only have time enough to hug one of you. So, I can either choose one of you little doinkers and give you a super awesome hug, ooooorrrrr, I can try to hug all three of you at once, but maybe drop one because it will be super heavy."

"You coulda just hugged all of us one at a time by now, duh," Hannah said, looking up at him and tilting her head.

"Oh yeah, smartie? Well now I **am** going to hug all of you and you're the one getting dropped," he replied, raising his voice at the end and grabbing all three of them as one. They squealed and squirmed and giggled as he picked them all up and lifted them off the ground and spun them around in two circles before softly placing them down in the grass. As Hannah came to rest, Stephen nudged her and she fell to her knees. "Oops, my bad!"

Hannah got up and curled her mouth in, trying not to laugh, even as her siblings and father were giggling around her.

"Alright kids, gotta go. It was great seeing you and I'll see you again soon. Make sure you behave for mom and dad or they'll sell you on *Ebay*, don't forget that," Stephen told the kids.

"No sir," Ethan exclaimed. "You said that last time you were here anyway."

"Wowzers, dude. Your kids are already knocking me for recycling my stuff. Tough crowd," Stephen said to Chris.

Chris reached over and hugged him one more time. "Drive safely buddy, OK. Call me if you need anything and I'll see you soon."

Stephen walked around to the driver's side of the car and rested his forearms on the roof, smiling over at the four of them, the two girls holding each other's hands.

"You're the best looking bunch of goobers I've ever seen. Have a fun day, guys," he said, before opening his car door and stepping in. As he sat in the cabin, he grabbed his phone and texted Chris with his new number, adding the note:

*<Everyone wants to 'live the dream' but some don't realize they already are. Love the whole bunch of you. Talk soon>*

He watched the four of them wave from the grass as he started the car and pulled it into the neighbors across the street, then backed out and headed in the other direction. He dropped the car in neutral for a moment, revving the engine to seven thousand RPM, sending the kids hopping up and down, he observed from the side mirror. He thumbed the button on the shifter and eased the car back into drive, then made his way out to the back roads that would take him to the Interstate and deep into Pennsylvania.

# Chapter 25

*The* drive into Pennsylvania took less time than anticipated, and so far, there were only two pee breaks. As he made his way across Route 80, almost an hour past Scranton, he began thinking about the girls that were freed. How they might be assimilating back into lives long stolen from them, the reactions of their families, the barrage of media clamoring for their story and interviews with their parents, the confusion and fears that would continue long into adulthood. He was resisting listening to the radio, logging into his Twitter account, turning on a television-even avoided going to his apartment-for his own self-interests. There was no harrowing tale to recall, other than his attack, and those pictures hadn't been completely painted yet. The girls, twenty-five of them, were trying to make sense of their lives-life itself-and how what they endured was even plausible never mind a reality they existed in for weeks, months or even years. Some may be unable to sleep, crying without provocation, afraid to turn the lights off while Stephen was driving his BMW on curved roads to go drink some of the world's best beers in a warm, safe place. He'd long been an advocate of the perspective argument-always positioning yourself in place of humility when self-pity crept it-but this elevated the concept to another stratosphere. How could someone ever complain about a bitter four-dollar coffee when there were little children being locked in cages?

Rain began to fall, and the roads were biting back at some of the throttle inputs Stephen gave the car, though the steering and suspension behaved impeccably. Each pitch and angle the road offered against the shocks created resistance that communicated perfectly where his hands needed to move-guiding the wheel, facilitating a steady line. The speed rose and fell as the turns opened and closed in the road and the eight-speed transmission blended the engine revs with road speed precisely, careful to factor the limits of adhesion in the slick conditions.

Up ahead about an eighth of a mile on the right he noticed a Convenience store, "Delray Deli & News". He decided to stop for one last pee break and a bottle of water, and confirm the last part of the directions, which the GPS was struggling with. He slowed the car and pulled in, easing up next to the side of the building and away from the two other cars and pick-up truck that were out front.

As he turned the car off and leaned forward to grab his wallet from the cubby space, he saw the corner of *The Alexander Circus* peeking out from underneath the front seat. Forgetting he grabbed it before leaving Heather's place, and where he left off before his world went dark, he picked it up and began thumbing through some of it, landing on a passage about fifty pages deep:

*Thirteen-year old's who look like fast food clowns and have Heavy Metal band patches on their denim jacket don't get laid. Even the girls that go to the shows where those bands play, they don't fuck those guys. Stephen was old enough at nearly fourteen to source his own haircut, though for some reason still allowed his mother to do it even though she was cockblocking him with the bright red nerd-fro. When your best friend is a kid that collects calculators, has asthma and a lisp, but he has girlfriend and you don't, you begin to question everything.*

The ends of Stephen's mouth curled upward, thinking back to a time when, wearing a similar outfit at twelve years old, a neighbor's little brother, no more than eight, came over to their yard and asked him if he could have five dollars. He said no, and the little kid punched him square in the stomach, causing him to keel over. The kid then pushed Stephen to the ground and said, "You're a dork", before laughing maniacally, which was echoed by three kids standing on the sidewalk who'd witnessed the event.

"You were right, kid. I am a dork," he said, before getting out of the car and hustling inside.

<#>

As the BMW made its way out of a long sweeping turn in the final stretch out to Sheriff McCabe's place, Stephen noticed a rolling field bordered in stone walls and swaying, rain-soaked trees. In the back-right corner of the pasture was an old farm house, red and white and dilapidated, just as the sheriff had described in his text. A few hundred feet down the road he saw a dirt driveway that lead out to the house, so he stepped onto the brake and slowed to make the turn.

The driveway was soaked and muddy, filled with potholes and bumps, so he decelerated the car and was careful to keep the nose from digging in. The sport sedan was great for traversing smooth asphalt at high speeds and dissecting abrupt turns in the road but failed miserably at rugged off-roading, with its low ride height. The suspension did its best to be kind but kicked, screamed and twitched with violence as he made his way up the hill towards the house in the field. He got as close as he could, parking out against one of the many stone walls. Up closer to the house he saw a Grand Marquis parked in an open carport and assumed it was the Sheriff's, confirming he was in the right place.

Steven turned off the car, grabbed his iPhone and went around back to grab the beers in the trunk. The rain had lessened, but he tucked the phone into his jacket pocket and pulled the hood up around his head, making his way up the dirt driveway that bent to the right and lead to the house. Before heading there, he kept straight along the wall and up over a small hill. The path angled left, and behind the stone wall-which also turned-was another large field along with a line of trees. In the distance, he saw a gap in the wall that led into the surrounding woods.

As he walked up into the other field he surveyed the area, lined with hundreds of trees, many barren, as winter still held firm. There were several green pines and birch mixed in, adding color to an

257

otherwise bland picture. In the upper right corner, resting alone and just beneath some overhanging branches was a small red shed, maybe 15 x 15 and in a state of disrepair much like the home at the bottom of the hill. For no reason beyond curiosity, he made his away across the saturated grass and over to it.

The door of the shed was cracked open so he pulled it forward and leaned his head inside. It was empty except for some dried grass and leaves on the wood floor, likely blown in through the two broken windows in the front of it. There were a couple hooks and a makeshift shelf on the back wall and a vague odor of old leather and burning leaves permeated the air. He made his way inside to take a deeper look.

In the right corner, on the floor, was a pile of about fifteen cigarette butts in a rusted metal plate. A couple looked recent but they could've been there for twenty years for all he knew. The walls, save for the hooks and shelf, were barren and worn. The roof had some tiny holes in it and some of the rain leaked down through and dripped onto the floor as he watched. Considering how old the shed likely was, it was miraculous it wasn't leaking worse that it was.

The windows had small shards of glass left in them, so he peered out into the field from inside, careful to not lean in too close. He watched as the landscape shifted and the air became discolored as the rain began to hammer the wet ground while it danced on the roof above, sounding like tiny stones poured across a cardboard box. He wished he had a cigarette, which was abnormal as he smoked only after having too many beers, which was infrequent. Maybe it was the residual smell of nicotine and ash that clung to the worn boards inside or an anxious mind. Regardless of origin, his desire to smoke was trumped only by his need to take a leak, so he wandered outside and unzipped right against the stone wall behind the shed. The overhanging branches provided decent cover but he was still getting wet.

He finished up, then started walking down the hill towards the house, and in the distance a figure emerged from behind a tree in the yard. He presumed it was the Sheriff, as the description of the property was spot on and the man coming towards him didn't look at all alarmed that another man was wandering around his yard.

"That how you Connecticut folks do it? Take a piss in someone's back yard before even saying hello," the man in the hat shouted up towards him.

Stephen smiled, walking in his direction, the bag of beers swinging with his momentum. "You don't need an animal like me using indoor plumbing. Best that I keep it outside," Stephen yelled back.

The man kept coming towards him, glancing over at his car.

Stephen watched him approach, about six feet of him in all, wearing jeans and a button up denim shirt along with a light brown Campaign hat. His hair was salty gray and as he got closer he noticed he resembled a younger Sean Connery, minus the beard.

"Sheriff Chuck McCabe, I presume?" Stephen asked, closing in on forty feet away from the man.

"You found 'em. Would know who you were just from all the pictures lately. Plus, not too many people pull into this place by chance. Have been told it's a little creepy," the Sheriff replied.

"Here? Oh, hell no. Love it. Especially on a day like this, with the rain," Stephen said, offering his hand out towards the Sheriff as he closed in on him. "Stephen Alexander. Pleasure to meet you, Sheriff."

The Sheriff shook his hand and smiled. "Hey, let's get you out of the rain here. I'm assuming that bag has some of those beers we discussed?"

"It does. Some of the best in the nation, as far as I'm concerned," Stephen answered. "You a big beer guy, Sheriff?"

"Please, call me Chuck, really. As for beer, I always had a taste for it but it wasn't until I met this woman whose son is a homebrewer and he gave me a bottle of this stuff-looked like orange juice, smelled like a pineapple-and just tasted like nothing I'd ever tried. He gave me a couple bottles of it, then some big cans from some Brewery in Vermont and, well; never knew beer could taste like that. Course I've been drinking whatever shit they've had on tap here and there for forty years.

Stephen chuckled, then stretched his arms out from his body several inches to maintain his balance on the slippery rocks leading up to the Sheriff's house. The home sat at an odd angle in relation to the street, with the front facing towards the back and the side almost parallel to the road. The red paint was dull and worn, chipping away all over, as well as its white trim. Other than the hundreds of trees and dense vegetation that bordered the property, there was no landscaping or flowers to speak of and the only color other than the home's paint and the abundant green was the tie-dyed metal sun ornament that hung next to the rear door the Sheriff was leading him to.

"That's an interesting piece," Stephen said, nodding his head up towards the colorful decoration next to the door as the Sheriff looked back at him.

"Ahh yes, the Hippie Sun as a friend called her once. One of the last remaining pieces of a failed marriage. Best thing she ever gave me, other than a cat who died awhile back," the Sheriff replied.

Stephen followed him in as he opened the door and walked inside, the doorway leading to a small mud room where several coats hung as well as another large hat. The Sheriff removed the one he was wearing, placing it on an empty hook. "Make yourself comfortable in the living room off to the right there, and if you want to hand me those beers I'll put a couple in glasses and the others in the fridge."

"Sounds great," Stephen said, handing him the bag. "You want me to take my shoes off? I wiped them pretty-"

"Oh God, no. I keep the place tidy but I'm not a lunatic. If they're dry then don't worry about it. Just go relax," the Sheriff interrupted.

Stephen watched him walk into the small kitchen, devoid of any decorative flair and awash in off-white colors and a natural wood table with four chairs in the middle of the floor. He turned and made his way through the arched wall and into the living room where the lack of enthusiasm theme continued.

On the wall behind the couch, Stephen noticed the Grand Canyon painting. It was too large for the space and out of place in such a drab environment, but the color at least brightened things up. In the corner, he noticed the acoustic guitar and went over and knelt in front of it. There was a fine layer of dust on the neck and body, but otherwise looked pristine. Stephen struggled with the six-string on and off for years, always failing to have that "ah ha" moment where weeks of study, practice and focus translated into a full understanding of the instrument or even a lick played with any fluidity or poise.

"You play at all," Chuck asked, walking into the room holding two small soda glasses filled with a honey colored, thick beverage.

"I don't know if you can call what I do 'playing' but I've had some time with the guitar. Never felt right in my hands, but I'm a music junkie so, always wished it had," Stephen answered.

"You have a favorite player? Or is that another of your 'Top Five' deals you mentioned?"

"Oh man, Chuck, I don't know. I've said for years now it was Stevie Ray Vaughan, and probably still is, but as the years pass I start leaning towards David Gilmour from Pink Floyd. The way he communicates with those freaking bends, such perfect intonation. Part of it likely owed to the fact I've seen Dave play several times and never got to see Stevie, though."

"I saw Stevie Ray, one time, down in Austin a long, long time ago, when he was first coming up. You could see he'd be one of the greats, watching him for five minutes. Scared the fuck out of everyone else there that day. But I agree about Gilmour, truly an artist with those hands. Never flashy but makes you wanna cry. Good deal."

"Wow," Stephen said, finding a place on the side of the couch and sitting, "Don't think I'd have ever figured you for a Floyd or Gilmour fan."

"You wouldn't be the first," the Sheriff replied, placing one of the beers down in front of Stephen on the coffee table, then sitting in the recliner ten feet away. "Most folks figure me for a Merle Haggard and Glen Campbell kinda guy, who, by the way, was a great guitar player as well."

"I agree. Fucking shame what happened to the poor guy's mind, though."

The Sheriff took a long, slow sip of the hazy, yellow-orange beer. "Holy shit, kid. You weren't kidding. Where did you say this was from? Oh, it's right on the can, dumbass. *Tree House.* Huh, I never made anything like this in my treehouse. Incredible."

"That's 'Julius', which is arguably their best. The guy Nate that brews these things is like the Gilmour of beer," Stephen suggested, getting a laugh from Chuck.

"I'm sure Tyler-the kid who I mentioned homebrews-has heard of these folks. I'll have to reach out to him and see what he thinks."

"I'd be shocked if he hasn't. They're killing it. Awesome folks, too."

Chuck took another long pull from the glass, then placed it down on a coaster resting on the chocolate wood table between the recliner and the couch. "So, Stephen, before I get on those Club Sandwiches-which are their own form of artistry-tell me why the long drive out this way. Everything alright, or just looking for an ear that shared in this experience of yours?"

Stephen picked up the glass of beer and took his own long, savored sip. "Never gets old, tasting this stuff." He put the glass down and nodded his head a few times before Chuck chimed back in.

"I hope that didn't sound harsh or abrupt-I mean you're welcome here any time, especially if you keep bringing this nectar-just wondering why you'd drive all the way out here to see me when half the world is hoping you'll talk to them instead," Chuck asked.

"No, not at all. I guess it was sort of random but I suppose after you reached out to me it felt like you may be a safe place to sort some of this shit out. Hell, you've got to be dealing with it yourself, no?"

"Which part are you referring to? The incessant phone calls? Lack of sleep? Nightmares? The doubts, second guessing or the overwhelming urge to move to the mountains and never come back?"

Stephen smiled and took another sip. "Well, I haven't had enough time to assimilate back into day to day living but I'm sure the nightmares are coming. The rest is already there, however."

"Listen, there's no way you could've prepared for something like this, kid, nobody could. With me, as fucked up as that whole situation became, at least I had the experience of seeing the worst of humanity and the darkness around corners. You walked into danger to save a little kid without a paycheck or the benefit of training. That takes guts."

"I don't know if it was guts or a reaction that I can't guarantee would be there every time. It may have just been a fluke, an anomaly."

"So, what? Is that what you're going to do, beat yourself up because it *might* not have happened if it was a different day, a different location, in the dark-whatever? Who gives a shit. You did it. That's the only story here."

"It's not that it's lost on me how this all developed and what the result was-I get that-I really do. I'm intensely grateful these girls were found and that I played a part but, you did the *real* work. The dirty work. You're the hero here, I'm just the one that pointed to the battlefield, you marched into war."

"Well, first, I don't think you can call it a war, as there was only one adversary and I had no idea what I was even looking for when I got there. Secondly, I had a weapon on me and backup at my disposal. Why are you so intent on deflecting, to pass it off to someone else? You're obviously forgoing a lot of money to sit down and talk about it-something that would be hard for most to pass up-yet it seems that's your plan, at least for now. Why?"

Stephen looked over at the guitar sitting on the stand. He recalled the time his sister Jessica took it up for several months as a late teenager and wrote a song called "Boys Are Dumb", which had two chords and only a verse of the same name. She eventually moved on to Piano and became quite proficient. By all indications, she still felt that boys were dumb, however.

"Do *you* want attention for this, Chuck? Excuse me if I'm getting too personal here but, have you given any interviews about it or do you plan to?" Stephen asked.

"Son, I've changed all my numbers and pulled the damn cord out of the wall. The last fucking thing I want to do is sit down with some chucklehead on TV and recount everything which was only me doing my job. In saying that, I don't begrudge anyone who had a similar experience speaking about it-whether in law enforcement or not-but for me it's just not who I am. I'm human and, sure, money is always tempting but I wouldn't feel right being paid to discuss the time I unhooked a Beagle from a chain link fence while on the job no more or no less than what happened out at that farm. That doesn't answer my question about you, however."

Stephen reached for the beer, took a quick sip and placed it back on the table before adjusting his position and leaning up against the side of the couch, facing the Sheriff.

"I feel embarrassed I suppose," Stephen exclaimed after a long pause.

"Shit kid, what the hell do you have to be embarrassed about? You charged into danger, saved a little kid, then set off a fuse that led to something almost unimaginable. I was there when that door opened. I watched those little girls led from their enclosures and brought outside-confused and terrified, gaunt and vacant-and as harrowing a moment as it was I knew that what it meant was that families who had their kids stolen from them would see their babies again.

Embarrassed? Be humble, sure. Be respectful, absolutely. But don't be embarrassed, son."

Stephen took the last sip of the *Julius* and held the empty glass in his hand, looking down into it, remembering the night in the hospital when he saw the video footage of the girls being released. The discussion among the panel of guests. The dozens of people that lined the halls of the hospital at his release and then stood outside his mother's place with signs.

"People are looking for me to be something I'm not. Maybe I distract them from what's going on in their lives or the country right now and it helps them feel unified-I get it. The thing is, it doesn't matter what their reasons are because the man they're looking at isn't worthy of their attention. I'm glad I did what I did-like I said-wouldn't take it back, but I don't need the world peering down into my soul, seeking answers or understanding. I have nothing to offer."

Chuck looked over at Stephen, nodding several times, then tipped back the glass of beer and took a sip before returning to the arm of his chair, fingers wrapped snug around the glass.

"So, what we're talking about here then *is* embarrassment, just not for the reasons I assumed. You steal something that day at the restaurant? On parole? Cheating on your wife? What is it?" the Sheriff asked, noticing a shift in Stephen's posture when he mentioned the wife.

Stephen fidgeted on the couch, then leaned back, stretching his arms over his body. "I'm not married. I couldn't be cheating-eh, it doesn't matter. Isn't it alright to not want people digging into your life, your business, without it meaning you're covered in dirt?"

"Well of course it is, and I feel the same way, but that's not why you're uncomfortable."

*...for a man that does a fair amount of lying...*

"Oh what, you're going to put me through the human lie detector bullshit you cops do now?"

"I don't think we need to sit in a room with my hands on your wrists, lock in stare with you, to figure out that you're distressed about all this for more than losing your anonymity. You didn't drive all the way up here for my Turkey Club and to give away beers. I'm no Priest but I've heard my share of confessionals, so, what is it that you need to say, Stephen?"

*A searching and fearless moral inventory.*

"Chuck, hey, if you're looking for a *Good Will Hunting* moment you've got the wrong guy, and I'm dumb as shit when it comes to math anyway," Stephen said in jest, fidgeting on the couch again.

"Levity will only further my suspicions," Chuck shot back.

"Just because I'm uncomfortable living under a microscope doesn't make me a criminal. It's a lot to be saddled with and I'm working my way through it, mentally and physically. You seem like a reasonable man, I'm sure you can understand that," Stephen said, his volume rising.

The Sheriff observed his growing discomfort and contemplated backing off but decided to keep pushing, leaning forward in his recliner.

"Reason is what's telling me to not let up here, son. First cop I ever knew, I was twelve years old, told me that 'everyone wants to tell you their story, especially when it's ugly' and he was dead on. Can't tell you how many times I've sat in a room and listened to men-and women-play tough and tighten up when they first walk in, then two hours later they've told you about every red light they ran and nickel they stole. I'm-"

"I'm not a fucking criminal I told you," Stephen interjected, leaning forward.

"And I'm not accusing you of anything unlawful here but the wisdom that cop shared with me applies to everyone; it's not exclusive to crooks. People want to unload their baggage, it's human nature.

Now you can continue to keep up this cat and mouse bullshit or you can tell me what's going on," the Sheriff replied.

*If you want to keep feeling like you're feeling, just keep doing what you're doing.*

Henry would repeat those words to Stephen hundreds of times from adolescence to shortly before he died. So simple in construct and meaning, yet so complex in its application.

Stephen downed the last sip of beer in the glass, then made his way to the kitchen. "I'm opening another can, you want one?"

"Absolutely," Chuck replied. "Why don't you take that bacon out of the fridge and set it out on the counter as well. At this rate, I'm going to need some food right quick."

Stephen found the package of Maple smoked bacon and laid it on the counter, then grabbed two more cans of the IPA's he brought and placed them down onto the coffee table in front of him before sitting back on the couch. He cracked open each one, producing a quick *Shnick-pfff* as they met the air outside their can. He poured two thirds of the can into his empty glass, then reached over and filled the Sheriff's, who had stretched his arm out towards him with his half-full glass.

For a minute or two, both men sat there and sipped the hoppy beers, saying nothing. The only sound either heard was the boiler in the basement that kicked on as the temperature fell and Chuck's index finger and thumb clicking against each other.

"My old man was a tyrant of truth," Stephen said, after lengthy silence. "Fucking guy abhorred anything bullshit, whether it was someone telling a story, a guy trying to score a chick, someone trying to save their ass after a mistake-hated lawyers and politicians, obviously-anything that wasn't genuine. Mostly he loathed the lies people told themselves because they destroyed the one telling the lie and those around them. Can't say I ever disagreed with him on that, though we certainly had our share of battles about when or if I was guilty of doing it. Guy was a drunk-alcoholic from the time he was a

267

teenager-admittedly told more lies than any politician on Earth for a good twenty-year stretch, but when he got sober he went on this crusade of truth. I'd get pissed off that he'd try and nail my ass to the wall bullshitting him about something, call him a hypocrite for all his years of far worse, and his response was always, 'What does that have to do with you?'-a 'Do as I say, not as I do' kinda thing," Stephen said, then downing a sip of his beer.

"He had a brutal fucking childhood, sinister alcoholic father, violence, all the shit nobody wants to imagine, and I understood why his disease made him have to lie for so long and why 'truth' would become so important but, it still used to piss me off because he was never wrong. He always knew. Guy should have been a cop himself, but, he was half hippie really, so, never would have worked," Stephen explained.

"Not as uncommon a pairing as you'd imagine, Chuck countered. "When did he die?"

"On Christmas day, three and a half years back now. Heart gave out."

"Jesus, Stephen, I'm sorry."

"Thanks," he said, rubbing the inside of his left hand with the thumb of his right. "Shitty day to lose anyone, never mind your old man, but, as much as his truth bullshit used to get under my skin I do miss talking to him. Smartest guy I've ever known and always found a way to get my ass back on course whenever I ran askew. My teenage years could have been brutal if he hadn't set me straight on some things. One particular day, he sorta mapped out a plan to keep my life from becoming unbearable, essentially building a roadmap for it. Simple yet brilliant, though I've driven way outside the lines for years now."

Stephen felt a melancholy wave pool up behind his eyes so he reached for his beer and took a long, measured sip.

"I can't say I ever had the same relationship with my old man, and I don't have any kids but, I envy love like that. Considering where he came from, as you mentioned, it's wonderful-if not fortuitous-that you had the relationship you did. Could have gone a different way."

Stephen kept his lips pressed firm against the glass in his hand, staving off an emotional flood as he thought about his father, steering his mind to neighboring pains.

Chuck saw that Stephen was stuck in a turbulent moment so he stood up and headed towards the kitchen. "Hey, I'm going to get this food started so-"

"Hang on a sec," Stephen interrupted.

"What's that?" Chuck replied, standing in the doorway.

"Come back."

Chuck made his way back to the recliner and sat.

Stephen's eyes were red and filled at the bottom with tears, Chuck noticed, as he pulled the beer glass away from his face. He left it about four inches away, calculating where he was willing to let this conversation travel, terrified of crossing the precipice. He nudged the bridge of his nose against the pint glass several times, plotted a course, then started speaking again.

"I'm not a criminal but I'm definitely guilty. Guilty of things I don't know if I'm ready to talk about yet-or that I won't be able to without coming apart," Stephen spoke, the words shaky and wavering as they fought through tears. "This whole damn thing, these girls, this entire fucked up situation is just this massive ironic clusterfuck."

"What do you mean?" Chuck asked, leaning forward in the chair and looking straight at Stephen as he wiped away moisture from his eyes and cheeks with his sleeve.

"I've been trying to sort out why-like the rest of you I guess-why this has been so hard for me to talk about. Why I can't embrace that I did something good that resulted in those girls being found but, I have an idea...been lying to myself again. The only benefit in not having a relationship with my father anymore is that there's no one to call me on my bullshit, but it was he that told me, not long before he died, that I had to be the one that did that anyway. That I couldn't just

269

wait for him to be the barometer, the checks and balances. I had to be honest not because I was coerced but because *it was the right thing to do*. Of course, he was fucking right, he was always right."

Chuck watched as Stephen fought back more tears, then went into the bathroom and grabbed a roll of toilet paper, placing it down in front of him when he returned. Stephen tore a few sheets off and wiped his eyes and then balled up the paper and tossed it on the coffee table.

"OK, so you're still not telling me *what* we're talking about here?"

Stephen took a breath and leaned back against the rear of the couch as he exhaled.

"I saved that little girl, Chuck, I did. I saved this little girl that wasn't even maybe ten years old that, in another ten years or so, I'd be staring at in the mall like some creepy fuck while she's with her friends. I helped set her free but ten years from now I won't be any better than the asshole that was trying to take her," Stephen said.

"Wait, whoa, what the fuck are you talking about?" Chuck questioned.

"For so long now, years, I haven't shown a woman any real respect. I've been a womanizing, misogynistic prick that took who and what he wanted and never cared about the fallout or what that must have felt like on their end. The only difference between me and a sociopath is that I did feel guilt-sometimes it would sideline me for a couple weeks here and there-but I always drowned it out by hopping into another bed. I was just like my old man, except he had the excuse of alcohol, but I was stone sober and I remember everything. I watched those girls come out of those cages and I know all that I *should* have been thinking about was how incredible it was that they'd see their family again but what occurred to me was that I've basically been doing the same thing. Imprisoning these women, dozens and dozens of them for almost ten years now with my bullshit, knowing full well that I'm never sticking around, using them for my own amusement like that twisted fuck was."

"Hey, Stephen wait a second here. Christ, I thought at first you were going to tell me you were connected to this asshole somehow or that you raped someone or-"

"No, nothing like that, but it's still..."

"Wait, hang on. I'll let you keep unloading but, unless you're also going to tell me that you abused these women or stole from them-something, then you've no business putting yourself anywhere near that scumbag. The two of you are light years apart," Chuck interrupted.

Stephen downed a sip of beer and continued. "I never laid a hand on a woman in anger. I never brutalized one with words. I never held one against their will or anything of the sort, but what I did was worse-I gave them hope. I lured them in knowing full well I'd never stay though I did everything in my power to suggest that I would. The day of the attack I was in a motel with the greatest woman I've ever known, yet cheating on another one that never did a fucking thing wrong to me."

Chuck looked at Stephen, perplexed. "Kid, wait a second, seriously. You're telling me that what's got you all twisted in knots in this thing is because you're a womanizer? You lied to women to get in their pants and so you're making the leap that you're as evil as the prick in that cellar? I have to say, frankly, I'm still confused."

"Women have never served a purpose to me other than for my own gratification, my own pleasure. I watch them move through my eye line a hundred times a day, watching the way the curve of their ass travels in their jeans or how long their eyes stay connected to mine. I judge their size, their shape, the way they smile or don't, the tone they use talking on their phone, the way they're dressed. Not the same as one might do with the population at large-as I know we're all guilty of-but instead to formulate an opinion on what their *worth* is to me. Like some asshole looking at animals at a meat market, sizing each one up, determining which ones will most satisfy his palate.

271

I'm no better than that dead man. The women that have been in my life just didn't know they were in cages."

Chuck stared at Stephen for a few seconds as his message began to resonate. He then got back up and went into the kitchen and started making the food, leaving Stephen to work through his grief, which was audible from the other room. Chuck had seen men cry in the past, dozens of times, but it was most often a relative of an accident victim at the hospital or a Perp that realized they were being taken away, but this was something else. This was a moment where the content of one's character was being exposed and examined for the first time without a filter or any dilution. This type of self-examination could kill people.

Chuck finished making the sandwiches and went back into the living room, placing one down in front of Stephen on the coffee table. He was leaning back on the couch looking out the front window, his eyes bloodshot and glossy, and his left leg bouncing up and down at a furious pace.

"Why don't you have some food, OK?" Chuck suggested. "Emotional stuff like this will suck all the energy right out of you, and these potent beers sure as shit don't help."

Stephen remained as he was.

"I guess where I'm still having trouble here," Chuck continued, sitting back in his recliner. "Is figuring out why this incident-you making a brave move in the face of danger-has opened up this particular wound. I understand the parallels you're trying to draw, in a general sense, but why now? Why this?"

Stephen leaned forward, rubbing his hands over face. "I don't know, but I feel like a fucking phony. I used to think I was Holden Caufield but in truth I'm everything he despised."

"Listen kid, I don't know you anymore than I know the guy who sells me the paper in the morning at the convenience store but I feel like I can get a general sense about folks, just from talking to them. In your case I have the added benefit of knowing about a deed you did that was ballsy and selfless so I'm confident in making a basic assessment here. You're a Lothario, a womanizer, maybe a user-sure-not going to argue that based on what you told me, and certainly that's something you're going to need to deal with. However, the fact that it's causing you this much distress clearly demonstrates you understand how damaging this behavior has been to these women and to yourself. I don't know if you're a phony, you seem genuine to me, but yeah, that could all be bullshit too. This is stuff for you and a shrink. She'll probably start with your mother, then move on to dad and so on-real textbook shit-but if I'm being honest, I need to say that I still don't see how this history of yours makes you so unworthy of praise for what you did saving that kid? A guy that just robbed someone's house but then saves a dog trapped on an icy lake doesn't have his good deed negated for that past act, does he?"

Stephen reached for the sandwich, clamping down on the bread, making the wheat toast crunch and crumble in his hands, then taking a sizeable bite.

"Wow, you weren't kidding about this sandwich," he said, the words dulled by the mass of turkey, bacon and bread tumbling around his mouth. "Fucking fantastic."

"It's what I put in the mayo. A blend of garlic, fresh rosemary and a touch of celery powder. And that I slice the tomatoes really thin and layer them instead of slapping on a huge hunk of gooey mess."

Stephen continued devouring the first half, sending crumbs and bits of bacon onto the plate he was leaning over, some bouncing onto the floor. He reached for the other half, then pulled back, feeling the expansion of the beer and food in his gut. He leaned back on the couch, grabbing a few pieces of the toilet paper Chuck brought in to wipe his face.

"So, listen to me, alright? I hear what you're saying and I can imagine how it might jam you up in all this, feeling like a hypocrite and such as you said, but it's not evil, it's not unforgivable," Chuck suggested.

273

"So, if you had a daughter you'd be OK with me dating her then?" Stephen asked.

"Oh, hell no," he answered, after laughing. "I won't even let you speak to my neighbor Eleanor and she's in her late seventies, asshole. However, it still doesn't warrant a lifetime of self-loathing, especially if you stop."

"I don't think I've ever had a shortage of self-loathing, Chuck, that's pretty much a constant. This is more self-realization. Accepting that who and what I am has contributed to a lot of other's suffering, and my own. I'm just saying it out loud, finally."

"So then, yes, maybe it's time for you to do that. I'd imagine it helps you heal and become a better human being in the process, but as I keep telling you, this character flaw of yours doesn't negate what you've done and it doesn't have to define you. Son, I looked evil dead in the eye in that basement. There was anger and hatred in those eyes that you don't possess."

"Shit, here I am rambling on like an idiot about myself and you still have issues you're dealing with from all this. Stephen said, wiping his eyes on his sleeve. "So, if you don't mind me asking, what was it like down there anyway, face to face with this guy?"

Chuck thought for a moment about the way he was killed by Amber. The brutality and rage in her attack and how it satisfied some sort of basal instinct in him, watching the man savagely ripped at and killed, though part of him was still grateful it was someone else that performed the deed. He would always know it had been her, as would some very close to the case as well as Amber herself, but he would take that secret to the grave if he needed to and spare her the intrusion from others.

"It's going to resonate for the rest of my life, there's no question. It's not an event that one could ever wash away. Not saying yours will be either, but...this was ugliness and depravity that even my years on the job couldn't adequately prepare me for. The sick fuck, his odd habit of playing a running clip of a fake fireplace in the

274

background of the cellar where he kept some of the more recent-or favorite-girls I guess. The rooms connected to it, damp and cold and filled with every textbook creepy artifact one might imagine in a place like that, and those God damned shoes."

"Shoes?"

Chuck was shaking his head, leaning back and then crossing his arms. "Yes. The freak had this pile of shoes up on his porch, stacked in this symmetrical yet inexplicable pattern, but right out in the open, not hidden anywhere. As soon as I saw it gave me the heebie jeebies but, as the days have passed and I had some time to sit with it it's given me quite a stir. Knowing every pair of those shoes belongs, or belonged, to someone he snatched up. Some little girl that probably got them from her mother or father at the mall or on her birthday, and then taken off their feet and stacked like little trophies on this guy's porch while these little girls, fucking *children*, are locked in cages nearby. Those final words, 'My girls and their pretty feet', he says, fucking monster.

I've seen a lot of shit in my time, much of it ugly, but this was just something altogether different. I'm glad the prick is dead, let's just leave it at that."

Stephen watched the Sheriff finish the story, his eyes and face *there*, in that place, in that moment of discovery and experience. His head was sunken back down, fixed on his knees, and his arms remained folded as he remained entrenched in the memories.

"A lot of people are glad he's dead. You did the right thing and I can't imagine, or I'd hope you wouldn't, lose a wink of sleep over that. Sounds like the creepiest motherfucker on Earth."

Chuck nodded, then popped out of the place his thoughts held him captive. "You going to finish that other half or you want me to wrap it up for tomorrow?"

"Uh, man, it was so good but I don't think I can finish it right now," Stephen answered, startled by his abrupt rise from the chair.

"No worries," Chuck said, picking up the plate and taking it out to the kitchen. "These things, you'd think, being on toast and all, wouldn't keep so well for next day but I find if I pack them tight in foil, toss in the fridge overnight they are incredible the next day."

"Hey, thanks a lot. For listening, for sharing your part in all this and for the food, everything," Stephen said, getting up from the couch.

Chuck stopped in the doorway, holding both their plates. "Where the hell do you think you're going?"

"I've burned up enough of your time and I don't want-"

"If you think you're going to attempt to hightail it out of here after drinking those beers you're out of your skull. Plus, your mind isn't right to be driving to the corner never mind back to Connecticut. I have a guest bedroom and a couch, you take your pick," Chuck interrupted.

"Hey, I appreciate it, Chuck but-"

"Enough. You're staying here and if you want to scurry out at first light then feel free but not before then. Understand?"

He looked over at the Sheriff, holding the plates, wide eyed and strong willed, and then flopped back down onto the couch. "Fair enough, and thank you."

"Don't mention it, kid. Only fee for staying is that you leave one or two of those Hop bombs in my fridge when you go," Chuck said, putting the plates down and fishing out foil from a drawer to wrap Stephen's leftover half.

"All yours, of course," Stephen replied.

The rest of the evening the two men sat on the couch and chair, conversing about their fathers, music, their dysfunctional childhoods and danced around the other specifics of each of their roles in the freeing of the girls. Neither went too deep or revealed too much, content knowing their actions resulted in something astonishing while still leaving residual scars for each of them and those that were saved. Stephen recounted stories of some past relationships, attempting to offer some clarity to the murky picture he painted Chuck earlier,

276

though under any light it was still dark. He also shared selected excerpts from the book he was writing about his childhood, eliciting numerous belly laughs from them both. As the night sky filled with stars and the pauses between stories grew longer, Chuck got up and went to the hall closet to fetch a pillow and blankets.

"You might as well just sleep here. Couch is more comfortable than that lumpy fucking bed in there, and it smells better. Always had the odor of wet dog in that room, could never figure it out," Chuck said, tossing the blankets and pillow over at Stephen's side.

"Yeah that's fine. Thanks again, Chuck. I'm still surprised I made the trek out here spur of the moment like that and sorry if it freaked you out."

"Not at all, anytime. I like the sound of this Heather gal, so why don't the two of you find your way up here soon once you get your head and this other shit all sorted out. She sounds like a lifer, pal, so do the work and don't blow this one."

Stephen laughed, "She is a 'life-er' as you say, absolutely. Haven't been real straight with her, either though. Need to sort that out and..."

"It was good talking with you, Stephen, and I'm glad you came up. If I'm being honest-in all this talk about truth et cetera tonight-I do understand why this behavior with women has been eating up your insides because it's some selfish and devious shit, need to stop that garbage. But, I still feel like that's not the only reason you're anxious. Seem to recall you eluding earlier to other items you weren't ready to delve into and, by my own unscientific assertions, feels like you're living with some guilt that stretches beyond what you've shared."

Stephen looked away and down at the carpet as the Sheriff's gaze held firmly at him.

"We don't need to discuss it, and I don't assume it's something twisted or deplorable, but I think it exists. Call it instinct, call it whatever you want but I'm going to leave you alone to work through whatever it is. Sometimes those demons we let ride around on us are only exorcised by our own hands when we're good and God damn ready-talking it out just won't help. Anyway, you get some sleep and I'll see you in the morning."

Stephen slid off his shoes and stretched out on the couch, his feet coming up over the end. "It was a good night. Thanks for the hospitality and the ear."

Chuck nodded and made his way into his bedroom and closed the door. Stephen pulled the pillow from under the middle of his back and moved the blankets to the floor as the temperature was quite pleasant. He stared up at the ceiling, noticing a reflection of moonlight off a metal pole that held a flower basket outside, which bent the light and sent it inside and onto the popcorn ceiling above. He watched the light flex and contort as the leaves on the plant were blowing in the night air, interfering with the beam and distorting its form.

There were more conversations to be had and many miles to drive in the morning, but in the moment all Stephen saw was the swing carrying him across the moonlit water. His feet, as always, never touched as he swayed up and down through the long arc; the colossal, radiant moon just over his shoulder. He rode the pendulum back and forth, one hundred and eighty degrees in a perfect rhythm, forgetting about full bladders and embarrassing behavior. The haze of sleep slid over him as the swing continued its travels, gently pulling him down into slumber before Chuck's astute words of observation could begin to sabotage his placid journey.

## Chapter 26

"*There's* a great spot for coffee as you head back onto the main road. Tiny hole in the wall you'd drive right past a thousand times, called "Mirabelle's". She does Breakfast and lunch and the coffee is the finest you'll get in this part of the state," Chuck suggested, standing in his doorway.

Stephen turned back towards him, looking first at the peak of the roof over the kitchen where a Mockingbird had landed and was chirping with bravado.

"I'll stop and check it out, definitely. Thanks for the food," Stephen said, holding the wrapped half of sandwich is his left hand. "And the conversation and perspective, I appreciate it."

"You have some miles to travel, my friend, literally and figuratively as they say, but if I was a wagering man I'd put a fair amount on you getting yourself together. Whatever else is still nagging at you, hey, figure it out, right? This situation we found ourselves in could either be one that elevates us to a better understanding of ourselves and our place in the world or another piece of baggage weighing us down. I'm going for the former, myself...or at least I'm going to try. I haven't always been a man that's given the relationships in his life the respect they deserved, either. Cost me a marriage and beyond. Something for me to take a peek at, I suppose.

Maybe both of us are damaged goods, yet we somehow seem to find our way to doing right by others when it's needed most. That's gotta mean something."

"I hope so."

"Oh, and you know at some point, in addition to the hounds coming at both of us for their own selfish wants, the families of the girls-and the kids themselves eventually-are going to want or even need a part of us. It may be a thank you, questions, tears or just some kind of closure they seek that they hope we can provide them. Don't shut them out, Stephen. Not that I think you ever would, but, you know. Something else to think about putting in that book of yours, I suppose, when you're ready."

Stephen smiled, nodding over at him. "I understand, and I will. Can't imagine not putting some of all this on paper, too, so maybe that'll be what I'll do. Anyway, I want to say, 'You're a good man, Chuck' but feel like I'm Linus talking to Charlie."

Chuck snorted, then pointed over to Stephen's left hand. "Hey, well you know that sandwich you got there is a hell of a lot better than some blanket filled with snot."

"True. Take care of yourself, and thanks again. I'll be in touch soon."

"Good deal," Chuck said from the doorstop as Stephen walked out into the field where he'd parked his car. "Drive safely out there."

"Will do," he yelled back. "Oh, and maybe call that woman from the Doctor's office. I'm sure she'd like to hear from you."

Chuck grinned before turning back into the house, then back around again. "She's just a close friend, wonderful woman. Nothing this old queer from Georgia could do for her."

Stephen tilted his head to the left, smirking. "Well I'll be a son of a gun, Charlie. Look at you."

"You're not the only one better served by honesty. Could use a tune up in that department myself. Not getting any younger," he replied, before nodding his head and heading back into his house.

Stephen watched him close the door, then fished his phone from his pocket as he walked to his car, noticing a text from Heather and a missed call from an unknown number.

*<My body and soul ache now that you're not here :( Could really use some more of the body ache stuff soon ;)>*

His face warmed reading her words on the screen, and he tapped out a quick reply before jumping in the car.

*{The body aches are probably just psychosomatic. It's a lot to wake up to, remembering that I was inside you recently #Pukefest}*

As the car started and he drove off, he dialed back the unknown number, curious who may have his new digits already.

*"Agent Duplas,"* the voice said over the speakers, after five rings.

"FBI Agent Duplas?" Stephen asked.

*"That very one. Mr. Alexander?"*

"Yeah," he answered, wrinkling his brow wondering how the agent had his new number. "I just changed my phone number yesterday and have barely given it out. How the heck did you get it?"

*"Do you want me to tell you what color shirt you're wearing now too?"*

Stephen looked outside both door windows, instinctively, then felt foolish knowing he was obviously joking.

"OK, so please just tell me you haven't bugged my girlfriend's place and if so, I can explain why she said, 'Oh come on, *already*?!' the other night. Twice."

The car door speakers crackled as Agent Duplas laughed. *"You're an amusing guy, especially for an Eagles fan. Sorry for the invasiveness here but I figured you may want to change your number so I had one of our techs run a search, grabbed the new one. Anyway, you have a quick second?"*

"For Big Brother? I have a full minute," he answered.

*"So, just wanted to see if I can get you in here soon if you're feeling up to it."*

"Sure, is there something you need specifically?"

*"Wanted to finish up the talk we had in the hospital and close out the file on that side of the investigation."*

"OK, no problem. Make any headway since we talked? Anything new?"

*"Nothing Earth shattering, but we did discover the names of these dummy corporations this guy set up, 'Juan PL Holdings' and 'Kinetic Detonation Systems', were just cheesy references to his sick bullshit. Juan PL is a reference to Juan Ponce de Leon-"*

"The Fountain of Youth," Stephen interjected.

*"Exactly. And the other one is just 'KiDS', we think. Not exactly clandestine shrouding, but it so often seems to be the case when these things come together that some of the external details are plain as day, and lack any creativity at all while the heart of the operation is tighter than a Submarine in a swimming pool."*

"Yikes."

*"So, what about you, have you set up anything with the media outlets yet? The press can turn on you in a blink and pretty soon they'll be trying to connect dots that have no business being connected, assume you're ducking out on them because you're somehow connected yourself, 'cause it's how they create their narratives."*

Stephen felt the tiny hairs on his neck come to life. "Wait, are you suggesting people might think-or you might think-I *did* have something to do with this? Cause that's-"

*"No, no-not all, sorry for making it sound that way. Not going to lie, of course we did a little digging as it's our job, but other than a credit rating that's dipped into the high six-hundreds of late and some website visits that won't exactly have you at the top of the list for Sainthood, there's nothing of concern there. The press though, those bastards will do whatever it takes to manufacture a story. Be cautious is all, whether you choose to not speak for a while and certainly when you do."*

"Jeez man, way to give a guy a heart attack."

*"Sorry. Just want you to be prepared.*

"Between the surveillance and suggestion the media might try to pulverize me, I'm in full shit-my-pants mode now, thanks buddy."

*"Ha, you'll be fine, I have no doubt. Thanks for calling me back and let's try to get together in the next few days if possible. The Connecticut State Police need to check a few things off their list as well, so we can make it a joint meeting, button things up."*

"Of course. Let me call you tomorrow and we can get a time squared away."

*"Sounds good. Oh, and Stephen do me a favor and keep the details of this conversation between us, alright? I mean, most of it is all out there over the airwaves but not every detail. We still have no idea who the scumbags are that some of these girls were likely going to be sold or shipped off to and if there's other kids that we may be able to track after poring through everything, continuing conversations with them, so, keep that in mind."*

"So, you think there could me more people involved? More girls locked up in who the fuck knows where? I hate to even ask, but…were there any bodies out at the guys place?"

*"Not as of yet, and we've had dogs and infrared devices all over it for days. Keeping fingers crossed. Sex trafficking of kids isn't unique to this case, it's a big industry, as deviant and ugly as it is. We hit the mother lode on this-with your help and others-and I'm still inclined to think the dead perp is the core of it all but it may spawn other leads, names, other avenues. We'll find him. You did an incredible thing, Stephen-I don't think that can be stressed enough. I've gone through countless hours of videotape where abductions were caught and bystanders just watched or turned away or were oblivious to what was happening or in the cases where they did get involved, didn't have any material impact. You took that fucker down and set off this whole thing. I'm sorry you had to pay with an injury and now the whole country's up your ass but it's a welcome relief to the political garbage of late."*

"Well thanks, I appreciate it. I'm still struggling with wrapping my head around it all-may be my whole life-but, I'm glad families were reunited, kids saved. Any challenges I may have pale in comparison to what they endured, and may continue to, I'm sure."

*"Right. I'll let you go, but please check in soon and let me know when you can come in."*

"Will do. Oh, and hey, I always heard you FBI guys were real stiffs, but I have to say you've nixed that stereotype."

The speakers whooshed with a couple quick exhales.

*"Hey, I'm a Raiders fan, we are some dynamic motherfuckers. Going to have to be considering where our team is headed now."*

Stephen chortled. "What a disaster that whole thing is. Good luck in the desert. Have a good day."

*"Ok thanks. You too."*

Stephen ended the call and stared out through the windshield and down the long road ahead of him. He needed to check in with Heather and give a heads up to his boss, who'd been immeasurably patient, without applying pressure or asking for a specific return date. The thought of working a desk, calling clients and asking if they needed parts for their various mechanical widgets, was excruciating. There was a temptation to parlay this event into a financial windfall and abandon work altogether but-just like the Sheriff-he had his own misgivings about profiting from these girl's suffering. It was yet another time where he could use Henry's wisdom to guide him towards the right choice but instead had to rely on his own shoddy moral compass.

Stephen pulled the car onto the road and accelerated up to 60mph, tapping the Scan button on the radio and stopping it as he heard the familiar piano opening of The Eagles "The Last Resort" fill the cabin. Don Henley had one of the best voices in any of the major rock and roll bands that came out of the seventies, he often argued, and the very top of any list of drummers who also sang. That final vocal fluctuation at the end of the song where his voice ascended into a higher register on the word "goodbye" never failed to raise his gooseflesh, and was one of his Top Five album closers ever.

He let the song envelope him and dissolve unwanted thoughts, though it failed with one that was recently awoken from a forced slumber. Chuck was keen, observant and clever and had no trouble discerning the deeper truth in Stephen's anxiety with his recent ascension into stardom. His relationships with women were a real concern needing attention, though it wasn't the epicenter of his anguish, and Chuck knew that immediately, though he lacked the knowledge to pinpoint what it was.

Last night was a sin of omission, by design.

Up on the left, Stephen noticed "Mirabelle's", the place Chuck mentioned, so he pulled into the lot and parked the car, intent on buying some of the coffee he'd raved about. As he exited the car he noticed a woman in her early thirties sitting on a bench outside the restaurant, wiping, presumably, the face of her young daughter with a napkin. The little girl cringed and squirmed as the woman licked the napkin before touching the girls face with it, cleaning what looked like chocolate off her left cheek and upper lip. The woman laughed as the girl fidgeted and moaned, though she too was giggling, continuing to lick the paper and then apply it to the girl's skin. As a young boy, Lillian used to perform the same maneuver whenever Stephen or his sister had food or dirt on their face, and it made Stephen bonkers. He'd wiggle and writhe and complain as his mother would dab the napkin on her tongue, then slide it across his face, soaking him from eyes to chin. He'd whine and twist and squirm, trying to pull away, but Lillian was relentless and wouldn't be swayed, and was often in hysterics much like the mother outside his car now. Although Stephen wasn't laughing when it happened, he'd sit in his room later and chuckle, recalling how absurd it was that she wouldn't just get some water from a faucet or take him to the bathroom and clean him up. It was always the licking of the napkin-a device she had with her at all times-and the slobbering of the face. Years later in his late-teens Stephen displayed his interpretation of the tactic to several friends and his mother while hanging out at the house by exaggeratedly licking a small towel and then rubbing it all over his buddies' head like a lunatic. It sent Lillian and the others into a maniacal fit of laughter and his dog Oscar into a tail chasing bark fest.

Stephen walked over towards the woman and her daughter, watching as the mother put the napkin into her pocket and then pick up the girl and lift her up over her head, making a "Whooooooo" sound before asking her, "See, now doesn't that feel better to not have chocolate chips all over your face." The little girl howled as her mother placed her down and took her tiny fingers into her own and led her back to their car. The vehicle, a damaged and tattered Dodge Neon with no hubcaps and some duct tape keeping one of the fenders on, was in shambles, echoing the attire worn by the two of them. The little girl was in beige pants and a flowery white top too big for her with holes in each garment, while the mom wore dirty jean shorts and a torn gray T-Shirt. Both had shoddy dental work and inexpensive sandals but what they both shared was genuine laughter and joy at being with one another in that moment, despite their misfortunes elsewhere. Stephen watched the little girl climb into the back seat of the car, her mother tucking her hand under her butt and easing her up, then climb into the car seat. Her mom strapped her in and then squeezed her cheeks with her right hand before kissing her on the top of the head and slamming the door. As she walked around the back of the car she looked over at Stephen and smiled wide, and he returned a grin before speaking.

"You're a great mom. That's beautiful to see," Stephen said, hoping it didn't come off creepy to someone he'd never met and was gawking at.

"Aw, thank you. Not every day is this easy, though. If you saw me at home with her you'd probably want to take that back," the woman replied.

"Somehow, I doubt that," he countered. "Enjoy your day."

"You too," she yelled back, before getting in the car and then smiling over at him once more before starting the car and backing out.

She slowed the car as she passed by, appearing like she may want to say something but then kept driving out onto the main road. He watched the car drive away and recalled the numerous times he and Jessica would leave whatever convenience store was nearest to their current home as children, their mother toting five to ten scratch-off lottery tickets that she'd buy each time, always letting the two of them scratch when they returned home. In all the years he could remember, the most he recalled Lillian winning was fifty dollars but she was never dissuaded in her quest. The inspiration, she claimed, being the time she'd forgone a chance to buy one at a grocery store in Stafford Springs, CT with her "last five dollars" and the man behind her won fifty-thousand bucks. The story was dubious at best, but the way it became embellished and inflated over the years was entertaining and always served to help him and his sister encourage his mother's expensive habit.

Most of his life was spent with two women, one shy, submissive and naïve, the other extroverted, reckless and cunning- though both were similar and unwavering in their affinity for him. They each showed him boundless affection and support, never holding back their obvious admiration and almost sycophantic love for his sense of humor, though they were both hysterical themselves. His mother was flighty, impulsive and vastly irresponsible at times but she was *there*, always, month in and month out, whether it was a new town or the same one at the end of its cycle. She made the mundane joyful and the morose comical, often verbally illustrating the absurdity of their current living situation to an uproarious farce, sending the three of them into fits of laughter. She'd cry some nights for hours at a time, usually a result of impulsive or poor choices, but she was the one that showed Stephen it was safe and therapeutic to lose yourself sometimes in despair, as it was often the only path to healing.

Lillian was, despite her many flaws, a mother that would lick the napkin before she cleaned all those things that tainted or troubled you, because, in doing so her way, it made it easier to laugh through the pain. In all those moments where he cowered and struggled as she wiped away at him he was laughing with her and never at her. She found her own healing in the offbeat healing of her children.

Jessica was distant and closed off lately, a byproduct of her recent indoctrination into her husband's Faith and his lack thereof but also because she long struggled with close personal relationships. Her protection and cloak of invisibility growing up was her introversion and isolation where Stephen employed extroversion and humor for insulation. Jessica found solace and community in Christopher's religion regardless of if she was being honest about her belief in its tenets, and this bolstered her confidence and dampened her anxieties, enabling her to engage in conversations not previously considered. The tension that often arose between them, Stephen knew, was his loss of the shy but witty partner in crime who would converse without filters or the embarrassment that her current beliefs had instilled.

Still, he reasoned, she held these beliefs of her own volition and for reasons valid and significant to her, and attempting to counter them at every turn was only driving them further apart. Jessica loved him unquestionably, and if there was any chance for their relationship to heal and strengthen he'd need to shelve the cynicism and condescension despite his divergent beliefs.

He looked down at his phone, and before heading into Mirabelle's to grab coffee he picked it up and dialed his mother's number.

## Chapter 27

*During* the ride home to Connecticut, shuffled, streaming music and drifting thought prevailed. He avoided news media and his phone, other than a brief chat with his mother and a text exchange with Heather, letting her know he was alright and heading back. For days, he'd been zipping from one place to the next, avoiding the necessities of his current reality and, although some of the dialogue and introspection was helpful, he was still circling around the edges of responsibility.

Lillian mentioned she was eager to see him again, and had texted a picture of the infamous "glamour shot" of the three of them in hopes it may dilute some of the tension. He didn't respond other than to say he'd be there soon, but the image brought a laugh and a lengthy smile. As he drew closer to his mother's house, his mind went to Henry. How the two of them would often dissect conversations they'd have with Lillian, expressing the same frustrations with her obstinate thinking and manic behaviors yet always arrive at a place of hilarity; her ability to infuse levity into madness and tumult was unmatched by anyone. Henry often said Lillian was the love of his lifetime, but that they were too much alike to ever have had a real shot even if the juice hadn't been an affliction and sent him wayward.

There were days when Stephen would pick up the phone and look at the Contacts section, scrolling down to the late middle of the alphabet, stopping on "Poppy", making sure it was still there. Many years earlier, Jessica had given Henry the nickname while fishing with

289

the two of them and although Henry wasn't enamored with it immediately, over time he warmed to it, often referring to himself with the moniker. Stephen would venture into his old voicemail menu from time to time and scroll to the end, replaying the last message he ever received from Henry:

*"Hey son, it's Poppy. Don't worry about what I said, really. I got myself into a little jam here and I always find my way out, you know that. You have more on your plate now than a fat guy at an all-night buffet so just do what you need to do. Poppy always pulls it together. I love you, kiddo, and stop arguing with your sister, asswipe. She loves you. Not as much as Jesus, but, hey, he was a way better dude than you. <laughs> Be happy, son, no matter what."*

He hadn't listened to it in months but he knew every word, each inflection and the exact cadence and pace of the dialogue. There were days where he'd listen to it ten or twelve times and let himself come apart, isolate indoors for a day or two, telling those around him that he was under the weather. Instead, he'd be crouched in the back corner of his shower for hours letting the falling water drown out his sobbing and the scalding heat of the steam remind him that he was still alive.

The entrance to his mother's place was empty, no news vans or people with signs gathered outside, so he signaled and pulled into the tree-lined driveway, his heart rate climbing as the car's RPM's fell. After he shut it down, he angled the rearview mirror towards him, looking at his face from several angles. The latest bandage on his head was clean and dry, though he was scruffy and unshaven and looked tired, his eyes bloodshot and sunken. Under his left eye, a little twitch had developed in the last several months and seemed to correlate with stress and anxiety, and it was currently wiggling like an inchworm trying to free itself from his cheek.

He stepped out of the car and walked up towards the house where Lillian was waiting in the open doorway, wearing gray sweatpants and an oversized white sweater with a Cocker Spaniel sewn into the front.

"Well, at least you dressed up for me this time," Stephen jabbed, making his way up the steps.

"Oh sure, coming from Howard Hughes over here. You look like you woke up under a bridge. When's the last time you took a shower, birth?" Lillian fired back.

Stephen grinned, passing her in the doorway, headed for the living room couch.

"I was making some tea, you want some?" Lillian asked.

"No thanks," he yelled back from the couch.

Lillian fetched her tea and a small plate of shortbread cookies and came back into the living room, placing the items in the center of the coffee table as Stephen pulled off his shoes.

"So, sounds like you've been a world traveler. Look like it too. You were in Pennsylvania with the Sherriff?" Lillian asked.

"Yeah, spent the night up there, talking and what not. Real good guy. He'd reached out to me and I figured might be nice to pay him a visit."

"I see. Well, that's great, I'm sure it was nice to talk to someone that's connected in the same way you are to this whole thing. How was he? Pleasant man?"

"Awesome guy, yes. Enjoyed talking with him."

Seconds passed after he finished speaking and Lillian clanked her tea cup against the pastel green plate it was on. The awkward silence stretched for almost a minute before Lillian chimed back in.

"So, Stephen, I wanted to-"

"Hey, listen, I know what you're going to say and it's not like we haven't been down this road before. We fight about one thing or the next and then one of us apologizes and it gets smoothed over for a little while. Aren't you tired of that, Ma?" Stephen interjected.

She put her cup of tea back down on the plate and let her back rest against the couch cushion, letting out a small sigh.

"I'm not trying to agitate you, I'm-"

"No, no, I understand, you're right. How do you propose we do that, is my question though?" Lillian interrupted.

Stephen leaned forward on the couch, placing his hands on his knees. "By not bullshitting each other anymore. By not having a fake fucking relationship that, at its best is comical and absurd, but at its worst is horribly dysfunctional. I'm tired of existing in this sphere of make believe and veiled anger, with under our breath jabs wrapped in truths we don't want to delve into. Let's just stop, once and for all. If it ends with the two of us indifferent to one another, well, so be it. At least it would be real."

Lillian's lower lip began quivering, and she took a deep breath before removing her own shoes and adjusting her position on the couch again.

"You left here last time in a huff because I suggested dealing with this very topic, Stephen-truth. I made some assumptions-assumptions I believe are valid-and you didn't want to hear it. So, what you're telling me now then is that you're willing to discuss these things about yourself as well? Not just the myriad of flaws you think I have, as seems to be the norm?

"Yes."

Lillian shot her eyes over to Stephen, hearing the one-word answer. He was looking straight at her, his eyes pained and his face sullen. She saw her little boy in that moment, the way he was the day he returned from lifting the brick off the bees. Confused, frightened and in pain-completely vulnerable. *"Vulnerability is the oxygen to the lungs of intimacy"*, Henry would often say to her, suggesting that the only way two people could truly connect intimately is if they exposed themselves without limit, bared their souls with no filter or protection. Henry often failed in his own quest to adhere to that principal once the alcohol took control but the message still had worth and validity.

"OK then. So where do we start?" Lillian asked.

Stephen rubbed his hands across his face and stood up, heading for the bathroom sink that was right in the hall. "Let me get some water first."

He ran the faucet and placed his mouth underneath, lapping up a few huge gulps before turning it off and plopping back down onto the couch, opposite Lillian.

"I remember the first time I saw your father do that, right in front of my mother in her house. She nearly had a fit. Never bothered me," Lillian said.

"Well, coming from a woman that lets the dogs lick her ice cream cone then continues eating it, I'd imagine not," Stephen said.

"Ha ha, yeah yeah, crazy old Ma with the dogs. I put them outside on the run, by the way, so they wouldn't bug you. Did you notice that?"

"I did, yes. So, that's a place to start…Mom, I love dogs, I love animals-I know you know this about me. You've somehow, over the years, managed to turn my issues with the thousand dogs and pets we've had in the house into 'Stephen doesn't like dogs' and that's patently false. I adore them, and have loved all those we or you've ever had. Yes, that latest one here with the lazy eye and loudest fucking bark on Earth is a challenge, but it has its moments. This isn't about the animals themselves, mom, it's about your inability or unwillingness to care for them properly. You, nor we, growing up, ever had the space to handle some of these animals and that in turn made them nuts and they ended up destroying the house. Plus, you were always working or out and Jess and I got stuck with much of the care and we were too wrapped up in our adolescent nightmares to be able to handle all that. Plus, these days, as you've made it very clear, you don't have the financial ability to take care of yourself never mind multiple dogs. They need vet visits, grooming, long walks, the right food; loving them boundlessly as you do isn't enough Ma, I'm sorry."

Lillian's hands were trembling. She nodded her head but said nothing.

"As for money, I've helped you more times than I can count in my life, from as early as I was first able to earn a buck for myself. I remember using paper route money to help you put the lights back on in Vernon, Connecticut. I was twelve. Anytime this comes up you get defensive and angry-hang up the phone or rush me out of the house. I've offered to help you move to a smaller place, get the dogs taken care of if you can at least agree to scale back to one, and that fits the space you're living in, and whenever that gets brought up it's as though I'm trying to stuff you in a nursing home on an island somewhere.

Then there's your health, Ma. I mean, at what point can I stop pretending that you saying, "I don't like doctors" is alright? I listened to that into your fifties and sixties and now you're over seventy, still smoking, eating whatever you want and as I watch you start to break down and suggest taking you to see someone it's still, "Eh, I don't like doctors." Well, you know Ma, I don't like watching you fall apart in front of me and neither does Jessica, and I know she's expressed these same concerns with you so don't pretend it's only me saying this because it's not."

Lillian was still sitting, her hands now resting in her lap, her body and face motionless and her eyes lost somewhere.

"You've told me, and I've heard through Jess many times, that 'You wish we were closer' and I've tried to address that as best I could, though maybe not as directly as I'm trying to today. There's an expression, Ma, that says 'don't set yourself up for failure', and I think it applies here. If you want us to have a comfortable, cohesive, healthy relationship then it needs to be with variables in places that don't doom it to fail. I can't tell you how to live your life, and I know you well enough to know that you're always going to do what you wish anyway, but I can't see how you expect us to grow closer if you won't do even those most basic things to take care of yourself and survive. I don't make a shitload of money, and I can't help you live the way you always choose to. I can't accept that you're "just an old woman" and some of your choices aren't affecting your health and well-being, and I

294

can't come visit and be mauled by multiple animals that aren't being cared for the way they deserve in a space not big enough for them to live. I'm sorry, and if that makes me a terrible person in your eyes, a bad son, well, then I guess that's what I am."

His mother leaned forward and took a sip of her tea, then cradled the cup in her hand as she let herself ease back on the loveseat into a comfortable position, sitting silent for a minute. Stephen watched her, looking lost in a place in her mind, and said nothing as she traversed whatever landscape her memories had pulled her into.

"When I was seven years old," Lillian spoke, resting her teacup on the table in front of her. "I was playing with a tattered doll my mother gave me, in the room next to her bedroom. She was talking to my father, your grandad, and my name kept coming up. So, I slid myself over towards the doorway and leaned down, laying my head on the floor so I could hear through the gap. It was my mother speaking, mostly, and she kept saying, 'You need to hug her, tell her you love her. She's your daughter.' And he wasn't saying much but at one point I heard him say 'I love my son, and that's enough,' before leaving the room as she cried out to him to return. She stayed in that room and wept for what seemed like days, as I lay on that floor listening to her. I wanted to get up and go to her but I was afraid, so, after a while I sat back up and just kept brushing my dolls hair, faster and with more intensity in each stroke, and later that day she came in and ran over to me, asking what I'd done. Apparently, I'd been brushing the hair on the doll with so much force and so many strokes that I'd pulled it all off and it was in a pile between my legs, but I was still brushing the doll's head."

Stephen bit his lower lip and felt his breathing become stuttered as he listened.

"A few weeks later your grandmother bought me my first puppy. It was a Springer Spaniel, this speckled brown and white mess of a neurotic dog I named Pickles for who knows what reason. I took that dog everywhere. It slept in my bed, I walked it, fed it, brushed it and then one day it was gone. I screamed and cried for weeks and never got an answer until I heard my father tell Ruthie that he gave it away. She screamed and yelled but he said nothing, and when the next dog arrived a couple months later I tried not to get attached, fearful of what may happen, but the little Collie got under my skin and I fell in love, of course. 'Betsy' lasted maybe two months and then there was a big fight between my father and brother and the next day she was gone too. I tried to ask Will if he knew what happened but he was lost in his own head by that point already, barely knew who I was."

"Mom, I've asked you about your childhood so many times and-"

"You know, Ruthie and my father had money, because he worked and they did have some family money but they never taught me about how it all worked. I always assumed certain people 'had' money and some didn't. They seemed to have enough to do what they wanted, take us to Cape Cod every year, buy a new car, fix the house when it needed repairs, but I never knew it was all leveraged, all debt. The first two dimes I had of my own I spent and I've lived that way ever since-that's not lost on me-I know who I am. Every new toy I bought as a child, every dress I spent too much on as a teen, every new car I couldn't afford that I bought while you kids were growing up was nothing more than a distraction from the torment of not being loved. It's no different than you and all these women, except the difference is you seek the distraction because you don't love yourself, not because they don't love you."

Stephen watched her continue speaking, massaging her own hands, the way Jessica often did but with less tension.

"As for doctors, well, that's a fear born of many parents. Between Ruthie telling me that my father's rampant alcoholism was merely him, 'not feeling well', and that he was always going to the doctors-though never getting better-and me being dragged in a hundred times for infections they could never figure out and treating me with Penicillin, which I was allergic to, seeing a doctor was

296

terrifying. When Will's condition worsened, I heard that 'he was seeing some of the best doctors in California' and a month later he was dead. I don't avoid doctors out of laziness or cost, Stephen, I do so only out of fear. I have control over my little, dysfunctional universe and it may be unhealthy and it may be chaotic to outsiders but it's *mine*."

Stephen put his head down into his hands, then rubbed his temples several times before getting up and moving to the other couch beside Lillian.

"Why didn't we ever talk about any of this stuff? I asked you about your father, growing up, all that shit many times and you never wanted to engage, and you've never had a problem speaking your mind, so why never about this?"

"I don't know if I have an answer, Stephen. Other than embarrassment I guess. Remember that guy from Boston, the recently divorced one with the beard named Kyle? Think you were maybe eleven at the time I was seeing him?"

Stephen nodded.

"Well, he encouraged me to talk about all this garbage when we were having problems and he basically told me I was a fucked up broad with daddy issues so I tucked it away in a box and haven't opened it since."

"*That* guy? The one with the chipped tooth who drove the heinous green van? Come on, mom, he looked like he sold bait in the Ozarks, he couldn't possibly have the mental fortitude to shut you down like that, really?"

Lillian smirked. "You know, he did. Maybe because it was the first time I was ever willing to talk about those things or because I thought I loved him at the time but when you expose yourself like that and someone rips your guts out, you close up quick. And tight."

He looked over at his mother and saw her sitting there, hands in her lap, the pathetic Cocker Spaniel pattern on her sweater looking like it was sewn in by a child with Parkinson's disease-blotchy, ragged and uneven-and felt his eyes fill up with tears. She was looking down at her knees, lost in the memories of those things she'd just spoken of and as vulnerable as he'd ever seen her. For most of his entire life he'd looked at his mother as the force that had pulled him away from his father, making impulsive and reckless decisions that induced endless stress and anxiety. He blamed her for the majority of negativity that existed in his life as a child and even now, though he rarely gave her the credit for what was good. Her welcome ear, her calming sense of humor, her boundless affection, her silliness, the spontaneity, the protective nature, but most importantly, her *presence*. He'd forgiven Henry for his misdeeds and idolized him even from afar while demonizing his mother, who stayed. Stephen gave a pass to Henry, knowing the hell his childhood was comprised of, while ignoring the obvious reality that Lillian had suffered in her own kind of hell. The alcoholic father, the detached mother, the suicidal brother-all known elements of her world yet Stephen never bothered to assemble them or delve any deeper.

"I love you mom. I do, and always have and I don't know why it's taken me so long to realize that I haven't been very fair to you my whole life, why I've boxed you out and judged you with different parameters than others," Stephen said, his voice trembling and tears leaking from his eyes. "I pulled myself so close to dad, because I loved him, of course, but also because I think I was afraid to get too close to you. You were all I had-we had, me and Jess-for so long. I suppose a part of me was terrified to let you all the way in. I used to cry some of those nights when you worked late at a second job, terrified you may not come home. With dad, he was always so far away and it was easy to allow myself to get close without really *being* close, if that makes any sense?"

Lillian sat up and turned to face Stephen, putting her hands on his, her own eyes now filled with liquid and her jaw and lips trembling.

"I know how much you loved Henry, Stephen-he did the very best he could for you kids considering where he came from. I loved him too, he was the funniest and most passionate man I ever knew and I'm so glad you had the years you did with him. I never wanted to replace him, or for you to love me more than him, I just wanted you to see me through the same eyes you viewed him."

He heard the sentence climb into his ears, and as it resonated, it tore into him as no words had prior. He looked at her for another moment, then began sobbing, his head falling into his mother's lap, as her own tears intensified. She stroked the side of his head as he wept, with forty years of pain, anguish and anger leaking from his soul and out through his eyes. Lillian wiped her face with a tissue from the box on the coffee table, continue to rub the side of his head as he lay there, beginning to pull himself together.

"Here, sit up honey. Let me get you some water," his mother said, stopping after she got a good look at his face. "Hang on a second, you have fibers from my sweater or something on your face."

He watched Lillian reach for a wad of tissues out of the box and bring it up towards her face and he pulled himself back several inches. "Holy shit, Ma, no way. Please tell me you weren't seriously going to lick that tissue and wipe off my face like it's nineteen eighty-one?"

She chortled, then dabbed the tissue on her tongue a couple times. "Come on, I'm your mother, we have the same DNA. Stop being such a baby."

He got up off the couch and snagged a tissue for himself from the box and wiped his eyes, then balled the paper and tossed it onto the coffee table. "I need to eat something. Feeling a little dizzy. Have you got any food here or you want me to go pick something up?"

"You just sit down and relax and let me make something, alright? You know how much I love to cook for you kids. It's about the only thing that gives me any pleasure these days, other than the dogs and Robert Downey, Jr.," she answered.

"Thanks, Ma."

Lillian made her way into the kitchen and prepared a meal of pork chops and garlic mashed potatoes, with a garden salad and crescent-shaped rolls that burned the roof of his mouth as he stuffed them in at a breakneck pace. The two of them ate as they laughed about various childhood memories and he recounted some of his talk with Sheriff McCabe. They talked about Jessica and the kids and their plans for the summer. Neither one mentioned their previous conversation or the money offered, agents, talk shows or anything connected to most recent events. As the conversation waned, Lillian went outside to check on the dogs and Stephen stretched out on the couch and fell into an hour-long lap, devoid of dreams, and full of rejuvenation.

<#>

"Did you drool all over my new comforter?" Lillian asked, peering down at his widening eyes.

"Yikes, how long did I sleep?" Stephen asked.

"About an hour," she answered, sitting down at the end of the couch next to him, as he pulled his legs closer to himself, then sat up. "So, I wanted to ask you, when we were talking about the conversation you had with the Sheriff, you mentioned he thought there was something else bothering you other than mounting every woman from here to Canada. Was he right?"

"Wow, way to hit the ground running after a guy has a nap, Ma, thanks."

"Well hey, you want a 'no bullshit' relationship, I think we've done pretty good today. Let's keep it going."

Stephen rubbed the sleep out of his eyes and took a sip of the water Lillian had placed on the table near him when he fell asleep. He looked over at the ridiculous picture of the three of them and chuckled. "You and that freaking picture. What is it with that thing?"

"Well," she said, picking it up and examining it closer. "Getting the two of you to sit still for anything was nearly impossible, and that was a wonderful day if you don't recall. I had just started-another-new job, we had a little money and we spent the day at Riverside Park and then did the photos afterwards," she answered.

"Holy crap," he said, remembering the day like it was yesterday. "I do recall that now. You even went on a roller coaster. Were you drunk?"

"No, but I probably should have been at the photo shoot because you two were making me nuts. Now, enough stalling, what else is going on with you," she asked, placing the picture back down on the table.

Stephen felt as comfortable with his mother as he had his entire life, but what had been haunting him for years now-more so since the hospital-was something he hadn't shared with anyone, nor had he planned to. It was living deep within him and inflicting torment daily but he'd learned to manage it, hoping someday it would no longer beckon.

"It's nothing I can't handle, Ma, really. It's just guilt...not seeing Poppy before he died."

Lillian's face wrinkled into a curious frown. "Not seeing him? It happened suddenly, Stephen, and he was three thousand miles away, how could you have seen him?"

He didn't want to dig into this wound, but she'd been so open and honest today and their relationship felt like it had moved to higher ground. Bottling things up was a practice he preached against, same as his father. What would Henry expect of him if he called and asked for advice on the situation? Any situation.

*Truth.*

Stephen straightened himself up on the couch and looked over at Lillian and smiled, she returning one to him.

"It's OK, honey. You can tell me whatever it is," Lillian assured him.

Stephen sat up and gathered himself, running his hands over the back of his neck, searching for words before he spoke. "Well...you know how rough things got with him at the end, with the drinking starting again in the last year of his life and his girlfriend, all her troubles?"

"Yes, Jessica has told me some of the details that you may not have, sure."

"So," he continued, then drawing in a sustained breath. "I was still with Christine then, you know that, and she was not sympathetic to his whole situation with the relapse and we'd just moved into the new place and things were getting chaotic."

"That bitch wasn't sympathetic to anything, but go on."

"Well, even less so to things that may take me away from day to day errand boy and bill payer. Anyway, Poppy had gotten bad in those last few months. I was still processing the fact that he'd started drinking again and as his situation was devolving, he called me from a motel outside of Vegas somewhere a few weeks before Christmas. He told me that a friend from AA was driving him back to San Diego and he'd left his chick for good and he was going into a dry out tank. Wanted to get sober and hook up with another friend who built houses and he was going to start running a crew himself once he was on his feet, had it all planned out."

Stephen took a breath, then gulping down the last sip of water in his glass. Lillian was sitting close, facing him, listening.

"So, he asks me how bad things were at home and I tell him it's a fucking nightmare and he asks me if I want to come out West, live with him a while and start writing together, like we talked about a lot over the years. I was so jammed up and stressed out at home that I impulsively told him yes and two days later I was on my way, driving out to California."

Lillian tilted her head, asking, "You actually left Connecticut and drove out there?"

"I did, but…I only made it to Utah."

"Wait, how did I not know that?"

"I told you, Ma, nobody knew about this, other than dad and Christine, and as you can imagine she freaked the fuck out. So, anyway, I get out to Utah and the entire time Christine is blowing up my phone, texting me pissed off, calling me a quitter, a loser, and so on. I'm ignoring most of it but then one night while I stop and see a high school friend, Jared Houle, the skier, you remember?"

"Always had the helmet head, the gel in his hair. Yeah."

"That's him. Well, I'm out at his place and I get a text with a picture from Christine and it's a drawing of a house and kids, a mom and dad and it has all their names on it, and a couple little notes like, 'We miss you Stevie' and 'Please come home we need you', written in their handwriting. It's followed by a text from her saying something like, 'I know we moved real fast and I haven't always been the most supportive person but I love you and me and the kids need you. I promise I'll do better.' I just came apart, Ma, you know? I was so emotionally spent anyway that-"

"I know you loved those children of hers," Lillian said, choking back tears as she spoke. "They were wonderful kids and couldn't have had a better man around than you and I know how hard the loss of them has been on you, honey. It was so hard to watch, the way they adored you, trusted you and knowing that if you wanted your own someday…"

She stopped herself from going further in fear it might open wounds too vast to mend in one night.

"I told you early on that she may use those kids against you. Jesus Christ, to go to those lengths though, ugh," Lillian said instead.

"I did love them, I still do. Think of them every day. I never realized, then, that it wouldn't matter what I did or how long I stayed, because as much as the kids loved me it would never change the fact that she was incapable of loving anything. So, after the text, I just crumbled and I called Dad and I told him that I thought I needed to go back. He was upset, concerned and worried for me but also, selfishly he admitted, wanted me out there, he said. He was certain we'd write the Great American Novel together and have celebrity friends and be the envy of every motherfucker that ever doubted us growing up. He sounded scared and manic and I was torn because I knew what I was going home to could turn to shit again quick but, I also knew that Poppy might pick up the bottle and head back to Linda in Nevada and I'd be left by myself, with nothing but a damaged, dysfunctional relationship and an alcoholic father and not a pot to piss in.

So, I drove home, against his wishes, choosing only the lesser of two things I feared. A week later he called me, sounding drunk, begging-not asking, begging-me to come see him. I reminded him how he always told me not to have a serious conversation with someone hammered because even though there may be truths in some of the words, there was too much noise, too much bullshit and no way to know what was reality and what was nothing more than the rantings of a madman. He hung up the phone. I texted him several times, again the next morning and then days later he finally called me back and left a message. It was short and sweet and sounded more like his normal self, telling me it was alright that I went home. I never responded, and, a week later it was Christmas and he was dead."

Lillian watched as Stephen's eyes pooled up. His mouth shivered as his breath became pronounced and choppy, his head slumping down into his chest.

"He died on some shitty fucking motel floor in El Cajon, California. Alone on Christmas Day. Some maid found him. Not his children or someone who loved him. He died all alone, on a cold floor in his underwear and a dirty T-Shirt. A week after he begged his son to come save him. Oh fuck," he said, letting himself fall into the couch, unable to control the wailing and onslaught of tears.

Lillian cradled his head, just as she'd done earlier, stroking his face and letting him get it out. She said nothing, but the tears in her own eyes were too numerous and heavy to hold and they fell on him as well. For several minutes, he sobbed and she lay with him, keeping her pain to a whisper and wiping her eyes with her free hand. Only when he grew silent did she speak.

"Your father died knowing that you loved him, and that will never be in doubt," she spoke through her own tears. "He and I talked a lot more than you might think-not so much in those last six months, but regularly-and he considered it a gift that you two loved him as you did, as it was his only real source of joy. That man lived a life that no child should ever have to endure and it's amazing he ever survived. The fact that he established a relationship with you two as well, you know, it's a bit of a miracle.

He hated Christmas. It was the most terrifying time for him in that house and his father would wreak unimaginable havoc. I don't say that in hopes it will make things any easier but instead maybe offer some clarity, some understanding. Your father never expected to live past thirty-five, Stephen. He said that to me at least a thousand times in the years we were together. In countless conversations we had in his late years, the only thing he ever talked about that saved him-not AA or his other two wives, girlfriends or whomever-was you kids. He adored you both and I fully believe it's the only reason he lived as long as he did."

"He was in so much pain at the end though, and alone and I should have-"

"You need to stop that, alright?" she interrupted. "I knew your father better than I've known any man in my life. He was a tortured soul and even in his best moments he wasn't *really* connecting with those around him, it was just a façade. The two of you were the only ones that he let get through and he adored that but it would never be enough, could never be, to silence the demons of that man's childhood. There's nothing you could have said, nothing you could have done, no place you could have been to stop your father from going down that road. He'd avoided his past for so long, drowning it in booze and pills, pacifying it with the love he had for his kids but...it always came back. This time it was just too much."

"Do you think he killed himself," Stephen asked, after a long silence.

It was the first time that he'd ever mentioned that possibility with his mother. The Coroner ruled the cause of death a Heart Attack, but Henry had been drinking heavily for days and there were pills found at his bedside, though only a small amount in his system.

"You know, darling, he may have, I don't have the answer to that. He said his whole life that he may 'do himself in' because his knees ached from all the work he did, he had back issues and his head was swimming with shit, but he said it mainly in jest. Though, I don't know how anyone could live as long as he did and *through* what he did and have it not be a possibility but, does it matter? He was in pain. Tremendous, all-consuming pain and his suffering ended. That's the only way any of us should look at it."

"I want to, and I understand what you mean, but I can't stop feeling like I failed him. I made the wrong choice and I left him out there to die all alone for a pathetic reason which was nothing more than my own fears. Now all these people who don't know a fucking thing about me are calling me a hero and don't realize I'm nothing more than a coward"

"Stephen, stop. Is there any part of you that honestly feels like, knowing your father as you did, that anything you may have said or done could have influenced his actions? You're talking about the guy who carried a pound of Marijuana over the Canadian border into the US, 'just to fucking see if I could'. If Henry was done with his job, a relationship, or this world then it would be by his choosing. If the ideas he had in his head for you two didn't come to fruition when you were out there he very well may have relapsed again, gone back to

Nevada or just pulled the plug anyway. You simply can't put this burden, *his* burden, on yourself."

She was right, about Henry, but that truth wasn't enough to cauterize the wounds or dampen the doubt.

"I hate that he died all alone, I can't shake it. On a day that was so hard for him."

"I know," Lillian said, stroking the side of his head. "But I can promise you that no matter what the circumstances were at the very end, he would never want you kids to suffer with those thoughts and I know it pains Jessica a lot too, but, your father never had anyone to guide him on the path of parenting, in making good decisions or thinking about repercussions, which I'm sure sounds familiar. I have to say though, considering, he did pretty well for himself. He cleaned up his act for more than twenty years and always had his shit together with money, unlike me. He could have turned out to be a colossal shithead and an abusive father and instead he turned out to be an alright lay and good dad. That's really all that matters."

Stephen smiled and felt more welling in the bottom of his eyes, but staved it off by abruptly changing the subject.

"OK," he said, sitting up and wiping his eyes on his sleeve, "so tell me about this agent guy."

"What? Right now? We can keep talking if you want honey, unless it's-"

"No, it's fine, and I appreciate everything you said mom, and I love you. I know I need time to work through the Poppy stuff, but I'm happy I finally brought it up, and glad it was with you," Stephen interrupted, then leaned over and embraced Lillian with a strong, extended hug. "All this attention lately, it's left me feeling so unworthy of adulation knowing the ways I've failed others and myself for so long I guess."

"Your father loved you to pieces, Stephen, and not one ounce of anything to do with where he ended up or his passing has a thing to do with you, and I don't want you to forget that," she said above a

307

whisper, as her head rested on his shoulder. "And as for the attention and your guilt or whatever it is, enough already-these items are not mutually exclusive. You did an incredible thing and, yeah, you've done some shitty things, mainly by thinking with that little six incher you have down there-and don't try to argue that point, I was married to your father and I caught you that time in front of the VCR watching *Dirty Nurses 4*."

Stephen laughed, not arguing his stature in that area or being busted self-gratifying years earlier. "Thanks Ma. I'm glad I came over and that we talked like this. It's been long overdue. No more bullshit, right?"

"Absolutely darling. But if you think I'm gonna stop hitting you up for twenty bucks here and there you're out of your mind. Hey, I'm just being hoooneest," she said, accentuating the word at the end.

"Oh Christ," he said, standing up from the couch, shaking his head, grinning.

"Hey, speaking of Jesus, after we sort out some of this media crap, you need to check in with your sister. She adores you, and I know that's not lost on you. Just because you don't see eye to eye on the Religion thing doesn't mean you can't find common ground elsewhere. If you look deep enough you'll see that she's the same little girl she always was."

"I know. I've been a shithead to all the women in my life since the Christine disaster. Well, and some prior, to be fair...eh, I have some housecleaning to do. This was a good start."

"Well whoever that Heather is that you mentioned talking to the Sheriff about, she sounds like a keeper so don't fuck it up by jumping in bed with every hussy that shakes her jugs at you now that you're a celebrity. The Sophia thing though, that's really over?"

"Yeah. It was the right thing, and a long time coming. She saw through me like fucking Superman looking through a clean window."

"Wouldn't anyone be able to see well through a clean window? Why does it have to be Superman?"

He rolled his eyes and looked over at her. "Shouldn't you be choking on some of those dry, death cookies right now?"

"Shit, I forget I just bought some more! I'll go let the dogs in and we can have a couple," she said, hurrying out of the living room.

"The Alexander Circus. Indeed," he said to himself.


The rest of the evening the two of them spoke about the media offers, the suggestions of the agent she spoke to, as well as an attorney that Jessica often used. There was a considerable amount of money offered by three different major networks and a wealth of interest from smaller cable shows. Stephen had decided on the ride back to Connecticut that, regardless of what choices he made after that point, the first place he would go and tell his story was the *Motormouth* show on Satellite radio. It was unlikely they'd offer him any money, as they were always crying poverty, but the host and oddball panel of characters on that morning show had been like an extended family of his for almost twenty years, and it seemed like the natural choice. Lillian wasn't thrilled, but he gave her his blessing to speak with whomever she chose to and bank whatever she could, and that significantly reduced her annoyance.

As the night was slipping away and Stephen found himself on the couch with a small, mangy white dog under his chin and a monstrous, golden behemoth at his feet, Lillian made her way into the living room to check on him.

"You want another blanket or anything?" she asked, looking down at him from behind the coffee table, wearing a fluffy, off white robe and reading glasses.

"No, I'm OK, thanks Ma."

"I'll take the dogs in my room. Hey guys-"

"No no, it's OK, really. They're comfy here and I'm alright. Maybe just leave your door open a crack in case they get up in the night and want to come in."

"Oh, there's no chance they're gonna leave you now, but I will. I told you, these freaking dogs worship you. It's like me in my teen years, the bigger the asshole the more I wanted to be with them. I didn't shit on their floor and chew their shoes like these guys will but, it's pretty much the same thing."

Stephen laughed and the little dog wiggled around but stayed put.

"You know Ma, you're really funny. One of the funniest people I've ever known. I don't think I've told you that enough, but it's true."

"Oh, I know, don't you worry. You wait till these cable TV hosts get a load of me. They'll be asking me to host my own show."

"I have no doubt," he said. "Oh, and hey so you'll set that up, the radio thing? I need to go see Heather tomorrow and then check in at work and I'll need to go home at some point…for at least as long as it'll be my home."

"I told you you're welcome to stay here. I have the extra bedroom, or the couch here and the dogs will be in a state of constant euphoria, that's for sure."

"I just may do that, Ma. I'll let you know."

"OK, and yes I'll set that up, or have that agent guy do it, something. He's probably going to want you to sign something though, you know how that works."

"Yeah, and as long as I'm not giving up a kidney or something I'll sign it. Just let me know."

"Sleep tight, Stephen. I love you."

"Love you too, mom. See you in the morning."

## *Chapter 28*

*Stephen* drove to Heather's place that morning feeling more optimistic and well rested than his first days back in the world. The talk with Lillian was cathartic, and although he wasn't foolish enough to believe it would solve all their problems or unwind forty years of damage they were both responsible for overnight, it was a gigantic step in the right direction. He'd call Jessica later and try to clear the air with her as well; dial back some of the tension that had built in recent years by being less critical and more empathetic. The conversation with Heather, however, was not one he welcomed having, though it was vital if he had any chance to turn the corner and stop repeating destructive patterns.

He pulled into her complex and parked his car, then texted her that he'd arrived. She welcomed him in the doorway of her unit, wearing a wide smile and her green chiffon bathrobe over baby blue PJ's.

"Hey handsome," she said.

"Hey beautiful," he answered, walking into her awaiting arms.

"I missed you," she said, then kissed his forehead and lips several times. "But it sounds like you had a great visit with that Sheriff and your mom, so, was a productive journey I guess?"

"It was, yes," he answered, after returning her kisses. He stood there in her arms grinning at her for a moment, then detached himself and made his way to the couch. "I feel like all I've been doing for the last few days is driving around, sitting on people's couches and crying, but it's been helpful."

Heather followed him in and joined him on the couch, nestled up close beside him.

"Well, there's nothing wrong with a good cry. I employ that tactic almost daily, and it's usually on the couch," she said playfully.

Stephen sniffle-laughed, then turned to look at her, taking in the beauty of the natural light that spilled in from the outside and how it illuminated her delicate face.

"You're unquestionably the most beautiful woman I've ever known. If there's a flaw in you, inside or out, my eyes are unable to see it," he told her.

She tilted her head, smiling. "Well, I have plenty but I'm also a sucker for compliments, so, you can keep going."

Part of him wanted to grab hold of her and pretend he wasn't the man that he was and just make love to her. Lay with her and rub her ears as she liked and laugh with her until it hurt, forget about the work that needed to be done, but she, more than anyone, deserved the truth.

Heather watched as his face grew sullen and his eyes shifted away from hers and she felt that inevitable drop in the gut that comes from discovering something awful is about to happen.

"Stephen, what is it?" she asked, resting her shaky hand on his leg.

"So," he said after twenty seconds of silence. "When I left here that other morning, a morning after one of the most enjoyable nights of my life, I had to return Sophia's call. That's her name, Sophia. I know I've avoided telling you that though I can't imagine why. Anyway, I called her and we spoke for a while and although it was *my* intention to end things with her officially, she did it of her own volition and left no uncertainty about it."

Heather's eyes widened, partly in fear, the rest in hopeful anticipation.

"It's not that I was bothered that it was her doing it rather than I, in fact, that took some of the pressure off, but it was the reasons behind the decisions. Reasons that were valid and fair but that I'd long ignored, and not just with her," Stephen continued. "I've been living a selfish existence, comprised of lies and bullshit for a long time now, Heather, and I'm terrified that I might never stop if something doesn't change."

She pulled back from him, unknowingly, several inches and her hand slid off his knee. "I don't understand what you mean. What have you been doing, you mean cheating on her with me? What lies?" she asked, pointedly.

"Cheating on her with you, yes, that's part of it but it's more than that. In that short conversation, she sized me up and broke me down and none of it was inaccurate. I've been using women most of life, taking what I want and giving very little back and often lying about my intentions. I've been faithful to very few people-and before you ask you are one of the few I haven't cheated on, you have my word-but that doesn't mean it might not have happened. You're the first person I've been with where that's not actively on my mind, and I know that sounds pathetic and awful and I'm not supposed to get credit for doing what's right but I'm just being honest," he said, his words rushed and tripping over one another.

She absorbed what he said for a moment, then, "Stephen, first, I knew that when we got together it was on shaky ground and I could end up losing you back to her, or, as Brianna pointed out numerous times, someone else because 'once a cheater always a cheater' but I decided to do something I hadn't done in many years-have *faith*. I know that sounds absurd considering our beliefs, or lack thereof, but I did it anyway because to me you seemed worth it. Maybe I was crazy, maybe I still am, but regardless, I had no illusions that you were someone who wasn't a risk but I fell in love with you-no wait, that's a lie because I had no choice in falling in love with you, it just happened. Anyway, I *chose* to let you all the way in because the risk

313

was worth the reward of all those other wonderful things about you. If you had cheated on me I definitely would have stabbed you in the face but it wouldn't have meant I didn't love you."

Stephen laughed, slowing the saturation in his eyes which he was determined to try and avoid happening for another day in a row.

"See, but what you're saying is exactly why this has been so hard for me, accepting this realization about myself and understanding why it's happened and why I let myself live that way, so carelessly and self-serving. I knew you were different, miles more evolved and self-aware than anyone I'd ever met and for the first time in my adult years I think I finally let someone peek behind the mask, as cheesy an analogy as that is, and you didn't turn away. You just loved me more. The fact that you love me at all is a miracle."

"Why, because you're not perfect? Because you did what a million other asshole men-and women-do out there while they're trying to 'find themselves' or test the waters as their other relationships fall apart? I've done the same damn thing, Stephen, I'm no saint. We didn't meet at a convent. I have my own battle scars."

"I know you do. I know everything about you," he said, sliding himself closer to her. "I know you have a Master's Degree in Sociology but do nothing with it because 'people are annoying'. You choose foods you love based solely on texture, with crunchiness being a big plus, and you're obsessed with Maple flavor, especially Maple syrup. Syrup that you only buy from "Stone's Farm" out of Vermont but for some ridiculous, fucked up reason that syrup, nor any syrup, can be anywhere near or on Pancakes, even though you love pancakes. I know that you think any other chocolate other than dark is pathetic, that you don't like fruit in your cake and that children and animals are immediately in love with you. I know that you *listen* to people, actually listen and don't just wait for them to finish speaking so you can say something else and that you're an unselfish lover and more beautiful to me each time that I'm lucky enough to see you."

Her eyes were foggy as she watched him finish what he said, still searching for something else he'd left out.

"I know that I've never loved anyone until I met you," he said, looking up with his own foggy eyes. "I've been broken for so many years, I...I don't know if it was ever even a possibility. Now I know it's a reality and I don't have a clue what to do, and I'm terrified that as time passes you'll see right through me and it won't be what you thought I was. You'll see me as what I am and not what you wished I was."

Her jaw shook and her eyes wept as she put her hands back on his before attempting to speak.

"Do you think I expected to feel this way about you? I saw through you right from the start, Stephen. I had more walls than Scotland Yard, and I knew what you were looking for with me, and it was the same thing I wanted from you, but see...that's never really the truth with people like us. We're just cowards that tell ourselves and those around us that we're 'cool being single' and don't have a problem with casual relationships but it's all bullshit. We aren't even original, we are who-knows-what-the-fuck-generation of idiots that trade deferred gratification for instant feeling. We slide into bed with someone just cute enough to dull the pain of knowing it's the very thing that's holding us back. We are the definition of insanity, Stephen."

Tears rolled from his eyes but he kept himself together, not wanting to impede her words.

"Do you remember that paper that you wrote right at the end of High School, the one that your Creative Writing teacher said made her nauseous?" Heather asked him, wiping away some of his tears with the thumb of her right hand.

"About the motorcycle?" he questioned.

"Yes, that one, but I'm talking about what you said at the end. The way you loved to blast up that quiet canyon alone at high speed because you believed that, 'the meaning of life lies on the thread which

315

binds it to death'. That's what I want, Stephen. I want to be right on the freaking edge of it, to feel like I'm terrified to lose it and that if I did I may never recover because I'm tired of pretending the other way is any kind of life. I want that with *you*. You and nobody else, and whatever it takes, whatever you need from me to get us there I'll give it you, or try the absolute best I'm capable. I promise."

He told her that story the afternoon they first had sex, him bragging about his early praise as a writer and fearlessness on a bike, and expected that she'd forget the anecdote as anyone might. The fact that she hadn't was the reason that he loved her.

"I think, for a little while, I need a friend," he said, after a long silence, his eyes leaking at full steam, his voice wobbly and cracking. "I have left so many fires burning and carried pieces of other souls with me into places I shouldn't have before us and now, with you, I need to clean up my world before it burns everything down. I need to spend some time not hating myself, whether that hatred is fair or not, and I need to-"

"Put your Oxygen mask on first," she interjected.

"Put mine on first, yes," he said, his cheeks soaked and red, lifting upward as he smiled at her through his anguish. "You're the only thing that's ever made sense to me, Heather. I only wish Henry could have met you because he would have adored and loved you like crazy, as I do."

"I feel like I know him. Through you, and through your words," she replied, tears rolling down her face and hitting her leg. "I'm so glad he gave you to this world, and to me."

With that, Stephen fell into her, his head landing against her chest. They cried together, as each took turns pulling the other one tighter. Neither one spoke for almost ten minutes, content in the words that had already been said. As Heather adjusted her position up against him, Stephen pulled himself up and looked at her, wiping his eyes on his sleeve before he spoke.

"I can't have children of my own. I know we've never talked about that and I don't know if you even want children, though you'd be an incredible mother, no question. I've never told anyone that other than my family. But, I think with everything that's happened I finally realized how significant the impact of that realization has been on me. When I met my ex, Christine, I was at a place where I'd convinced myself that I was OK without children and that the connection to them I always had even from adolescence wasn't real. When I met her children, however, and became bonded to them and then they were gone..."

Heather pulled herself up close and tight against Stephen as his words trailed off and the wellspring began again. She said nothing for several minutes, just stroking his fuzzy, unshaven head and trying to keep her own tears at bay as best she could. When he grew quiet, she spoke.

"I can't imagine a man that would bring more joy, more comedy, more peace and more love to a child's world than you, Stephen," she said, her words wobbly. "There are other ways to have kids, and a father is defined by the relationship he has with his child, not his DNA. These are conversations for another time, I know, but...I love you and they are conversations I look forward to having. For now, find that peace that you need, and...well, you know where to find me."

They stared at one another, saying nothing as a minute passed.

"I'm not going to lie and say that it won't be difficult for me," Heather said, breaking the silence. "That we won't have our own hills to climb when it comes to trust going forward, if forward's where we're going, but, go bandage your wounds and set yourself straight. Yes, from now on I will read every freaking text you send, every email, take hair samples and inspect your clothes with a black light, but, I'll be here, babe."

Stephen chuckled, then reached his arm around and pulled her against him for what felt like the millionth time that day, saying nothing, feeling everything. As several minutes passed, he gathered himself and looked at her before speaking again.

"There's a part of the book that you didn't read-the only chapter I gave a title to-and it's been on the Notes app in my phone for a while now. I don't know why I've never printed it out but I suspect part of it must be the fact that I've gotten so far away from the message, the meaning of it. I need to find that place again. I will.

It's called, 'The List', and it's a moment between my father and I that...well, you know, why don't I just let you read it," he said.

"I'd love to," Heather replied, her eyes still watery.

Stephen went into his phone and attached the chapter to an email, then sent it to her.

"Read it tomorrow, if you don't mind," Stephen asked, his voice strained. "After I've left."

"I will," she responded, smiling over at him, a lone tear jumping from her left eye and rolling down her cheek.

That night in bed they lay next to one another, he on his back and she with the side of her head on his chest and his arm draped over her neck. They said very little else, kissing just once, and letting the fingers of sleep reach for them within moments of one another.

There was no plan, no timeline nor any agenda, but the lack thereof only served to solidify their shared belief that they would find themselves in the right place, together, before time got away from them.

# Chapter 29

{*****}

*The List*

"*Listen*, I talked to your mother and she's assured me that you're going to stay here for at least these next three years. Get you all the way through High School," Henry said, sitting on the edge of Stephen's unmade, cluttered bed.

"Yeah, well, I'll believe that when it happens," Stephen said, fidgeting against the headboard he leaned on.

Henry laughed. "I know you've been bounced around a lot and that's caused some real grief for you and Jess but I promise you-even if I have to build a fucking house in this town myself-you kids aren't moving, so it's a non-issue, capisce?"

Stephen shrugged.

"Hey, you made it through the hardest damn year of any kid's life, OK-Freshman year in High School. You didn't get your ass kicked, you said you made a couple friends, you're gonna stay parked here for the duration so what's the problem?" Henry asked, wiggling Stephen's knee that dangled over the edge of the bed.

Stephen started to speak, then caught himself.

"So, if this is the part where you tell me you're gay, fuckin' A man, rock on. I live in San Diego, son, remember? Not only are most

319

of my friends gay, but I can tell you that would do a hell of a lot for your wardrobe. These rock band concert shirts every day? Jesus Christ, Stephen," he said, rolling his eyes then erupting into a stuttered, snorting belly laugh.

"I'm not gay. I'm not *anything*, that's the problem," Stephen answered, stifling Henry's laughter.

"Well you're something, because your mother tells me you whack off like you're trying to win an award. You think she doesn't know why socks get crispy, son? No dirt, just crunchy and streaks that shine. Come on."

His father leaned over laughing again, this time causing Stephen to smirk as his face grew flush.

"I just don't know who I am, who I want to be," Stephen said, as the color left his face. "If I'm going to stay here for another three years of High School I don't wanna be just be 'some dork that moved here'. If I finally have a chance to make some roots and settle in then…I want to be liked."

Henry stopped laughing and slid closer to Stephen on the bed, grinning at him.

"I hated myself so much at your age," Henry said after ten seconds of silence, "hated my face, my body, my life so much that if it wasn't for the booze I would have never survived. It insulated me from the terrors that the average zit-faced teenager lays awake at night fearing. Not always, but enough to keep me from jumping in front of a train."

Stephen pulled his knees tight against his chest.

"Here's the thing, this life of yours-even with you staying here through High School and without you having 'the bug' like I did, is still going to be a mishmash of poetry and tumult, ya know? You're going to fall in love with some Suffield, CT little cutie and she's going to smile at you and you'll get hard as a fucking anvil, walking around with a boner and a stupid look on your face twenty-four seven. Maybe she tells you she loves you, you tell her back and it's euphoria as you

320

never thought possible. Then two weeks later she's wearing the captain of the soccer team's Varsity jacket and not meeting you at your locker in the morning and you're ready to drop a toaster in the bathtub. You're going to be a clusterfuck of raging hormones, awkward movement, clumsy, stuttered dialogue and poor decisions, and you'll probably get your ass kicked at least a few times-this is all inevitable, Stephen-and I can promise you it's not only the 'dorks' that are dealing with it. The kids with money just hide it better. Yeah, and of course, some kids are just cooler than you. I mean, a "DeathTomb" shirt? Who the fuck is that ridiculous band and on what planet do you think that awful shirt will even get you near the ballpark of getting laid?"

Stephen tried to contain his laughter with a bit bottom lip and looking off towards the wall to his left but failed as Henry came apart himself. The two of them laughed and snorted for a minute before Henry got up and fished something from his light brown leather camera case he was always carrying.

"Let me show you something," Henry said, sliding back onto the bed and opening a small notebook not much larger than his hand. "You see this? I've had this tattered, time-worn piece of shit since you were six years old. Gargantuan Irish fuck at the second AA meeting I ever went to gave it to me, told me to write down every twisted, sick thing I ever did, thought about, got away with, desired-that 'searching and fearless moral inventory' I've mentioned. Well, because it took me many more years to get sober for good, the thing was basically just a recipe for the depraved, filled with all the horrible shit I'd done. When I decided the booze had to stop I didn't want to start off negative, depressed and terrified-though I sure as fuck was-so instead I made a list of people I admired and would love to be like. It started out as celebrities, athletes, Aristotle, JFK-though maybe avoiding Dallas-and evolved into not just specific individuals but character traits. I still have that finished list, right here in this book."

Stephen leaned forward, reaching for it.

321

"Eh eh eh, no way, pal. This was mine, you need to make you own," Henry said, pulling the notebook back against his chest.

"I'm your son, I'm sure there's lots on there that would be the same on my list," Stephen suggested.

"Oh, you're *my* son, huh? I dunno about that saffron tumbleweed up on your head, there," Henry quipped, pushing his hand into Stephen's chest, toppling him back onto the bed.

Stephen turned red, trying to hold back a smile, then pulled himself back up against the headboard with his knees at his chest.

"Listen," Henry said, tossing the notebook back into his leather bag and leaning up against the doorway threshold. "You make your own list. Figure out who and what inspires you, what qualities you want to emulate and just *become that person*. But stick to it, and don't crap out. You do that, and you'll figure out who you are in no time."

"Yeah but…"

"Oh jeekers, I was waiting for the 'yeah buts'," Henry interrupted, rolling his eyes. "Don't overcomplicate this, you dork. Just trust what I'm telling you."

Stephen smirked, as Henry laughed.

"I'm not, I was only going to say that, if I make a list of people or characteristics I admire or want to mimic then, won't I just start becoming someone else? Just me, pretending I'm something I'm not?"

Henry peered over at him, then walked back to the bed and sat down, placing his hand on Stephen's shin as he spoke. "See, but that's the beauty of this-you already *are* this person. 'The List' is just a mechanism to remind ourselves, keep us on course, force us to remember those elements of our soul that are organic, intrinsic, but we're too scared to nurture. It's easy to be an asshole when you're fourteen and brimming with testosterone and adrenaline-being compassionate is fucking terrifying."

"Yeah but-I mean, yeah well," Stephen started, before Henry's laugh followed by a snort paused his words.

"Yeah but nothing," Henry interjected, turning towards him on the bed, his eyes glossy.

Stephen watched Henry's eyes well up and his face reddened as he looked off to his left at the eggshell wall.

"You're my son. You're the most beautiful, lanky, skinny, hysterical, kind, awkward, intelligent, clown-headed human being I've ever known. You're poetic, loving, patient and brave and you love animals despite the insanity they often bring your life. You care about people, you ask questions, you love to learn, you help people and you stick up for the underdog. You have more to give this world at fourteen than some do in their whole lifetimes, Stephen, and that's true even amidst all the turbulence both you and Jessica have sustained as kids, much of that my fault-not just your mother.

You don't *need* a fucking list, Stephen," Henry said, his words working through trembling lips. "You just need something to remind you that you are all these things every day and not let the fears suppress who you are. A perfect, screwed up, wonderful kid with giant feet and an average sized wiener."

Stephen chuckled as his eyes fogged up.

"I don't understand why I'm so scared," Stephen questioned, wiping his lenses.

"You know what my first AA Sponsor said to me when I knew I was finally ready to get sober," Henry asked, dabbing his eyes on the bedsheet. "I came to him after my first meeting in years, stone sober for three days, and I begged him, 'Joe, Joe what the hell do I do, man? I'm going out of my mind here. How do I make it through this?', and you know what he said?"

Stephen shrugged.

"He said, 'Suffer. That's what you do.', and I understood him immediately, though I was terrified, of course."

"Suffer?" Stephen questioned.

"Oh Christ, maybe you're not as smart as I thought," Henry quipped, then laugh-snorted as Stephen blushed. "Yes, suffer kiddo.

Meaning, these years are going to be brutal, especially if you allow yourself to be the man I know that you are. Choose compassion over bullying, empathy over disdain and kindness over torment and there will days when that will leave you all alone. It's not going to be easy, but if there's any kid out there that can do it, it's you. Your sister too-I don't mean to be leaving her out of this-it's just that, well, she's a lot more attractive than you and probably smarter so her road is going to be a lot less bumpy anyway."

Stephen flipped off Henry, and they both wrestled around on the bed until they slid off, landing on the floor, which sent Lillian in to investigate. She asked them why they both looked like they'd been crying and if everything was OK, to which Henry replied, "Jesus Lill, you never told him he was adopted? Shame on you for making him wait this long, and that he had to find out it was a rodeo clown from Oklahoma." Lillian rolled her eyes and fired back that the car Henry parked in the driveway looked like, "A Hearse for dead garbage", which made no sense but sent them all into hysterics. Shortly after, Jessica made her way into the room, plopping down onto the bed in between Henry and Stephen, asking if she could have five dollars for a record she wanted. Henry pulled a wrinkled bill from his front left jeans pocket and handed it to her, instructing her that it "had to be an Elvis record though", which she giggled at.

That night, under the light of a half-moon pouring through his window and a hallway bulb spilling in, Stephen made his list.

{*****}

# Chapter 30

"*I've* been to New York City a hundred times, Ma, versus your 'once in the late seventies with Dad to buy weed', I think I'll manage," Stephen said into the phone, pacing in the hall outside the Guest Suite at the Satellite radio office.

Lillian jabbed back at him that she'd been there half a dozen times and it was never for weed, only Quaaludes.

"It's amazing my head doesn't look a football and I can get an erection, between the two of you. I gotta go."

She wished him luck and asked him to call her after the interview was over, and that she loved him.

"I will. Love you too. Oh, and let me know the details of the *Today Show* thing. If I should stick around here a couple days and if you're coming in or what," he mentioned, referring to the interview she'd coordinated with the Agent she secured. "I can't believe I'm saying this, but, I'm sorta looking forward to that. The world has no idea what they're in for, two Alexanders on live television."

Lillian laughed and told him again not to get lost in the city.

"OK now you're annoying me. Go eat a shitty, dry cookie and try not to die. Love ya," he said, tapping the end button on his phone as he walked back into the room.

His attire consisted of sunglasses, a white baseball hat and a black pea coat-as conspicuous as he was willing to muster for the short walk from his hotel to the radio studios. As he passed the Julliard School on the way over he noticed a group of folks outside that appeared to recognize him, one that followed him for several hundred feet until he pulled out his phone, pretending to call someone, then peering back at them over his shoulder. One of the conditions of setting up the interview on the *Motormouth* show was that it wasn't publicized, so he could head into the city with his half-ass disguise and not be swarmed at the studio building. Once the interview wrapped, he figured, he'd have to deal with whatever onslaught followed.

As he settled into the brown leather couch in the Guest Suite, he noticed an unshaven man enter from another door with a Diet Coke and a navy-blue sweater with a plaid button-down shirt coming up through the collar. He smiled over at Stephen, who'd just removed his baseball hat, then popped open his soda and took a sip. Stephen recognized him as a local New York Stand-Up Comedian that had also been in several films over the last ten years.

"Hey, Connor Kelly , right?" Stephen inquired.

"I believe so, yes," he answered.

"Cool. I just watched a Netflix special with you, something to do with New York Restaurants and eating."

"*What's the Deli, Yo?.*"

"Yeah, that was it. Really funny, loved it. "

"Thanks a lot. This whole island is obsessed with food, it's all anyone talks about anymore, besides the Subway prices going up and how the rats are bigger now. You know, I go on after you and my guess is that I lose about ninety-seven percent of those listeners so, think you could mention the special in your spot?"

"Pitch your Netflix special? I don't have a fucking thing to talk about, sure, why not."

"Great. Really, that's fantastic."

"Do you want me to see if I can get Gary to say on air, 'This segment sponsored by Conor Kelly and his brilliant Netflix special, *What's the Deli, Yo?*'"

"I like the way you think. Must have recovered nicely from that rap on the head you got there."

"Yeah it still stings a little, and I can't count past twelve or piss straight but I'm healing exceptionally."

"I mean, it's brave and all that you charged that guy, saved the girl but, the whole 'hero' thing, maybe a bit strong, no? I mean the cop, whoooooaaa, of course, no question, but, uhh..."

"You know, I've wrestled with that too. Keeping me up nights, hiding from the press until now actually but-oh wait, I'm sorry, do you know what the 'press' is? I shouldn't have presumed that, though I know they must have been camped outside your place after your stint in those *Frat Men* flicks. Real edgy shit, man, with the whole 'old guys going back to school and partying again' thing. Original too," Stephen said, rolling his eyes with exaggeration.

With that comment, Connor's resolve broke and he leaned to his side, silently laughing with his hand on his belly.

Stephen walked over to him and nudged him off balance on the couch.

"I saw you at *The Comedy Cellar* a few years back," Stephen said, standing over him, smirking. "Fucking killed it."

The main door opened and a man with a mustache and curly brown hair leaned in, asking, "Mr. Alexander, ready in ninety seconds for you, OK?"

"Oh sure, yes," he replied, feeling his intestines drop about three inches.

"Great, just meet out here in the hall in a minute and I'll walk you in," the man instructed before stepping back into the hall.

"Got it," he answered, then drawing in a long, deep breath and holding it.

"Jesus, if this rinky dink operation has you all twisted I'd hate to see what the morning Network stuff is going to do to you. Some hero," Connor jabbed.

Stephen shot out his held breath and cracked up, partially due to the well-crafted joke and the rest being obliterated nerves.

327

"I work a desk, wear *J.Garcia* ties to the office and my hands are as smooth as combed cotton. I saw a neighborhood kid shoot a Robin out of a tree with a BB gun when I was eleven and I cried for ten days straight. I don't know what the fuck I'm doing here either," Stephen said.

"Well, you did what a lot of the bums I grew up with might not have," Connor said, sitting up on the couch. "Don't take this away from yourself. And see if you can crowbar in my show in Jersey this weekend when you're out there. Ticket sales are softer than I'd like."

"Zero's a pretty soft number. You got it," Stephen jabbed.

"We're ready for you," the man in the mustache said, peeking in the door.

"OK," Stephen told him, then turned back towards Connor. "Hey, somehow your babbling calmed my nerves, I appreciate it."

"I've made a career out of it. Yours, well, I wouldn't put away those Garcia ties just yet, it's all I'm saying," Connor said, extending his hands up in a 'slow down' motion.

Stephen smiled and watched as he took another sip of the soda, then motioned with his head to get out into the hall.

"Shit, right. See ya," Stephen said, zipping out through the door. "Where do you want me?"

"Just stand right here, we're good. Another few seconds and we're back from commercial and he'll be doing the introduction, then I'll walk you in," the man said.

Over the speakers that hung on the wall Stephen heard the last seconds of an IT company promising to protect your email servers. As it ended, he heard Gary Morse begin speaking.

*"Ladies and gentlemen, we're back, and as I told you yesterday and reminded you again today, we have a mystery guest on the program this morning, and I'm not going to lie, it's a big one. It's huuuuuge, as the Commander in Chief might say, as massive a guest as this stupid operation has ever had, that's for certain. So, I want to thank the callers and those on email for their guesses but no, it's not*

328

*'some YouTube guy' or Screech from the TV show. Great guesses, and yes, they'd be good gets on any normal day but this is no normal day, my friends, because this day we have a bona fide celebrity in the house. A national hero, an elusive gentleman who's so graciously allowed us to be the first place he sits down and talks, very likely because he was struck on the head and hasn't fully recovered but I digress. Anyway, enough of my bullshit, will you please welcome to the Motormouth program, for the first time since he was whacked on the head by some scumbag trying to kidnap an innocent girl in Connecticut and who is now dead, thanks to some other hero out in Pennsylvania-Stephen....Alexander!"*

"OK, here we go," the man said, placing his arm behind Stephen's back and leading him into the Studio.

The chilly temperature grabbed hold of him, slowing his gait, and it was difficult to see Gary with the lights in his eyes. He was ushered over to a plush purple couch and let himself fall into it before the man escorting him handed him earphones and motioned for him to slip them on. Stephen looked to his right and saw two of the regular personalities on the show behind Mics as well as the resident Voice Over guy, George, who was often asked for his take on segments of the show, responding in his deadpan, baritone voice and injecting hilarity into the program without even trying.

"Mr. Alexander, how the fuck are you brother? Seriously, hang on a second here," Gary said, getting up from behind his Mic and out of his seat to walk over to Stephen. "I'm not a big hand shaker or hugger but I'm giving you a damn hug my friend. I have a daughter and two sons and if anyone ever tried to nab them, well, I'd be thrilled, the ungrateful dicks but I'd still appreciate someone trying to save them."

Stephen stood up as he approached and Gary leaned into him and hugged him, patting him on the back before he broke the embrace.

"Seriously, you deserve that. I'm so glad you're here on our show and it's an honor, truly. OK, I need to go back to my seat, it's freezing over here. Tom, do we pay the oil bill here, what the hell is going on?" Gary questioned, walking back to his chair.

The lights were coming at Stephen from every angle as he slid back down onto the couch. White and blue lights down from the ceiling, pinkish lights off to his sides and green lights running the length of the floor. He could barely see the host or his sidekicks, but in the earphones, could hear clear as a bell in his blindness.

"I have to say, I'm rather impressed myself," the gray-haired announcer said, his booming voice filling Stephen's ears in the tiny speakers on his head. "He's a big score for this show, and I second what Gary said, sir, very honored to have you here."

"Thank you, I appreciate it very much but, you know, I'm just a guy that walked into something weird and tried to fix it," Stephen said.

"Oh please, come on," Gary interjected. "I know that's what people tell you you're supposed to say but fuck that, brag a little. You deserve it, dude."

"I would have not only *not* gotten involved, but probably would have also pissed my pants knowing it was happening and I did nothing," the chubby sidekick, Marty said, inducing laughter from those in the room.

"Seriously, I'm just so honored that you chose to come in here and talk with us and before you get into it all, can I just say that you chose us over some other venues that were offering you some big bank to hear from you first, am I right?" Gary asked.

"Well, yes and no. I mean, I did decide to come here before anywhere else but, I've decided to make the rounds at a few other spots, after strong encouragement from certain individuals who I won't call out on the air," Stephen replied.

"Oh, what like agents and lawyers. Those pricks will be pimping you out till you're ninety if they can make a buck," Gary said.

"Not exactly. Was something I resisted at first but as I thought about it more I arrived at the same place everyone else is. Meaning, if this had happened to anyone besides me I'd be a guy on the sidelines wanting to hear from them too, with all that ended-up transpiring from that one event."

"You aint kidding, and yeah so have you talked to any of these girls, met any of them, their families, anything? None of the families has really said anything yet, and I know the kids are too young but everyone's going to want to hear from them too, obviously."

"Right, of course, and no I haven't, really," Stephen said, electing to keep his discussion with the mother Diane between the two of them. "But I suspect that may happen down the road. Those girls have a lot more on their plates than I do. These families torn apart, now brought back together and all the shit that goes along with that, not to mention the healing they'll need to do for months if not years following this."

"It's a total mind fuck, it really is. If I'm you, I'm just sitting around all day going, 'What if I hadn't gone after this guy and all these girls are still locked up for who knows how long' and probably making myself nuts!"

"I've done plenty of that, yeah, among other inner dialogues."

"So, not to sound horribly insensitive here, considering the subject matter of this whole thing but, have you been able to parlay your newfound fame into getting some chicks or what? The women must be all over you."

Stephen chuckled. "I've pretty much been in seclusion since this unfolded and when I'm not I have been keeping a tight circle. There's a woman that I do enjoy being all over me, however."

The room laughed, filling up the headphones.

"Oh shit, well, you have to tell us about her," Gary urged.

"I'm not going to drag her into this. She knows who she is, and I hope she knows that I love her. That's all I need to say about that."

"Awwwwwww," Gary said, then joined by the others in the studio. "OK, so I need to know everything about that day but first, you mentioned money before and that always intrigues me so, obviously, we aren't paying you a dime but, what do you stand to make from all this? You could end up a millionaire, no?"

Stephen reached down at his feet where the man who walked him in had left a bottle of water, turning the cap off and taking a long sip before answering the question. "You know, I've given that a lot of thought in the last twenty-four hours and I realized that…the families of these girls have, in some cases, spent years without one of their children. It's probably put them in hospitals, therapist's offices, sent them all over traveling, trying to chase down leads, and put these poor people in a bad way for so many reasons. There's also families out there right now with missing kids that don't have the resources to do what they need to or to even stay afloat. I felt like I needed to help them after this. So, I'm donating anything that I'm paid by the media to a fund to assist them. I can't take money for this, I can't profit. I helped a little kid that was in trouble, that's what I did."

"Wow," Gary responded. "I don't know if I could be that selfless. I mean, you're going to have people hounding you and in your business for a long time. You don't feel like you deserve something, a piece of the pie?"

Stephen wished Henry was there, sitting on the couch next to him. He wished he could see his son doing the right thing, finally, instead of listening to him seek approval for selfish decisions. He wished he had a chance to show him that he could be the man that Henry was sure he was-with or without a list-but had not yet fully become before he was gone. He wished he could stack piles of change on the wooden floor and listen to Jessica laugh every time it fell. He wished he'd been there at the end, but he was going to stop tearing himself down because he wasn't.

"You know, I'm writing a book about my life, or some of it, it's called 'The Alexander Circus'. About my childhood, about my old man, Henry, my mom, Lillian and my younger sister, Jessica. I'm calling it a novel for now, but it's *my* life, really. I've thought about adding some chapters in at the end about this experience, especially if

332

I meet and talk with these girls and families someday. I'm sure it could be therapeutic for all of us on some level, but, I guess we'll just see how that evolves.

Anyway, for years now I've been critical of some of the things my parents did, or didn't do, mainly my mother, and probably held on to some resentment for things I shouldn't have. When I think about a lot of that and then imagine what those kids went through I feel foolish. It wasn't always an easy time for me growing up but I had love, I had shelter and lots laughs to go with the tears. Those girls had all that stolen from them when they should have been playing with dolls or riding a bike or on a beach somewhere. So, I can't say I feel like I really deserve anything from all this, ya know? I've had a pretty good life, and it's not over yet."

Gary looked over at him, and then to the others in the studio, nodding at them. It was silent for about ten seconds and then, "Yeah, yeah of course, you're right. But you're going to keep the money from the book, right?" he said, cracking himself up after he finished.

"Oh, fuck yeah, of course. Come on, I'm a good guy, Gary, but I'm not *stupid*."

The room laughed collectively and Stephen joined them, easing himself back into the couch, getting comfortable, as he peered around the room. He would answer their questions and offer his perspective for the next hour and a half as the studio and the world listened.

The night before, in the hotel, he lay in bed anticipating the morning to come-what he may say, the questions he'd be asked, who might be there and so on. He felt himself grow anxious and despondent, so he called his sister Jessica who, for many of their years, had always been able to calm him in times of peril with her hushed tone and benevolent sensibility. They spoke for a while and her voice and words relaxed him, as always, and he thanked her. He then asked her if she was happy, and she replied-though somewhat flummoxed by the question-that she was. He told her that he loved her, then let her go. Shortly after, he got up from the bed and made his way to the bag he'd packed and pulled out the red envelope that the beautiful blonde at the hospital dropped in his lap. He recalled her gaze, fixed on him, hoping for a reaction in their brief exchange. He ran his fingers over the back of the envelope where it was sealed, cautiously edging his pinky finger underneath, prying it upward. Then, looking in the mirror on the closet door, seeing himself, he stopped. He walked the card over to the trash can, folded it twice, then dropped it in, making a *Falump!* sound as it hit the metal sides and bottom.

"There's nothing in there for me," he stated, staring down at it, then offering a smile to only himself.

As he returned to bed that night, waiting for any residual anxiety to fall away, he imagined himself on the swing as slumber lurked around the corner. Starting at the bottom-its equilibrium position-he pushed his feet forward and then curled them under himself. He accelerated upward-pulling on the ropes as he stretched his legs outward-then slid backwards quickly as the momentum shifted with his legs turned under. The arc widened under the moonlight as his speed gathered, and he could feel the warm night air rush past his face and whoosh through his ears. He swung back and forth, grazing the top of the iridescent ocean water with his toes but never relaxing his legs enough to let them fall in. As he continued the pendulum for several swings, he thought about Henry. Soon after he thought about Lillian, and then it was Jessica. Moments later it was Heather, and her image resonated and remained with him as his motion began to dissipate, and just before it ceased she was joined by two little figures standing beside her.

For years of his life he had these crazy, wonderful, complex people all around him, doing all that they could to love him, despite their own limitations and dysfunctions. More recently, he had a woman that showed him unconditional love and support, offering honest understanding and empathy, though he'd known her less than a year. He spent his restless nights swinging, afraid to let his feet feel the water because of the unknown, while disregarding the known, which held firm beneath him and had never faltered in so many years.

As Stephen rocked the swing fore and aft once again, finally reaching the top of its rearward arc-hovering in suspense for a moment-he let his legs dangle freely as he fell forward. The heels of his feet hit first, then his shins plunged in and the resistance stopped his travels dead as the lukewarm water raced up his legs and sprayed up over his chest and face. He sat there, motionless, looking over his shoulder at the luminous midnight moon, wiggling his feet in the tepid ocean, grinning to himself.

"I miss you, Poppy," he said through misty eyes-gazing past the moon-just before sleep reached down and carried him away, and just as the swing was slowly pulled back skyward, through a cloudless night sky, not to be seen again.

*The End*

48850124R00192

Made in the USA
Middletown, DE
29 September 2017